the christmas club

After an extensive career in radio and television in Ireland and the UK, Stephen Price stepped off the media rollercoaster to concentrate on writing. *The Christmas Club* is his second novel. His first novel, *Monkey Man*, was published by New Island in 2005.

the christmas club

STEPHEN PRICE

**NEW
ISLAND**

The Christmas Club
First published 2006
by New Island
2 Brookside
Dundrum Road
Dublin 14

www.newisland.ie

The moral right of the author has been asserted.

ISBN 1 905494 34 3

British Library Cataloguing in Publication Data.
A CIP catalogue record for this book is available
from the British Library.

Book design by New Island
Printed in the UK by Mackays

10 9 8 7 6 5 4 3 2 1

1

'I'm not coming – you're mad!'

Dionne sipped her coffee. 'Excuse me, but officially, you're the loony.'

Oona sighed and looked away with that vulnerable yet bravely coping expression that everyone who knew her knew so well.

'Thanks. You know, I've been told to try to take my mind off things, for the sake of my health. See my friends – people who make me feel positive about myself.'

She wrenched a stubby Gold Bond away from its neat row of companions, firm in the pack. A waitress sailed past, arms loaded with prodigious chicken dinners for the porcine family wedged around the next table. Beyond the windows of Wynn's Hotel, gobbets of sleet tipped headlong into Dublin's Abbey Street. Dionne's apology sat perfectly with the artificial holly pinned to the oak panelling.

'Sorry. Just trying to cheer you up. I mean, after last night…'

'I was fine last night.'

'You kept bursting into tears.'

'I was upset. I was upset about my life being totally crap, but that doesn't mean I'm headed back to the nuthouse or anything. It's just the Surmontil.'

'The what?'

'Surmontil. It's an anti-depressant, but one of the side-effects is that it makes me weepy.'

'Poor babes.'

'Actually, they want to put me on this new stuff called Prozac, when it comes on the market. It's very exciting.'

'Good for you.'

Oona snorted. 'Okay, imagine you discovered a shop in Dublin that sold Miss Selfridge at discount prices, and you were the only person that knew about it.'

'Miss Selfridge would never come to this feckin' dive.'

'Well, that's how brilliant Prozac is supposed to be. Then I won't have to depend on my friends to help me feel positive about myself.'

'Don't be like that.'

'Hey – you're the one who wants to spend Christmas up the arse-end of nowhere with some bloke you met in a pub, and you call me a loony? He could be an axe murderer for all you know.' Oona grinned maliciously. 'Lock you in a cellar and never let you go, like *The Collector*. Nasty, nasty thing.'

'Rubbish. It sounds perfect – big house, by the sea…'

'Mmmm. Romantic.'

'It's not like that!'

'Dionne Brady, I'm depressed, not blind. I saw you last night, outside. You shifted him, didn't you?'

'No!'

Oona cackled. 'You're such a liar. You tried to hide it when I came out, but you did, didn't you?'

Dionne grinned. 'Maybe just a little bit.'

'And now you want to drop everything and follow him off to God knows where, like a lovesick teenager.'

'No! There's nothing…*indecent* about this. It's a chance to get out of town for the holidays. Actually, when I said I'd go, I was thinking of you.'

Oona cackled all the more. 'Yes, you were thinking of me holding your hand while you cop off.'

'I was thinking how the change might do you good.'

'Oh, be honest. You so badly want to go, but you don't want to go on your own. Stop pretending this is about me.'

Dionne could feel her hangover kick in. She'd made it through the half-day at work with the buzz of the previous night still on her, and with the help of a little extra make-up. The thing about architectural drawings was, hangover or not, you could poke quietly away at them until everything clicked. Myles O'Brien, the senior partner at O'Brien Fanning Tate, was fond of saying that people, not planning, were the awkward part of getting anything done. That he was fond of saying it while standing in Dionne's personal space was something she would tolerate until fully qualified. Another year, Mr O'Brien, then you better watch your fat backside. People are only awkward for as long as you allow them to be.

Take Oona as another example. Oona could be a downright pain. She was unpredictable and attention seeking, and Dionne suspected that her so-called depression was mostly an excuse to act the maggot. However, in this instance, she was absolutely right – Dionne needed back-up for her snap expedition, and, given the time of year, her choices were limited. Because persuasion had failed, she decided to gamble.

'Forget it – I shouldn't have presumed. A quiet Christmas with your mum is obviously what you need.' She took one of Oona's cigarettes without asking, in a manoeuvre designed to aggravate her almost as much as the prospect of Christmas with her mother. Oona glared with grey, glittering eyes, then took a sulky swallow from a gin and tonic murdered with ice.

'I wish you'd buy your own.'

'Melissa's coming.'

'*What?*'

Dionne nodded beatifically. 'It will be lovely for her. Lovely to get away.'

'I don't believe you!'

'I rang her this morning. She's mad keen. Couldn't make it for lunch, but she's definitely coming. Started packing already, bless.'

'You're kidding!' Melissa's father, in poor health since for as long as anyone could remember, had passed away in June. If Melissa had socialised only sparsely before then, she had barely left the house since. Her mother had died having her, so now Melissa was alone. Dionne wasn't kidding – she was lying through her teeth, but like all good liars, she knew not to gild the lily. Instead, she changed the subject to give Oona time to nibble at the bait.

'I like your hair.'

'I don't. I don't like anything about myself right now.' Oona's mouse-brown mop had been cut short and razored at the back, like a boy's. Her whole outfit screamed 'boy'. Black Levis, a tatty Fred Perry shirt, a navy bomber jacket, Doc Martens and a thick leather belt. She'd also put on a bit of weight during her stay in St Eunan's. And her skin wasn't the best either. Oh, where to stop? All the more reason to be gracious.

'Rubbish, you look great.'

'I look like shit, so shut up.' She lifted a knapsack from the floor, rummaged inside and came up with a luridly coloured circular tin. With the businesslike indifference of one touching up her lipstick, she smeared fingertip-fulls of its contents, a pungent orange paste, beneath her ears. A sharp, fusty smell fought with the reek of chicken dinners.

'What is that stuff?'

'Tiger Balm.'

'Pretty whiffy, isn't it?'

'You wear Opium, so what would you know? Now, run this crazy scheme of yours past me one more time.'

Dionne ignored the slight. Gotcha. 'It's like I said – big house, fantastic location, free holiday.'

'Yeah, but where is it?'

'On the north coast.'

'Of Northern Ireland?'

'Are you mad?' Oona frowned, and Dionne continued quickly, 'Jesus, no, this place is in Donegal, by the sea.'

'That narrows it down to within about a hundred square miles. What did he say it was called?'

'Dun…Dun something. Dunratty. No, that's not it, I can't remember. But it doesn't matter. All we have to do is take the bus to Letterkenny, and he'll pick us up from there. Simple.'

'Great, I'll just go home and tell my mum, "Hey mum, I'm off to the middle of nowhere with Dionne Brady to stay with some northerner she shifted outside the Stag's Head last night. So toodle-pip, and enjoy Christmas on your own."'

Dionne stood abruptly. 'Look, we'll tell you all about it when we get back.'

'Who said I wasn't coming?'

'You did.'

'Wait a minute, I wouldn't miss this for the world. Christ, a ringside seat at one of your seductions…'

'You have a bad mouth, Oona Tyler.'

'Wild dogs wouldn't keep me away!'

Slowly, disguising her triumph, Dionne sat down again. 'But what about your mother?'

'Oh, she'll book a turkey dinner in the Burlington with all her batty friends and get totally arseholed and have a fabulous time with me not there. The way it's been lately, she'd probably pay you to take me with you.'

'You shouldn't be so hard on yourself.'

'Well, it's true.'

It probably was true, Dionne reflected. In August, Oona had stolen two hundred pounds of her mother's savings and disappeared, turning up three weeks later, naked, in Berlin's Tiergarten, with seemingly no memory of how she'd come to be there. She hadn't been assaulted – the park police had simply found her wandering happily but somewhat blankly through the trees at four o'clock one fine morning. Repatriated with no small amount of bureaucratic trouble, Oona had been dispatched directly to the secure wing at St Eunan's for treatment, from whence she had emerged in October, relatively stable but greatly subdued. She'd been skulking around her mother's apartment ever since, and it was part of Dionne's calculation that by now, Tyler mother and daughter might be glad of a break from one another.

'There's only one thing I need to know for sure.'

'What?'

'This place has central heating, right?'

'Of course it has – do you think I'd go anywhere that didn't have central heating?'

'No, you'd rather slit your wrists.'

'Exactly.'

'I'm not sharing a room with you or Melissa. I want my own room.'

'He said there's plenty of space.'

'What if he's lying, to lure us all up there and lock us in a cellar with the decaying corpses of all the other women he's murdered over the years?'

'The bus leaves tomorrow at two.' Dionne rose again. 'See you at the station. I'll get this.' She opened her purse and placed two banknotes on the table.

'I'll get my own.'

'Don't be silly, benefits of having a job.'

Dionne joined a bus queue on neighbouring O'Connell Street. Of course, it being cold and wet, and this being Dublin, there wasn't a taxi to be had. She caught sight of herself in the window of Clery's department store. In her black PVC coat and boots, she looked way better than anything they had on display. The alternate pink and green lettering on the inside of the glass exhorted her to

RING IN 1989 AT CLERY'S NEW YEAR SALES

The sleet had eased, but she carefully adjusted a woollen beret over her white-blonde hair. She was thinking of having it recoloured and curled, a bit more like Kim Basinger's – because people often told her she looked like Kim Basinger, with her high cheekbones, big lips and slightly hooded, jewel-blue eyes. And who was she to disagree? But maybe the hair could wait until after the holidays – it looked better than fine, and she had other demands on her spending money, like clothes that said 'winter, in the countryside'– though not from Clery's. She gave her reflection a congratulatory smile, then hopped on a bus.

Alone at the table in Wynn's, Oona stared at nothing in particular. Her eyes filled with tears.

After a ten-minute journey, Dionne alighted in Ranelagh. Once a country estate, Ranelagh had been overrun by Dublin's middle classes in the late nineteenth century. The sedate maze of red-brick streets still maintained an air of gentility, home now to legions of old ladies lost behind net curtains. Melissa's house occupied a corner site. The front door was set back from the pavement up a patterned tile path, half-blocked by an overgrown yew, of a green so dark as to be almost black. Dionne often wondered about this tree, not least because one had to step sideways to avoid it, but also because, according to the faded white lettering painted on the skylight above the door, the house was called 'The Garden'. Why call a house that, if all you're ever going to plant is one single, not very pleasant tree? The rear of the house, Dionne knew, was just a concrete yard. If she owned the place, that tree would be the first thing to go, and the sappy name would be next. She pressed the bell, a cracked ceramic button mounted on a brass ring. It rang languidly, muffled by distance. Eventually, Melissa opened the door.

Everything about Melissa was long, except her hair. She had a long face, a long neck, long arms, long legs. Her nose was long, but not overly large, her features balanced by enormous brown eyes and thick eyebrows. She kept her black hair in an elfin cut with a heavy fringe. Her clothes were as simple as always – a grey blouse, black pedal pushers and thin leather pumps.

As she crossed the threshold, Dionne's fantasy refurbishment of Melissa's home continued unchecked. The flock wallpaper in the hallway was a disaster – those walls needed painted, not papered, primary colours offset by white. The worn carpet on the stairs, held in place by metal rails – that staircase would look much better naked, stripped back to the wood. The dowdy furniture in the first-floor drawing room was mentally consigned to the dump, and replaced by leather, chrome and glass. The day would come (Dionne swore this to herself) when she, too, would own a house as big as Melissa's, but properly done up. For now, she could only envy her friend for having all this space to herself, even if it badly needed redecorating. Perhaps this was her way of grieving, leaving everything untouched.

Dionne didn't remove her PVC coat, and declined an offer of herbal tea. She was conscious of the risk she was taking – there was nothing to stop Oona from telephoning Melissa to check if she really had agreed to travel north for Christmas, so Dionne knew she had to act fast. She chose a wooden chair by the black marble fireplace. Melissa sat on a worn sofa opposite. Dionne took a deep breath.

'This is about Oona.'

Melissa nodded, wearing the faint smile that was her stock response to anything anyone ever said to her.

'I'm worried about her.'

Melissa raised an eyebrow.

'You know what she's been like since she got out of hospital – hanging around her mum's place, making no effort to get on with her life. Well, I took her into town for a drink last night, to try to cheer her up a bit, and I'm afraid my plan worked much better than expected.' Dionne paused to give Melissa a chance to voice curiosity, but she merely moved her head slightly. 'I was really careful not to let her drink too much, and she was sort of snivelling away to me, crying into her beer. Then, we got talking to this guy, a northener. Natter, natter, nothing unusual. But next thing I know, doesn't he invite us up to Donegal for Christmas – and doesn't Oona agree to go!'

'That sounds…charming.' Melissa's voice was almost as faint as her smile.

'That's what I thought – no big deal, and when I rang her this morning, I thought she'd have forgotten all about it. But no, she was still deadly serious about going, so I met her for lunch to try to talk her out of it, but she says she's catching the two o'clock bus tomorrow, and there's nothing I can do to stop her.'

Melissa shrugged. 'Perhaps a holiday is just what she needs.'

'You may be right, and I don't think this guy is trying to get into her knickers or anything – but you know how she rushes headlong into things. Like, one minute she's sitting there moaning about how crap her life is, and the next she's away with some stranger.'

Melissa shrugged again. 'She's her own woman.'

'Ah – but is she? The thing is, I feel kind of responsible. I mean, what if she went up there and suffered a relapse? I don't think we should let her go on her own.'

Melissa stopped smiling. 'We?'

'This guy said he had loads of space. He said anyone could come.'

'I'm sorry, but what exactly does any of this have to do with me?'

'Well, first of all, I'd appreciate a bit of help with Oona. To keep an eye on her. She listens to you. Mostly, she just gets bolshy with me. But more importantly, the doctors say she should be with her friends, people who make her feel positive about herself. You know, that time she took the head-staggers and ran off to Berlin – maybe that would never have happened if the three of us saw a bit more of one another. And the hospital afterwards, that must have been awful. We can't let that happen again, we owe it to her. If we go with her, then we can make sure she comes back in one piece. Look, I know we've all been busy, me more than anyone, but last night just sort of set me thinking – here's a big house, in a fantastic location, a free holiday…'

In Dionne's professional opinion, whoever built Tallaght needed shooting. Row upon row, street upon street, of featureless pebbledashed corporation housing, divided by stark expanses of open grass where the locals were somehow meant to disport themselves. Perhaps the town planners of the 1960s had entertained utopian visions of grateful slum-clearance families eating picnics outdoors or holding inter-street games; more likely they wanted the far-flung suburb built as cheaply as possible, and had left grass in the place of proper civic amenities, like shops, libraries and swimming pools. It had come as no surprise to Dionne, during a primary school project, to discover that the name 'Tallaght' came from the Irish for 'plague cemetery'.

By the time she made it home, laden with shopping bags, she could barely walk in the PVC boots. She tugged them off in the cramped hallway of the little house and popped her head around the living room door – crowded, as usual, the TV blaring in one corner. The kitchen was worse, her mother having commenced the feeding of the five thousand, and Dionne hurried upstairs before she was ordered to help. She closed the door of the bedroom that she shared with three sisters, and spread the clothes she'd bought on one of the bunk beds. She reached under the bed and came up with a large tartan holdall. Then she took a small key from her purse which she used to open a metal locker at the foot of her bed – a crude but effective precaution when sharing a room with three sisters. She selected more items of clothing hanging within and began carefully folding them into the holdall.

2

The day they lynched the corporals, Singer realised he was in the wrong job. Up until then, things had been going well, as once again Belfast erupted into front-page news. The latest round of atrocities had brought the world's media back onto the city's dreary, dangerous streets, and Singer had built up a decent portfolio of clients – mainly French and German picture agencies – that couldn't or wouldn't send their own photographers to Northern Ireland. In March 1988, he had as much work as any freelancer could hope to handle. Until then, based on past experience, he also thought he had the stomach for it.

On Sunday the sixth, British undercover soldiers had executed three IRA members in Gibraltar. They had been attempting to bomb a military parade, but the summary nature of the killings had plunged Belfast into yet another of its periodic cycles of psychotic violence. During the ten days it took for the bodies of the 'Gibraltar Three' to be flown home, riots raged around the clock, punctuated by regular gun battles.

Singer, who owned a small brown brick terraced house on the edge of the city centre, made hay while the sun shone. His girlfriend, Stacey Edwards, from Andover, Massachusetts, sat in their miniscule living room, drinking and smoking, doing her utmost to advance her thesis on War and Statecraft for Boston University over the babble of two radios and a television set that she was too terrified to turn off. Theirs was a relatively quiet street, removed from any immediate rioting, but Stacey could still hear the sporadic echo of automatic gunfire in what she sincerely hoped was the middle distance. Sometimes the news bulletins explained the gunfire; more often they did not.

She slept on the sofa so as not to miss Singer at the odd times he returned, dirty, exhausted and exhilarated. Their kitchen doubled as his darkroom, and he would close himself away almost immediately, rushing to develop his latest material while eating cold from the pot whatever she'd left over. Then, when the prints were hung up to dry, Stacey would be admitted to help him pick, in a token way, the dozen or so images to be dispatched to the agencies. Thus she would learn where he'd been and what he'd seen. This was their 'together time'. She would want to be held, he would urgently want sex. If she demurred, he would fall silent, blowing a hairdryer over the prints, ostensibly to speed up his work but mainly to sabotage any further conversation. If she succumbed, she would come away feeling even more squalid and frightened than before, whereas he would smoke afterwards and pour a tumbler of whiskey, which he would swallow before collapsing into their only armchair. She would then extinguish the radios and the television to let him sleep, but usually, after about an hour, he would start awake in an opulence of swearing, pull handfuls of pictures from their pegs in the kitchen, and jump in his battered coupe to wire them from a newspaper office downtown. With Singer gone again, Stacey would restore her electronic companions to life, sit down at the living room table, and try to remember what she had wanted to say about War and Statecraft.

On Wednesday the sixteenth of March, a funeral crowd several thousand strong saw the Gibraltar Three to their graves. Surrounded by industrial units, marshy wasteland and a motorway, it's difficult to imagine Milltown Cemetery as a way station to some better life beyond. To the west, Belfast's Black Mountain looms, like a threat. That day, two helicopters hovered high above, their racket a relentless psalm. As the huge cortege entered the cemetery, Singer thought it odd that, apart from the helicopters, the security services were nowhere to be seen. No doubt there were many soldiers and policemen crouched behind the blast walls of the barrack directly opposite the cemetery gates, but perhaps some higher authority had deemed it unwise to exacerbate the already ugly mood of such a large body of people. The grim distraction of burying the dead had briefly becalmed the topography of hate.

Having snapped the standard news pictures of coffins carried from hearses, Singer, along with scores of other cameramen, stood atop gravestones and tombs to capture the interments proper. He had begun to zoom in on the faces of individual mourners, which often told the most eloquent stories of all. He did so surreptitiously, as not everyone who attended such events welcomed the attention.

Then, from behind, two muffled blasts made him jump, and someone jostled sharply against the equipment bag slung at his side. He looked over his shoulder, half-expecting to see a paramilitary firing party, at the same time knowing that the noises weren't the cracking snap of guns. Shouts of 'Get down, get down' erupted from the men around him, followed by delayed-action screaming from the women.

At first, he saw nothing more remarkable than the drab expanse of the cemetery stretching down to the motorway. Then he noticed a small, stocky man with a tweed cap and a moustache, walking about fifty paces away from the funeral amongst the gravestones. As he watched, about two dozen youths moved towards the man, who turned, hurled a small object, then continued on his way at a light jog. The object exploded off to Singer's right in a puff of grey smoke, sending some of the youths diving or falling to the ground. The screaming trebled in volume. He brought his camera up, sweeping the graves with his telephoto lens. For a few seconds, he panicked, unable to pick up on the now-running man, but then his target stopped and pulled out a handgun, pointing it, it seemed, straight at Singer. The gun cracked five times, and Singer's tummy tingled the way it always did whenever he snapped a 'seller'.

The man threw another grenade, casting a pillar of mud and water high into the air, then vaulted the barrier onto the motorway, followed by a large gang. Singer jumped off his tomb and began running, following the path that the bizarre attacker had taken. As he moved away from the shrieking crowd, he heard a megaphone voice appealing for calm. Two small boys huddled, crying, behind a slate gravestone. Singer took their picture and ran on. A woman in a blue coat with blood seeping from her neck staggered towards him. He snapped her in passing. He practically fell over a group of young men his own age, kneeling around another young man, who lay flat on the ground. He stopped, reeled off a few exposures, but one of the group shouted 'hey' and reached towards him. He dashed on, his camera bag bouncing off his hip. The ground dropped steadily, and he couldn't see what was happening on the motorway. A large part of him didn't want to. Another part of him knew that he had to.

As he reached the road, he heard the whoop of sirens. A line of armoured grey Land Rovers had stopped on the far carriageway. Policemen with green helmets and long plastic shields scuffled with the shouting mourners. Of the moustachioed man, there was no sign. Panting for breath, Singer took a few last shots as the riot police jumped into their vehicles, back doors closing as they moved away. There was nothing on the motorway for the furious mourners to throw, although a few aimed pointless kicks at the armoured jeeps.

Singer stormed into the house, waking Stacey from a nightmare in which her mother's neighbour's dog was eating her little brother's face. Her mother's neighbour in Andover didn't own a dog. The sofa cushion sopped with hot sweat, because she had fallen asleep with the gas fire turned up full. The tiny room stank like a crematorium. Singer cranked up the television news, which showed someone attacking a funeral – what kind of place was this? 'What's going on out there?' Stacey croaked, her throat dry.

'We don't know his name yet, some incredible nutter. Chucked four grenades into an IRA funeral, but not just any IRA funeral. Lucky for him, the cops caught him before the crowd ripped his head off. He killed three people, but nobody big. I got most of it, some really good stuff.'

Not quite awake and not quite listening, Stacey contemplated Singer – large, heavy-set, dark hair ruffled, brown-black eyes buried in a frown behind a prominent nose. She always thought he looked Polish, but he insisted his forebears were Welsh. He lifted his camera bag off the living room table and, Stacey noticed, her thesis and pushed through the kitchen door.

'This lot will keep us in fags and booze until Christmas,' he called back at her, 'but I better hurry up and...' His voice fell silent.

'What? What's the matter, honey?' No reply, so Stacey dragged herself upright and stepped into the darkened kitchen. By a feeble red bulb, Singer studied one of his spare cameras.

'Turn the light on,' he said quietly.

'Are you sure?' Once before, she had lit the fluorescent strip without asking, and he had cursed more violently and for longer than she had hitherto imagined was humanly possible.

'Turn the light on,' he repeated. She flicked the switch at her shoulder. The colour had drained from his face. He held the spare camera out to her. At first she saw nothing amiss, then she noticed an uneven lump of grey metal, about the size of a matchbox, embedded deep in the back of the camera body. 'Came straight through the canvas, look,' he explained, holding his equipment bag up for inspection. There was a hole in the side, big enough for him to push three fingers through. 'I thought someone bumped into me.'

'What is this?' Stacey held the damaged camera at arm's length, like an unloved pet.

'Shrapnel. From a grenade.' She nearly dropped it, so he took it from her. 'It's okay, I didn't use this one, so I haven't lost anything. Be a pal and pour me a drink there, would you?' She didn't move. With his back to her, he started measuring developer. 'Okay, don't pour me a drink, but would you knock out that light? And don't stand in the doorway.' She turned off the light, pulled the kitchen door closed, and stood in the middle of the living room, looking at herself in the antique oval mirror that hung on a chain above the fireplace. Wearing one of Singer's tatty old jumpers, with her long chestnut hair matted around her face and black circles governing her eyes, she recognised almost nothing of her reflection.

Singer spent the next day in a newspaper office downtown, wiring his clients photographs of Michael Stone – as the perpetrator of the 'Milltown massacre' had now been named. When he returned that night, he found Stacey crying inconsolably on the sofa. She'd run out of milk and cigarettes and had been too frightened to walk to the corner shop for supplies. He made her a hot whiskey and poured a stiff measure for himself. The gunfire continued until daybreak.

On Saturday the nineteenth, he awoke with her on top of him. For a moment, he didn't recognise his own bedroom. Because of his sporadic rest pattern, when he slept, he did so near-catatonically. She held him by the neck, and moved herself slowly against him.

'Don't go to work,' she whispered, pulling the heavy patchwork quilt up over her exposed back. Beyond, the air was cold and damp. Beneath, it was warm and delicious. She kissed him full on the mouth. He only half-reciprocated, because his tongue felt like a pub carpet. He thrust himself up against her, and she exhaled into his ear, flexing to give him what he wanted. 'Please,' she whispered, 'don't go to work. Please.' She kissed his nose.

'Jesus, States, you know I have to.' She came off him abruptly, and lay down with her back to him. As he dressed, the quilt shook gently with her sobs.

On his way across town, he stopped at a hardware store, where he bought a small aluminium stepladder. The funeral of Kevin Brady, an IRA man killed during the cemetery attack, was due to pass down Andersonstown Road within the hour. Singer knew that there were no high points where he could shoot over the crowd. And there was going to be a crowd. He also knew that he had taken Brady's picture in Milltown, lying dead or dying on the ground. But the shot had been rushed, and obscured by the young men huddled around.

He folded down the rear seat of his coupe and tossed the ladder inside. As he drove on, he realised that the sick feeling in his stomach was fear. The March air was heavy with it; every breath drew more dread into his body, along with the smoke from the cigarette in his fist. His hands still smelled of Stacey. She was right. Fear was the only sensible reaction to what this city had become. Halfway to Andersonstown, he pulled into the kerb and almost swung the car around. If he felt like this, how must she feel? At least he had had the dubious benefit of growing up with this madness. Stacey, on the other hand, hailed from an affluent suburb of Boston, where violence was a tough game of college football. A year previously, her academic mentor in Belfast, who also happened to be Singer's uncle, had charged him with chaperoning the newly arrived Stacey to a political rally, to gather material for her thesis. Instead, Singer had taken her to see a riot. She'd moved in with him ten days later.

It was a small thing that swung it – he decided he'd feel foolish returning home with a brand-new, unused stepladder. So he parked two streets away from the funeral route, extracted his camera bag and the ladder from his car, and walked onto the Andersonstown Road, away from Kevin Brady's final destination, the same cemetery where he had lost his life. He reached a junction where the rest of the press had congregated. His colleagues had obviously been warned not to approach the cortege, which was assembling about a quarter of a mile away. Even at funerals, journalists and cameramen often share a bit of relaxed banter. On this day, there was none. Angry-faced stewards stood along the roadside. Significantly, Singer noticed, they weren't talking amongst themselves either, but staring silently at the bystanders, as if intent on studying everyone in the crowd. Again, apart from the inevitable helicopters, the security forces were nowhere to be seen. If the mood at Milltown had been ugly, today it was ferocious.

A line of black taxis, driven by IRA members, chugged slowly down the road. The hearse had started moving. Singer opened his stepladder and climbed halfway up it. One of the stewards, a square-headed man with a grey buzz cut, stared at him. Singer held up his camera. The man sneered and looked away. After Milltown, everyone was under suspicion. The line of black taxis rattled past. The hearse drew closer.

Perhaps it was the incident of the shrapnel, perhaps it was because of Stacey, but after taking a few shots, Singer checked behind himself. That was why he was one of the first to see a small saloon car approaching the funeral up the otherwise empty Andersonstown Road. He snapped it. The car sped through the advance guard of black taxis, which stopped. Singer snapped it again. Incredibly, the car kept coming. A murmur spread through the crowd along the pavement, rising quickly into a cacophony of shouting. 'Look out! Look out! Jesus, look out!' The car reached Singer's junction just before the hearse, then swung sharply into the side street, avoiding a collision. But the street was jammed with onlookers, and there was no passage. It skidded to a halt, then, engine screaming, reversed back into the main body of the funeral. The stewards pelted forward, punching the windows and kicking the doors. One of the black taxis reversed and deliberately blocked off any escape. In a savage, collective movement, the crowd fell roaring on the little car, joining the stewards, punching and kicking it as if it were a living thing. It stalled, jammed in a heaving sea of bodies. A man ripped open the boot of the black taxi, and came up with a wheel brace, which was quickly passed into the throng that stood jabbing at the car like killer bees. Metal crunched against glass.

Hands laid hold of Singer's waist and tugged him backwards off the stepladder. With the camera glued to his face, for an instant he had the sensation of drifting through space. He fell heavily, landing on top of whoever had pulled him. 'Fuck's sake!' exploded from beneath. He thought that the crowd had turned on him, that somehow he was next, and clutched his camera to his chest, waiting for the first boot to swing smashing into his head. The square-headed steward seized his stepladder and disappeared with it into the convulsing crowd. Then he felt a push from below and rolled sideways. A fat little man with appalling body odour extracted himself with a final shove, leapt to his feet and ran after the steward.

For a few seconds, Singer lay looking at the pavement, and the shoes shuffling around his face. Stay down, don't watch. Stacey had been right – don't go to work today. He stood up. Behind him, metal railings protecting a shop window gave him something to wrap one arm around while he jammed a foot onto the narrow sill, gaining just enough height to start snapping again, over the crowd. The steward smashed Singer's ladder across the windscreen of the car, which hung inwards like a sagging white duvet, but didn't completely break. With every swing of the ladder, the crowd gave a gut-wrenching howl. One of the side windows gave way beneath the wheel brace. Several arms reached in, to grab whoever was inside.

Suddenly, the mob pulled back, and a young man Singer's age emerged bodily from the window, holding a pistol. He had a small moustache, brown hair and wore a green jumper. Through his telephoto lens, Singer once again had that momentary effect of his subject appearing to look his way. Singer could tell by the man's face that he knew he was going to die. The man raised his pistol. At that moment, he could have shot any seven of the hundreds who bayed for his life. Instead, he pointed the pistol skyward, and fired into the air, looking desperately around, as if appealing for some last-minute understanding, a single shred of sanity in the seething sea of hostility. Singer, who until that instant assumed he was watching a rerun of Milltown – a reckless psychopath attacking a crowd – saw that the man hadn't wanted to hurt anybody, that this was all some atrocious mistake. He just wanted to explain, but when he saw that he could not, he lowered his gun, and the crowd fell upon him.

So many people tried to strike him as they dragged him from his car and into the black taxi that they mostly struck one another. Then, with another roar from the crowd, a second man was physically hauled from the smashed-up vehicle. He wore glasses, but they were quickly punched from his face. As he, too, was bundled into the taxi, a middle-aged woman – from her dress a journalist – ran forward and tried to intercede. Her bravery earned her a punch and she stumbled off, holding her face. To the turbine-like screaming of the mob, several mourners climbed into the black taxi on top of the two unfortunates and it moved off, seriously overburdened, rear doors flapping like the wings of a lazy raven. It gathered speed and disappeared down a sweeping bend of Andersonstown Road.

Looking for fresh meat, the mob began pushing and heckling the television crews, who stood out because of their equipment. Singer unstrapped his camera and stuffed it into his bag. The stewards shouted for the mourners to rejoin the forgotten cortege, but they hadn't a prayer. Singer crossed the road to the female journalist he'd seen punched.

'Are you okay?'

Her skin was that of a fifty-year-old who smoked, and she had a red welt on her left cheekbone. Her hair was groomed and dyed reddish-brown. She wore heavy hooped earrings and a patterned neck-scarf against a brown trouser suit.

'They're going to kill them,' she pronounced in an unusually deep voice. 'What I want to know is, where are the cops? We're five minutes' drive from the biggest police station in Belfast, and the helicopters can see what's going on.' She pointed upwards at their noise. 'So where are the fucking cops?'

A medium-sized man with thick glasses and prominent front teeth practically fell up against them, pushed by the milling crowd. He wore an anorak and carried a heavy, plastic-wrapped television camera at knee level.

'What do you want to do now?' he panted.

'Follow the story.' The woman strode off briskly in the direction the taxi had taken. Singer and the cameraman exchanged a look, then struggled after her. Singer felt dizzy, disembodied. He knew that anyone following the victims would seem conspicuous, so he glanced backwards after a minute or so of fast walking. Sure enough, several youths had peeled off from the crowd and were running down the road in pursuit.

'I think we'd better...' Singer began, with absolutely no idea of how to finish his suggestion. Better what? Make a last stand, and get beaten under the crushing weight of boots and fists, like the men from the car?

'Stupid, stupid, stupid,' the woman growled to herself, marching with her head in the air. The gang of youths caught up, shouting unintelligible insults. The woman halted abruptly and, hands on hips, roared at them to fuck off. She was old enough to have mothered any one of them, and her vehemence caused them to freeze, open-mouthed. Singer braced, but after a moment's hiatus, the yobs laughed, then dashed onward, leaving their little group alone again on the wide, featureless road. They continued walking. The clamour of the mob faded behind. For the first time that day, Singer felt how cold it was, and saw that the clouds threatened rain. His body was half-numb with fear, yet somehow his legs worked. The road bent steadily to the left.

Then they heard several flat cracking noises, like small fireworks. The woman, still leading, began to run. Up ahead, engines. As the road straightened out, they saw three black taxis pull away from a spot of waste ground, close to the walls of a sports park. The woman and her cameraman ran faster. Singer could easily have outstripped them both, yet he fell slightly behind. It was like running in a dream, where the harder you try, the slower you go.

What was left of the two men lay stripped, battered and shot on the cracked concrete of the waste ground. Singer could see absolutely no resemblance between the face of the man who'd fired the warning shot from the car and either of the poor, helpless items sprawled before him now, in spreading puddles of their own dark blood. Nor could he see any connection between human beings who could laugh, sleep, play with their children and those who could do a thing like this. His hands shook as he extracted his camera from his bag. The woman reporter stood silent while her colleague calmly shot footage. The gang of youths collected at the far end of the waste ground, admiring the handiwork of their elders. Singer took two photographs, one of each man, but suddenly he remembered some other victims from long ago, trapped in a blast-mangled car. His eyes filled with hot, stinging water and he lowered his camera, because he couldn't see. The woman took a handkerchief from her pocket and offered it to him. He blew his nose.

A skinny, white-haired priest in a long black frock coat came from nowhere, pushing his way through the gang of youths. They stood out of his way, naughty boys before his palpable anger. The priest knelt beside the dead men. Singer knelt too, and took three more pictures of the priest administering the last rites. He felt that tingle in his tummy, and nearly threw up. Policemen emerged from the gathering crowd. Singer hadn't heard the sirens. He wanted to lie down, like the dead men, but struggled upright and made to leave.

'Hurry up!' the woman reporter hissed at her cameraman. Fumbling, he extracted a tape from the tray of his machine. The woman stuffed it down the front of her trousers and closed her jacket. 'I'd get out of here if I were you,' she muttered to Singer. 'Those cops will start confiscating cameras any second now.'

Singer returned unchallenged to his car and drove downtown to a newspaper office, where he developed his film and wired the grue-some results to his clients. He performed every action mechanically, as the newsroom floor gathered round to ogle his work. When he finished, he put his negatives in an envelope and posted them, with a scribbled note, to an old schoolmate who lived in London. Then he went and sat alone in a dismal little pub where he knew he wouldn't meet any other journalists, and drank whiskey, and smoked.

Later that night, he returned to a dark, empty house. Even before he switched on the living room light, he knew that Stacey was gone. The space no longer smelled of her, just of photographic chemicals, stale cigarette ash and a faint tinge of damp. The table, habitually cluttered with her papers and books, was naked apart from the note. It read,

> *Sorry. I can't do this any more.*
>
> *Love,*
> *Stacey*

The top story on the television news identified the two men as British army corporals, Derek Wood and David Howes. It said that they'd stumbled into the funeral by accident. They were – apparently – Signal Corps, a pair of electricians. It showed footage of Corporal Wood firing his gun in the air, but not what happened afterwards. The photographs of the bodies, Singer's included, wouldn't appear until the morning papers came out, when they would sicken the world. The second item on the news dealt with unconfirmed reports about a poison gas attack somewhere called Halabja, in northern Iraq. Thousands dead, mostly women and children. Another conflict – one that made Northern Ireland look like amateur night out.

Above the sofa, the wall was thick with overlapping prints of Singer's best shots, held in place by brass pins. Silhouettes threw petrol bombs, buildings exploded, coffins were carried, men wearing black balaclavas cradled weapons galore. In the middle of the mayhem, Stacey had pinned a photograph of herself, taken on the morning she'd moved in, sitting in the sunshine on the pavement outside, laughing at something Singer had just said. He knelt on the threadbare carpet in front of the gas fire, trying to fight a rising tide of memory, but he could not, so he curled up on his side and cried harder than he had for many years, until his face felt as swollen as the victim of a mob. He was still lying there the following morning, when the police kicked down the front door.

3

Pizza, or more correctly, the absence of pizza, ended their relationship. Ronan was mildly allergic to cheese – it gave him headaches and could even bring on his asthma – but now, the mere thought of the dreadful stuff bubbling, melted across a layer of processed tomato, was enough to cause him severe emotional distress. In the past twenty-four hours, he had lost his girlfriend, his job, his home and, worst of all, most of his books – because of a non-existent pizza.

Food, it seemed, was still the enenmy on the foetid, wallowing ferry home from Liverpool. A mere whiff of the offal dispensed by the ship's cafeteria had disabused him of any urge to eat, and had almost disabused him of his last meal, a tangerine consumed at Euston Station. He had had to run for the deck and gulp fresh air to recover. The lounge bar, if anything, was worse, every table overrun by unshaven oafs in denim jackets and their lard-faced women, swilling beer and stuffing themselves with chips from paper plates, the atmosphere solid with cigarette smoke and the stench of urine mixed with bleach. And that had been before the ferry set sail. When it did, it hit the winter swell of the Irish Sea, and the scene on board had degenerated into something from the bowels of hell itself, as every mouthful consumed by Ronan's fellow travellers came spewing back up again.

Huddled in a corridor, where the air was marginally less foul than that of the main passenger areas, and marginally less cold than the November night outside, Ronan sat on his scuffed leather suitcase with the collar of his grey cashmere overcoat pulled up around his ears. What a fitting place to contemplate his misery, he thought. How bitingly ironic it was, for example, that he should now be fleeing London to throw himself on Singer's hospitality when, eight months previously, the situation had been precisely the reverse.

He'd been happy before Singer's visit, that much was certain. Happily installed in Linda's flat (until last night, he'd thought of it as *their* flat), practising at playing married couples. He'd had a decent job – not one, perhaps, to be overly proud of, but one that permitted plenty of spare time for his precious books. Most of all, he'd enjoyed the satisfaction of having escaped Ireland in general, and Belfast in particular. And then Singer had turned up and ruined everything, with one simple, apparently disposable remark. Or had he? It exasperated Ronan to think that such a minor off-hand insult might have triggered such a catastrophe. Surely life was never so precarious?

Queuing to disembark in Belfast, he was torn between relief at quitting that floating purgatory, and desolation at returning to his native city. Contacting his parents was, for the time being, out of the question. As far as they were concerned, he was prospering in London. His father, whose actual achievements in life were far outweighed by the importance he attached to them, had only recently desisted from delivering telephonic lectures about the need to shape up and settle down. Big in Pensions Administration, he'd been incandescent when Ronan had taken English Literature at Canterbury instead of the Northern Ireland Civil Service entrance examination. While unconvinced that editing a trade magazine for Linda's father constituted actual work, he'd at least stopped complaining. It was inconceivable that Ronan should now turn up on the man's doorstep to announce that, apart from his professionally useless degree and a suitcase full of books, he was back to square one again. And it was too early to lie and simply declare himself home for Christmas. There would be questions – what about your job, where's Linda? No matter how distasteful the prospect of stopping with Singer might be – and Ronan was certain that it would be distasteful – nothing could be worse than letting his parents know he was home again.

'Enjoy the match, eh, son?' The query jolted him out of his reverie. A patently tipsy steward held the sea door of the ferry open to the icy air beyond. He leered at Ronan's puffed-up black eye and the gash on his brow whence it emanated. The paper-stitched wound jarred horribly with Ronan's circular reading glasses and his carefully combed red hair.

'Football? Certainly not,' Ronan sniffed. 'I suffered a road traffic accident, if you must know.'

'Oh, so they have cars in England now that will fight you, do they?' The steward threw a playful jab in the direction of Ronan's temple. Tugging at his suitcase with both hands, he lurched onto the gangplank to the guffaws of the steward and several rancid voyagers. Welcome home, to that legendary Belfast wit.

He splashed out on a taxi to Singer's address, for the walk with that suitcase at three o'clock on a frosty morning would most probably have killed him, assuming some roaming sectarian gang didn't first. Singer's street confirmed his worst fears. Ronan had grown up in a quiet, opulent suburb in the south of the city. This neighbourhood, close to the bombed-out heart of town, had been built sometime around the turn of the century. No doubt, like the horse-drawn tram, it had seemed quite modern and possibly even sanitary at the time. Now, with smashed streetlamps and several of the houses boarded up, it looked ready to be razed. Number 12 gave off a muted red glow through the single ground-floor window. Ronan knocked, and when there was no response, he felt inside the letterbox for the key on a string that Singer had promised to leave if called away.

The red glow came from a bulb in the kitchen. Ronan used it to detect a lamp-standard, which he lit to reveal a room barely big enough for three adults to sit in; a small sofa and one armchair huddled round a gas fire, hemmed in by a mahogany table and a matching cabinet, both supporting unfeasible towers of photographs, newspapers and books. Further layers of photographs and newspaper cuttings were tacked to the wall, adding to the claustrophobia. A television and two radio sets clung on where they could. There was a note taped to the television screen. It read,

> Ro, gone to Tyrone. Two killed in bomb. Make yourself at home, S.

Ronan made himself tea by the red bulb. The kitchen counter, he noticed, harboured several empty whiskey bottles and a half-full one. He silently cursed Singer for not being a red wine drinker, then carefully lit the gas fire in the living room, aware that one errant spark might be enough to send not only the paper-stuffed room but the entire street up in flames. Which, given how he felt, would be no bad thing. He sipped his tea on the edge of the sofa, and waited for his host to arrive.

'Did you get those negatives I sent you?'

Not so much as 'hello, how are you, and would you mind putting me up for the next ten days or so?' Instead, Singer had simply materialised on Ronan's doorstep in Clapham one chilly afternoon the previous March, unannounced. Ronan hadn't laid eyes on him for nearly two years. They had attended boarding school together, some tottering Edwardian pile on the North Antrim coast, where Singer had spent most of his time arguing with the teachers, and Ronan most of his hiding from the other boys. Singer had refused to participate in sports on ideological grounds, denouncing soccer and rugby as surrogates for warfare. Because of who he was, instead of being beaten, Singer had been relegated to the school library every Wednesday afternoon, which is how Ronan had made his acquaintance, himself excused from physical activities on the grounds of his asthma. Gradually, they had become friends. Singer confessed to Ronan that the real reason he mooched off sport was that he hated being part of any group that he wasn't in charge of. Ronan admitted to Singer that his asthma wasn't so bad, and that he just detested exercise.

At university, they had kept in touch, Ronan dreaming amongst Canterbury's spires, Singer studying photojournalism at some suitably proletarian polytechnic in central London. Upon qualifying in the summer of 1986, Singer had raced off home to 'cover the war', while Ronan had seamlessly taken up with the comfortable and comfortably off Linda McAleese, a Business Studies graduate and the only daughter of the fifth-biggest building contractor in the south-east of England. Linda was neither good looking nor particularly ambitious, but then, neither was Ronan. They had moved up to London when Linda's father had rewarded her graduation with a starter flat in Clapham and a fabricated job choosing décor for his housing developments. Soon afterwards, like God, he had created yet another job, asking Ronan to edit a new trade magazine for building suppliers. As an intellectual activity, it was shameful, but as a salary for doing next to nothing, it was perfect, and at least Ronan's link to apparent future wealth, however negligently acquired, had served to silence his own father over his prospects from 'writing bloody poetry'.

'Did you get negatives? I sent them by post.'

'Singer. Jesus. Come in. What are you doing here?'

'I don't think they followed me.' Singer peered around the quiet south London street, but made no move to enter. 'I drove to Dublin and flew from there.'

'Followed you? Who followed you?'

'Nobody. That's what I said.'

'What on earth are you talking about?'

'I sent you some negatives two days ago. Do you have them?'

'And it's very nice to see you, too.'

'Do you have them?'

'Is this what you mean? It arrived this morning...' Ronan poked around atop a hallway commode, and came up with a brown envelope.

'Bloody hell, Ro. I said in the letter for you to hide this away, and what do you do but leave it lying beside your front door?'

'But I haven't opened it yet, so how would I know what it says? Is this from you?'

'Yes. Don't you open your mail?'

'Rarely before lunch. Anyway, why are you posting me things, then coming all the way over here to pick them up again? Have you joined MI5 or something?'

Singer grabbed the envelope and stuffed it inside his leather jacket. 'Let's go to the pub, and I'll explain everything.'

Ronan had been wandering since breakfast in Yeats's *Seven Woods*, working from home being one of the advantages of editing the *South-East Construction Review*. Reluctantly, he fetched his coat.

'He's had a rough time of it. A very rough time.'

Several hours later, Ronan stood propped against the stone sink of the small but bijou flat kitchen. Linda, not finding him home as expected, had begun ringing around the local hospitals, little realising that her boyfriend sat less than a minute's walk away in the Britannia public lounge and bar. The cause of this highly uncharacteristic behaviour lay snoring on the sofa. Linda had taken an instant dislike to Singer, for leading her boyfriend astray. 'You don't know what it's like back home,' Ronan finished, looking nobly down at her, then immediately negating his imagined superiority by clumsily pushing his glasses back onto the bridge of his nose.

'I don't want to know!' she exclaimed. 'Bunch of bloody paddies killing each other!'

'Your father's Irish,' he reminded her.

'Well, I'm not!' she snapped. 'I was born and bred in Maidstone, and my mother's from Kent and I'm a Kent girl through and through! I've never set foot in Ireland, and I never will!' For the first time, Ronan found himself wondering whether Linda's mother stood like this, arms folded, when she was angry with his father-in-law to be. 'I thought you'd been hurt, fallen under a train or something, when I came home from work and you weren't here for such a long time...' Her voice dissolved in a squeak and she buried her face in a pair of dainty, undersized hands. She stood quaking, so Ronan stepped forward and tried to get his arms all the way around her.

'There, come now, everything's fine. I was only gone a few hours. Singer landed out of the blue – there was nothing I could do.'

'But why is he here?' Linda's large, slightly bulging eyes peered up into his. Her thyroid was subject to fluctuations, which explained the eyes and, partly, her weight.

'Darling, he's had a terrible time of it. The police broke into his house, looking for photographs of a double murder.'

'Whaaaat?' she shrieked, pushing him away.

'It's okay, he's not charged with anything.'

'I don't believe it!' She stamped a dainty, undersized foot. 'You bring somebody like that into my home?'

'But darling, he hasn't done anything wrong! He's a photographer, not some sort of criminal! From a very good family, as it happens, only they're—'

'I don't care!' She stamped her foot again. Although groggy with alcohol, Ronan could see that none of this was helping. Inspiration struck.

'Look, what about supper at Roberto's?'

'What?'

'Come on, just you and me. I don't think Singer wants to eat, anyway.' A rasp from the sofa confirmed this supposition.

'But I'm not dressed...'

'Balls to dressing, you look wonderful the way you are.'

And so, over spaghetti carbonara with garlic bread for Linda, and a tomato and basil salad (no mozzarella) for Ronan, the shock of Singer's initial impact on their daily routine was temporarily dissipated. They sat late at the window table looking onto Clapham High Street, drank lots of red wine and made love for the first time in months when they returned to the flat, giggling as if they were students once again.

The following fortnight was the most tiring Ronan had endured in years, for keeping Singer out of Linda's way made fearsome demands on his sobriety. Getting rid of him by day posed no difficulty, as Singer had announced that all he wanted to do was to rephotograph the great Victorian municipal cemeteries he'd documented as a student. No matter how much he drank the night before, he was up early each morning, disappearing off to Highbury, Kensal Green, Norwood, Nunhead, Brompton, Tower Hamlets or Abney Park. The problem was that he came back in the evenings with reams of pictures of stone angels, sarcophagi, mausoleums and obelisks in various states of overgrown decay. These he would spread across the living room carpet to discuss in great detail, thrusting his favourites at Ronan who, while he could fully appreciate the aesthetics of Victorian funerary symbolism, grew uncomfortable when Singer's eyes would suddenly fill with tears, in particular over a monument he'd photographed in Kensal Green, which bore a stone relief of a shrouded woman, and the laconic legend 'Ninon'.

'That's all it says, Ro – "Ninon". Just her name, nothing else. No date, no explanation – nothing. Whoever lost Ninon must have died of a broken heart, you can feel it when you stand there – the pure, simple grief. I can't do her grave justice, no matter what way I shoot it. But I completely understand it.'

Then one night, the living room door opened and there stood Linda, staring down at Singer's carpet of death. She had had to be worked with for hours afterwards, and mollified with a very large helping of Roberto's bucatini all'amatriciana with extra bacon and pecorino, washed down with rivers of Barolo and two servings of homemade tiramisu. After that, Ronan took to hustling Singer straight off to the pub the instant he returned from his excursions. It was hell on the liver, and even worse on the lungs, but at least that way Linda's sensitivities were spared. On occasions when contact couldn't be avoided, Singer was exceedingly polite towards her, never returning any hint of the animosity she openly displayed towards him, but it was one evening in the Britannia when the fateful moment finally arrived.

They'd downed five or six pints. Singer had been alternately enthusing over that day's batch of morbid photographs and fretting about whether the Belfast police would still be after him. Wearily, Ronan assured him that they wouldn't, and suggested that Singer might be overreacting in the wake of what had been, in fairness, a traumatic experience. He went to the gent's, and when he sat back down again, Singer changed the subject away from himself for the first time since his arrival.

'So how did you first meet the Kraken, then?'

'Pardon?'

'Linda. How did you two meet?'

'No, you said something else there. What did you say?'

'Never mind, slip of the tongue. How come you're together?'

'What's a Crack-in?'

'Forget it. I'm just asking you about Linda, because you're obviously going to get married, what with you beavering away for Daddy's newspaper and all of that…'

'It's a magazine, not a newspaper. And it was at the Wine Tasting Society.'

'Eh?'

'Where we met. The university Wine Tasting Society.'

'How marvellous. Look, I'm off in the morning.'

'Where to? I'm surprised there's any graveyards left for you to drool over. Or are you moving on to the hospital morgues?'

'No, I mean I'm leaving London. I think I'll slip over to Paris while I'm here and visit a few clients. Most of them only know me as a voice on the phone – it would be good to put a few faces to names. To be honest, it's more of an excuse to stay away from Belfast.'

Ronan tried to disguise his elation. 'Well, as long as you're sure...I mean, it's been great to see you and all that, but if duty calls. As it happens, I have to get busy with the next issue of the *Review*.'

'The *Review*? Sounds quite highbrow, when you call it that.'

Ronan snorted. 'Muck and brass, you know yourself.'

'Don't I just.'

The following morning, after Singer had gone, Ronan took his sore head to the *Oxford English Dictionary*, in the office space he'd created in the living room. Now, what was it he'd said? Crack-something.

Cracknel? Not a biscuit, no.

Cracksman? Hardly a burglar...

Cracow...now that was just silly – try under 'K'.

Krakatoa...

Kraken /kra:ken/ n. a large mythical sea monster said to appear off the coast of Norway. [Norw.]

Ronan threw the dictionary against the wall. He couldn't decide what angered him more – Singer calling Linda a sea monster, or his missing a literary reference. Not one, but two! Tennyson *and* Wyndham – that smug fucking bastard!

After that, it had started with the little things – things he either hadn't noticed before, or had noticed but pretended not to care about. Like the way she ate. She always stuffed far too much food into her mouth, leaving her cheeks puffed up like a hamster's, and her dainty, under-sized lips straining to close in an 'o'. Worse, her eyes glazed in an unseemly fashion when she chewed, as if the very act of nourishment rendered her semi-conscious, like a baby on the breast. But the mouth and the eyes, in terms of incipient irritation, paled in comparison with the herding. The herding drove him mad.

Ronan liked to pick delicately at his food. He contemplated each morsel before he consumed it, and ate slowly, rarely finishing a full serving. Linda, on the other hand, ate with the steady rhythm of an industrial machine, eyes glazed, cheeks overstuffed, her knife and fork constantly herding her food around on its plate. She guided peas into neat corrals, pushed pasta into easily plundered heaps, bisected bacon then arranged the pink slices in a row, like aeroplanes on a runway, destination Linda's gullet. Her knife and fork never stopped fretting, cajoling her food around, like the feelers on a huge blue crab Ronan had seen once in the aquarium of the Natural History Museum. The feelers had mesmerised him, scrabbling for morsels as if completely independent of the otherwise immobile crab, herding tiny specks in the water towards the flap in the exoskeleton, which opened like an o-shaped mouth, seemingly much too small for the sheer bulk of the squatting creature that it fed…but those feelers kept frantically herding, and the crab kept cramming morsels in, growing bigger and bigger and…

Kraken.

No! Don't think that! She's not!

Then there was their living room. With Singer gone, and the sofa-bed folded away, Ronan saw the space where he and Linda spent a large portion of their lives as if for the first time. They didn't socialise. Linda hated pubs and rarely went into them. She liked Roberto's, but only on nights when it wasn't busy, so they stayed indoors at weekends. After dinner in the small but bijou kitchen, the living room was where Ronan and Linda passed their evenings – which would have been fine if they'd both liked watching television. Linda loved television. The first two items she'd purchased for the flat were a large white sofa-bed, which she'd had placed across the middle of the room, dividing it almost exactly in half, facing the second item – a massive television set. The 'TV' half of the room sported a shaggy white rug that Linda liked to stroke with her dainty, undersized feet, but mostly these stayed tucked up beneath her on her sofa, as she gorged on a relentless diet of *Neighbours*.

Ronan, on the other hand, detested television and rarely watched it for anything other than the news. It genuinely mystified him why anyone would care a single jot about a bunch of oafish Australians whose profoundly dull lives furnished the fodder for these torturous soaps, so he spent his evenings lurking behind the sofa, propped in a leather recliner, with his back to both Linda and the television, blocking the pair of them out with the earphones of his Sony Walkman. He would read, from the books lovingly arranged on the shelving that enveloped 'his' half of the room. A roll-top desk bearing an electric typewriter and a brass reading lamp completed 'his' décor.

Linda's half of the room had a glass coffee table for television snacks, and magnolia walls, which were bereft of decoration apart from a large, purple-framed print of Renoir's *Les Parapluies*. Privately, Ronan considered *Les Parapluies* chocolate-box art, but he kept that opinion to himself, because Linda's father had apparently told her she looked just like the woman with the basket. She didn't, but she often wore her hair that way anyway. And there they would sit, in their living room, night after night, he bogged down in Borges, she stranded like a beached whale, devouring garbage.

Kraken.

No! You love her!

That July, Linda's father, obviously at her behest, invited Ronan on a family holiday for the first time. The day before they left, a postcard arrived from Paris, a black-and-white image of Oscar Wilde's grave. It read,

> *Ro, still haven't made it home, but have run out of money so
> no choice now. La Rive Gauche or the Falls Road? Life is full
> of harsh decisions. Spent the past two months bumming around
> a film school, did a short course. But the agencies are demand-
> ing dead bodies, and I must eat. Amanecera y veremos, S.*

Ronan had been to Spain before, but never this kind of Spain. Puerto Banus consisted of a marina, a supermarket, one street of designer-label shops and another of gaudy nightclub-style bars. Rising untidily from the parched hills all around were sprawling enclosures that jealously concealed a proliferation of apartments and artificial oases of vegetation and pools, their greens and blues so intense as to be almost damaging to the eye. The heat was unbeliev-able, and Linda's father, mother and younger brother, Teddy, all of whom shared her blimpish body shape, sweated terribly at the least effort. They didn't tan when they sunbathed so much as baste. After a swim, they would spend the hottest part of the day – from noon until five – hermetically sealed inside their luxury apartment behind double glazing, with the air conditioning turned up full. Everything inside the apartment was white – the walls were white stucco, the floors white marble and the furniture a thick, white-painted cane.

Linda's father was particularly proud of his living room bar, made from the same white-painted cane, stocked with a seemingly endless supply of Bacardi and tepid cola. The apartment was completely bereft of books, but Ronan, having anticipated that situation, had brought a plentiful supply.

In the evenings when it cooled, the McAleeses liked to change into their good shorts, skirts, shirts and sandals and promenade along the marina, admiring the floating fibreglass palaces parked there by various Arab princelings and Lebanese arms dealers. Linda's father had only one topic of conversation, and that was when the time came for him to buy his yacht (within the next twelve months or so, if projections were correct), whether he should 'go Sunseeker or Azimut'. Sunseeker, he explained, was the more desirable brand. Azimut yachts were every bit as good and better value for money, but not as prestigious a name. It was a tough one, Ronan agreed.

'You can research it for me when we get back.'

'But I know nothing about boats,' protested Ronan.

'Yachts, they're yachts. Never call them "boats". You know nothing about building supplies either, but you still manage to fill a magazine every month.'

They ate out every evening. Several times, Ronan tried to persuade Linda's mother to let him cook prawns from the supermarket on the perfectly serviceable but never-used barbecue nook on the patio, but she would laugh and say something about holidays not being for dishes. Ronan knew for a fact that the woman never did dishes at home either – her housekeeper did. So they hopped from restaurant to restaurant along the seafront, Ronan desperate for a spot of paella. The McAleeses refused to countenance paella, because it had 'bits' in it. However, the restaurants would only cook paella for two or more, and the smell was driving Ronan wild. He would order sea bass instead, which was fine but not nearly as good, he supposed, as the paella being consumed at nearly every other table. Fresh paella, Tabasco sauce and a squeeze of lemon – heaven! The McAleeses would stare at Ronan's sea bass oddly, as they herded well-done lumps of steak and mountains of chips around their plates, cheeks stuffed, eyes glazed. 'A good steak' was the highest compliment any McAleese could ever pay a dinner. When Ronan finally cracked, and insisted on paying out of his own pocket for two portions of paella and to hell with the consequences, Linda's father said he wouldn't hear of Ronan paying for anything, ordered the paella on his behalf, then huffed for hours afterwards when Ronan failed to consume the entire contents of the massive iron pan.

They had been on holiday for about a week when one morning, sitting in the shade nursing Umberto Eco's latest opus, Ronan glanced up and saw the au pair. The McAleeses were enjoying a family splash, dominating the pool like a herd of hippopotami. Then a man emerged onto the patio of a neighbouring apartment. He was middle aged, but trim and tanned teak, with thick black hair and heavy sunglasses. He perched on a sun lounger, opened a folder of papers and began prodding at them with a pen, oblivious to his surroundings, as if he were sat at an office desk. Next came a woman, forty-ish, with a one-piece black swimsuit pulled tight over a body that was too thin, too muscular and too tanned – if her husband was teak, then this woman was ebony. Her hair was sculpted into an alarmingly blonde bob, her eyes and most of her face hidden behind huge sunglasses. She, too, climbed onto a lounger and opened a magazine.

Then, out ran two children, a boy and a girl, holding hands with a breathtaking young woman of about twenty. Squealing, the children tugged the young woman down the grassy slope to the poolside, where Ronan hunched beneath a pine. She was immaculate – tall, but not Amazonian, full hipped, yet not matronly. A purple bikini strained to control a magnificent bum and two beautifully proportioned breasts. Large red lips framed a wide white smile; she had a pert little button nose, green eyes, freckles and short, gamine brown hair. Her skin was golden brown like the children's, not hideously overdone like her employers', nor watermelon-red like the collective McAleese pelt. The children shrieked in French, broke her clasp and water-bombed the pool. Without breaking her stride, the young woman dived in after them. For an instant, Ronan held her frozen in mid-air, lusciously, at full stretch, before she disappeared below the surface, smoother than a knife dropped in a snowdrift. I will never have a woman like that, Ronan thought as he waited for her to surface. Never.

A gut-wrenching scream came from the far end of the pool. Linda sat on her father's shoulders, like the Michelin man riding a bull walrus by the neck. He clasped her legs, each pink thigh twice as thick as his head. Teddy pushed his father by the chest, enough for the amazing tower of flesh to totter, then come crashing down, causing a tsunami of turquoise water that spread in all directions, practically emptying the pool. At Ronan's end, the stunning au pair wrapped a gorgeous, protective arm around each of her charges, gathering them close under her glistening breasts. Linda's head reappeared, eyes tight shut, spitting foam. She reached for a ladder and hauled herself out, waddling across the tiles, the water tumbling off her in streams. Panting, she flopped backwards onto a poolside lounger, which promptly collapsed beneath her weight. The other McAleeses hooted with delight. Ronan felt himself hesitate before reluctantly picking himself up to go and see if she was hurt.

Don't say it. Don't even think that name, don't! Goddamn you, Singer!

The end came in the last week of November, when London was cold and wet, and Puerto Banus just another pouch of photographs forgotten in a drawer. They now bickered constantly, every minor exchange a petty point-scoring exercise, he cringing at her whinge-ing, she stung by his sighs and sardonic silences. The wedding had been scheduled for the following July. 'We want you two tied up and in the river for the nineties,' as Linda's father had put it. For the recep-tion, Linda's mother wanted a marquee in the enormous back garden of her brick mansion in the outskirts of Maidstone. What with so many royal weddings, marquees, she maintained, were all the rage. Linda, however, wanted Chilston Park Country House Hotel. It had dawned on Ronan that 1989 would not be a stress-free year.

It was a Tuesday night. Ronan had endured, by his standards, a rather taxing few days, thinking a lot but writing little on the equally dull subjects of luxury yachts and building supplies for the looming dead-line of *The South-East Construction Review*. Linda came home from work, poked her head through the living room door, grunted a greet-ing, then began foraging noisily through the kitchen. What little train of thought he had gathered was irrevocably derailed. She poked her head through the door again. 'There's nothing to eat,' she announced.

'I had stuffed vine leaves for lunch. There's a few left, in a can in the fridge.'

'Ugh!'

He sighed. 'Okay, I'll walk to the supermarket. Could do with some fresh air anyway.' He nearly added that inspiration was about as likely to strike in the supermarket as it was in the living room, listening to her pulling cupboards apart like a starving bear.

'I'll come with you. We haven't been shopping together in ages.'

At that point, alarm bells should have gone off in Ronan's head, because there were actually a number of very good reasons why the two rarely went shopping together. At the supermarket, Linda proceeded to load up the trolley with bags of potatoes, pasta, oven chips and frozen fried rice. Next came boxes of burgers, reconstituted chicken sticks, biscuits and bacon. They argued over whether to buy a chicken frozen or fresh. Linda mocked Ronan for wanting to spend three pounds on a tiny jar of saffron, and point-blank refused to let him buy chickpeas to make his own humus. Nor did she see the point of purchasing tomatoes and onions to make pasta sauce, when it came ready-made in jars. Ronan, in turn, tried to explain, eyes raised to heaven, that it was wasteful to buy Brie, Philadelphia, Boursin and Cheddar all at the same time as he wouldn't eat any, and most of it would go off. Then, at the checkout, he found he'd forgotten his wallet, so Linda paid instead, with a supercilious smile on her face that made him want to ram the trolley through the supermarket window. They didn't speak on the way home, and when they reached the flat, he pointedly left her to put the shopping away in the kitchen, returning to his typewriter. That was when he heard her moan, 'Oh, no! We forgot to buy pizza!'

He ignored her.

'I don't believe it – we have no pizza!' Louder, this time, but still he ignored her. She stood in the doorway.

'I said, we have no—'

'Darling,' he snapped, punching a key on the typewriter much harder than necessary, 'if you wanted pizza for your dinner, you should have bought some. You did, after all, buy just about everything else.'

'But I want pizza!' Her voice upgraded from whinge to whine.

'Well, unfortunately you appear not to have—'

'I just want pizza!'

'Jesus!' Ronan exploded out of the chair and stormed past her into the kitchen. The plastic bags bulged on the counter. His thin arms flailing, Ronan tore at them, and as they ruptured, items fell to the ground.

'Here we are!' He held up a bag of white flour to Linda, who watched him, eyes wide. 'We have flour!' He slammed it onto the kitchen table, splitting the bag. 'Butter!' Slamming the butter raised a cloud of flour. 'Eggs!' Slamming the eggs wasn't such a good idea, but it sure looked dramatic. 'Milk!' A carton burst over the growing mess. 'Crappy tinned tomatoes!' Linda jumped at the bang. 'Cheese! In fact, we have every cholesterol-soaked piece of fodder known to man! I'm sure that even you could make a pizza out of that! And if you can't, then why don't you cook something equally thick and tasteless, and enjoy it all the same!'

He barged past her, back to the living room, and flung himself into his chair. He stabbed viciously at the typewriter, hitting the keys in nonsensical order, covering them in flour from his fingers. He glared at the paper as if it were Linda's face. From the kitchen a low wail started, rising like an air-raid siren. After a minute or so, it quieted into little choking sobs. At this point, he was evidently supposed to go to her, and say sorry. He didn't.

'Is that what you think of me?' She filled the living room doorway, sniffling. 'Is that what you think of me…thick…and tasteless?' He punched a few keys. 'Ronan!' She crossed the floor and put a dainty hand on his fingers, pinning them to the machine, which protested with a buzzing noise. 'At least acknowledge that I exist!'

Before he said it, he knew that he shouldn't.

'Okay, you exist. Now fuck off.'

She pulled back as if punched, then turned on her heel and stalked out to the kitchen. Ronan pretended to study the page before him. Seconds later, the toaster hit him squarely on the temple, just above the right eye. The fact that she hadn't slammed the door should have warned him, but then, physical violence was not one of his areas of expertise – indeed, as he felt around for his glasses, it occurred to him that the blood squirting from his forehead across the typewriter was by far the most he'd ever seen in his life. The fact that the blood was his seemed strangely irrelevant.

He didn't emerge from the Accident and Emergency ward of St George's Hospital, Tooting until well after midnight. He'd been forced to wait for hours, holding a bathroom towel to his forehead before a doctor could see him, then a few hours more for an X-ray. A nurse cheerfully informed him that it was better in any case not to sleep when there was a possibility of concussion. After all that hanging around, it took the doctor less than five minutes to sterilise and close the wound with a couple of paper sutures. Still, Ronan assumed that by now Linda would be sick from worry and guilt, and correspondingly apologetic, humbled and compliant.

As he stepped from the taxi in front of the flat, he stood on something. He peered down and saw that it was a book. How odd. Looking around, he then saw through the gloom that the pavement was strewn with books. Dazed, it took him a few seconds to comprehend that the books were all his, from his shelves in the living room. Horror washed over him when he saw that his electric typewriter had been smashed violently off the concrete path of the diminutive front garden. A few more of his possessions – a Sony Walkman and a couple of cassette tapes – had been tossed on the gravel, while four of his shirts – good ones – lay draped across the privet hedge. Enraged, disbelieving, he stuck his key in the front door. It was bolted from the inside, so he hammered with the knocker. At first it seemed as if Linda might have abandoned the flat as well as his worldly goods. He ran at the door with his shoulder, but under his slight build, it was never going to give. The noise, however, caused the hallway to illuminate. He heard the bolt unfasten, and drew a deep breath, pumping himself up to gush indignity. And there stood Linda, wearing a face he had not only never witnessed before, but had not, even in nightmares, imagined to be part of her plump, helpless repertoire. The snarling timbre of her voice was also completely unprecedented.

'My father's on his way up from Maidstone with two of his men. If I were you,' and she reached behind herself to dump a large object at his feet, 'I'd be gone before they get here. Unless you fancy having your fucking books shoved up your arse, one by one. Which, now that I think about it, you probably would.'

The door slammed, the bolt slid home, the hallway light extinguished. By the streetlamps, Ronan saw that the large object was a scuffed leather suitcase he'd bought at a flea market in Canterbury. He had no chance of fitting all his poor, abused darlings in, and even if he had, he couldn't have carried them. The tears he wept while packing from the pavement were for the books, and not the girl, he left behind.

He awoke to find Singer crouching in front of him, adjusting the gas fire. For several seconds, he had absolutely no idea where he was.

'Hi, Ro.' Singer hoisted his camera bag onto the table and walked past him into the kitchen. Ronan heard the spray of a faucet, then the low roar of an electric kettle starting to heat. Glasses clinked. He sat up and took in the cramped room, which could easily have passed for the nesting box of a magpie with an eye for a picture. The right side of his face felt numb. He touched his cut. It was dry, it hadn't seeped, and the swelling had started to subside. He pushed his glasses up onto the bridge of his nose. Still in his leather jacket and with the smell of cold air clinging to him, Singer handed him a hot whiskey, then subsided into the armchair and pulled it up to the gas fire.

'So, my man, what in the name of holy shit happened to you?'

'Do you remember that night in the pub, when you called Linda a Kraken?' Ronan thought that Singer frowned into his drink for just a split second too long before answering.

'No.'

'Well, you did.'

'What's a Crack-in?

Ronan sipped his whiskey and breathed out heavily, tapping his chest. 'I'm here because the Kraken is awake,' now he was certain he detected the barest of smirks behind Singer's exaggerated frown, 'and by God, I wakened her.'

4

Ronan had been right about living with Singer – it was distasteful.
Not because Singer himself was possessed of any particularly noxious
habits; indeed, his host was often away. Rather, because his self-esteem
had plummeted hand-in-hand with his circumstances. Until that
dreadful night in London, he had believed himself cosy and secure,
yet also independent. He was like a spoiled housecat weaned on
warm cushions and chopped liver which overnight finds itself
dumped in a faraway ditch. He didn't know how to respond, so he
inured himself against his grim new reality by sleeping a lot, and
reading everything in Singer's house.

Singer's library, if one could flatter the random piles of books with
such a title, concentrated heavily on art, history and film. He also
possessed coffee table-sized tomes of photography of every conceivable type – landscapes, fashion, reportage, arthouse, nudes. If Singer
appeared in the evenings, the two would huddle at the gas fire and
chat, smoke and demolish a bottle of whiskey.

Sometimes Singer wouldn't return until very late, then when he
did, he would slump in his armchair and listen to Mahler's *Adagietto
from Symphony Number 5 in C sharp minor*, which he played on an
ancient turntable cached inside the mahogany cabinet. This piece of
music, Ronan decided, was the most lachrymose he'd ever heard.

He suspected he knew why Singer listened to it, but when a man is unhappy himself, he cares little for the misery of others.

Belfast had calmed down considerably compared to earlier in the year, in the sense that people were being killed on a weekly rather than a daily basis. The city centre, a square mile of Victorian architecture lined with bomb-damaged 1970s shopfronts, was barely worth visiting, and Ronan did not dare show his face in the peaceful southern suburbs of the city, where he risked being spotted by his parents. So, like Stacey before him, even though the sound of gunfire was relatively infrequent, Ronan rarely left Singer's house except on necessary missions to the odd little corner shop at the top of the street. Cigarettes and tobacco, it sold in abundance. Soft white bread, too. Milk, tins of revolting corned beef and, for some unfathomable reason, pineapple chunks, were the only other forms of sustenance it offered, and Ronan wondered if the ailing proprietor perhaps feared a nuclear war, not merely a sectarian one.

Once, overcome by hunger, he walked for twenty minutes to reach the nearest supermarket. There, he was confronted by a total absence of peppers, celery, avocados and even garlic from the vegetable display. The staff had never heard of olive oil. He had returned home vexed and empty-handed. As December rolled in and the days grew ever darker, he felt all the more trapped. He slept longer, and washed less. Every afternoon, upon rising, he asked himself how he would ever escape the decrepit little street he now called home, with its incessant din of helicopters hovering high overhead.

One morning at three a.m., after a semi-somnolent drinking session before the gas fire, Singer answered his question for him.

'I've had enough,' he announced.

'Yeah, bed,' Ronan affirmed, through the unlit, half-smoked roll-up stuck to his lower lip. He had taken to smoking roll-ups for economic reasons.

'No, I mean I've had enough of...*this*.' Singer gestured with his hand. The needle of the record player bounced repeatedly off the end stop, making a quiet, constant scratch.

'Thank God. If I never heard Mahler again, it would be too soon.'

'I wasn't referring to the music.'

Ronan felt the hot swill of many whiskeys turn chilly in his tummy. Was he on the verge of another eviction? 'Listen,' he spluttered, 'you've been very good, putting me up and all that, I just need more time to—'

Singer interrupted him. 'Don't be silly, I wasn't talking about you either. Stay as long as you like.'

Ronan's panic subsided. 'Oh. What have you had enough of, then? The evils of Thatcherism?'

Singer stood, tore a handful of photographs from the wall and tossed them contemptuously to the floor. Ronan peered owlishly at the random images of armed men and burning motor cars, as if seeing them for the first time. When he spoke, Singer's voice was thick with drunken dejection.

'I've had enough of scrabbling around in the filth of this rotten little place, looking for bits of shit to sell. I feel like a thief, always turning up to steal people's worst moments.' Ronan was taken aback, for it was somehow unacceptable that his apparently capable friend should reveal himself as being also adrift in the sea of uncertainty. There was room for only one drowning man in their relationship.

'I thought photojournalism was your calling. You always said that the world needed to see what this place was really like.'

'The world has seen enough. I've seen enough. Anyway, things are quiet. It's hard to take photographs the agencies want to buy when nobody's getting murdered.'

'But the killing never stops for long.'

Singer's eyes flashed. 'That's precisely it! So what am I to wish for? What they did to those poor corporals? What they did to...' He paused, pursed his lips and then drained his glass, shaking his head. Ronan knew what his friend had been about to say, but also knew better than to pursue it.

'But if you gave up your work, what would you do?'

'I have absolutely no idea.'

'Then we'd both be unemployed.'

Singer laughed sourly. 'We make a fine couple, don't we? The best education money can buy, and look at us. Do you know that everyone else in our class at school went on to become a either a solicitor or a dentist?'

'Who told you that?'

'I got an invitation to a class reunion last year. It had a list of every-one's name inside, and their current profession. Dentists, most of them.'

'I'd rather die than be a dentist.'

'I bet they earn good money, though.'

'Imagine having to look down people's throats with a hangover. You couldn't pay me to do that. What did it say beside our names?'

'Nothing, just a blank.'

'Did you go to the reunion?'

'Gimme a break – reunions are strictly for saps.' He started up the narrow stairs. 'But on the subject of glowing careers, I'm off to Dublin in the morning. They're refusing to extradite some priest. The Brits want him on explosives charges, would you believe. I'll be back on Saturday. Be ready to go, first thing.'

'Go? Go where?'

'I don't know. Anywhere but here.' He climbed the stairs and closed his bedroom door. Mystified, Ronan stared at the ceiling as Singer's discarded boots thudded across it.

The weather turned to winter, and for two days Ronan didn't speak to anybody, except for the decaying proprietor of the corner shop, and then only to state his desired brand of tobacco. He felt himself slipping over into another, ghostly world – a parallel universe of empty pavements, dark alleyways and depressing news bulletins that seemed to emanate from a distant planet.

On the third day, he was startled from his coma by a clatter from downstairs. He sat up in bed. His head felt numb. He pulled on his glasses to peer out the window. The terrace opposite was smothered in white, like an over-iced Christmas cake. The snow-muffled silence outside magnified the racket from below. Ronan pushed his feet into his burgundy carpet slippers, wrapped the eiderdown around his pyjamas like a cloak and descended. He found Singer stomping in and out of the front door, dumping sundry items – pots, pans, blankets, even his darkroom equipment – into the open boot of his car, his feet trailing generous measures of slush into the living room with each return journey. It was as if he intended to move house. The chill air seized Ronan's throat and made his chest feel tight.

'Close that shagging door, it's Baltic out there!'

Singer lifted three bottles of whiskey from the kitchen counter. 'Can you describe it to me – I've just driven up from Dublin through that lot, with a blazing hangover. I thought I told you to be ready to go? Look at you, you're not even dressed!' He wrapped the bottles of whiskey in a black combat jacket.

'Are you deranged?' Ronan wheezed. 'I'm not going anywhere in that snow! Why, I'm sure if we turned on the radio, they'd be telling people not to make non-essential journeys.'

'This is an essential journey. Essential to my sanity.' Singer strode out to the car and placed his precious package in the boot. He returned with more slush. 'And you shouldn't do everything the media tells you to.' Ronan shuffled into the kitchen and groped around the gas cooker.

'Where's the kettle?'

'I just packed it.'

'But I want tea!' He could feel himself fighting for air, and coughed.

'Get dressed. I'll buy you breakfast on the road – could do with some myself. And bring that blanket you're wearing.'

'Why? Where are we going?'

'North Donegal.'

'What? You may as well try to reach Reykjavik, in this weather.'

'You find me a place to stay in Reykjavik, and I'll be there. The further away from Belfast, the better. The best I could organise at short notice is north Donegal. Look around you.' Singer stopped packing and gestured at the little room, the armchair and sofa pulled tight against the gas fire, pathetic and grubby in the morning light. 'It's Christmas next weekend – is this what you want? You and me sitting here, staring at each other?'

'But why do we need so much stuff?'

'Get yourself together, and I'll tell you in the car. Are you all right, by the way? You look kinda…'

'Wait, wait,' Ronan coughed again, long and hard, and began to retch. He stumbled into the kitchen, returning with a large green tin and a saucer. He plonked himself down at the table, clawed open the tin, and emptied a pile of green–grey powder into the saucer. 'Gimme your lighter,' he whispered.

'Jesus, what's wrong with you? Your face is purple!'

'Gimme your fuckin' lighter!' Ronan's voice was a high, thin rasp. Singer dug in his pocket and handed him a lighter. Ronan set fire to the powder in the dish, which smouldered briskly, producing a grey column of smoke. Leaning over the smoke, he gulped it in greedily, breathing more deeply every time he took a lungful. Singer stood with his arms folded, rapt at this novel display. After a few minutes, the powder burnt itself out and Ronan flopped back into his chair. His face was pale, skin bluish around the eyes and mouth, but his breathing had returned to normal.

'Are you okay?'

'Sorry. Asthma attack. Got it just in time.'

Singer lifted the green tin, inspecting it. 'I recognise this smell. Your room at school stank of this.'

'Potter's Asthma Remedy. Old-fashioned, but it works. I just need to sit for a minute.'

'Yeah, look, I'll get the kettle from the car and make you a cup of tea.'

'Forget it. I want wine.'

'Eh?'

'I said, "I want wine".'

'Bit early, even for you.'

'If you really must insist on dragging me off to some arctic tundra, the least you can do is buy me a few decent bottles of wine to take with me. That way, I can die like a gentleman.'

Day became evening as the car slithered from motorway to minor road. The landscape was like a clean, puffed-up pillow, until it started snowing again, and their surroundings disappeared behind an endless curtain of falling white feathers. Ronan had been right – snow was general, over Ireland. Tightly wrapped in his grey cashmere overcoat, he fell asleep in the passenger seat. When he awoke it was dark, and he'd never felt so cold in his life. The road had been reduced to a single track, and had merged seamlessly with the surrounding countryside – which appeared mountainous in the pitifully small cones of light thrown out by the car. Singer steered gingerly, easing forward mainly by guesswork.

'What time is it?'

'Late.'

'Are we there yet?'

'Yes. But I thought I'd drive around in circles until you woke up.'

'Where are we?'

'This would be north Donegal.'

'So are we there yet?'

'I'm not sure. I've never been here before, and this bloody snow makes everything look the same. Do me a favour, and roll me a cigarette.' Ronan fumbled for his tobacco. Cigarettes, at least, were warm things.

'This place we're staying – you never told me what it's like.'

'It's a big old house, by the sea. That's as much as I know.'

'Who owns it?'

'Some people. I've never met them before.'

'How will we know when we get there? There's no road signs or anything.'

'We go north, until we hit the sea.'

'How come you picked this place? I mean, why here, and not somewhere else?'

'My Uncle Lucius did some diving up here.'

'Diving? I thought he lectured at the university?'

'He does, Professor of European History, but he used to dive when he was younger. Back in the early seventies he led an archaeological team that salvaged a wreck off this coast. Spanish Armada.'

'Wow. 1588?'

'That would probably be the same Armada, yes. Anyway, the house we're headed for is where Lucius stayed when he was diving on the wreck. He mentioned it once, and when I asked, he still had the number of the woman who owns it. I rang her from Dublin, she said the house was available, so here we are, looking for it.'

'But there are no houses around here.'

'Should stand out like a sore thumb, then.'

Ronan lit two shabbily rolled cigarettes, and passed one to Singer. 'You have no idea where we are, do you?'

'Shit.'

'Pardon?'

There are two kinds of car crash. There are those that happen instantaneously, where everyone involved is caught completely by surprise. When Singer didn't answer, Ronan looked out the windscreen, and saw that they were gathering momentum down a very steep hill. He realised that he was about to experience the second kind of car crash, where those involved have just enough time to understand that they might die. He writhed on his seat like a skewered reptile, spitting his cigarette onto his overcoat.

'Stop! Stop this fucking thing! *Stop!*'

'I'm trying! I'm trying!' Singer spun the steering wheel this way and that, but the car flew onward. He yanked on the handbrake – nothing. The hill, which steepened with descent, ended in a hairpin bend hemmed by thick stone walls.

'Ssshit!' Singer hissed again.

Ronan could see the treeless countryside for miles around, carpeted in a bulging, flawlessly uniform layer of snow that reflected blue light from a richesse of stars. Then the stone walls filled the windscreen, there was a tremendous bang and an explosion of glass. The car bounced twice and stopped in a mound of bright, swirling dust thrown up before the headlamps – which Ronan could see were still working, which meant he was still alive. Singer exhaled and laid his forehead against the steering wheel.

'Out! Let me out!' Ronan clawed at the door.

'Relax – we're okay!'

Thrashing wildly, Ronan threw himself bodily into the snow, rolled over, then stood and shook himself off.

'Bastard cigarette! Ugh! Nothing looks worse than a burn-mark on cashmere!'

'Never mind about my car,' Singer muttered, climbing out his own side.

'Which you crashed, on a journey that you insisted on making! I knew this would happen!'

Singer walked back along the tyre tracks through the newly deflowered snow to a narrow gap in the stone wall. He patted a wooden post at one side of it. A metal hinge hung like a broken limb, and the fragmented remains of the car's wing mirror lay strewn below, glinting brighter than the ice.

'Used to be a gate,' he announced. 'We're not the first to have gone through it. If I'd hit that wall, we wouldn't be standing here talking to one another.'

'If you'd listened to me back in Belfast, neither of us would be standing in a field in the middle of nowhere, knee-deep in snow!'

'Quit whining,' Singer leaned his hands on the car bonnet, 'and help me to push.'

'You're joking. Surely we should summon assistance.'

'How should we "summon assistance"? We haven't passed a house for ages, and we haven't seen another car since we crossed the border.'

'That's because everyone else in this wretched wilderness has had the good sense to remain indoors!'

'Shut up and push.'

'If I get short of breath, I might suffer another attack.' Ronan plunged his fists in his pockets. Then he screamed, urgently retracted his right hand, and waved it in the air.

'Found your cigarette, have you?'

Ronan huffed for the next half an hour or so, until eventually the road ran through a small forest, crested and plunged into a valley. Singer drove in low gear, very slowly. A faint yellow light appeared up ahead, lonely and out of place in the winter wasteland. As they drew closer, they saw that it came from an old two-storey house that stood to the left of the road. The walls had been whitewashed, but not in recent memory. Singer stopped and killed the car engine but not the headlamps.

'I think this is it.'

'What? We've driven for five hours through a blizzard and cheated death just to see this? Where's the sea?'

Singer opened his door and climbed out. Reluctantly, Ronan followed. His feet crunched softly on the snow. The light didn't shine from any of the house windows, which were discouragingly dark, but from a weak, wall-mounted lantern that vaguely illuminated a flat metal sign above the wooden front door. The sign was faded, and patches of rust had erupted through the enamel, but they could make out a smiling tortoise, carrying a large glass of black liquid on its back. In anaemic pink lettering, the legend above the tortoise commanded,

Have a
GUINNESS
when you're TIRED

'Gosh,' Ronan breathed, 'it's Chukwa.'

'Who?'

'In Hindu mythology, a giant tortoise called Chukwa carries the world around on his back. His feet represent the four corners of the earth. We've obviously found one of the corners, probably the furthest-flung.'

'I have to say it looks more like a beer advertisement to me.'

'Singer – take my word for it; maybe this was a pub once long ago, but not any more. They just forgot to take the sign down.' He hung back as Singer tried the wooden door, which opened to reveal a dark corridor with another closed door at the far end, visible as a yellow outline. Ronan's voice fell to a forceful whisper. 'We're like those idiots in horror films who don't turn back when they should! We can't go in there, this is someone's house!' But Singer walked on down the corridor and opened the second door, hesitating momentarily, before stepping into the light. Swearing under his breath, Ronan followed. Halfway down the corridor, he bumped into an old-fashioned pay phone, which protruded solidly from the wall. The phone chimed, and Ronan swore some more.

The room beyond smelled of cooked meat, milk, spirits, beer, tobacco and polish. Some of the odours emanated from a glass-fronted, 1950s-style refrigerated display counter off to the left, which doubled as one arm of an L-shaped bar counter, the other section being three paces directly in front of them, this made of a rich, dark wood that stretched to the linoleum-clad floor. Tall, thin stools of the same dark wood were drawn up in front of both the fridge and the bar counter proper. To their right stood a single round table that serviced a black plastic-leather bench set into the wall. The fridge exhibited glistening prisms of processed ham fringed with orange crumbs, thick parcels of fatty bacon tied with string, cubes of cheddar cheese wrapped in greaseproof paper and a stack of pyramidal milk cartons. The two walls behind the L-shaped counter were taken up with uneven rows of wooden, cream-painted shelving that stretched upward to a disproportionately high ceiling. These shelves were home to a thriving population of tin cans, containing everything that could be conceivably tinned, from creamed rice to shoe polish to prunes and mushy peas. Bottles of paint stripper, paraffin, sarsaparilla and bleach peered down from the loftiest levels, and below these were more bottles, of whiskey, gin, rum and vodka – one of each inverted into a glass optic. The shelves were also home to numerous ceramic spirit flagons with dark blue writing on the sides, interspersed with fully intact brass artillery shells, some highly polished, others brown and corroded. Two ship's lanterns, one green, the other red, stood out amidst the clutter, as did, suspended high behind the fridge, a heavy old railway station clock with roman numerals, strict black hands and a face the colour of brandy butter. According to the clock, which didn't so much tick as clunk, it was nearly half-past ten.

From the ceiling above hung blue nylon ropes, green netting, aluminium frying pans, several pairs of black Wellington boots and a cluster of pink plastic buoys. But what struck Ronan most were the knives. A wide variety of bladed instruments dangled down from amongst the nets, suspended overhead like so many swords of Damocles. Some were modern fishing implements, with rubber handles and plastic sheaths. Others were plainly antiques – Ronan noticed several cavalry sabres, a Gurkha *kukri*, a pair of basket-handled cutlasses, an elegant but evil-looking rapier and a nest of ill-intentioned daggers, dirks and bayonets.

Singer settled carefully onto one of the barstools – saying nothing, but smiling lopsidedly to himself each time his eyes found some item stranger than the last. Ronan remained standing, his attention taken by the wall to his right, which was papered with yellowing maritime charts and a pictorial guide to the manifold species of crustaceans and fish one might expect to encounter in the North Atlantic. The clock clunked away the minutes as the two studied their surroundings. Ronan eventually beckoned Singer over to point out two black-and-white photographs hanging beside the door by which they had entered. The first showed a harbour with two small trawlers tied up inside it. An enormous wave stood over the harbour, as high again as the wall itself. In the second picture, the wave had just broken, consuming both harbour and boats in a frightening mountain of white spray.

They turned away from the picture to see a woman standing behind the bar – they started slightly, as neither had heard her enter. A shadowy alcove off to the right of the shelving must, Ronan guessed, hide a passage into a dwelling area. The woman was middle-aged, small, wore undyed peppery hair and a bottle-green cardigan. Her face was disapprovingly impassive, like that of a church caretaker who'd seen generations of sinners come and go.

'Gentlemen,' she stated, flatly.

'Good evening. We're looking for Dunaldragh.'

'This is Dunaldragh.'

'Glad to hear it. My name's Gareth Singer. Would you be Mrs McFall?' Ronan had not heard Singer use either his first name or such a polite tone in quite some years. The woman nodded curtly.

'I am.'

'In that case we spoke yesterday, on the telephone.'

'We did that.'

Singer eased himself back onto the barstool. 'Are you still open?'

'We are.'

'Could I have two pints of Guinness, please, and two large whiskeys – hot, if you don't mind.' The woman nodded abruptly again, and set about her task without indulging in any further conversation. Ronan perched himself gingerly on a barstool, as if he had no right to be there, which, in Mrs McFall's presence, was rather how he felt. She served the drinks, boiling an electric kettle behind the bar counter for the hot whiskeys. When Singer paid, she took his money and disappeared into the dark alcove, re-emerging some minutes later with his change and a big old iron key, which she placed on the bar. It looked like the key to a castle, or maybe to a castle's dungeon, Ronan thought.

'Thank you. The house – how do we find it from here?'

'Keep on going down this road until you can go no further. Will that be all for now?'

'Just one thing.' He pointed towards the photographs of the wave engulfing the harbour. 'Those pictures – where were they taken?'

'From the Pier House.'

'The Pier House?'

'Where you will stay.' Mrs McFall nodded at the iron key, then withdrew, leaving Singer and Ronan alone again. They finished their drinks in silence.

Singer drove as directed. The road became a laneway, a vigorous tuft of grass down the middle having triumphed over the ancient tarmacadam. At least it was free from snow, dropping steadily downhill beneath the level of the surrounding countryside, first through a tunnel of gorse and skeletal fuscia, then through a rocky defile that eventually opened onto a flat gravel apron where a dozen wooden fishing boats stood on ramshackle trailers, propped haphazardly upright by planks and metal poles. The pair stepped from the car to the sound and smell of the sea. They sneaked through the stranded vessels, as if not to disturb a menagerie of sleeping monsters, and found themselves standing on the stone cobbles of a pier. Beside them, glassy black water surged, licking the harbour lip, before subsiding down the slipway with a slap and a suck. By the light of the moon, they could see that the pier was about four paces wide and some forty paces long, running roughly parallel with the shoreline. Beyond it, jagged outcrops of rock punctuated the star-spangled surface of a horseshoe-shaped bay which, judging by the hiss of the wash, had a pebble beach. A single yellow light behind and above the bay had to be that of the pub. Singer climbed a flight of worn steps onto the sea wall. An arm of the Milky Way arched spectacularly overhead, making him feel dizzy, exhilarated and slightly sick. He turned north and a chill upward draught clasped his face. He looked down. Less than a step away was a sheer drop over the far side of the harbour, which ended in seething blackness. Down there, beyond the miniscule shelter of the harbour, was the real sea – always ready, always waiting. He descended the steps much more respectfully than he'd climbed them, and scuffed a boot against a gleaming cobble.

'You know it's cold when there's ice this close to the sea.'

'I know it's cold,' replied Ronan, 'because my trousers have frozen to my fucking legs. So we've found the pier – any idea where the Pier House might be?' Singer, lost in the menacing magic of the place, had momentarily forgotten their reason for being there.

'What do you suppose that is?' He pointed to the landward side of the harbour, which was a steep jumble of sharp black rock. Where that rock ended and the pebble beach began, a dark shape sat slightly apart. Even in the bright moonlight, it could have easily been mistaken for another outcrop, but as Ronan squinted, he thought he could make out a long, irregular roofline. The pair walked back through the boats and spotted an opening, a rough track that wriggled across the sea-grass beyond the shingle beach. They came to a low, dry-stone wall, interrupted by a crooked wooden gate. Behind it stood the Pier House.

Singer fumbled with the gate, found the latch and heaved it open. 'Wait here. I'm pretty sure I can squeeze the car up, then we can see what we're doing.' Ronan opened his mouth to disagree, but Singer strode off back along the path, so he stood and stared at the house, while the house stared back at him. Suddenly, the walls came alive with a luminous white glow, the windows gaping like plundered tombs. He stepped backwards and fell on his rear as the house shone with its own radiance, then, as quickly as it had come, the weird illumination vanished. For an instant, Ronan panicked, summoning every ghost story he'd ever heard as a child. Then, as he picked himself up, he saw the same spectral flash far out to sea. How odd – he'd thought they had travelled as far north as possible. The lighthouse must be on an offshore island. He waited about a minute for the beam to sweep round again, then took in the house with greater equanimity.

The main building was two-storied, quite a bit bigger than the pub but not whitewashed, faced instead with weathered sandstone that made it blend with its surroundings, in spite of its size. A rectangular porch stood proud from the ground floor – Ronan counted two bay windows on either side of it and five smaller windows up above. The angled roof was of heavy, irregular slate that sparkled with frost. A stubby chimney stood at each end, and a slightly taller one not quite in the middle. A single-storey set of outbuildings stretched from one side of the house inland. Turning around, Ronan saw that the front elevation diagonally overlooked the harbour, facing north-west. Beyond the seaward gable, the smash of water on the shingle alternated with the knocking of millions of rounded pebbles, dragged along after each wave as it withdrew. He inhaled – the cold and the salt stung his throat, but he had never tasted anything cleaner. Each exhalation from his lips formed a cloud of mist that lingered a few seconds before dissolving in the sharp night air.

A revving engine and a pair of headlamps heralded Singer's arrival. The car slid past Ronan through the gate, then swerved violently to the right. The grass within the wall was even more unkempt and hummocky than that without. As Singer wrestled with the car to direct light onto the front door, Ronan saw that he had narrowly missed colliding with a waist-high stone plinth that stood halfway between the gateway and the house. He walked over to inspect it. Singer joined him.

'Nearly destroyed the bastard thing. What is it?'

Ronan felt around for his cigarette lighter. 'Silly place to leave it, whatever it is.' He flicked the flint and held his lighter aloft. A corroded, green copper plate stamped with roman numerals was embedded in the top of the plinth.

'The needle's gone,' Singer rubbed the plate, 'but I could swear it's an old sundial.'

'Whoever put this here was either an incurable optimist or else plain mad.'

'Perhaps both.' Singer produced the iron key. 'Shall we find out?'

The lighthouse beam swept over them again as he inserted the key into the porch door. Expecting a struggle, he was surprised when the lock turned as easily as a modern mechanism, and the heavy door opened inward without a sound. The porch windows admitted enough moonlight to show a second door leading into the house proper, which bore panes of patterned glass of the kind Singer remembered from old sweetshops as a very small child. A twist of a round wooden handle opened this door in turn, then he paused, as beyond was pure pitch black. For all he knew, his next step might have led him onto a solid floor, or else over a drop as final as that which lay beyond the harbour wall. Ronan shoved him between the shoulder blades and he fell forwards. It was a stone-flagged floor.

'Hey! You could have…'

'What? Stood here freezing to death? Get a move on! Find a light switch!' Singer grunted and began to feel the wall to his left. Ronan stomped his feet. 'Hurry up, or I shall lose a limb to frostbite. Haven't you found a switch yet?' Singer stopped moving.

'Yes. But I'm indulging my fetish for rubbing up against walls in strange houses in the dead of night.'

Ronan sighed and sparked his lighter again, which, to his eyes, did nothing but thicken the gloom. However, Singer must have spotted something, because he reached out and seized the lighter, then bustled off, laughing.

'I don't believe it.'

'What?'

'Check this out.'

Ronan saw his lighter spark anew, then another object caught fire in a greasy orange tongue of flame, which became a yellow ball of light as Singer added the glass pipe and trimmed the wick of a copper oil lamp and picked it up, like a figure from a book of nursery rhymes. Half-expecting to be greeted by cobwebbed portraits of some frightening family, Ronan was taken aback to see that the hallway was home to nothing more than a modest hall table where Singer had found the lamp and, fixed on either wall at just above head height, a long row of black iron hooks. Grey-painted wooden panelling clad the walls up as far as the hooks, above which was plain white plaster. The hooks were empty, apart from the last on the right, which at first glance appeared to have a severed head suspended from it, although on closer examination the sinister object turned out to be a very dusty old gas mask.

Ronan murmured. 'What *is* this place?'

A wide wooden staircase climbed from the hallway into shadow, and two doors stood at either side of its foot. Singer chose the left-hand one. Beyond it, twin rectangles of stars appeared suspended in the darkness. It took him a few moments to comprehend that he was looking at windows, at the far, seaward end of what must have been a very large room stretching half the width of the house. Holding the lamp aloft, he saw that between the starry windows was a fireplace, big enough for a child to stand in. To his left, a pair of bay windows gave onto the harbour. The rattle of the beach could still be heard, but faintly, as in a dream.

'Oomph!' Ronan grunted as he collided with something. Singer directed his lamp to reveal a giant, misshapen sofa that resembled the consequences of some tormented furniture-maker's brutal desire to stuff as much horsehair as humanly possible into an acre of stressed brown leather. A legion of tarnished brass tacks strained to hold the miscreation together. Gathered around the yawning fireplace sat the gargantuan sofa's matching armchairs – each looked capable of swallowing a man whole. Feeling a faint heat, Singer approached the fireplace, and sure enough, the remains of a turf fire gave off a little warmth, and also the sweet, earthy smell that permeated the room.

'Hey. Maybe Mrs McFall isn't such a fierce old biddy after all.'

'Great. Do you think she'll come and tuck us up, and read us a story?'

The lighthouse beam flashed through the windows, casting the room in momentary stark relief. Singer noticed a veneered wooden box standing against the landward wall. Brown bakelite knobs surrounded a semi-circular glass dial.

'Oslo,' he read, 'Stockholm, London, Berlin, Rome. People used to listen to cities, Ro. Imagine sitting down at night, to listen to a city.' He turned one of the knobs and the dial glowed, then a soft crackle of static came from the front of the cabinet. 'Valves,' he announced. 'They'll take a minute to heat up. Amazing this thing works at all, the age of it.' Sure enough, very remote martial music could be heard battling to penetrate the hiss.

'Look here.' Ronan peered down the far side of the radio and nudged something with his toe. Singer squatted with the lamp to reveal a car battery, with a wire running from each terminal in behind the set. Ronan sneered. 'Tell me – when you asked to rent this place, did your good friend Mrs McFall mention anything about electricity?'

'Jesus,' Singer admitted after a short silence. 'I think you're right. No light switches, no electrical appliances apart from this thing.' He patted the radio and held the lantern aloft again. On the high mantelpiece stood an assortment of candles in brass sticks and tin holders. A table behind the horsehair sofa was home to a substantial porcelain oil lamp, with an opaque white globe the size of a man's head. Singer began to laugh.

'I don't know what you find so funny,' Ronan snapped. 'We can't possibly stay in a house without electricity!'

'Why not?' Singer sounded genuinely pleased, which annoyed Ronan further.

'Well, for starters, how on earth am I going to chill my white wine?'

5

Singer awoke to a blessing from the Infant of Prague. The podgy plaster icon raised two fixed, benedictory fingers from its position on the narrow fireplace, close to the foot of his iron bedstead. Feeble sunlight struggled to penetrate the salt-caked glass of the sash window, while an absence of curtains allowed the sea breeze to whistle unimpeded through several gaps in the warped wooden frame. Rising to a chorus of broken springs, he saw by the size of the harbour wall that the tide was low. He was still fully clothed, apart from his boots, which lay kicked across the uneven, time-darkened floorboards. He watched the harbour for a while, then wandered out onto the landing. He hadn't looked into all of the rooms, as there were quite a few, but judging by the dim corridors that stretched away on either side, it seemed that the entire upper storey of the Pier House was floored with the same scuffed planks as his bedroom. If there had ever been carpet, it was long gone. He descended the staircase.

Ronan lay stiff as driftwood across the horsehair sofa, head and limbs sticking out from beneath the blankets Singer had heaped upon him before retiring. He had managed to revive the fire with lumps of turf from a willow basket, and Ronan had plonked himself down before the flames and refused to move any further. Singer had stepped out to the car to retrieve a bottle of whiskey, and returned to find

Ronan snoring. So he'd sat in the dark for some hours, watching the stars through the gable windows.

Now, seeing the room in daylight for the first time, he saw that the landward wall bore a variety of pictures hanging by thick cord from a high cornice. A few were engravings of sailing vessels, and several were photographs, dating, by the looks of them, from the turn of the century. One showed five moustachioed, uniformed men, standing in erect, self-conscious poses before the Pier House. They weren't soldiers, their attire was more maritime in appearance – dark, double-breasted jackets with bright buttons, small lapels, tall collars with ties and peaked caps. The front of the house looked immaculate – the porch and windowsills were painted white, and where all was now sea-grass, there had been a neat gravel drive. The sundial stood intact in the middle of the drive, and Singer noticed that the missing gnomon or needle had been delicately ornate.

Another photograph showed the pier itself, with a single-masted schooner sitting at half-tide. In yet another, the uniformed men made a second appearance, this time standing more at ease on a wider, lower pier that was plainly not the one from which the house took its name. Other men, in baggy jackets and flat caps, worked to either load or unload a large wooden rowing boat tied to this mysterious pier, and a huddled group of women in rough shawls, bonnets and skirts looked on, smiling. One of them held a swaddled baby, and two skinny dogs sniffed the ground around their feet.

Ronan sat up, like a corpse from a coffin, clearly enunciated the phrase 'Crash, bang, wallop!', then flopped down again to continue snoring, louder than before. Singer smiled and turned on tiptoe to leave. As he did, he saw that the wall on either side of and above the doorway was entirely taken up by an impressive collection of cloth- and leather-bound books. He selected one at random, opening it at the title page. It read,

GUNNERY INSTRUCTIONS,

SIMPLIFIED

FOR THE

Volunteer Officers of the U.S. Navy;

With hints to

EXECUTIVE AND OTHER OFFICERS

BY

LIEUT. EDWARD BARRETT, U.S.N.,

BROOKLYN NAVAL YARD, 1862

Singer gently returned the book to its place and closed the door behind him. He sat on the staircase to pull on his boots, lifted his black combat jacket from one of the hallway hooks and walked through the porch into the morning air. Although bitter, it was also sunny. He followed the path to the harbour, where he carefully climbed the same steps as the night before. The drop on the far side was only marginally less intimidating now that he could see it, ending on razor-sharp rocks exposed by the tide. A steady breeze blew onshore, shredding any remains of sleep.

Daylight didn't flatter the Pier House – it seemed much more dilapidated than it had by night. Still, it exuded an air of unkempt solidity, as if its worn grey façade, the veteran of countless storms, knew it would weather a few more yet. To the east of the house, the shingle beach arched for about a mile, ending in a riot of brown rock that rose into a bulging, rounded mountain. On its seaward side, the mountain had been bitten away to reveal coal-black cliffs, white along their crests from snow, and along their feet from an unbroken line of surf, thrown there by a restless, gunmetal sea. Behind the shingle beach, mounds of sea-grass rolled far inland, in mellow contrast to the dramatic harshness of the rest of the landscape. Overlooking the sea-grass, Singer could see the faded whitewash of McFall's pub peeping through a clump of trees, the only other building visible from the pier.

To the west, the view was blocked by a steep, heather-coated headland that plunged into the sea in an escarpment of rocks like serrated knives. Perched on top was a rectangular stone tower. Singer thought he detected the outline of a hairpin path leading up to it. A low, distant booming indicated that the headland quite likely protected Dunaldragh Bay from the North Atlantic proper. At the tip of the headland, the same jagged rock punched up through the water in a series of grass-tufted islets that receded untidily towards the horizon. Singer scanned them for signs of the lighthouse they'd seen the night before, although none looked big enough to support a building of any size.

'Them's the Garvan Isles. You'd get seals out there in season, but not at this time of year.' The nasal voice came from behind and below. Turning around, Singer saw an intensely red face looking up at him, topped by thick white hair streaked yellow with nicotine. Wire-brush eyebrows presided over small, cobalt eyes, and the smile exposed a gap between the two front teeth. The man climbed the steps. He was a good head-and-a-half shorter than Singer, but was even more thick-set in the chest and shoulders. He wore a stained burgundy sweatshirt with the sleeves rolled up and black corduroy trousers stuffed into a pair of Wellingtons. 'That's Saddle Rock.' He pointed out one of the islets that, sure enough, resembled a horse saddle dropped by some giant, godly hunting party. 'How far would you say that is from here?'

'About a mile?'

'Wrong. It's exactly two miles from the end of the pier. Distances over the sea, they're deceptive all right. Things always look closer than they are.'

'I saw a lighthouse last night. I can't see it now.'

The man's arm swung towards the north-east horizon, like the boom of a yacht caught in a gust. At first, he seemed to be pointing at a low, pregnant silver cloud trailing dark streams of sleet that curved like spilled ink in the wind, but then a diamond wink of white penetrated the curtain. Singer thought he could discern two mounds like giant whale snouts rising out of the sea.

'When that shower moves, you'll see it clear, but that's Inistrahull, Ireland's most northerly island. How far do you think that is from where we're standing?'

'Three, maybe four miles?'

'Would you believe me if I told you it's seven?'

'Since I'm not from around here, and you plainly are, I'd say I have no choice.'

The man laughed and stuck out his hand. 'Manus McFall.'

'Singer.' Fingers the size and colour of butcher sausages crushed Singer's hand. The man laughed all the more.

'When I first met your Uncle Lucius, I asked him if he was a singer by name or by nature.'

'And what did he say?'

'Right there, on the spot, he gave me to a rendition of 'The Foggy Dew'. It was brutal, I have to say.'

'I'd be no better.'

Manus laughed some more. 'We'll avoid that territory, so. Are you in the history game, like him?'

'I read, but I'm not a professional historian, if that's what you mean.'

'You're like me then. Interested, but self-taught. I learned a lot from Lucius.'

'Were you here when he salvaged the wreck?'

'Sure, I worked for him. His team used my boat for the entire dive — summer of '73, that was.'

'Where did it go down?'

The boom-like arm swung north-west. 'Over there, just inside the Garvan Isles. They made it into the bay, then hit a rock. A lot of ships have sunk outside the bay, and the current rips them to pieces, but as it was, we brought up all sorts — cannon, jewellery, coins, a gold cross. And when we weren't out over the wreck, we were up in the pub. Those were good times. So you're not a teacher, like him?'

'No, I'm a photographer, for the newspapers.'

'Jayz. No shortage of news where you're from — Belfast, is it?'

'You could say it's been a busy year. I'm glad to be away from it.'

'It's unusual, to have anybody here in the winter.'

'Glad to hear it. Tell me, the island…'

'Inistrahull.'

'Is it inhabited?'

'No. The lighthouse-keepers came off last year. Would you believe that light is now run by a computer in Dublin?'

'Doesn't seem right, does it?'

'It does not. The rest of us came off long before, between the wars.'

'The rest of us?'

'I was born out there. The walls of our house are still standing.'

'Why did you leave?'

'Bad times. When the fishing was bad, everything was bad. There were twelve families then, but they all came off when I was five years old, in 1928. Bad times, but times change.'

'And what about this place?' Singer faced the Pier House. The sky had darkened and the crumbling building seemed to frown.

'That was built by a big landlord, but the lighthouse commissioners took it over during the First World War.'

'Yes, I saw the photographs. But why would they want to be ashore, when their lighthouse is seven miles out to sea?'

'Because this place was very important to them. Remember that air travel is only a recent thing. For centuries, every ship that sailed between America and Scotland or the north of England had to pass here – it was like a highway. The light on that island had to be kept burning no matter what, so there were three keepers assigned to it at all times, sometimes more. If the winter was rough, the keepers' families came ashore, and the Pier House is where they stayed. It was like a barrack, if you can imagine that.'

'But it's yours now?'

'It's not mine, it's the wife's. Are you married?'

'God, no.'

'Well, if you ever do tie the knot, you'll quickly find that what's hers is hers, and what's yours is hers also.' This homespun maxim set Manus laughing again. 'Her father bought the house for next to nothing when the commissioners finished with it. The house, and all the land you see behind the shore, over there to the far side of the bay. But the land's not much good – not even sheep will eat that oul' sea-grass.'

'And what did your father-in-law have against electricity?'

'No one's lived in that house for near on forty years. It's way too big for us. I do my best to maintain it with what little we have. As your uncle often said, it would be a sin to let it go. But we only got the electric up at the pub in recent times, and I never saw the need to bring it down here.'

'Don't get me wrong, I'm not complaining. No television, no phone – it's perfect.' A handful of small hailstones bounced off the wall at their feet, carried on an icy blast.

'I'd better show you how to light that range or you'll have no hot water either.' The two set off towards the house. By the time they reached it, the hail was pelting down in stinging lumps the size of children's marbles. Manus led Singer up the hallway and through the door opposite the living room. It opened into a huge kitchen, with a long oak table dominating the near end, and at the far end a cast-iron range that was so big it looked like a steam locomotive that had crashed into the house and been left there. A door at the far end of the kitchen gave onto a corridor that ran under the stairs, along the rear of the building. There were a number of lesser rooms off it, one a pantry with cold stone shelves, and another was stacked with turf. Manus filled a bucket, then began showing Singer the intricacies of the range, opening doors and pulling levers. He explained that once the fire got going, it heated an inbuilt boiler that supplied water to the kitchen and bathroom. It was old-fashioned, but better than nothing. He hadn't lit it the previous evening, because once started, the range needed constant feeding. Singer thanked him nonetheless for having left a fire in the living room, mentally trying to reconcile the gregarious Manus McFall with his taciturn wife up the road.

The rattle of the kitchen door alerted them to the entrance of a pale, blanket-clad entity that drifted uncertainly to the chair nearest the door, and sat delicately down. Ronan's face looked very different without his spectacles, more chiselled, with larger, red-rimmed eyes.

'Someone please tell me – where in God's name am I, why is it so cold, and how do I summon room service?'

'Manus, allow me to introduce my good friend Ronan Doherty. He's a scholar and a poet, although this morning you'll have to forgive him for looking more like something the cat threw up.'

Ronan squinted as a blur approached, seized him by the hand and squeezed hard enough to make him yelp. 'Aoow! Charmed, I'm sure. Now I'm crippled as well as blind. Singer! What the hell have you done with my glasses?'

'I removed them from your drooling face and put them safely on the mantelpiece. You can thank me later.'

'Fetch them, please. If I go back in that room, I might never find my way out again.'

'Don't go putting ideas in my head,' Singer muttered as he left on his errand.

The blur, attempting to make conversation, addressed Ronan cheerfully. 'So, I take it you're a Belfast man, too?'

'I wish I could claim otherwise, but yes.'

'Are you really a poet?'

'I dabble, yes.'

'Welcome to the Pier House, I hope you enjoy your stay.'

'At present, survival is taking precedence over enjoyment.'

'Well, maybe you'll feel better once you cosy up to this girl.'
Manus patted the range as Singer returned with Ronan's glasses.

'Heat. Must have heat.' Ronan dragged his chair from the table
across the stone flags to the range and sat tight up against it, pulling
his blankets tighter. He looked plaintively up at Singer. 'Breakfast
now?'

'What am I, your ma?'

Manus roared with laughter. 'It'll be another twenty minutes
before that's hot enough to cook on.' He addressed Singer. 'Come
with me, we'll leave the ashy pet to warm his toes.'

'What's an ashy pet?' Ronan asked, not at all sure that he wanted
to be one. Manus laughed all the more and beckoned Singer through
the hallway and out the front door. The hail had passed and the weak
sunshine fought hopelessly with the icy breeze again.

'Here's something else I want to show you,' Manus spoke over his
shoulder, walking around the side of the house, away from the
harbour. 'How to get up above, in half the time it takes to walk the
road.' He set off through the hills of sea-grass behind the house,
following the line of the shingle beach at first, then cutting inland
along a path that wended its way through the hummocks then gradually upward, eventually entering a copse of wind-sculpted trees. On
the far side of these, a rusty gate set in a stone wall gave onto the road,
almost directly opposite the pub. 'The fishermen use it,' explained
Manus. 'They stop with us before they set out, and after they come
in again.'

'Where do these fishermen actually live?'

Manus waved vaguely inland. 'You'd have driven past a cluster of
houses last night, set back off the road. That's the village. Not much
to look at in the daylight, let alone the dark. But there's a post office,
a school and a church.'

'Do you fish yourself?'

'Crab and lobster. I still have the boat all right, but I only use it to
set the pots. Look there now.' Manus turned Singer around, showing
him an elevated view of the bay, and beyond it, the rounded twin
peaks of Inistrahull, standing clear of the water. Singer could easily
make out the white tower of the lighthouse on the western hill.

'You'll have to take me out sometime.'

'If we get a calm day, I will. I'll ring Dublin and let them know.'

'Let them know what?'

'The lighthouse commissioners, Irish Lights – they own the island now. You need their permission to land.'

'You have to ask to visit your own home?'

'This is my home,' Manus patted the wall of the pub, 'and there's been a lot worse than the lighthouse commissioners owned land around here, let me tell you.'

Shortly, Singer returned along the sea-grass path, holding aloft a tray with a loaf of bread, a carton of eggs, a parcel of bacon and two glistening pints of Guinness balanced upon it.

The cold sunshine persisted, so Singer crammed the now-scalding range full of turf and proposed a walk along the beach. The two sauntered east across the shingle, with fussy, hectoring waves breaking close to their feet. Singer updated Ronan with the information he'd gleaned from Manus.

'It certainly is all very different,' Ronan mused, stooping to pick up a lengthy piece of driftwood that he studied, then used as a makeshift staff, lending him the air of a pilgrim.

'It's wonderful. I've only been here a night and I feel better already.'

'But no shops, no cinema, no electricity, one pub – what the hell are we supposed to do with ourselves?'

'What we're doing now. Walk. Talk. Drink. Not be anywhere else. Gather driftwood for the fire. And you never know, there could be other things besides.'

'Like what?'

'Hmm. I'm sure we could get past that if we tried.' They had reached the end of the beach, to be confronted by an untidy jumble of brown and black boulders, where the sea had long ago provoked the mountainside into falling away in what must have been a dramatic landslide. Without answering Ronan's question, Singer jumped onto the first barnacle-encrusted stone, then scrambled upwards, leaping from rock to rock. He was agile for a big man. When he had climbed a certain distance he stopped, hands on hips, peering off to where Ronan couldn't see.

'Come on up!' he called down. 'It's easy!'

Ronan took much longer to reach the flat, high rock where Singer waited. As he dragged himself onto it, a spectacular view unfolded. Standing upright, he felt dizzy and steadied himself on Singer's arm. Beyond, the cliffs stretched for miles, high and sheer. If the bay behind them seemed wild and isolated, then the coastline beyond was intimidating, vastly primeval – indeed, Ronan wouldn't have been surprised to have seen pterodactyls wheeling around the precipices, rather than gulls.

'I hope we get some stormy weather while we're here.'

'Why?'

Singer smiled, as if he knew something Ronan didn't. 'A storm would make me feel more part of it.'

'Part of what?'

'This.' Singer swung his arm out, encompassing the rocks, the cliffs, the sky, the sea and the island.

The hailstones caught them just as they set back along the beach, so they bolted through the sea-grass up to the pub. Still, it was a good ten-minute run, and by the time they burst into McFall's, they were wet and panting, skin pink from exertion and the flaying of the hail. A red setter sprawled across the bar-room floor. It raised its head at their entry, then flopped back into its doze, beating its tail off the linoleum when Singer scratched its tummy. However, when Ronan stooped to give it a token pat, it jumped up as if kicked and barked at him. He recoiled and swore. The dog cowered beside Singer, licking his hand.

'It's not me you need to say sorry to, boy, it's this fellow here.' Singer patted Ronan's arm. 'Nice Ronan, see?' The dog growled. When Singer moved his hand away, the dog licked him. When he touched Ronan again, it growled. Singer repeated the experiment several times.

'Bastard doesn't like me.'

'He's a good boy, yes he is!' Singer knelt before the dog, making a fuss of it. The dog pawed at Singer, greeting him like a long-lost friend.

'Stupid breed,' Ronan sniffed. 'You know, they haven't got the sense that God gave geese.'

'I'd say quite the opposite. I'd say Mister Dog here has impeccable taste. Haven't you, Mister Dog?'

'Gentlemen.' The two looked up. Mrs McFall stood behind the counter, once again having materialised noiselessly.

'What's this fellow called?'

'His name's Michael.'

'Michael. Yes, you are.' The dog fawned over Singer all the more.

'Do you sell smoked salmon?' This complete non-sequitur from Ronan caught both Singer and Mrs McFall by surprise. Her expression altered for the first time, from forbidding gaze to outright frown.

'Don't be silly, of course they don't sell—' Singer began.

'Do you sell smoked salmon?' Ronan repeated the question to a near-hostile Mrs McFall. He turned to Singer. 'Breakfast was all very well, but I rather prefer smoked salmon with scrambled eggs, bacon gives me heartburn. I'm just thinking ahead, to tomorrow morning. The only way to eat scrambled eggs is with smoked salmon and a pinch of tarragon.'

'Hey, you're not in some bloody London deli now.'

'Don't panic, I brought a whole jar of dried tarragon.'

'We have two kinds of salmon,' Mrs McFall interrupted. 'This…' she placed a tin of salmon on the counter before Ronan, rather harder than necessary, then walked off into the house. Singer sat on a stool and put his head in his hands. The dog sat at his feet. '…and this!' Mrs McFall returned, with a very large frozen fish, which she dropped on the bar counter. The fish was black and silver with a red slit up its belly. It wore an aghast expression that precisely mirrored Ronan's.

'No, that's not what I meant.'

'How much is it?' Singer asked.

'Five pounds.'

'For the whole fish?'

'Five pounds.'

'Singer, we'll never manage all that for breakfast.'

'You're looking at dinner, not breakfast.'

'Hmm. I suppose we could stuff it with water chestnuts, if they have any.'

'I vote we stuff you with water chestnuts. You let that fish be – I'll handle this.' Singer placed a ten-pound note on the counter, addressing Mrs McFall. 'Can I have a roll of tinfoil, a bag of flour, a tin of baking soda, a tin of yeast, a pint of buttermilk, a packet of butter and two pints of Guinness, please.' Mrs McFall gave a curt nod and set about business without another word. Michael wagged his tail.

'What's all that stuff for?'

'So as I can build a bomb, and plant it under your bed.'

'I don't have a bed.'

'Then pick one, there's no shortage upstairs.'

'So what's the stuff for?'

'Have you ever eaten roast salmon with freshly baked soda bread?'

'No.'

'Then you haven't lived.'

'Hmm. If we're making bread, we should jazz it up a bit. Excuse me.' Mrs McFall glanced up from packing a cardboard box. 'Do you sell fresh caraway seed?'

Singer placed his forehead against the bar counter. Michael barked.

Ronan sat as close to the kitchen range as he tolerably could. Now that it had been running for several hours, the room had heated up considerably. The warmth and the lunchtime beer had relaxed him somewhat, and, for the present, he couldn't think of anything to complain about. He watched with mild interest as Singer stuffed an object the size of a human head, wrapped in a cotton tea towel, into the oven.

'Listen carefully to me. You have to take the bread out in an hour's time. Got that?'

'Why?'

'Because if you don't, it will burn. When you take it out, put it on the table to cool.'

'No, I mean why do I have to do it? Why can't you do it?'

'Because I won't be here.'

'Eh?'

'The other thing is, see that bucket? I've filled it full of turf. Keep the range burning, don't let it die down. Do you think you can cope with that?'

'But where will you be?'

'I have a message to do.'

'What sort of message?'

'To be honest, I won't know myself until I get there.'

'Get where? What the hell are you talking about?'

'I'll be back by dinnertime.'

'Being wilfully mysterious about simple everyday matters doesn't make you big or clever. Would it not be much easier just to tell me what you're up to? I hate the way you never explain things.'

'On the contrary, I'm explaining exactly what I want you to do while I'm gone.'

'Bossy swine. So where are you off to?'

'Come here. I want to show you something.' Singer beckoned Ronan towards the living room.

'I also hate the way you always change the subject when you…oh. Goodness. What have we here?' Singer stood behind the living room door and gestured at the bookcase wall. Ronan pushed his glasses back on his nose and began peering at their spines. '*Inishowen – Its History, Traditions and Antiquities,* by Maghtochair. Hmm. Yes. And look. Is that an original Lady Gregory? Surely not…'

Singer sidled out the door. 'I'll be back after dark. Do you think you can light a lamp without burning the house down?'

'What? Hmm, yes.'

'One last thing – keep your hands off my fish. It's defrosting in the pantry, so don't you go rubbing it with sun-dried goat's cheese or anything.'

'Don't worry about me.' Ronan selected a tome. '*A Book of Saints and Wonders.* If this imprint is 1906, then it's a first edition.'

'And you'll remember about the bread?'

'Yes, yes, of course.' Ronan only vaguely heard the sound of Singer's car leaving. Absorbed in his new treasure trove, where each discovery seemed more unusual and fascinating than the last, he barely noticed the time pass, until the light dimmed to the point where he had difficulty reading and he was forced to work out how to light an oil lamp without burning the house down. Then he remembered about Singer's bread and ran cursing into the kitchen.

6

The bus from Dublin to Letterkenny stopped in every town in the midlands to disgorge one set of smelly passengers and absorb another. At every halt, the driver descended to manhandle bags in and out of the luggage compartment, and each time he flogged the groaning vehicle back into motion, it jerked fitfully forward at a pace somewhere between that of a tired marathon runner and a lame horse. Oona loved travel, but for her 'travel' meant leaving Ireland, on an aeroplane or a boat. Bouncing through the nation's bogs on a rickety bus with Dionne Brady's head in her lap – this wasn't travel, it was torture.

Dionne had fallen asleep even before they'd cleared Dublin. By now, she had managed to smear a fair portion of her generous facial make-up onto Oona's jeans – presumably her heavy cosmetic scheme was meant to compliment the blue velvet cape, high-heeled lace-up boots and turquoise beret she wore, an outfit which would have been perfectly appropriate had their coach been horse-drawn and attended by handsome servants bearing glass slippers, rather than diesel-driven and crowded with rednecks bearing bottles of cider. Perhaps, in Dionne's dreams, she was indeed being whisked away into some fairy-tale winter fantasy, but the reality for her waking companions was somewhat less than magical, and it seemed hardly fair to Oona that the instigator of this hell should sleep peacefully all the way through it.

Across the aisle, Melissa sat bolt upright, looking straight ahead, as motionless and composed if she were watching an opera or ballet. Her face glowed pale between her black hair and a black polo neck – she had the quality, as ever, of an entity from some other dimension where beauty and silence were normal attributes, sent to impassively observe the sordid realities of this one. It really was quite extraordinary to see Melissa this far from her Ranelagh retreat. Oona was both slightly afraid of and at the same time fascinated by Melissa. Not that Melissa was overtly intimidating – on the contrary, she was utterly unpretentious, a good listener, and when she did speak, she did so with intelligence and honesty. When it came to intellect, Oona knew that Melissa was at least her match. When it came to looks, there was no contest, but since Melissa was so private, it was hard, even for Oona as the plainest of the three, to feel jealous of her. Dionne was the go-getter in that department, the one with the right combination of confidence and glamour. Any time they'd competed for male attention, Dionne had beaten Oona hands down, but since Oona liked immature, messed-up young men and Dionne despised them, such occasions had been relatively rare.

Melissa, on the other hand, had never been a player. For while both Oona and Dionne had cut determined swathes through the traditional teenage pastures of boys, pubs and parties, Melissa had barely dabbled, being drawn out only on rare occasions, her father's failing health and the absence of a wife to care for him conspiring to keep her indoors. The Montgomerys had been wealthy enough to afford daily visits from a private nurse, which allowed Melissa to attend school and to intermittently pursue her only other outlet, drama classes at the Gaiety Theatre. Certainly, it had always seemed odd to Oona that an introvert like Melissa should be interested in acting, but since she never discussed it, the subject remained unexplored. When they were eighteen, Oona had heard a rumour via a friend of a friend about a dalliance between Melissa and one of her drama teachers, but had failed to uncover any evidence beyond that single, uncorroborated whisper. During one of their regular soirées in Melissa's kitchen, Oona had put the allegation to her in a 'you'll-never-guess-what-they're-saying-about-you' context, but had received only a faint smile in return.

The companionship between the three had developed through being socially excluded at school. Melissa was unpopular because her silence was interpreted as aloofness; Oona's obsessions, most of which were utterly alien to the teenage female mind, ensured that she was regarded as the class weirdo; and Dionne was shunned because she came from a poor family. Not that one would have automatically known, looking at Dionne, that her father was a sometime car mechanic and petty criminal with nine children, as she was never anything less than impeccably turned out, her appearance a testament to the triumph of willpower over circumstance. But at any upmarket all-girls school, the have-nots will invariably be found out, singled out and kept out by the bourgeoisie-in-training. Dionne had paid her academic fees by working evenings in a supermarket. Her response to her lack of privilege had always been to try twice as hard. At university, she had laboured her way through a degree in architecture and was now the only one of the three with an actual job. These days, Melissa scrimped by on the small sum left by her father, while presumably trying to decide precisely what a first in Philosophy might practically achieve for her. As for Oona – well, there wasn't much demand for graduates of any sort in Ireland these days, and none whatsoever for drop-out geologists suffering from depression.

Since Melissa was in many ways unquantifiable, Dionne was the yardstick that Oona alternately measured herself against and beat herself with. She considered herself more intelligent than her friend, and had definitely had the more comfortable upbringing, yet Dionne had more money, better clothes and, most of all, a well-planned future.

Oona was certainly unwell – several top doctors were convinced of that – but her recent sojourn at St Eunan's had shown her that sickness is relative. She was not as sick, for example, as the girl who had lacerated her arms with a bread knife, convinced she was a prominent politician who had lost the 1987 general election. In reality, the girl was a seventeen-year-old waitress from Monaghan.

Neither was Oona as sick as the fifty-year-old woman in the bed opposite, who had recited the rosary non-stop, black beads pressed to her lips like an infant sucking on a blanket. And she wasn't even in the same universe of illness and pain as the young woman who had hanged herself with a shoelace tied to a hook on the back of the ward bathroom door the evening after she was committed. Why the poor woman hanged herself, the nurses refused to say, which, according to the other inmates, almost certainly meant she'd been sexually abused.

The daily regimen of drugs at St Eunan's had made Oona feel dopey by day and feverish at night. For morning exercise, the resident psychotherapist would set up a portable record player in the gymnasium and force the entire population of the female ward to dance to the Irish national anthem. Again and again, wearing only those mortifying disposable paper aprons that don't tie properly at the back, the ones where you're convinced everyone can see your arse, waltzing in circles to 'A Nation Once Again', clutched by the psychotic waitress from Monaghan, her arms livid with purple scars.

Best of all – and Oona would never have believed this had she not seen it with her own eyes – on her third day, when she'd finally been allowed a walk through the grounds, accompanied by an orderly, she'd come across a crazy golf course. There they were, all the loonies in their dressing gowns, playing crazy golf. Oona had practically collapsed laughing, and the orderly had pinned her to a park bench, believing her mirth to be the onset of an episode.

Later that week, she'd accidentally sat at the canteen table reserved for girls with severe eating disorders and had wolfed down her lunch, causing one of her fellow non-diners to burst into tears and fling her tray at the wall. Grasping desperately for some form of normality, she had been delighted to learn that St Eunan's taught pottery as a form of therapy, and had a workshop equipped with wheels and kiln. But her lousy luck had followed her even into the madhouse – for the entire duration of her stay, the pottery teacher was off sick, suffering from what else, it was rumoured, but depression. So Oona had spent most of her time in the smoking room, where one of the oldest inmates, a woman in her eighties, held daily court, talking non-stop about her lengthy career as a prostitute in the most obscenely graphic terms any of them had ever heard.

It was obvious that the inmates of St Eunan's were people who had palpably suffered, whereas her own instability had no traumatic cause. Unlike many of the others, Oona had never been raped, beaten or subjected to a particularly unhappy upbringing. Indeed, if anyone she knew deserved to be mentally ill, it was surely Melissa Montgomery, yet she had responded to the oddities of her childhood by clinging firmly to the rails rather than flying off them. This was doubtless why she found Melissa's grace and stability a bit unsettling – her own sense of identity had suffered a setback, having left St Eunan's with the distinct sensation that she was only pretending to be sick, like Randall McMurphy in *One*

Flew Over the Cuckoo's Nest. Ironically, the thought made her more depressed still.

The bus shook violently and hissed like an asthmatic dragon. All noise and movement ceased, there was a brief hiatus, then the overhead lights flickered on and the rest of the passengers rose as a single body and tried to disembark all at the same time. The driver stood, his cap pushed back, accepting the muttered thanks of each huddled form as it pushed past him into the night. Dionne sat bolt upright.

'Are we there, so?'

'You've slept on top of me for six hours.'

Dionne's eyes widened and she tore open her handbag, which looked as if it had been made from a Siamese cat.

'Shite – my face has come off. Don't anybody move. Lipstick. Where's my lipstick?'

Oona spotted Singer first, standing in the darkness against his car, arms folded. He stepped forward with a smile and helped Dionne descend from the bus. Oona watched as Dionne fell into his arms, kissed his cheek and babbled something about luggage, her voice assuming the higher pitch it always did when she was excited or embarrassed. Oona hadn't thought Singer particularly attractive when they had met two nights previously – she preferred smaller, thinner, more lost-looking types than this burly, hugely confident-looking man. But she did notice, as he shook her hand, that he held it for slightly longer than necessary.

'Three of you, that's great. Welcome to Donegal.'

'Well, you did say I could bring who I wanted!' Dionne hung off Singer's arm, giggling and squeaking.

'The more the merrier, we have plenty of space. Gosh – are you sure you brought enough clothes?' Singer hauled Dionne's gargantuan tartan holdall from the luggage compartment, and staggered with it towards his car. Dionne laughed uproariously, as if Singer had cracked the funniest joke in the world.

Ronan was loathe to unwrap Singer's bread from the cotton tea towel. He knew from the smell that all was not well underneath, and resolved to lie furiously about having taken it from the range one hour to the second after Singer's departure. The range! Jesus! He dived for the turf bucket, lifted the iron hatch above the fire and began stuffing lumps inside, blowing frantically to get them to catch. Nothing happened, so he grabbed his oil lamp from the table and searched frantically for something flammable. The cupboards beneath the old ceramic sink held nothing of use, so he ran along the corridor at the back of the kitchen, tearing open doors as he went. The sole occupant of the first room was a very large dead fish, wrapped in tinfoil, recumbent on a cold stone slab. The next room held turf, turf and bloody more turf, so he stumbled outside through the back door and made his way along the rear of the house and into the nearest outhouse, which had large double doors but also a smaller, latched entrance. Inside, most of the floorspace was taken up by a car-shaped object, hidden under a dirty tarpaulin cover. However, there were rows of crude shelving on the walls, bearing paint-pots, bottles of bleach, glass coffee jars full of nails and screws, and – there! That had to be something – a tin drum stood in the far corner, with an inverted funnel on top. Ronan unscrewed the cap, sniffing. Of course – paraffin for the oil lamps, perfect! He looked around, selected the biggest coffee jar of nails from the shelves and emptied the contents on the floor. He used the funnel to fill the jar with the purplish liquid, then returned through the house to the range, where he tipped the lot into the hatch-hole, standing carefully back as he did so. Again, nothing happened, but there was a funny smell. He fetched a box of matches from the kitchen table, and struck one. He leaned over, and dropped it into the hole. Before it even made contact with the smouldering turf, there was a bang, and a blue fireball erupted from the hole. Ronan's glasses protected his eyes, but a loud hissing and distinct smell of burning told him that his hair had gone on fire. He lunged for the sink and splashed handfuls of cold water over his head. Swearing venomously, he dried himself on a tea towel, which, he noticed, was left covered in bits of frazzled hair.

'Bugger you, Singer, this is all your fault!' he announced to the empty house, grabbed the oil lamp and went in search of a mirror. There were none to be had on the ground floor, so he trudged up the stairs, which ended before a large window made from the same patterned, frosted glass that was used in the porch. He turned about and found himself in a corridor running the entire upper width of the house, with doorways on each side. One by one, he began trying the rooms, starting with the seaward-looking one directly in front of him. This was obviously where Singer had slept, for carrier bags stuffed with cameras and assorted paraphernalia sat beside the fireplace, watched over by the Infant of Prague.

'I hope your new tenant roasts in hell,' Ronan snarled at the icon. Most of the other rooms were similar to Singer's – an iron bedstead and fireplace, bare floorboards and a view over either the harbour to the front or the sea-grass dunes at the back of the house, barely visible now in the dusk. The last two rooms at the eastern end were different, however. On the seaward side, the corner room was double the size of the others, and panelled entirely in oak. It overlooked both the harbour and the pebble beach, having front and gable windows deep enough to sit in. Inistrahull light winked at Ronan from beyond the bay. The centre of the room was dominated by a heavy four-poster bed, spectrally bereft of its hanging drapes, which must have been long removed. A wardrobe and a dressing table made of the same dark timber as the bed added to the relatively opulent feel of the place, and Ronan looked in the time-speckled mirror of the dresser to see that his eyebrows and fringe had, indeed, suffered noticeable singeing.

He was examining the damage, swearing softly, when he saw a gaunt female face looking over his shoulder. He jumped and swung around, but the room behind him was empty. He went cold and made to flee, but stopped halfway across the floor and forced himself to look again in the mirror, positioning himself as he had before. It was possible, just possible – yes, the spotted, occluded mirror had the effect of making the room behind him seem somehow more alive, and if he looked from the corner of his eye, the blemishes on the glass could well have formed a face, his imagination supplying the details. He snorted and left, but resolved nonetheless not to occupy what was by far the most commodious bedroom.

The last room on the landward side was a bathroom, with enormous ivory porcelain fittings and brass taps gone dull with age. A slightly better, newer mirror above the sink showed that his eyebrows would look a bit funny for a while, but Ronan reckoned that a wash and brush might disguise the disruption to his hair. Actually, a good soak might dissolve some of the disruption his entire body and indeed mind had suffered over the past twenty-four hours, so he tried the bath taps, and sure enough, after a bit of banging and spitting, one of them began to spew hot water. Feeling cheered, he returned downstairs to the living room, where he got some candles down from the mantelpiece. In the kitchen, he poured himself a generous glass of red wine, hauled his overnight bag up to one of the back bedrooms and rifled around for the lavender bath salts he knew he'd packed. He rummaged past his tin of Potter's – no need for that, thank goodness – ah, there they were. Also at the bottom of his bag was the Sony Walkman he'd salvaged from the disaster outside Linda's flat, which already, now that he was reminded of it, seemed much longer than a month ago. He had only one cassette tape, *It Will End in Tears* by This Mortal Coil. Still, it was enough. Becoming almost jolly, Ronan planted three candles at the bottom of the now-full bath, emptied a generous dose of salts into the steaming water and set the oil lamp on the cistern. He stripped and eased himself into the tub, which was a gigantic free-standing affair, not one of those horrid modern plastic inbuilt things that barely wet past one's waist. He removed his glasses, donned his headphones and pressed play.

As the music lilted along and his stresses soaked away in a lavender-scented fog, he sipped his wine and stared at the ceiling. Perhaps this wouldn't be so bad after all. Although the house lacked modern conveniences, there was something quite splendid about it too, something that spoke to the aristocrat manqué in Ronan. The huge dimensions of the rooms, the sense of space, almost of grandeur – the house, once one adapted to it, would most likely prove quite comfortable, certainly compared to Singer's hovel back in Belfast. Ah, Belfast – now there was yet another unpleasant memory that had already begun to fade. Perhaps it was the other-worldliness of this place – what was it Singer had said? The thing about being here was that you weren't anywhere else? Something like that. Now that he thought about it, technically the Pier House was his home, as he currently had no other. Ronan could easily envisage a fortnight or maybe more of working his way through the bookshelf downstairs, wrapped up snug on the sofa before a crackling driftwood fire, while Singer scrabbled around his shagging cliffs. A couple of pints in the evenings, and plenty of time in between to consider the future, come up with some sort of plan to get life back on track again. Ponder one's prospects from a kingly position of calm, as it were. And who knows? Perhaps the odd verse might even spring to mind…

He closed his eyes, slipped down further into the bath and held his wineglass upright on his chest. Your one from the Cocteau Twins that sings on some of the Mortal Coil tracks – what was her name? Elizabeth something. What a voice. Ronan drifted, on Elizabeth Something's voice. Art, love and longing. Now there was a woman, he wagered, that wouldn't waste her time watching *Neighbours*. He tried to picture what Elizabeth Something looked like, but couldn't. Come to think of it, he wasn't sure he'd ever seen her photograph. Instead, unbidden and from nowhere, the au pair from Puerto Banus walked into his mind, purple bikini stretched across the curves of a rudely ripe body. She was minus the two children – indeed, the lush, central oasis of the apartment complex and the swimming pool were entirely devoid of people, not a McAleese in sight. It was warm and sunny, but not uncomfortably hot. This time, before the au pair dived into the pool, she smiled at Ronan. Halfway through her dive, time froze as it had before, and once again, he was able to ogle her stretched, suspended figure just before it hit the water. He held her there in mid-air, admiring the curve of her back, the pertness of her bum, the neatness of her calves. Then he allowed her to continue, and she was in, she was under the cool blue water, then she surfaced, still smiling at him. She swam over to the nearest ladder and climbed out. The water sluiced off her light-brown skin as she walked over to him, and stood close. He kissed her where her shoulder met her neck. She tasted like a warm cappuccino. She put her arms around his waist, so that her wet breasts crushed up against him, then, green eyes shining, she stuck her tongue in his mouth, while at the same time pulling at his shorts, making it clear what she wanted, and the track ended and Ronan heard someone say 'oh' and his eyes blinked open and the woman from the mirror in the bedroom was staring at him through the steam in the bathroom. He yelled 'Aarggh!' and at the same time he saw that he was bleeding. He lunged for his glasses, pulling them onto his face with one hand as he tried to cover himself with the other. Not one, but three female faces peered at him through the door, their mouths hanging open. The smallest and nearest held an oil lamp. She said, 'We're really sorry – we thought you were a murder victim.'

She retreated, slamming the door, and Ronan heard clattering footsteps, then the sound of laughter echo along the hallway. He erupted from the tub, clutching the empty wine glass, which must have tipped over as he fantasised.

'We need to fetch tobacco from the pub.'

'Jesus, what happened to your eyebrows?'

'Never mind. We need to go to the pub, right now.'

Ronan stood before Singer in the kitchen, who was unpacking purple-black bottles of wine from a cardboard box on the table. Three women sat at the end of the table closest to the range, each with a glass of wine from a freshly opened bottle. One was blonde to the point of albinism, one was dark and very pretty, and the one who had spoken to him upstairs had short brown hair and a knowing face.

'Ronan,' Singer announced, 'meet Dionne Brady, Melissa Montgomery and Oona Tyler, all from Dublin. Dionne, Melissa and Oona, this is my good friend Ronan Doherty.' The women smiled, eyes bright with amusement – or maybe it was just the reflection of the oil lamps – and Ronan nodded.

'Look, I bring you treats from Letterkenny, decent Rioja, most of it. However,' and Singer pulled the cotton tea towel away from his soda bread, which was blacker than the wood of the table and clunked heavily upon it, 'if you won't tell me what you did to your eyebrows, can you at least tell me what happened to my bread?'

'Singer,' Ronan repeated, through gritted teeth, 'the pub!'

'Umm…yes, well, okay…I could certainly do with, uh, some more ingredients for soda bread. Ladies, please make yourselves at home, we'll be back shortly.'

The pair made their way through the sea-grass, Singer putting himself at an immediate advantage by carrying a torch extracted from his car.

'So why the sudden urge to buy tobacco? You could have borrowed some of mine.'

Ronan stumbled into hummocks in the gloom, kicking out at them in fury.

'This isn't about tobacco, and fine well you know it!'

'Oh?'

'This is about me according you a damn sight more courtesy than you've shown me, by not yelling at you in front of your fancy women!'

Singer laughed. 'Excuse me?'

'Don't fuck about! Who are they, and what are they doing here?'

'Look, first of all, I apologise for them finding you like that. When we arrived, the house was completely dark, so I thought you must be up in the pub. I gave them a lamp and let them explore while I unpacked the car. I swear, if I'd had any idea you were in the bath,' and his voice took on a mirthful edge despite his attempt to sound serious, 'I'd have kept them downstairs. So I apologise. That was my fault, and I'm sorry.'

Singer's apparent sincerity rather back-footed Ronan. He'd been ready for a right old screaming match, à la Ronan v. Linda, but obviously wasn't about to get one. That was the longest explanation Singer had ever offered him for anything. He grappled around for something to keep his anger broiling.

'Never mind about upstairs – the point is, you should have told me they were coming in the first place!'

'I didn't know they were coming.'

'Bollocks, where have you been then? Did you just pick them up off a street corner in the next town? Is the best brothel in Ireland just over the hill?'

'Don't be offensive. They're three perfectly decent girls, as it happens.'

'Then what are they doing all the way up here?'

'I invited them…'

'Right! Why couldn't you have just said so in the first place?'

'…but I didn't know they were coming.' The two emerged from the trees, onto the road.

'Singer, you're making less sense than usual, and Christ knows that's saying something. Now, give me one good reason why I shouldn't pack my things and go. I think you've been downright rude, inviting people without telling me, yet here you are trying to turn the tables, like it's me who's being unreasonable!'

Singer halted before the pub door. He looked Ronan in the eye, under the feeble light of the tortoise sign, and held him by one shoulder. 'Ro, look. I've said I'm sorry. Here it is. You remember I was down in Dublin for that stupid priest thing before we came here?' Ronan nodded. 'Right, well, that turned out to be a bit of a goose chase, so I knocked off early, went to the pub and had a pint, exactly the way we're about to do now, okay?' Ronan pouted and made to pull away from Singer's clasp, but found that he couldn't. 'Listen to me. So I'm there, at the bar, and I get talking to the blonde one, Dionne. As you do.'

Ronan snorted. 'As *you* do.'

'Look, we were just talking, you know? She's with her mate, that one Oona. But Oona isn't saying much, just sits there snivelling into her drink, so Dionne chats to me, okay? Well, one drink leads to another and we end up chatting for quite a while, the rest of the evening as it happens, and, uh, well…' Singer coughed, released his grip, and looked away 'The thing is, right, I, uh, kissed her outside the pub.'

'What?'

'We were both totally arseholed. But anyway, there we are, and out of the blue, she asks me what I'm doing for Christmas. So I say I'm coming here, and the next thing I know she's invited herself. She just asked me outright could she come, and I was kinda surprised, so I said "yeah".'

'I never knew you were such a pushover.'

'I didn't think she was serious. I thought she was just plastered. Well, she was plastered, but when she made me promise to meet this bus, I seriously didn't think she would show, not in a million years. But today, it was kind of niggling at me, and a voice in my head told me I had better meet the bus, just in case. That's why I didn't say anything, 'cos I was pretty sure she wouldn't be on it. I bought a case of wine in Letterkenny, so it wouldn't be a wasted journey either way.'

'If you're expecting me to roll over for a case of wine…'

'No, all I'm saying is, I meet the bus, thinking I'm totally wasting my time, and off step the three of them. Just like that. And now here they are. What was I supposed to do, send them home? The tall one, Melissa, I've never met her before in my life. As for Dionne and Oona – I know them about as well as you do. Actually, not nearly as well, from what I gather.' Singer started to laugh.

'Buggering hell,' Ronan tapped his foot, crinkled his face and looked into the night, in the direction of the Pier House. 'I don't know…it's just sort of…unexpected, that's all. I mean, what's the next few weeks going to be, me hanging around while you get stuck into your private harem, is that the plan?'

'Don't be silly.'

'Gimme a break. You've already admitted to a physical relationship with one of them.' Singer grabbed Ronan by both shoulders and kissed him on the lips. Ronan writhed. 'Urgh!'

'There. I've kissed you outside a pub. Do we have a physical relationship?'

'Get off me, you freak!'

'Well, that's all that happened between me and Dionne. So what?'

'So what is she's sitting in our kitchen. Do you think she's come all this way for nothing?'

Singer crumpled slightly. 'No.'

'Poor Singer. All these women chucking themselves at you.'

'Stop it.'

'Well, what are your intentions?'

'Jesus, what are you, her father? Look, the plan is there is no plan. *Pasa lo que pasa*, you know?' Singer made his way through to the bar. Sighing, Ronan followed. It was empty, as usual, an Aladdin's cave with nobody to admire it. Ronan drew out his tobacco pouch as they settled onto two barstools. Almost immediately, Manus emerged from the shadows behind the bar. His face was serious, unsmiling.

'Two pints, please…' Singer began, but Manus lifted the flap in the bar counter, and beckoned them through it.

'Come here, quick, c'mere till you see this!' After a moment's hesitation, the pair followed him, down a short dark corridor that gave onto a kitchen, nowhere near as big as that of the Pier House, but with a more modern, cream-coloured range in one corner, and a television burning beside it. Michael lay sprawled in front of the range and growled quietly without looking up when Ronan stood near him. Mrs McFall was nowhere to be seen. 'Look here.' Manus turned the sound up on the television. The picture was a night-time scene, with what looked like a large, indistinct bonfire, filmed from the air.

> '…*Scottish town of Lockerbie, where a Pan American jumbo jet, flight 103 from Frankfurt to New York, is believed to have crashed earlier this evening. Initial reports say that the aeroplane, with over 250 people on board, disappeared suddenly from the radar screens, just under an hour after taking off from Heathrow, where we can confirm it took on British passengers. I repeat, the picture we're seeing now is from Lockerbie, a small*

market town in the Scottish Borders region. It's not yet known whether there have been casualties on the ground, but officials are already calling this Britain's worst aviation disaster…'

'That's about a hundred and fifty miles due east of here,' Manus said softly. 'Twenty minutes later, and they'd have been out to sea in front of us.'

Singer bent to pat Michael, who stopped growling. 'Do me a favour, Manus.'

'What's that?'

'For the rest of my time here, please don't tell me any more news?'

'I'm sorry! What have I done?' Dionne, her face buried in her hands, spoke through her fingers. She and Oona sat at the kitchen table with an oil lamp between them. Melissa had lifted another lamp and wandered off into the house again, alone. Oona sipped her wine.

'I don't know – what have you done?'

Dionne spread her arms out. 'Look at this place! It's like a feckin' morgue!'

Oona smirked. 'I quite like it.'

'But how can you? No central heating, no light, no television, no phone, no cooker, no fridge, nothing except that feckin' weirdo in the bath!' She let out a small, mock-hysterical shriek.

'Either he had a gun in his pocket, or else he was really pleased to see us.'

'Ugh! Listen, I've a good mind to walk right out of here, and I would totally understand if you two came with me.'

Oona snickered. 'I'm more than happy with what I've seen so far.'

'You filthy bitch! He's ginger, for fuck's sake!'

'Dee, I don't get it. You drag us all the way up here, we've barely sat down, and now you want to leave? I mean, I thought you liked this Singer?'

'Okay, okay, I like him, but now it turns out he's a big fat liar.'

'How so?'

'He said he had a brilliant house by the sea.'

'He does have a brilliant house by the sea. I think it's amazing.'

'It's fucking freezing!'

'Not in here. I'm toasty.'

'I mean the bedrooms! Did you see them? I thought there was central heating!'

'Ah, but did he lie about central heating, or did you, when I asked you?'

'That's hardly the point,' Dionne whimpered.

'Every bedroom has a fireplace. Or,' Oona grinned malevolently, 'you could always take the ginger fella in to warm you up. He's certainly capable.'

'Nooo!'

Oona half-sang, 'You should be so lucky, lucky lucky lucky...'

'Melissa!' Dionne called out. There was no reply, so she walked to the kitchen door and yelled into the hallway. 'Melissa!' She returned to the table, poured herself another glass of wine and downed it in a gulp. 'You were right. That Singer probably does have a cellar full of dead bodies. Yuck. Him and his creepy friend. This is not what I expected, not at all.' Melissa stepped quietly through the door. 'Ah, there you are. We thought you'd been eaten by giant spiders. What do you think? I think it's totally bizarre here, and I'm not sure we should stay.'

Oona sparked up a cigarette. 'And I think Dionne's being totally wet.'

'Ha! When I think of the arm-twisting I had to do to get you to come with me!'

Melissa gave Dionne an odd look. 'Persuasion takes on many different forms. But if you're asking for my opinion, then I want to stay. I like it here.'

'But you don't know these people at all.'

Melissa raised an eyebrow. 'And you do?'

'Go, girl,' Oona chipped in. 'I vote we stay. I'm so glad you twisted my arm, Dee.'

Dionne sighed and dragged a chair up beside the range. 'Gimme a cigarette, would you, babes?' Oona threw her one and tossed her lighter after it. 'Fair enough. I just want everyone to be happy, that's all. That's all I ever want. If you two are happy – well, I'll sleep on it, and see in the morning.' She yawned. 'I'm bloody knackered after that bus.'

Melissa smiled at Oona, less faintly than usual. Oona smiled back.

7

Singer padded down the staircase in his socks so as not to waken anybody. He figured that if he got the range going nice and early, by the time the women arose, the kitchen would be warm, and that would be one less thing for Dionne to whinge about. She'd made him light a fire in her bedroom, and when he'd cracked a joke about a maid coming to rekindle it every morning, she hadn't laughed. She had rejected the panelled bedroom because it was too big and cold, much to Oona's delight, who'd said she'd always wanted to sleep in a four-poster bed.

The cluster of dirty wine glasses he'd expected to find loitering on the kitchen table stood gleaming in a neat parade beside the sink. Someone had cleaned, swept and mopped the entire room, and the front window had been lifted to admit a flow of sharp air. Rubbing his eyes, he crossed the hallway to the living room and poked his head around the door. It was full of morning sun. Melissa sat on the rug before the enormous fireplace. Her back was poker-straight, her eyes were closed and she wore only a long-sleeved black leotard. Gracefully and apparently effortlessly, she lay flat, then, using her arms and legs, pushed her pelvis, then her entire back and head off the floor, forming a curved, bridge-like position, which she held. He rubbed his eyes again, feeling suddenly torn between wanting to watch, and thinking what a pervert he'd seem if caught doing so. He made to withdraw, but the door creaked audibly as he did, so after an instant's blind panic, he coughed and stepped noisily into the room. Melissa now had one of her legs stretched horizontally outward. She brought it down, then raised the other. She had very long, beautiful legs. Singer meandered awkwardly across the floor and sat on the sofa. Suddenly, she kicked and raised both legs directly into the air, standing on her hands. She held, then slowly allowed her feet to come down the far side, somehow folding herself neatly into the lotus position. She opened her eyes. They were of a brown so dark as to be almost as black as her hair.

'Good morning.' A faint smile.

'Sorry for interrupting.'

'You're not. I'm finished.'

'You're, uh, very fit.'

'Not really – it's my morning routine.'

'A bit like me and my five-mile jog.'

'You jog every morning?'

'No. I just said that to impress you.'

Again, the faint smile. 'You must show me how to light the range. I've never seen anything like it before.'

'Nor has anybody under the age of a hundred and twenty, I should imagine. But listen, you don't have to—'

'I want to know how. I'm an early riser, and would like to make tea.' She stood and walked towards the kitchen. Singer followed, giving his eyes another good rub, in case she looked back and caught him staring at her bum.

'Thanks for clearing up, but you really didn't have to. Aren't you cold?'

'No.' Melissa stood barefoot before the range, hands on hips, feet arranged like a ballet dancer at repose. He fetched the turf bucket and spent the next five minutes demonstrating his technique. She watched in silence, then thanked him and left. Somewhat dazed, but not unpleasantly so, Singer stood by the slowly warming iron giant, waiting for a kettle to boil. The tide, he noticed, was slightly higher in the harbour than it had been the previous morning, but the sea in the bay was utterly calm, with no wind or swell to disturb it. He heard the front door open then close gently, and watched as Melissa walked off across the sea-grass towards the harbour, dressed now in black pedal-pushers, monkey boots and a long black hooded raincoat. His eyes followed her onto the harbour wall, where she climbed 'his' steps and looked out to sea.

'The French Lieutenant's Woman, eh?' he enquired of the whiskey bottle as he poured a generous splash into his teacup.

The hairpin path up to the stone tower was steep, and Dionne made particularly heavy going of the ascent, wearing her high-heeled boots, a tan leather coat trimmed with white faux fur and a matching hat that made her head look like a giant snowball. Oona, who wore a blue anorak, watched as Singer held Dionne by the arm to keep her upright – every so often, Oona thought that her friend tottered and squealed rather unconvincingly, requiring Singer to grab her waist as well as her arm, as if he didn't have enough to contend with, hauling his camera bag over one shoulder.

The tower itself overlooked the open sea and the land around, for many miles in all directions. To the south, dumpling-shaped hills gleamed in the snow. Across the bay, the eastern cliffs rose like impossible ramparts – even the waves had abandoned their assault, for now. From this elevation, the island was a jewel-green brooch, held in place by the white pin of the lighthouse. To the west, the land retreated in a maze of inlets, culminating in a distant flat-topped mountain that resembled a titanic ship's hull, cast upside-down during some primordial storm. To the north, the Atlantic stretched away in a rich, benevolent blue. Fronds of cloud stretched across the upper atmosphere, like lace curtains blowing through the pavilions of heaven.

'Next stop, America,' Ronan pronounced.

'That's where those poor people were going, wasn't it?' Oona shaded her eyes and looked to the east, in the direction of Scotland, as if she expected to see a pillar of fire.

'Doesn't bear thinking about. It fell from thirty thousand feet…' Ronan had tuned the valve radio in the living room into the BBC World Service over a late breakfast, and he, Oona and Dionne had listened to reports about the Lockerbie crash, shaking their heads, sipping their tea. 'Manus said another twenty minutes, and it would have come down out there.' He nodded northwards.

'Manus?'

'Authentic local type – owns the pub, and the house.'

'What do you suppose this thing was?' Oona patted the seaward wall of the tower. It had once had a door and windows, but these had been filled in with rubble stone.

'Obviously a lookout of some sort. The walls are very thick, so it's old, definitely pre-war.'

'I want to buy it and live in it. Then I could be on permanent watch.'
'What for?'

'I don't know,' she laughed. 'Sea monsters? Pirates? Terrorists?'

'Hi. Mind that for me, would you?' Singer emerged at the top of the path, with Dionne wrapped around one arm. At first, Ronan thought he was being charged with Dionne, deposited after a torturous climb like a piece of awkward luggage, but instead, Singer set down his camera bag, selected a camera from within, walked to the cliff edge and stepped over it, dropping immediately out of sight.

'Hey – where's he off to?' Dionne approached the drop warily.

'Somewhere stupidly dangerous to take a photograph, I should expect.' Ronan and Oona joined her. Below, they saw that the nose of the western headland was steep, but not sheer, a grassy slope that eventually met a forest of schist and quartzite pinnacles. These dwarfed Singer as he scrabbled amongst them. To his left, a frightening gorge cut into the land, the walls of which were at least a hundred feet high. The ocean surged into it, even on this calm day, booming as it hit what Oona guessed must be a cave at the end of the crevasse.

'That's a fault.'

'If he falls in, it will be his fault. He's a reckless sort, our host.'

'No, I meant that ravine. It hasn't been eroded, it's a fault in the rock.'
'Oh.'

'I wouldn't mind getting a closer look – professional reasons.' To Ronan's astonishment, Oona sat on her backside and bummed her way down through the grass before climbing enthusiastically after Singer.

'Oona! You silly cow!' Dionne grabbed Ronan's shoulder. 'Sorry, I don't like heights. Why didn't you stop her?' Ronan frowned, pushed his glasses up on his nose and buried his chin in his purple scarf. Melissa appeared to his left and walked off the edge as casually as if she were descending an escalator in a department store. Within seconds, she had caught up with Oona, and Dionne watched with growing horror as the pair scaled a broad finger of rock that overlooked the gorge. Singer already lay flat on top of it. As Oona and Melissa climbed towards him, he turned and gestured at them to approach the edge on all fours. Soon, all three lay huddled together, peering into the abyss.

'Jesus, my friends have gone completely mental!' Dionne squawked.

'Then they're in good company,' Ronan assured her. Above the sound of the sea, they heard a faint, high-pitched whistle. They glanced upward for whatever gull might be hovering, but there were none. The whistle came again, in three long blasts. They realised that the noise was manmade, and looked around in puzzlement.

'What is that?'

'No idea.' Ronan drew Dionne back from the edge, close to the tower, solid and safe compared to the vista below. The whistle sounded yet again.

'It's coming from...' Dionne pulled Ronan back towards the top of the path. 'Look. Down there, in front of the house. Some man, waving his arms.'

'Hold on.' Ronan went to Singer's bag and found a camera with a telephoto lens. He used it to study the Pier House. Manus stood by the sundial. He put one hand to his mouth and beckoned with the other. A second later, the whistling noise reached their ears again. 'Speak of the devil. That's Manus, and I think he wants to talk to us. Wave back, to let him know we've got the message.' Dionne raised a hand, and gave it a ladylike shake. 'No, he hasn't seen you, look, he's whistling again. Try harder.' Dionne pulled the white snowball hat from her head, and waved it around like a cheerleader. 'Good, well done. He's got that all right. He definitely wants us to come down. I wonder what's wrong?'

They returned to the headland drop and yelled and waved Dionne's hat until the others looked up from the gorge. By the time the entire party made it back to the harbour, Manus could be seen pottering around the deck of one of the smaller boats, a coastal fisher with a forward cabin, that perched atop its trailer. He jumped nimbly out at their approach, his broad, gap-toothed grin on full display. He hooked a chain from the front of the trailer onto another chain, wrapped around a rusty winch at the head of the slipway.

'What's up, sir?' Singer enquired.

'Will you not introduce me?' Manus shook hands with the three girls in turn, smiling like a sun-god.

'Is everything okay?'

'It is, if you want out to the island.'

'Seriously?' Singer was delighted.

'I told you I'd organise it. I rang Irish Lights, and they gave me the nod. But we need to go today.'

'How so?'

'There's bad weather coming.'

Ronan looked up. 'You'd hardly think it, the sky all around is completely clear.'

'You take my word for it, there's storms on the way. It won't be a white Christmas, but it sure as hell will be a wet one.'

'I suppose that's a real sea-faring thing, having a feel for the weather long before it happens,' Ronan commented to the rest of the group.

'No, I watched the forecast on television. Now, gimme a hand to put this boat in the water. Hold her steady while I get the winch.'

With the boat afloat and the engine throbbing, Oona and Melissa scrambled aboard. Dionne stood on the pier.

'I'll get seasick on that thing, I just know it. And this is my good coat.'

'Oh. Well, hold on a minute, we can't very well leave Dionne alone…' Singer began.

'Actually, I'll stay too,' Ronan hastily volunteered. 'I don't want to be sick on my good coat, either.'

'Are you sure?'

'Go. Do your island-hopping thing. We'll be fine.'

Dionne threw her arms around Singer and kissed him on the cheek. 'You come back to me, d'you hear?'

'Don't worry, we're in good hands.'

Dionne made as if to kiss his cheek again, but this time hissed in his ear, 'Don't let Oona do anything stupid, okay?'

'What d'you…?' But she put a gloved finger to his lips.

'Shhh. Enjoy your trip.'

Within a few minutes, Ronan and Dionne were reduced to figurines, stood at the end of the pier. The boat rounded the eastern tip of the bay, and they were gone.

'Let me drive!' Oona jiggled up and down with excitement, crammed beside Manus in the cabin.

'When we're clear of the rocks, you can take her across the sound.'

'Good! I've always wanted to sail to Scotland, ever since I read Enid Blyton. There's one where these incredibly annoying children with a parrot have an adventure on an island with a secret agent called Bill.'

Manus laughed. 'The nearest part of Scotland's forty miles away. You'd want more than my little boat to be sure of getting there.'

'But we're headed for Inistrahull, right?'

'That's right.'

'Then we're off to Scotland.'

'Excuse me, missy – I was born on the island, and my father always told me I was an Irishman, just like him.'

'Ah. But geologically, Inistrahull is a part of Scotland. Lewisian gneiss, same rock as the Western Isles. It doesn't occur anywhere else in Ireland.'

'Dear Jesus – are you trying to tell me I've been a Scotsman all my life?'

'Technically, you were born on Scottish soil, yes.'

Manus roared. 'A bloody Scotsman! Well, I'll be…what did you say your name was again?'

'Oona. Can I drive now?'

As the boat hugged the eastern cliffs, Singer and Melissa stood aft, gazing upward. Even on this calm day, the view was breathtaking. Wordlessly, she touched his arm and pointed. Halfway up one of the dizzying rock walls, a lone sheep stood on a tiny ledge, which, as far as they could see, had no conceivable way either on or off it. Unconcerned, the sheep munched greedily at the grass around its feet. Suddenly, the boat swung north, away from the cliffs. Caught unawares, Singer fell backwards onto a wooden bench, and Melissa was pitched forward, into his arms. She righted herself instantly, but that didn't stop Oona from cackling wildly as she spun the wheel straight. Manus braced himself against the cabin door, shaking his head and laughing. The boat struck out into the swell of the open water, towards the island.

'The first thing we do is wait here, and wait for them to come.'

Manus tied the boat to a low, wide harbour, which Singer recognised from one of the photographs hanging inside the Pier House.

When Manus bade everyone be silent and still, Singer looked about, half-expecting to see the ghosts of women clad in shawls and bonnets. But instead, after about a minute, a doe popped its head over the incline beyond the harbour, then another, and another. Manus was chuffed.

'There's our reception committee.'

'How on earth did they get here?' Oona demanded. 'They're not native, are they?'

'The lighthouse keepers brought a pair out fifteen years ago. Now there's a dozen, including the stag. He keeps to himself, except when his ladies are in season. Of course, they're the nosey ones, they'll follow us around.'

'Oooh, Manus,' Oona flung her arms around his neck, and feigned to swoon. 'Help me, I'm in season.' Everyone laughed, and the does pricked up their ears. 'God,' she broke loose and walked towards the animals, which sidled away, 'I wish it were that simple. Be in season. Get serviced. Eat some grass.' Manus threw Singer a look, who shrugged and followed Oona.

They climbed the eastern hill first, the upper half of which was enclosed by a low stone wall. Inside the wall was what resembled one side of a street of small terraced houses, not unlike Singer's home in Belfast. A squat stone turret stood at the end of the improbable little street, with the circular remains of a large corroded cast-iron mechanism leaning up against it.

'The old light,' Manus informed the group. 'I remember these houses full of families. Then they built the new light in 1958.' He pointed to the west end of the island, to a tall, white-painted concrete needle with a black lamp on top. A two-storey blockhouse stood beside it. 'Now you see why the commissioners needed the Pier House. Back in the old days, when the winter turned rough, the families were sent ashore and lived there. But when they built the new light, things had moved on. The keepers worked in three-month shifts, and their families lived elsewhere.'

'How do I volunteer?' asked Oona.

'You can't – the keepers were replaced by computers, last year.'

'It must have been so beautiful to have lived out here.'

'Yes, but not all the time.' He walked them towards a piece of slate poking lopsidedly out of the ground, beyond the walled enclosure. It read:

In Loving Memory
of
WILLIE
the beloved child of
John & Maggie Glenville
Died
October 1891, aged 6 months

'Poor little thing.' Oona's eyes moistened. 'Out here on this old rock, all on his own. He must be so frightened.'

'He was a keeper's child. All our people are buried ashore.'

'Why's that?' Singer asked.

'Lack of space. There was never a church on the island, nor a priest. We're all in the graveyard, over in the village.' Manus gestured towards the mainland, which, from where they stood, looked like another universe, seen from a distant age. Oona knelt and pulled weeds away from around the baby's grave.

'I'm going to find him a flower,' she announced, still on the verge of tears. 'The wee pet – all those birthdays and Christmases that have come and gone, with no one to visit him.'

'You won't find flowers at this time of year,' Manus remarked.

Oona walked off down the hill, towards the rocks of the southern shoreline. Manus again looked at Singer, who glanced at Melissa, who shook her head slightly, as much as to say, 'Leave her to it.'

On the low-lying ground between the two lighthouses, which seemed narrow enough for a determined wave to wash over, a cluster of dry-stone gable walls stood at odd angles, the sole survivors of what Manus assured them had been a very pretty little hamlet, or *clachan*, the walls of each house whitewashed, thatched roofs held down by fishing nets to stop them from blowing away. With the cold sun shining, the air still and not a noise to be heard above the rhythm of the sea, there was a serene, timeless feeling about the place. Manus stood by a chimney, surrounded by nettles. He pushed them back with his boot, revealing a hearthstone in the ground.

'I came into the world on a settle bed right here.' He pointed to the left of the fireplace, black streaks still visible up the flue. 'The king's bed, we called it.'

'Because it was big?' Singer took in the tiny dimensions of the ruined room, wondering how a bed of any size could have fit into it.

'No, because my parents slept in it, and my father was the king.'

'King of what?'

'King of the island,' he laughed. 'Don't worry, you don't have to bow to me, it's not hereditary. The king was elected by the islanders, and he settled disputes, wrote letters for those that couldn't, and most of all, dealt with the landlord's agent whenever the rent was due. Nobody ever had enough to pay the rent, so it was my father's job to get the agent drunk when he landed and send him on his way until the following year with a few coins, and everyone's debts written into his book.'

'The landlords couldn't have been that bad if they let people off year after year?'

'We were lucky – others weren't so humane, but they got what was coming to them.'

'What do you mean?'

'Do you think your friend is okay?' Manus asked Melissa, obviously changing the subject.

'I saw her climb back up the hill.'

'Is she okay, though?' Singer picked up the thread. 'She seems a bit…'

Melissa gave one of her faint smiles. 'With Oona, whatever happens, happens.'

Singer recalled the instruction Dionne had issued him on parting. 'I suppose I better go see what she's up to.'

'Fetch her down,' Manus commanded. 'I have sandwiches and beer in the boat.'

Singer found Oona kneeling by little Willie Glenville's grave. On top of it, she had arranged white quartz pebbles in the shape of a flower.

'Told you I'd find one.' She seemed quite pleased with herself.

'By royal decree, you are summoned to a garden party. The king's son has laid on a feast.' Singer told her the story of Manus's father as they walked down to the ruined houses. Manus picked a sheltered spot with a view, and they ate huge ham sandwiches with lashings of mustard on them as they watched the white, brown and blue of the mainland across the silver sea. Oona used a little hammer from a pocket of her anorak to uncap the beer bottles. Manus eyed it.

'Live in a rough part of town, do you?'

'This is my sample hammer, your highness. Remember how I explained why this island is a part of Scotland?'

94

'Jayz, how could I forget?'

'Well, the chances are this is also the oldest thing you've ever stood on, much older than the rest of Ireland – eighteen hundred million years, or thereabouts. I've often read about Inistrahull, and now that I'm here, I want to take some of it back for a closer look.' She stood. 'Come on, your majesty, and I'll give you a crash course in basement granites.' She pulled Manus by the hand towards the exposed rocks at the shore, while the does looked on. Singer watched Oona and Manus poking around the rocks for a while, then stalked the deer, using his telephoto lens to reel off a few exposures. When he'd gone a certain distance, he turned around and composed several surreptitious portraits of an oblivious Melissa, who sat upright on a boulder, staring out to sea.

'I'm in architecture, yes. But I want to get into property, and the first property I intend to get into is a place of my own.'

'You still live with your parents?'

'And five brothers and three sisters – talk about a crowded house. I can't wait to move out. What about you?' Dionne sat at the kitchen table. She sipped a glass of white wine and smoked while Ronan stood, poking gingerly at Singer's salmon with a knife.

'I live in London.'

'What do you do?'

'I'm in publishing.'

'What do you publish?'

'I suppose there's only one way to do this…' Ronan frowned and hacked into the flesh of the fish about halfway along its body. He grunted with the effort. 'I'm in magazines. But I'm taking a break for a few months, to catch up with my own writing. There. That's one, anyway.' He lifted a thick, inelegantly cut steak away from the now-bisected body and commenced chopping another. After seeing the boat off, Dionne had declared herself hungry for lunch, and Ronan had remembered Singer's salmon, by now perfectly defrosted in the pantry.

'What do you write? Novels?'

He wrinkled his nose. 'God no, any fool can write a novel. I write poetry.'

'Oh. How long have you known Singer?'

'About ten years.' Ronan bridled inwardly at the change in subject and clattered an iron frying pan onto the range. He sliced a knob of butter into it, followed by the chunks of fish, then rummaged in a cardboard box and sprinkled a generous pinch of dried herbs from a small glass bottle.

'So you know each other from school?' He nodded in reply. 'Just like us, then. What's his family like?'

'I never met them.'

'So you're not that close.'

'No, it's more…' He paused, wiped his hands on a dishcloth and poured himself a glass of white wine which Singer had chilled by the simple expedient of depositing it on an outside windowsill overnight.

'Yes?'

'I'd rather he told you himself, actually.'

'Told me what?'

'He never talks about his family.'

Dionne smiled and played with her hair. 'Come on, you can't say something like that and then not tell me.'

'Yes I can.'

'No you can't!'

'Well, if it ever comes up, you didn't hear it from me, okay?'

She puckered her wine-wet lips and drew a manicured finger and thumb along them to show that they were sealed.

'I've never met Singer's family because they're all dead.' Her mouth fell open. 'They were killed by a car bomb, in 1972.'

'No!'

'Yes.'

'But how come he survived?'

'No idea.'

'You mean you've never asked him?'

'He never talks about it.'

'How come you know about it, then?'

'Northern Ireland is a small, poxy hole, where everyone knows something about everyone else.'

'Sounds just like Dublin.'

'When Singer arrived at boarding school, some guy teased him about cars backfiring, and Singer beat the shit out of him.'

'You both went to a boarding school?'

'Oh yes.'

'How come?'

'In my case, because my father thought it would make a rugby-playing high achiever out of me. I think Singer's uncle sent him there because he had nowhere else to go, really.'

'How awful.'

'Yes, I hated every second of it.'

'No, I mean, to lose your family.'

Ronan snorted. 'I wish I could have lost my family.'

'That's a dreadful thing to say!'

'You don't know my father. Look, as far as Singer's concerned, I haven't told you any of this stuff, okay?'

'No, no, of course not.' Dionne walked over and hugged his shoulders. 'But thanks for telling me anyway.'

He rattled the frying pan and made a fuss of lifting the salmon steaks onto plates, hoping she wouldn't notice how red he'd gone. But of course, she did. As they ate their lunch, he contemplated the butchered remains of the once-proud fish, its thawed mouth open in a semblance of shock.

'Do you know what, I think I see a curry in our very near future.'

She cleaned her plate with a piece of bread. 'Dee-lish. Now, that alone made the journey here worthwhile. I'm glad Singer talked me into coming.'

'Sorry?'

'I said it was delicious, thank you very much.'

'No, what you said about Singer – he talked you into coming here?'

She laughed. 'He practically begged me to, on Friday night. He was very keen. He even rang me yesterday morning, to make sure I was on time for the bus. He can be very persuasive, when he wants to be.'

Ronan frowned at his empty wine glass. 'Yes, he can, can't he?' He stood abruptly and fetched his coat from its hook in the hallway. 'Excuse me, I have a message to do, up at the pub.'

When he left, Dionne smiled to herself and poured another glass of wine.

That night, Singer knelt before the fireplace in Dionne's bedroom. Dionne sat on the bed, brushing her hair. She had spent the afternoon unpacking. All around the room, different items of clothing hung on hangers from the cornice. It was, Singer had remarked, like stepping through to Narnia. Dionne had asked him what Narnia was.

'Thanks for doing this. The room should be lovely and cosy by the time I'm ready for bed.'

He struck a match and held it to the mixture of turf, newspapers and firelighters. 'You'll have to remember to keep it fed.'

'You'll have to remember to remind me.'

Flames rose from the fireplace, their yellow glow augmenting the oil lamp on the chair beside Dionne's bed. Manus had set out from Inistrahull well before dusk, but by the time he and Singer had winched the boat out of the water, the day had faded. Now, Singer sat on the floor beside the sputtering fire and turned to face her.

'Dionne, can I ask you something?'

'Please, call me Dee,' she spoke gently. 'All my friends do.'

'Okay.'

'Can I call you Gareth?'

'All my friends call me Singer.'

'Why?'

'If you were called Gareth, which would you prefer?'

'So, what do you want to ask me?' Her eyes reflected the lamp-light, and the flame lent deeper shades to the pale blonde of her hair.

'Why did you say that about Oona, on the pier?'

'Hmm. What did I say about Oona on the pier?'

'You told me not to let her do anything stupid.'

'That's right, so I did.'

'Did you mean not to let her fall out of the boat, that sort of thing?'

Dionne didn't answer immediately, but moved the stroke of her hairbrush away from him, leaning her head with the direction of the pull.

'How was Oona, on the island?'

'She was grand. I don't think Manus has met too many girls like her, though.'

'Have you?'

'I thought she was funny.'

'Funny how? Funny strange, or funny amusing?'

'Amusing, and witty.'

'She's not exactly shy and retiring, is she?'

'No, that sounds more like Melissa.'

'Look, I said what I said because there's something I think you should know about Oona. We all love her very much. Melissa and I, we've always looked out for her, all the way through school. She's a lovely person. But she's also quite sick.'

'I'm sorry to hear that. What's wrong with her?'

'She's mentally ill.'

'Bloody hell. She seems pretty normal to me.'

'That's the sad thing about it. She's fine, ninety per cent of the time. The problem is that every so often, she goes totally nuts. I mean, really, really nuts. Back in the summer, she stole a shitload of money from her mum and disappeared. We all thought she was dead, and there was, like, a serious panic, police involved, everything. She didn't turn up for a whole month, and then, guess where?'

'Where?'

'Berlin.'

'What was she doing in Berlin?'

'We don't know. She won't tell anybody. I'm not so sure she knows herself. When they found her, she wasn't wearing any clothes. So they sent her back to Ireland, and it was as if she'd lost her mind. She was committed for six weeks afterwards. Locked up.'

'Holy shit.'

'That's one of the reasons Melissa and I decided to come here, to give Oona a break. She's been very depressed since that whole episode. Stuck in a rut. But you need to be careful with her.'

'What do you mean?'

'How can I put this...she forms attachments far too easily. She latches onto people, gets very up, hyper almost. But for every up, there's a down. She likes to be the centre of attention, and when she isn't, there can be hell to pay. Does that make sense?'

'Maybe...I don't know.'

'Well, my advice is, don't let her latch onto you. Always bear in mind it's best to keep a bit of distance. For her sake, if not for yours.'

'Right.' Singer stood and dusted his hands against his black jeans. 'I better go and see if Ronan's okay with dinner. Salmon curry – imagine doing that to a perfectly good fish.'

Dionne laughed. 'He's a sweetie, you let him be.'

'He's an arse.'

'You don't mean that.'

'Don't worry, we enjoy fighting.'

'He's very fond of you.'

'He thinks I'm a savage.'

'Ah, you say that, Mister Singer, but you don't mean it.' He moved towards the door. She put out a hand, and stopped him. 'I said Oona was *one* of the reasons I came here.' She gathered her hair at the back. 'On the mantelpiece – my clasp.'

'Uh, yes. Here.' He passed her the clasp, but she didn't take it. Instead she stood, with her back to him.

'Put it in my hair. Not there, further up.' He fixed the clasp as best he could, then she turned around and in a quick, smooth movement, draped her arms around his neck and gave him a baby kiss on the lips. He coughed and kissed her dryly on the forehead in return, and opened the door. She pouted, then smiled, released her arms and sashayed through it. They descended the stairs. As they entered the kitchen, she reached up and pecked him on the cheek before sitting down at the end of the table already occupied by Melissa and Oona.

'Pass me a glass, babes,' she asked him. He fumbled somewhat, then poured her a generous measure of wine, stopping to top up the other two girls, before escaping to inspect Ronan's work on the range.

'What have you done to my fish?' He sniffed at one of the pots.

'Tinned tomatoes and pineapple chunks, nothing fresh in that excuse for a shop, of course.'

Singer poked at the curry with a wooden spoon, as if prodding a dead thing.

'Ah. But where else could you buy rubber boots at ten o'clock at night, if not McFall's?'

Ronan snatched the spoon off him. 'Get your filthy hands off my cuisine.'

'I just feel sorry for it.'

'Well, don't.'

'Decent afternoon?'

'Read a bit, dozed a bit. You?'

'Serve that muck up, and we'll tell you all about it.'

Across the kitchen, Dionne sipped her wine and reached for a cigarette.

'So, is your fire well and truly lit?' Oona asked her, with a good-humoured sneer. Dionne winked. Melissa smiled faintly.

They dined by candlelight, somewhat less than heartily. Eventually, Oona pushed away her half-empty plate and sat back with her wine glass.

'Well, at least we solved the mystery of the tower on the hill.'

'Really?' Ronan, for the first time in his life, tried to finish a main-course portion, as if, like an officer in the trenches, he had to lead by example.

'Manus says it was a Lloyd's signal tower, from the days before radio.'

'You mean, as in Lloyd's of London?'

'The insurers, yes. They always wanted to know when ships had made it safely across from America, and the tower was used to observe them as they came and went. But the islanders were very naughty.'

'How so?'

'Coming back from America, captains and crews used to smuggle goods on board, to sell for themselves. On their way past Inistrahull, they would drop off bales of tobacco and barrels of drink, and come back for them later, to dodge the excise men. The islanders hid stuff for a fee. Manus also said that later on, they used to sail out to meet the big ocean liners, and sell them fresh fish. They even sold fish to German U-boats, during the First World War. Apparently the U-boats used to surface nearby, and hang out.' She sighed. 'It's just sooo Enid Blyton. Or Erskine Childers. I just wish I could have been there.'

'Hmm. Dunaldragh hasn't always been the god-forsaken spot it is today, obviously.'

'I'm glad it's godforsaken,' Singer chipped in.

'Yes, but all this other stuff,' Oona enthused, 'you can still feel it, can't you? I mean, I wouldn't be surprised to see ghosts walking up and down the stairs.'

'I hope I don't see any feckin' ghosts,' Dionne squealed. 'This place is creepy enough as it is.'

'Well, I think there's a ghost in my bedroom,' Oona announced matter of factly.

'Oh shut up!'

Ronan stopped eating. 'Why do you say that?'

'Because when I'm alone in there, I don't feel alone.'

'You wish,' Dionne snorted.

'Look who's talking.'

'What do you mean?' Ronan persisted. 'Have you seen anything…unusual?'

'No, but that room feels totally different from all of the others.'

'Because of the oak panelling and the four-poster bed. That room has been in every cheap horror movie you've ever seen.'

'No, it's not that. Not horror. Whatever it is, it's not malevolent.'

'Should we summon an exorcist just in case, though?' Singer's tone was drier than the desert.

Oona laughed. 'In case I turn green and start crawling across the ceiling.'

'The windows in that room used to have bars.' Melissa's quiet voice silenced the others.

'Excuse me?' Oona's wine glass halted just before her lips.

'You can tell. The windows were barred, from the outside.'

'How do you know?'

'This morning, I brought you up a cup of tea. I noticed, when I looked at the view.'

'You noticed what, exactly?'

'Bring the torch.' Melissa lifted a candlestick. The others followed, sharing significant glances, unsure whether to be more surprised by what Melissa was saying, or the fact that she was saying anything at all.

In Oona's room, Singer shone his torch through the glass of the side window. The lighthouse responded, throwing a white beam back. Sure enough, the sill bore four circular lumps of iron, cut almost level with the stone. Protruding from the architrave above were four corresponding lumps. The same was true of the front window.

'She's right,' Singer announced. 'You see this a lot in London, where they cut down iron railings for smelting in the war. There used to be bars here.' He walked off, and they heard doors open and close as he checked the other bedrooms. 'Nope, no other rooms were barred,' he announced upon returning. 'Now why would anyone want to block these two windows?'

'Perhaps this is where the lighthouse keepers kept their sex slaves,' Oona giggled.

'Perhaps this is where they kept people like you locked up!' Dionne exclaimed. Then, hurriedly, 'I didn't mean that. I was only joking.'

'Of course you were,' Oona agreed airily.

Ronan averted his eyes from the faded mirror of the dresser. 'Perhaps the bars were to keep people out, not in. Maybe they stored valuables in this room.' He gestured at the heavy panelling and the dramatic bed, which had a rather undramatic blue sleeping bag laid out upon it.

'Sorry,' whispered Oona. 'But it does get bloody cold up here.'

'This room is...richer than all the rest. Better appointed.' Ronan warmed to his theory, telling himself inwardly there'd been nothing in the mirror that night. 'This building was a barrack. So maybe this was the commanding officer's quarters. Maybe he had documents that had to be kept under lock and key.'

'To run a lighthouse?' Oona sniggered. 'Not exactly a job for the secret service, I would have thought.'

'Still, you don't know. This place has been around for a long time, it's seen two world wars. People thought differently back then. And there may have been a military dimension, what with all the ships passing by.'

'Maybe you're right,' Singer agreed. 'I found a gunnery manual on the bookshelf downstairs.'

'A what?' Oona sounded thrilled.

'For Yankee naval gunners, from the American Civil War. Quite extraordinary.'

Oona pulled at Singer's sleeve. 'Will you show me that? Please? Please?'

'Uh, if you want.'

Oona twirled like a ballerina, then flopped onto the denuded four-poster. 'Anyway, folks, this is my bedroom, and you're all very welcome, any time. I feel like I should throw a pyjama party, but the atmosphere is more S&M, don't you think? Mistress Tyler, and her parlour of willing slaves!'

Dionne snorted and left the room, followed by an uncertain-looking Ronan and a broadly smiling Singer. Melissa sat down beside Oona on the bed.

'What you said about feeling something in here – were you making that up?'

Oona took Melissa's hand and held it up for scrutiny, twisting it around. 'No. You have beautiful nails. I see a tall, dark stranger.'

'Do you feel it now?'

'No. There were too many people. It's shy.'

Ronan slumped in an armchair by the fireplace in the living room, toasting his legs. In spite of the light from four oil lamps and several candles, the far reaches of the room remained in shadow. Rain spattered noisily off the seaward windows – the first taste of the bad weather Manus had predicted. Ostensibly, the company presented a peaceful, even charming tableau, with everyone sipping from wine glasses and reading books selected from the shelves. Yet Ronan felt restless. He had an 1858 edition of *Select Poetry from Chambers's Repository and Miscellany* open at Byron, but some long-dead student had underlined words and phrases from different poems with brown ink and squiggled little numbers all over the margins, which distracted him. More distracting still, on the overstuffed sofa, Oona lounged close to Singer, cooing over the gunnery manual that sat open on his knee. Dionne, who obviously had about as much interest in gunnery as Ronan had in Byron, perched on Singer's far side. Oona wore jeans and a brown V-neck jumper, had her legs pulled up underneath her and dabbed a strange-smelling paste under her ears from a little tin in her hand. Dionne, on the other hand, sat stiffly, with one arm awkwardly stretched behind Singer along the back of the sofa. She smiled whenever he addressed her, but otherwise looked slightly miffed. She wore a black skirt with woollen tights and a white, open-neck blouse that, Ronan noticed, strained its buttons across the chest, revealing a black bra underneath. Ronan had last seen a chest like that…where? Puerto Banus? He quickly shifted his gaze away.

Melissa sat cross-legged on the carpet before the fire. She cradled an 1897 Baedeker guide to Egypt on her lap, her face a study in elegant absorption. Ronan thought that Melissa looked more like Audrey Hepburn than anyone he'd ever seen. That said, Ronan had never actually watched an Audrey Hepburn film, rather he knew of her existence through his mother, who bore no resemblance whatsoever to the former star, but kept a number of pictures in her bedroom. For her generation, Hepburn had been 'it', and his mother's bedroom was like a private shrine to the woman. Ronan's parents had slept separately for as long as he could remember, and it had come as quite a shock to learn that not everyone over the age of fifty behaved likewise. With a shudder, he recalled some of the noises that had emanated from Linda's parents' bedroom in Puerto Banus during siesta time.

There, now he was staring at Dionne's straining buttons again. The top of her bra was frilled, and her skin above was as white and soft as her blouse. He raised *Chambers's Miscellany* as if to see better by the oil lamp, but held the book so he could peek over the top of it without being caught.

8

During the week before Christmas, 1988, the new inhabitants of the Pier House settled into a daily routine of sorts. Melissa continued to rise early, while the rest surfaced in dribs and drabs, according to how much they'd drunk the night before. Mornings were spent walking, either along the beach or up around the western headland. As the weather became more blustery, the snow around receded, but it was still cold. Singer took to spending lunchtimes at McFall's pub, where he would sit at the bar, sipping Guinness and chatting to Manus. If any of the others followed him, he would chat to Manus anyway, while the rest sat huddled around the table, warming their hands with hot ports and marvelling at the quixotic collection of objects festooned about the place. In the afternoons, the company would lounge before the living room fire, reading and dozing, some even returning to bed to sleep off the lunchtime port. In the early evenings, after the failure of Ronan's salmon curry, Singer and Melissa took up cooking duties by unspoken but very definite consent, peeling, chopping and slicing in almost total silence, while Ronan, Oona and Dionne formed an aperitif society around the living room fire. Singer had somehow managed to wire Ronan's Walkman into the back of the old valve radio, and the same Mortal Coil tape was played over and over, a soundtrack to the hours slipping by in calm, collective contentment.

Dionne's pretext for dragging Oona along to Dunaldragh – that the change would somehow do her good – had actually worked, ulterior motives notwithstanding. Many subtle elements combined to make those few days delicious, not least the novelty of the situation. There was the frisson of forging new friendships and renewing old ones, a luxurious sensation of spending time unstintingly, without distractions or demands from the outside world. Time, indeed, seemed to slow down, and the only indication of its passage came from the relative brightness of the sky or from the clunking clock that hung in the pub. The envy that Oona had sometimes felt for characters in films or books who stepped into fictional worlds seemed somehow due to her now. She loved the sea, she loved scouring the beach with Ronan for driftwood and she loved watching the harbour from her bedroom window. She loved having to carry a candle stub in a tin holder to go upstairs at night. She loved staying up late, drinking, talking and smoking – so much so that on Christmas Eve morning, herself, Ronan and Singer found themselves still gathered around the embers of the living room fire as the windows on either side of the fireplace faded from black to grey and the chiding of gulls could be heard down the chimney. Melissa had long since retired, and Dionne lay asleep on the sofa, covered by her faux-fur coat, blonde hair spread like a fan across the rough leather of the cushions.

'Damn and blast,' Ronan pronounced, shaking an empty bottle into his glass, 'we're in a no wine situation.'

'I'll fetch more from the kitchen,' Oona volunteered.

'Oh, I think you'll find we've drunk everything in the kitchen. In fact, I believe I can say with total confidence that we've polished off every drop of alcohol in this house.'

'Ah, but you're not drinking with amateurs now.' Oona picked herself up from the floor and weaved into the shadows at the far end of the room, disappearing out the door. Ronan, who had prominent red wine stains on either side of his upper lip, blinked at Singer, sprawled in the armchair opposite. They heard light, creaking footsteps on the floorboards above, then Oona returned, bearing a green bottle and wearing her anorak. 'Gordon's finest,' she announced. 'Been saving it for emergencies. But you have to earn it. Come on, let's go and watch dawn, from the watchtower.'

'You've got to be joking.'

'The air will do you good.'

'I assure you that it won't.'

'Singer, are you going to be a big pansy fop like your friend here?'

Singer stood slowly and took the bottle from Oona. 'I never drink anything stronger than gin before breakfast.' He broke the seal and toasted them, before taking a generous nip. 'Ahh,' he breathed. 'Breakfast.'

Oona laughed and weaved off again towards the hallway to find her boots. Ronan stared up at Singer with the fixed intensity of one who has consumed more than enough alcohol.

'So, a romantic stroll with one of your wenches, huh?'

'She's not a wench, and she's not mine.'

'I wouldn't like to get in the way of anything.'

'Anything like what?'

'Her hair is beautiful, isn't it?' Ronan nodded at Dionne, curled up on the sofa.

Singer looked down at Dionne, as if noticing her for the first time. 'Yes, I suppose it is.'

Ronan stretched a hand out. Singer passed him the bottle and he sipped from it, retched and coughed. 'I despise gin,' he croaked. 'It makes me silly, and I always smell of carrots in the morning.'

'This is the morning,' Singer pointed out.

'Bugger. So either it's this poison, or a cup of tea.'

'Or you could just go to bed.'

'And leave you alone with all these drunk women?'

'The only object of my desire is actually sitting in your lap, at present.' Singer reached out to take the bottle back, but Ronan clutched it to his chest.

'My precious-s-s,' he hissed. Then he took another swig, which stayed down this time.

By the time they reached the summit, the gin bottle was nearly empty, most of it consumed by Ronan on the path up, his face twisting at each swallow. They stood by the tower, Ronan by now swaying perceptibly as the winter sun crept out from behind the mountain across the bay. To the east, the sky was clear and the island languished in the new light like one of its Mediterranean cousins. But a bitter gust blew in from the west, where, out to sea, a line of grey thunderhead clouds approached, like battleships in formation, queuing up to bombard the shore. From inland, a bell pealed, faintly but insistently. Oona shuddered and put an arm around both men's waists, pulling them to her.

'I hate that sound. I really do hate it.'

'Iss jus' a bell,' Ronan slurred.

'Bells mark time. Bells are evil.'

'Where the nashty bell?' Ronan looked around. 'I make it shtop.'

'It must be coming from the village.' Singer felt unexpectedly odd, with Oona's arm around him. He felt even more unusual knowing she held Ronan the same way.

'Wha' village?'

'There's a village a few miles inland. We drove through it the night we came here, we just didn't see it. There can't be much to it, but Manus said there's a church.'

'You never tol' me about any village.' Ronan looked at Singer accusingly, then pulled on the bottle.

'You never asked. And go easy on that gin.'

'He never tol' me about any village,' Ronan informed Oona, as if Singer were guilty of a heinous crime. 'I been here a week, and not sheen any village.'

'I'm glad we can't see it. But why are they ringing that bell on a Saturday? Today is Saturday, isn't it?' Oona wondered.

'Christmas Eve,' Singer snorted, 'so God only knows.'

Ronan, still staring at Oona, lunged forward suddenly and tried to kiss her on the mouth. She yelped and pulled back, letting go of both Ronan and Singer, shielding her face with her hands. Dropping the gin, Ronan flung his arms around her and tried to kiss her again.

'Hey!' she squealed. 'Stop messing!'

Singer reached out and held Ronan's shoulder. 'Down, boy.' Oona broke loose from Ronan, who in turn tried to pull free from Singer's clasp. Singer released him and he stumbled back awkwardly, falling to the ground, his glasses flying off his face.

'Christ,' Singer muttered, 'he's even drunker than I thought. Must be the fresh air.'

'Or the bottle of gin he's just necked. My bottle of gin.'

Singer bent to lift him, but addressed Oona. 'Are you all right?'

'Yes − is he?'

'Fuck the pair o' ye,' Ronan interjected. He had a black mark on one cheek, where his face had touched the peat.

'Come on, crazy horse.' Singer hauled Ronan onto his feet as easily as if he were uprighting a child. But Ronan's knees promptly gave way, so Singer pulled him over to the steps of the bricked-up tower doorway and sat him down. Oona retrieved his glasses, then knelt carefully before him and placed them back on his face. She tousled his hair as he stared at her, stupidly.

'I don't mind putting out on the first date,' she smiled. 'You just never told me this was a first date.'

His head lolled. 'Frsssnit,' he hissed.

'Pardon?'

But he answered only by slouching further against the steps, grinning sardonically. So she stood and joined Singer, who'd wandered over to the edge of the headland drop to peer down at the sea. Waves exploded into the gorge, their habitual booming now accompanied by a lower, bass rumble.

'Sorry,' Singer said. 'I've never seen him do anything like that before.'

'Forget it – he's completely hammered. We should get him back down to the house before he gets any worse.'

'You're right, we should. I just wanted to see the waves. They're getting bigger, there must be quite a storm on the oooof...' he gasped, and flew outward over the edge. Oona screamed as Singer fell, bouncing off the slope below her feet before rolling head-over-heels towards the jagged schist beyond. Ronan stood beside her, arms outstretched in front of him. He had caught Singer square between the shoulder blades. Oona held her hands to her face as Singer writhed in mid-bounce, grabbing at the grass with both hands. He slid, face down and boot first onto the shale, throwing up a shower of loose stones before jarring to a halt against the base of the rocky pinnacle that overlooked the gorge.

'You fucking idiot!' she shrieked at Ronan, punching him on the shoulder. He looked at her with a confused expression as she sat on the edge and dropped after Singer, half-sliding, half-scrambling down the slope. When she reached him, he lay perfectly still, clumps of grass clutched in each fist.

'Are you okay? Speak to me! Are you okay?'

'I don't know,' he answered through gritted teeth. 'Nothing feels broken, but I'm not moving in case anything is.'

'He pushed you!'

'You don't say.'

She looked back up the slope. Ronan was no longer there. Whether he had moved away from the edge or left altogether, she couldn't tell. She patted Singer's nearest arm, then leg.

'No bones sticking out. Not on this side, anyway.'

He grunted and rolled over onto his back. 'That's great news. Is my ribcage exposed? Is my spine sticking out through my stomach or anything?'

She laughed. 'No, but you're very dirty.'

He put on a mock-seductive voice. 'Darling, you have no idea.'

She slapped his leg. 'Now don't you start, too. What, am I giving off some sort of fuck-me smell this morning?'

'Ow! I've just fallen off a cliff, and she beats me!' Oona stood and tugged on his left arm. He picked himself up and leaned against nearby rocks. 'Jesus. Bastard could have crippled me!'

'He could have killed you. Is he a bit of a psycho, despite appearances?'

'Believe me, this is completely out of character. At school, he was the biggest geek of them all. I don't know what's gotten into him.'

'Gordon's gin, about eighteen fluid ounces of it. He practically wolfed that whole bottle.'

'He doesn't even like gin.'

'You could have fooled me. Hey – where are you going?'

Singer turned around and, stiffly at first, began climbing the pinnacle. 'Let's get a proper look at the waves while we're down here.'

'Shouldn't we go back up to the tower to see if Ronan is okay?'

'Yes, we probably should.' But he kept climbing. After some hesitation, she followed him. The top of the pinnacle was flat and about the size of a generous car-parking space. Lying on her tummy, peering into the gorge, Oona felt like a seabird, suspended in mid-air, viewing the cliffs in a way that no human ever should. Far below, the rocks glistened blackly, a yawning throat that swallowed wave after wave. The pair lay side by side for some time, hypnotised by the motion of the water, the noise and the dizziness of the drop – indeed, an observer looking down from the tower could have been forgiven for thinking that they had fallen asleep, in the most dangerous place imaginable. Eventually, she tapped him on the shoulder.

'Hey. I've haven't had a chance to say thanks. So, thanks.'

'Thanks for what?'

'Thanks for bringing us here.'

'I didn't bring you – you brought yourselves.'

'No, I meant in the sense that you invited Dionne. She really likes you, you know. It's been quite a while since I've seen her this keen on anybody.'

'I didn't invite Dionne – she invited herself.'

'Well, that just shows how keen she is.'

'I'll admit I encouraged her.'

'Right, so the feeling's mutual?'

'Actually, I encouraged her because I was hoping she wouldn't come alone.'

Oona felt a sudden chill inside. 'Pardon?'

He sat up abruptly. 'I think we should go and check whether my psychotic friend is still alive.'

'Hey, don't change the—' But he slid off the landward end of the pinnacle, and she had no choice but to follow him. On the walk back, she opened her mouth a few times as if to restart their conversation, but he wore a distant look that dissuaded her. However, what little he had said disturbed her much more deeply than Ronan's drunken advance. The latter was nowhere to be seen around the tower, nor on the hairpin path down to the harbour. Instead, they found him snoring soundly, face down in the hallway, covered by coats and with a pillow under his head. Melissa sat on the bottom step of the stair-case, wearing her leotard, pondering the prostrate form.

'Ah. There you are. I couldn't move him, so I tried to make him comfortable.' She took in Singer's torn, muddied clothes. 'What have you been doing?'

'Spot of early morning cliff-diving.' He knelt by Ronan, pocketed his glasses, then, holding him under the arms, began pulling him back-ways up the staircase, his heels clunking off each step. Ronan mumbled, but remained limp. 'Goodnight, then, ladies,' Singer called down. Melissa and Oona watched the odd couple disappear into the gloom, then went into the living room. Dionne moaned from the sofa.

'Ohh, my head. What time is it?'

'Eight,' Melissa informed her, sitting on the rug. Without another word, she started into her morning exercise routine. Oona crawled onto the sofa beside Dionne, who stretched.

'Hi babes. You're up early.'

'I haven't been to bed.'

'Eh? Why not?'

'We went for a walk – me, Singer and Ronan. There was a bit of horseplay up at the tower, and Ronan sort of pushed Singer down a steep hill.' Better to keep Dionne informed – up to a point. Eventually, women deduct much more from what they're not told than what they are. Still, Oona censored any mention of her gin, Ronan's crude pass at her and Singer's cryptic remark up at the gorge. That sort of detail could be open to misconstruction.

'Singer? Where is he? Is he all right?'

'He's fine. They're both upstairs, sleeping it off, and I intend to join them.' Dionne's eyes widened. 'I mean, I intend to join them upstairs, in the privacy of my own room. To sleep,' she added, a tad weakly.

'You should have woken me. I'd have liked to have gone for a walk, too.'

'You were out for the count, and to be honest, I'm sorry I bothered myself. God, I'm tired.' She was even more sorry she hadn't scuttled straight off to bed upon returning, feeling suddenly very guilty without being able to articulate why. She made to leave. Dionne touched her arm. Her face was puffy with sleep and her hair in a rarely seen state of disarray, yet her look had a menacing focus to it.

'Is there anything going on between you and Singer?'

The question inflated Oona's nameless guilt. 'God, no! How could you ask me that?'

'If nothing's going on, then you won't mind me asking.'

'Hey – I went for a walk because I happened to be awake. End of story.'

Dionne's look softened, but only slightly. 'Sorry.' She rubbed her eyes. 'God, I must look crap. I guess I'm just…I don't know where I stand. We've been here five days now, and he hasn't…well, you know. He hasn't even tried to kiss me again, let alone anything else. I don't know whether he likes me, or if he even wants me to be here. I'm back to thinking I shouldn't have come at all.'

Oona took her hand. 'Dee, you're tired and probably a bit hungover. We're having a lovely time.'

'I'm not.'

'What you said about Singer – is he aware of any of this?' There are black lies, white lies and lies by omission. Oona's question, she knew, fell into the latter category.

'Oh, I don't know what he knows. I can't tell what he's thinking.'

'Maybe he's shy.'

'Perhaps he just kissed me that time because he was drunk.'

'Hey, sometimes men need things spelled out for them – in neon letters ten feet tall.'

Dionne smiled at that. 'Sorry,' she repeated. 'I shouldn't take it out on you.'

'Don't be silly.' Oona climbed off the sofa, trying to appear unhurried. 'I have to sleep, is all. Night-night.' She bent and kissed Dionne's forehead. 'Or should I say, good morning.' As casually as she could, she fled for the stairs. Dionne's conciliatory smile disappeared the instant Oona turned her back, and she sat a while, frowning at the fireplace. Melissa finished her routine with her usual dramatic handstand, ending in the lotus position.

'I shall be going for one shortly, if you still want one.'

'Hmm?'

'An early morning walk.'

'Err – no. I think I'll get more sleep.' Dionne followed Oona up the stairs. Melissa remained, sitting upright, smiling faintly to herself.

Singer yawned. He'd been having a dream about hovering, like a seagull, amongst the graves of Milltown Cemetery. Oona was sitting beside a crooked headstone, weeping and eating an apple. She couldn't see him and he couldn't fly over to her. Someone was stroking his feathers, or was it his hair? He opened his eyes – he was facing the wall. Judging by the light reflecting off the aged, yellow-white plaster, it was mid-afternoon. Someone, he realised, was definitely stroking his hair – he wasn't dreaming. He made to roll over in the bed, but he couldn't, because that someone was tucked tightly in behind him.

'Sorry,' she whispered. 'I didn't mean to wake you.'

He twisted his head, looking over his shoulder with one eye. 'Dionne. Jesus. Hi.' He turned his head away again, mind racing. Did I go to bed with her? No. Are you sure? No. Jesus, I didn't, did I? Am I naked? No – you have a T-shirt and…yes, just move your leg slightly…yup, you still have your boxer shorts on. But my legs are bare, and I just felt – yes, hers are bare, too. I can feel them against mine, smooth, warm…and quite nice, actually. I can't tell if the rest of her is bare, too. Okay, a good way of second-guessing the situation is – are you sore? If you've had sex, you'll be a bit sore. Does it feel sore? No – *that* doesn't feel sore, but now that you mention it, every other part of my body aches like fuck. Well, Ronan did push you off the headland. God! Yes! Now I remember! Bloody Ronan. I went to bed alone, and I haven't had sex with anybody, at least not wittingly…

She resumed stroking his hair, talking now in a low voice, from her throat. 'Your face changes, when you sleep. You look less grumpy.' Her hand moved down and began rubbing his neck.

'Ouch.'

She stopped. 'Does that hurt?'

'No. I'm just very stiff.'

She resumed kneading his shoulder. 'I heard you fell.'

'I didn't fall – I was pushed.'

'Naughty Ronan. I shall have to have words with him. I'd be very upset if anything ever happened to you.'

'Thanks.'

'Can I ask you something?'

He stayed facing the wall. He knew what was coming, so he pretended to be less awake than he actually was. 'Uh-huh?'

'When we kissed in Dublin last week – did that mean anything to you?' Her hand stopped massaging, a significant pause. He knew he had no choice other than to roll around and face her now, which he did, drawing his breath sharply, as if his body hurt more than it did. Even with her hair draped around her neck and shoulders, he could see a black bra-strap, which implied, thank Christ, that she'd still have her knickers on. Actually, seeing her violet-blue eyes and full lips so close again reminded him why he'd kissed her in the first place. Why not just do it again?

'Did it mean anything to you?'

'I asked first, but take an educated guess, mister.'

'I'm sorry, I've been drinking red wine and gin and my mouth tastes disgusting.'

'I don't mind.'

'I do.'

'You could always go and brush your teeth, if that's all that's stopping you.'

He drew a breath. 'Dionne…'

'Dee.'

'Dee. My future isn't very clear right now. I haven't a clue what to do with myself, or whether I'll even stay in Ireland. I don't want to be unfair to you.'

'Let's not worry about the boyfriend-girlfriend thing, we can work that out later. Let's just do what we both want to do.' She smiled. He smiled back.

'I like you.'

'Good. That's all I wanted to hear you say.'

'But I don't know what I'm doing. After I leave here, I have no idea how I'm going to earn a living, except that I'm not going back to photojournalism.'

'Why not? You must be good if you're making money out of it.'

'Because I'm sick of people killing each other. For a long time I thought...I felt I had a duty, almost, to photograph what was happening...'

'Because of what happened to your family?'

His tone changed abruptly. 'Ronan has a big fucking mouth.' He bumped the back of his fist off his forehead. 'Let me give you a word of advice - never do a friend a favour. They won't thank you for it.'

'Sshhhh. Don't be cross with him. I was being nosey – I cross-examined him.' Singer harrumphed and frowned at the ceiling. 'And don't you dare,' she kissed his lips and slid a hand up the front of his boxer shorts, 'be cross with me. Oops,' she held on to what she found and giggled, 'I see that you're not.'

For the rest of their stay, he would marvel at himself for not giving in. How very un-male, and how utterly unlike him, not to take what was on offer, and stuff the consequences. Dionne, by any standards, was a beautiful woman. But instead, he forced himself to think about seaweed on the beach. He thought about dustbins, about vomiting, about being naked in public, and when none of that worked, he remembered the two corporals, lying butchered on the ground, then three other bodies, trapped in the burning wreckage of a car. That worked.

'What's the matter?' she whispered. 'I thought you liked me?'

'I do, but I need a bit of time. It's nice, just to lie like this.'

She moved her hand up onto his chest and snuggled up beside him, nestling her head on his shoulder. 'Time is the one thing we seem to have plenty of in this place.' He placed his hand on hers and yawned, pretending to fall asleep. Soon, she actually did fall asleep. When her breathing slowed right down, he very gradually edged out from underneath her, dropped between the bed and the wall, then crawled through the dust beneath the bedstead, cursing inwardly every time a floorboard creaked. What if she were to wake up? How would he explain what he was doing under the bed? The thought nearly made him burst out laughing. He wriggled across the floor, stood up, gathered some clean clothes and his boots and tiptoed out the bedroom door, closing it very, very softly behind him.

He snuck into the kitchen and began to put on his trousers.

'Look at this.' Melissa sat at the head of the table. Singer jumped, tried to pull his trousers on more quickly and practically fell over. She folded her arms, and gave him a sceptical look. Before her on the table were a book, a pen and a sheet of paper.

'Bloody hell,' he muttered. He went to pour himself a finger of whiskey, then remembered that the house had been drunk dry. He muttered 'bloody hell' again, poured a glass of water instead, and sat next to her.

'Ronan was reading this book the other night, he left it open on the floor.'

'Poets are notoriously untidy.'

'That's not what I meant. I'm just telling you how I noticed, by accident.'

'Noticed what?'

'Look.' She held up a tatty brown leather hardback – *Select Poetry from Chambers's Repository and Miscellany*. It was open at Byron, and he saw that different letters, words, phrases and whole stanzas had been underlined in brown ink, and numbered.

'These aren't our books! What does that ginger freak think he's doing?'

'Ronan didn't do this. Look closely.'

'Oh, right. I see what you mean. That's not biro…it's old ink, from a nib.'

'You've almost got it.'

'Sorry, I'm more than a bit hungover.' She held a forefinger up to his nose. Heaven preserve me from crazy women, he thought.

'I pricked myself with a needle yesterday.' Sure enough, a small spot blemished the white whorl of her fingertip.

'There's been a lot of accidents around here lately.'

'I did it on purpose, to draw blood. Then I did that.' She showed him a brown blotch beside a poem called *The Ocean*. 'Can you see, it's gone nearly the same colour as…'

'Are you trying to tell me that somebody annotated Byron in their own blood?'

'Well, one would assume it was their own.'

He rubbed his eyes. 'I can't handle this.'

'Pay attention, I'm perfectly serious.'

'That's what worries me. Look, Byron was a looper – maybe his fans were all nutbags, too. Wild romantics, devouring his poetry by moonlight, with a goblet of laudanum in one hand and a sharpened dagger in the other.'

'Possibly. But there's more. Do you see these numbers?'

'Don't tell me – this book is the key to the Holy Grail?'

'Don't be facetious. Look – every number corresponds to something underlined, but the numbers aren't consecutive. It makes no sense, until you flick back and forward, and write things out in the order they've been numbered.'

'I'm sorry, Melissa, if we haven't been very good company for you.'

'Shut up and read,' she commanded, with a trace of impatience – the first emotion of any sort Singer had noted since her arrival. She pushed a page, bearing her own handwriting, in front of him. 'I've used a slash instead of numbers.' The page read,

> Freedom, can it be, that this is all remains of thee? /
> I deem myself a slave
> For this will be my grave /
> I am dumb / In vain - in vain / forget me /
> My father a tyrant / despot /
> My voice sounds crush'd / by /
> the minions of luxury / Winter presides /
> I dwell in the dark / ill-starred / foreboding /
> destined to die / beneath the trackless mountain
> unseen / my memory long perished /
> Few are my years, and yet I feel
> The world was ne'er designed for me.
> I must not think, I may not gaze
> On what I am – on what I was /
> I look upon the / past /
> As on a place of agony and strife
> Where, for some sin, to sorrow I was cast.
> A world which vanquished me only /
> Where nothing, save the waves and I
> May hear our mutual murmurs sweep /
> The night-winds sigh, the breakers roar /

My / hearth is desolate /
I am sorrowful in mind
For I have from my father gone,
And have no friend / whom I love /
Trust not for freedom / oh servile offspring,
in dusty darkness hid. /
They're long to tell and sad to trace, each
Step from splendour to disgrace. /
I have become the spoil of our infection.

S o p h i a C l e m e n t s

Singer frowned, then read the transcript again, this time aloud.
When he finished, he set the page down.

'Jesus. Whoever Sophia Clements was, she was one unhappy
bunny.'

'It would seem so.'

'Or else she was a self-dramatising, hormonal teenager who'd read
far too much Brontë.'

'I think this has something to do with the panelled bedroom.'

He laughed. 'You think this explains the barred windows?'

'Maybe. All that stuff about freedom, and "I dwell in the dark",
"the night-winds sigh, the breakers roar", "in dusty darkness hid",
"beneath the trackless mountain". Imagine being locked in that room
a hundred years ago – that's exactly how you'd describe it.'

'How seductive. Our very own Gothic melodrama – poor tragic
Sophia, banished to the Pier House, imprisoned by her despot of a
father – something like that?' Melissa nodded. 'Okay,' he continued,
'let's try to stand it up by knocking it down.' He lifted the volume of
poetry. 'First off – this book could have come from anywhere. The
Pier House was a barrack for over forty years, books probably came
with each new arrival. There's a Yankee gunnery manual in the living
room – does that prove the house has some connection with the
American Civil War?'

'Of course not.'

'Right. So there's nothing to say that Sophia Clements, whoever
she was, ever set foot in Ireland, let alone in this house.'

'Nothing except this.' She rose and walked out of the kitchen,
down the hallway. He sighed, but followed. She opened the porch

door, then the front door and stepped outside. The wind gusted over the sea-grass, and there was water in the mouth of it. The surf bashed on the beach, hurling the pebbles around. She walked to the sundial, crouched down and pulled matted lumps of dead grass away from its base. An inscription was cut into the plinth, lichen-veiled and soil-stained in places, but plainly legible. As Singer walked clockwise around it, he read,

> in illis."
> : Clements :
> "Tempora mutantur
> nos et mutamur

He struggled to recall his boarding school Latin. 'Time…change… something else changes. Blast, is there a dictionary on those shelves in there?'

'"*Tempora mutantur nos et mutamur in illis.*" It means times change, and we change with them.'

'Have you already looked it up?' She smiled, more broadly than Singer had ever seen her do. It was the kind of smile that would stay with a man.

'No. I just remember my Latin better than you do. I don't know where the quote is from, but it shouldn't be too hard to find out. The important thing is the family surname. You would agree that links the book to here?'

'It would seem so. How long have you known about this?'

'I saw it on my first morning here. Just the tops of a few letters, peeping through the grass. So I took a closer look.'

'You see a lot.'

'I have good eyesight.'

'Any other surprises you'd like to share?'

'One or two, but let's concentrate on Sophia for now.'

'This quote seems a bit stuffy, compared to her Byronic message – if that's what it is. It doesn't sit with her style.'

'Sophia Clements didn't put this inscription here. Her father did.'

'How do you know?'

'Try this – you said yourself a landlord built this house, before the lighthouse commissioners took it over?'

'According to Manus, yes.'

'Have you ever asked yourself why anybody would build a house this size here? In the mid-eighteen hundreds, when getting to Dunaldragh must have been like travelling to the moon?'

'Manus said there was lots of sea traffic.'

'Yes, but how much of it stopped at this little harbour? It can barely hold a few fishing boats. All the big ships would have passed far out to sea. The lighthouse, the tower – this place is geared towards watching sea traffic, not accommodating it.'

'Okay...'

'Okay. Mister Clements is a big, rich landlord. He has a daughter called Sophia, but there's something wrong with her – don't forget, "I am dumb", "My voice sounds crush'd". Or maybe she's brought shame on the family, taken a lover, gotten pregnant – whatever it is, he needs to get her out of the way. But he can't bear to lock her in a hospital or an asylum, so he builds this place, far away from anything. He pays retainers – a cook, a few servants – to look after her, "the minions of luxury". He allows her reading material, but nothing that would let her get a message out, like pens, paper or ink. There's no escape, no outside contact. Sophia, locked in her room, records her plight the only way she can. If she writes coherently in the book, or rips pages out, the servants will notice. So she annotates, using the most popular poet of the day, one that others would be likely to read – on the off chance the house had visitors. Or maybe she bribed one of the servants to deliver the book to someone, and they never bothered. Or maybe she just did it for herself, and no one was ever meant to see it. Meanwhile, her father sticks this sundial out front, as a message for himself, more than anything else. It's of absolutely no practical use, so maybe we have to see it as a symbol, a sort of self-justification for what he's done. A statement of hope that one day, Sophia, or her circumstances, will change, and whatever is wrong will be okay again. Time heals all wounds, that sort of thing.'

Singer left a long pause, staring out to sea, before saying, 'Do you know what?'

'What?'

'You should talk more often. It suits you.'

'I speak when I have something to say.'

'You certainly do.'

'You're not taking me seriously.'

'Why do you think that?'

'Ooh, Singer, will you show me your gunnery manual? Please? Please? Would you take me seriously if I was a bit more flirty and quirky?' He froze. Not only had Melissa imitated Oona's voice perfectly, she had also captured her face and body movements. It was as if she had momentarily become her.

'Do that again.'

'Pour me a glass of wine, would you babes? While I sit at this table, and pretend to everyone else that I've just had sex with you.' Dionne, to a tee. Her tart, affected ennui, her throatiness.

'Stop that! You're freaking me out!'

'Stop that! You're freaking me out! But I'm only doing what big bossy-boots Singer tells me to!' She didn't quite have his lower notes, but his northern accent and tone of surprise were spot on. He laughed and spun on his heel, stuck for words. Melissa resumed her bland, faint smile – her mask to the world, he now realised.

'Was that your other surprise?'

'One of them.'

'I think we should go and talk to Manus. If he's half the amateur historian he says he is, then he'll know a lot more about this house than he's already told us. Plus, he promised me another salmon for Christmas dinner, so we may as well collect it. Then I better get my ass into Letterkenny and buy more wine, or there'll be mutiny in the ranks.'

The pair climbed into Singer's car and drove off up the lane. If either of them had looked back at the Pier House, they would have seen Dionne watching them from an upstairs window, her expression hard to fathom.

McFall's pub was empty, as usual, so they sat at the bar, swords hanging over their heads. When, after about five minutes, Manus failed to appear, Singer called his name up the back hallway. About a minute later, Mrs McFall shuffled from the gloom. She was pale, her face pinched as if she'd taken ill. She looked even less welcoming than ever, if such a thing were possible.

'Manus isn't here, so?'

'No.'

Singer saw there was no point in quizzing her about local history. 'Okay. I was to pick up food for tomorrow.' Without speaking, Mrs McFall lifted two cardboard boxes up onto the counter, then went off and returned with a whole frozen salmon, wrapped in newspaper, which she unceremoniously stuffed into one of the boxes, tail stiffly aloft. 'What do I owe you?' He dug around his pocket for money.

'Pay me later.' She disappeared back down the hallway without another word. Singer and Melissa lifted a box each and left.

'Life and soul of the party, huh?' He started the car engine and pulled onto the road, away from the sea.

'Pay me later,' Melissa intoned, in Mrs McFall's sepulchral brogue. 'I am busy disposing of my late husband's body.'

Oona came down to the kitchen at dusk, swaddled in a tatty tartan dressing gown and a pair of thick socks, to find Ronan seated at the table, inhaling smoke from a saucer before him. He coughed horribly, emptied powder from a green cylinder into the saucer and set fire to it with a match. The smoke billowed again and he sucked it, eyes closed. She hesitated in the doorway, as if she'd caught him in yet another embarrassing act.

'S'all right, s'all right.' He waved her in. His face was as red as his hair, which stood on end. Behind crooked glasses, his eyes were slits.

'Are you okay?'

'Yes, yes. Spot of asthma, brought on by a monumental hangover.'

'I feel pretty grotty myself. This helps.' She walked over to him, produced a small tin from her dressing gown pocket and smeared orange paste on his nearest temple. He recoiled.

'What the devil is that?'

'Tiger Balm. It will open your sinuses right up and help your headache.'

'Smells like aviation fuel.'

Oona laughed. 'It's probably stronger. Hold still.' She applied more paste to his temples and neck. For some reason, she felt obliged to touch him, to prove that she wasn't afraid – which she wasn't. He sat meekly, crinkling his nose. She could not believe that this poor creature had tried to kiss her. Singer, on the other hand, what he'd said this morning…she banished the thought, because, unlike Ronan, that was unsettling. 'Anyway, you seem no stranger to stinky medicine yourself. What is that stuff?'

'Potter's Asthma Remedy. It's pretty old-tech, but it works.'

'I've heard of that. If you eat it, you get the maddest hallucinations.'

'You're not supposed to eat it.'

'Which is probably why you get the maddest hallucinations.'

'I should think it tastes foul.'

'I hope you have a plentiful supply.'

'Why? Are you asthmatic, too?'

'No. It's going to be banned from sale soon.'

'How do you know?'

'There's very little about popular medication that I don't know. It's an area of interest, you could say.' She slipped her tin back into her pocket and filled the kettle at the sink. 'Cup of tea?'

'Please.'

She busied herself, deliberately not speaking for a bit, to give Ronan a chance to apologise for his behaviour that morning. But he didn't – he just sat at the table, rubbing his forehead and spluttering occasionally.

'I feel like I've been raped through my eye sockets,' he moaned at one point, but that was hardly the self-excoriation she sought. So she served the tea and sat across the table from him.

'Fancy a breath of fresh air? Walk up to the tower, maybe?'

'God no,' he snorted, as incredulously as if she'd suggested walking to Dublin. 'I'm far too shagged for that. Where do you suppose Singer is?'

'At the bottom of a cliff somewhere?'

'Excuse me?' His voice convinced, but she couldn't read his eyes behind his glasses. When she didn't reply, he sipped his tea. 'I see his car's gone. I hope he's had the sense to go to Letterkenny – we're all out of wine.'

'You're lucky Singer can walk, let alone drive to Letterkenny.'

'What do you mean?'

'What else do you remember from this morning, apart from being all out of wine?'

'Not a lot. Must have been pretty squiffy. Sat up most of the night, didn't we? I presume that's why I feel so horrendously horrendous.'

'I think that probably has more to do with the bottle of gin you drank.'

'What?' Again, his tone convinced, but something about his pained expression did not.

'Don't you remember anything about…' The door opened behind her, and Dionne strode over to the range, wearing a black backless dress that left very little to the imagination, either above or below the coccyx. Her platinum hair was tied up in a severe bun and she wore black silk stockings with high heels. Ronan's eyes trebled in size – Oona thought that only his glasses prevented them from popping out. Dionne stood facing the range, her weight deliberately balanced on one leg to tilt her hips, and held her hands up to the heat.

'Where's the rest of the gang?' she purred over her shoulder.

Singer and Melissa found the supermarket in Letterkenny a daunting experience. Just a week in Dunaldragh had conditioned them into another mindset entirely – it was like being plucked from one century and dumped into the middle of the next. Fluorescent strip lights, the day-glow colours of the products and displays and most of all, the crowds of people, combined to make them nervous and in a hurry to leave town again as quickly as possible – which they were attempting to do, having packed the boot with as many cases of wine as it would take. Singer was swerving through the shopping traffic on the main street, raining a steady stream of oaths on the other drivers around him, when a dog ran onto the road, barking furiously at the car.

'Christ – another crazy local.'

'Stop! That's Michael!'

'So it is.' He pulled over. The setter ran to his door, jumped up and pawed the window. Singer got out, folded his seat forward and held the door open. 'Good boy, good Michael – get in! What are you doing here, eh? You're thirty miles away from home – get in, you daft mutt, before you get knocked down.' Instead, Michael ran back across the road, stopped on the far pavement and barked again. Melissa joined Singer.

'I've seen enough Lassie films to know he's trying to tell us something.'

'We're not in a Lassie film, we're in Letterkenny!'

'Same difference, come on.' She tugged him through the traffic. The setter ran up to a nearby pub, where a barrage of voices fought with the muffled squealing of penny whistles and poorly tuned fiddles. It turned towards them and barked some more.

'Okay, okay, keep your feckin' fur on, we're coming…'

It trotted into a narrow entry at the side of the pub, which reeked of stale beer and uric acid. They found Manus stretched out behind a stack of crates, snoring like thunder. He had a nasty cut beside one eye – not, Singer thought, from fighting, more the kind you get when you bash your face off a wall or a pavement through being insensibly, paralytically drunk. Singer crouched, called his name and shook his shoulder while the dog sniffed and whined.

'This goes to show that the outside world is a bad place, and bad things happen when you venture into it. What do you reckon – hospital, or home?'

'Home – he's just out for the count.'

'Jesus. First Ronan, now Manus – and I thought I was supposed to be the resident alcoholic.'

'You are,' she answered, flatly. 'But you drink all the time, so you have better tolerance.'

Singer didn't have an answer for that, so he went and fetched his car over to the alleyway. Lifting Manus under the arms was nothing like lifting Ronan, and they had to settle for half-carrying, half-dragging him towards the open car door. As they heaved him into the rear seat, Manus threw an arm around Singer's neck, pulling him close.

'Declan! Declan!' Singer tried to retreat and nearly had his head severed.

'Aow! Manus! I'm not Declan! Let me go!'

'Declan!' Manus insisted, crushing Singer's face into the wool of his jumper. 'Declan,' he mumbled, falling back into his stupor, and, as his arm relaxed slightly, Singer wrestled free. Rubbing his neck, Singer showed the dog in beside its master. He turned to Melissa as he started the car.

'Check my face. Have I lost a nose or an eyelid or anything?'

'Haven't you ever wondered why McFall's never has any customers except us?'

'Until tonight, I'd have had to say no. But now that you mention it…'

'Who do you suppose Declan is?'

'The bouncer who threw him out? The last man to buy him a pint? Someone he once killed with his bare hands? Who knows? I've had enough weirdness for one day – let's go home.'

Nonetheless, as he hoisted Manus into McFall's, Singer couldn't resist asking Mrs McFall about Declan. She dropped the bar counter, which she had been holding open for them to pass – until then, nothing in her demeanour indicated that having her husband delivered home in this condition was particularly unusual. The counter slammed, causing Michael to jump and unleash a fresh volley of barking. Her hand trembled as she reached to open it again.

'Here, lay him here.' She indicated a small sofa in the back living room. Singer just about made it, with Manus's arm over his shoulders. Mrs McFall tipped water from a kettle on the range onto a tea towel, knelt and tenderly began cleaning the cut on his face. Singer and Melissa may as well have ceased to exist for all the attention she now paid them, so they patted Michael and left, pulling gratefully up outside the Pier House a few minutes later. The ground floor windows glowed with orange light from the oil lamps, candles and an open fire that burned within – just like a scene from a Christmas card.

9

On Christmas morning, the front windows of the house shook in the teeth of a mounting gale. Rain cracked across the panes in sporadic lashes, and hissing jets of air pushed their way through the gaps in the frames. Doors slammed abruptly upstairs and down, as rogue currents careered along the corridors. Outside, the roar of breakers on the shingle was constant, the water whipped white by an onshore wind. Fist-sized gobbets of foam flew across the flattened sea-grass, while waves half the height of the Pier House detonated against the end of the harbour, sending spray soaring in all directions. A grey, billowing barricade blocked the sky beyond the mouth of the bay, unleashing fusillades of hailstones almost horizontally. Out to sea, nothing could be seen – not the island, not even the lighthouse.

Melissa exercised alone amongst rickety piles of books stacked around the room. She heard the front door open and the sudden pressure hike swung the living room door ajar, which in turn knocked one of the book stacks sprawling across the floor. Singer came crashing in, wet as a drowned man.

'It's brilliant out there,' he panted, 'bloody brilliant.' He peeled off a sopping combat jacket and hung it in the hallway. A camera clung to his chest underneath it. He strode into the room like a conquering hero. 'I've been down on the harbour. It's amazing, the sheer energy being unleashed. After breakfast, I'm going up to the cliffs at the tower.'

'Is that wise?' Melissa sat cross-legged, wearing her faint smile.

'Probably not,' he grinned, 'but I need my head cleared, after last night.'

At dinner, Singer had shown the others Sophia Clements's annotated message, provoking considerable excitement. Melissa had allowed him to do all the talking, and when he didn't mention finding Manus in Letterkenny, neither did she. Oona had been practically beside herself with glee at the thought of sleeping in what she was positive must be Sophia's old room, and Ronan insisted on searching through other poetry books for further clues. When none were found, the hunt had widened, as, one by one, they examined every volume on the living room shelves for more evidence of Sophia's existence. Even Dionne, who, stalking around in her heels and microscopic black dress had at first seemed nonplussed by Sophia's poem, joined in what became a very jolly wine-and-literature party, as the five gradually forgot their higher purpose and became distracted as they uncovered a hidden world. Large tomes that bore the appearance of encyclopaedias turned out to be bound collections of *The Illustrated London News*, from the 1850s through to the First World War. Accounts of the great fire of Hamburg and reports from the Indian Mutiny and the Crimean War were accompanied by intricately engraved plates, but more fascinating still were the advertisements for products as diverse as Miller's Saponaceous Rose Tooth Cream, Newbro's Herbicide and Professor Wilson's Magneto-Conservative Garments for the Dispelling of Giddiness.

The highlight of the evening was Dionne's discovery, in an anonymous box file, of dozens of issues of an American magazine called *Sun Bathing Review*, dating from the 1940s. Ronan had earnestly pointed out how the black-and-white female nudes had all their pubic hair airbrushed out, to conform with archaic obscenity laws – for the magazines were the pornography of their day, he explained, published under the then-acceptable pretexts of naturism and health. That he expounded his thesis so fulsomely while leaning directly over Dionne's barely clad bosom did not escape notice, and the others had collapsed laughing when Oona passed around copies of *Sun Bathing Review* for a vote on which naked tennis player or javelin thrower should be Ronan's next girlfriend.

But with regard to Sophia, the trail went cold. There were no more verses underlined in blood, no sequestered daguerreotypes and no revealing letters fell out of upturned hymn books – although an assortment of ancient railway tickets, feathers, faded ribbons and even a folded temperance leaflet from 1902 that had all been used as bookmarks lay in a heap on the occasional table. As wine gained the upper hand, they had almost felt themselves part of the long-dead era the pages depicted, reading them by oil lamp, in a room whose décor, furniture and architecture were authentically of the period. All they needed, Oona had remarked, were corsets for the ladies and whiskers for the men, and they could have been a formal salon from the 1880s, rather than some happenchance gathering of suburban misfits from the 1980s.

Now, the morning after, the scattered books needed tidying. Melissa finished her stretching and commenced the task, still wearing nothing but her leotard against the chill of the room. Singer changed into dry clothes, lit the range and the living room fire and then helped her. By the time the others descended, all evidence of the previous evening's time travel had been carefully tucked away back onto the shelves, safe behind row upon row of cracked leather and cloth spines with faded gilt lettering. While Ronan, Oona and Dionne blearily chewed toast and sipped mugs of tea around the kitchen range, Singer donned a black woollen hat and a heavy jumper and announced his intention to watch the storm from the tower.

'You're mad!' Ronan called after him as he set off out the door. However, when Melissa and Oona began kitting up to follow, Dionne immediately leapt up too.

'Come on,' she tugged at Ronan's cardigan sleeve, 'you have to escort me.' With a puzzled frown, Ronan collected his overcoat. 'Everybody, wait for me!' Dionne ordered before pelting off up the stairs. Ronan, Oona and Melissa stood in the hallway, listening to the wind hammering at the front of the house. After a short silence, Oona gave Melissa a little hug, their anoraks rustling.

'Merry Christmas, you.' Then she hugged Ronan, repeating the wish.

'Goodness – I completely forgot!'

'It's easy to forget things here,' she smiled. 'That's why I love it so. Did you get me a present?'

'Yes, pleurisy. I'm about to give it to you now, the moment we step through that door.'

She nudged Melissa. 'I know who he reminds me of. The Ghost of Christmas Past.' Indeed, with his pencil-like frame lost in a grey overcoat and his pale, bespectacled face peering through the gloom, there was more than a hint of the Dickensian in Ronan's appearance.

'Humbuggery,' he snorted.

'Seriously, though – there is one thing missing, which we really shouldn't be without.'

'What – gold? Frankincense? An Easter egg?'

'No, a tree. We haven't got a Christmas tree. Even if you can't be arsed with the religious bit, a tree is still nice.'

'I think it's silly to kill trees and bring them indoors,' Melissa stated. 'It seems so perverse.'

'Are you feeling okay?' Oona asked her.

'Fine. Why do you ask?'

'Because it's daytime, and you're speaking. It's positively chatterbox behaviour for you to proffer an opinion before dinner. Anyway, about our tree,' and Oona gave Ronan an extra-large nudge, 'what'cha gonnna do about it? I mean, you're a man, right? You're meant to fetch things like wood and fresh meat.'

Ronan harrumphed and Melissa gave Oona a covert, but steady look. The stairs creaked and Dionne descended, in her faux-fur coat, high boots and snowball hat.

'Shall we go for this silly walk, then?'

'Dee, you can't go like that! It's at least force eight outside, you need something waterproof!' Oona grabbed a tatty spare anorak off a hook.

'I am not going anywhere,' Dionne sniffed, 'dressed like a fucking farmer.' She flounced down the hallway but regretted her impetuousness almost the moment she stepped outside. All the way up the hairpin path, she clung to Ronan's arm, which from his point of view was absolutely fine, but every so often, the wind seemed to take a deep breath and then try, with renewed venom, to blow them clean off the hillside. Then, Dionne clung to him all the more tightly, not because she was reassured – his body felt lighter than her own – but she imagined that if they should indeed be lifted and dashed on the rocks below, he might at least cushion her fall.

When they reached the exposed summit, the terrain flattened out, but the wind flattened the four climbers, practically reducing them to their hands and knees. The blast of air was tremendous, like a moving wall. They struggled into the lee of the watchtower, where they could at least breathe, stand upright and hear themselves speak. The bay below was a mass of surging breakers, all crawling on top of one another, competing to die on the shore. The tops of the eastern cliffs shredded a hurtling stream of black-grey cloud, while the sea smashed with mordant anger against their obsidian foundations.

Oona unzipped her anorak. Spreading it with her arms, she ran out of the shelter of the tower and was instantly picked up and hurled bodily backward a good thirty paces onto hummocky heather where she bounced, rolled and came to a stop.

'Yahoooo!' she screamed, but the others only saw her open her mouth, for her trill of delight was ripped from her lips and carried far inland. She stood and charged into the wind again, this time running up a peat-covered boulder before opening her coat – she blew higher and further, sprawling through the heather, limbs flailing. Melissa dashed out to join her and they leapt off the boulder hand in hand, shrieking, the atmosphere filling their lungs.

'My friends have gone completely buckshee daft.' Dionne huddled against the wall of the tower, still clinging to Ronan's arm.

'You say that every time we come up here,' he observed.

'I wonder where Singer is?' Oona panted on her back as the heather whipped her cheeks. 'He said he'd be up here, didn't he?' Melissa lay on her stomach, hood pulled tight over her head.

'Perhaps he's been blown all the way back down the hill, through the pub door and onto a barstool.' They laughed.

'Christmas Day, the pubs are shut. You don't think…'

Holding onto each other for support, they stood and battled their way to the edge of the headland. As they peered over, the sea level at the foot of the sloping cliff seemed to drop away suddenly, retreating in a torrent of infinite sluices. Then, as if alive, the water gathered itself into a hill, the top of which, nightmarishly, seemed almost level with their elevated position. It was as if the ocean sought to mock the imagined security of the headland, shape-shifting to mimic it in form and dimension. With a low, eerie rumble that sounded like the earth's crust tearing itself open, the improbable mountain of water fell slowly forward and collapsed against the headland, disintegrating with the force of an atomic blast, sending great plumes of spray rebounding off the serrated schist formations below. The gorge to their left boomed as if some giant demon were slamming his fists against the loudest drums in hell, and a raging geyser of spume exploded upward out of it. Melissa spotted him first, clinging to the back of the pinnacle overlooking the gorge, just before it disappeared under tons of tortured, falling sea water. She tapped Oona's shoulder and pointed, and as the pinnacle re-emerged from its titanic drenching, Oona saw him too, shaking his head and laughing. The airborne spray from the impact rinsed over the pair of them, wetting their faces, burning their eyes with salt. Another gut-shaking rumble signalled another wave on the way. It was even bigger and more fearsome than the last.

'You could have gotten yourself killed! That was really fucking stupid!' The five stumbled back down the hairpin path with the gale in cold pursuit. Singer was so wet all his clothes were the same dark colour as his plastered-down hair. His eyes, however, glittered.

'Not really.' He seemed surprised at the anger in Oona's voice. 'I found a good place to hold on. I'm like a barnacle. It would take an awful lot to tear me off.'

'I don't know if you noticed, but there was an awful lot coming at you.'

'Believe me, it's a safe place just to hang on and enjoy the show.'

'There was more than enough drama where I was standing, thank you. Dionne nearly fainted when she saw you.' Dionne was refusing to speak to Singer at all and she struggled along twenty paces behind, still clinging onto Ronan, but with her fur hat and coat so wet she looked more like a clubbed seal than a human being.

'I got some good photos, but there's something else about being down there – it's an amazing feeling.'

'You're an adrenalin junkie.'

'No, it's more like a religious experience. Fear, majesty, awe – when those waves come at you, it's like being slapped around by God.'

'Bit of a masochist, are you?'

'Spank my bottom and I'll tell you.'

'Grow up. If it's religion you want, go to church.'

'Sorry – I'm an atheist. Mankind hates taking responsibility for anything, so it creates gods to carry the can. But when one of those waves breaks around me…well, for a few seconds, I feel like I might be wrong, and maybe there's something more out there. Not some bloke with a beard, but I feel small before the goddess nature, you could say.'

'Well, hallelujah!' Oona snorted.

As they crossed the sea-grass in front of the house, Ronan excused himself from Dionne's grip and trotted off towards the beach. He returned moments later, dragging a piece of tree that the sea had stripped of its bark and bleached creamy white.

'Ho ho ho,' he announced as he wrestled it through the porch and dumped it in the hallway. They peeled off their coats and boots, and noticed an orange oilskin hung off one of the hooks, dripping water onto the stone flags. The kitchen door squeaked and Manus popped his head around it. A dark, coagulated cut decorated one eye, which had bruised but not closed.

'Youse must be foundered, you critters. Get in here and warm yourselves.' He'd brought a bottle of brandy and one of port down from the pub, and steaming hot drinks awaited them on the table. The range had also been stoked to furnace-like levels – perfect for drying jumpers, jeans and socks on the metal rail above. 'Bejasus, what have you killed?' he demanded of Dionne as she hung her sopping faux-fur out to dry. When she just sniffed, he addressed the others. 'I beg your pardon for letting myself in, but I didn't expect you to be out in that weather. I came down to wish you the season's greetings, but more importantly, I want to apologise for—'

'And a very happy Christmas to you too, Manus!' Singer interrupted. 'As it happens, we're delighted to see you, because we've been wanting to ask you about something – who was Sophia Clements?' Manus stood with his mouth half-open.

'Yes! You have to tell us, we're dying to know!' Oona drew a chair up to the table, clutching her steaming glass, all ears. 'What happened to your face, by the way?'

Manus glanced at Singer, who gave a near-imperceptible shake of the head. 'Well, I, uhh…I forgot to buy Mrs McFall a Christmas present, so this was her Santa box to me.'

'Proper order. Now, what about Sophia Clements?'

Manus studied the five faces studying his. 'Can I ask why you're asking?' His voice had a note of caution in it. 'Did someone up at the village tell you something about the house?'

'We haven't been up to the village.' Singer sipped his drink. He fetched *Chamber's Misecellany* from the sideboard and showed Manus the annotations in blood and Melissa's summary of them. Oona began to explain their assumed significance, but stopped at a look from Singer. Manus was silent for quite some time as he read the message several times over and studied the numbered segments of Byron's verse. Finally, he sat back, shaking his head.

'Well, well. I've often heard this story, but to see proof of it after all these years…this is the first time I've ever seen her handwriting.' He patted the book gently, almost reverently.

'So who was she?'

'Have you ever heard tell of Lord Leitrim?' The five shook their heads, rapt. 'Well, Leitrim was a big landlord, very big. Back in the mid-eighteen hundreds, he owned Donegal – the entire county, and three other counties, too. And – pardon my language, ladies – he was a right bad bastard.' Manus stopped and unconsciously rubbed his cut, as if unsure how to continue.

'Bad how?' Singer enquired.

'An all-round nasty piece of work. When he evicted tenants, he was notorious for helping with the evictions himself. Usually, landlords stayed well away from that sort of thing. A lot of them didn't even live in Ireland, but those that did allowed their gangs of thugs or the constabulary to do their dirty work for them. Kept their own hands clean. But Leitrim, he was ex-army and had a taste for the rough stuff. They say,' he paused, and glanced around, as if embarrassed, 'that he also had a taste for young women. That he would sometimes demand his rent that way, and if he didn't get it, then eviction was the alternative.'

Ronan snorted. 'Why, that's positively medieval!'

'Don't forget, the time we're talking about wasn't long after the Famine. Half a million died, two million emigrated. In some ways, it was worse than the Dark Ages. You see, not only did Leitrim own the land, but he was also the law, the justice for the peace. He could do what he liked – and he did, until he was stopped.'

'Stopped?'

'Leitrim was killed, in 1878. His carriage was ambushed near Milford, about twenty miles from here.'

'Who killed him?'

'They were never caught. A huge reward was offered, but Leitrim was so hated, the men who did it got away with it. The people never gave them up.'

'Did Leitrim build this house?' Singer asked.

Manus nodded. 'William Sydney Clements, the third Earl of Leitrim. Who knows,' he gave Ronan a half-smile, 'he may once have sat where you're sitting now.' Ronan looked distinctly uncomfortable at the thought.

'So, Sophia was his daughter?' Oona seemed chuffed.

'I don't know. Leitrim built the Pier House in 1861, and Sophia, whoever she was, was sent here shortly afterwards. I assume she was family.'

'"Sent" as in against her will?'

'The way it's told, Leitrim wanted her out of the way.'

Singer turned to Melissa and bowed. She acknowledged his tribute to her deductive skills with her faint smile. 'Why?' he asked.

'She went mad.' Manus coughed. 'My father reckoned it was caused by, er, syphilis. He said she had the scars on her cheeks as an old woman.'

'Your father knew her?'

'Oh yes,' Manus smiled. 'She lived to be the same age as I am now, sixty-five. When Leitrim died, she inherited the northern part of his estate. She owned the village, and a good bit inland. She also owned the island, and it was to her agent that my father paid the rents – or didn't, as was more often the case.'

'But how could she inherit if she was mental?' Dionne interjected, then, at a sharp glance from Oona, blushed slightly. 'You know what I mean – if she was so unwell, why would she be given property?'

'Leitrim left a will,' Manus responded. 'He must have wanted her to have it. Anyway, my father said that apart from the scars, there was nothing wrong with her – a nicer woman you couldn't have hoped to meet. She was easy on the people, let everyone pay what they could. Probably didn't do her bank balance much good, but when they set about burning the landlords' houses, no one ever thought of harming her.' He looked around the walls of the room with a slight smile. 'It's probably the only reason this place is still standing – because she was a decent woman. She died in 1909, and what was left of her family came and took what they could carry, then sold the house to the commissioners. She's buried up in the chuchyard,' he added.

Dionne persisted. 'But how could you be so mad you need locking up one day, and somehow be okay the next?'

'Dee!' Oona protested.

Manus looked as if he wanted the ground to open and swallow him up. 'Well, uh, apparently the way syphilis works, it sort of goes through you, then after a while you can be okay again. It's always there, in the body, but it can stay dormant for many years. So they say...'

'Hold on – I can see Dionne's point,' Ronan interjected, a tad pompously. Still, Dionne nodded gratefully at him. 'Let's back this up a bit; I can see why a rich landlord might build his beloved daughter a private sanatorium to recover from some nasty disease. I can even see why he might build it up here out of the way, to spare himself the social disgrace. But why put bars on her bedroom window?'

Manus pursed his lips and developed a sudden interest in the woodgrain of the table. There was a hiatus, and a burst of hail clattered against the kitchen window. Then Melissa spoke, softly. Her habitual faint smile seemed to have momentarily deserted her.

'It depends who gave her the disease.'

'What?' Oona asked. 'You mean like a lover? Someone she might elope with? Someone who might try to steal her away?'

'Or a father, who didn't want anyone to know how much he loved his little girl.'

In the porch, Manus turned to Singer, who was seeing him out.

'Why did you not tell them?'

Singer shrugged. 'Because everyone has a right to party how they please.'

'I wasn't partying.'

'Well then, even more reason for your business to remain your own.'

'It's not like me to get as bad as that. I just wanted to apologise.'

'No need – if you ever find me that way, then you can return the favour. And since you own a pub, I'd say the odds are pretty good.'

'The wife said one of the girls was there too.'

'Melissa. She wasn't offended either, just concerned you were all right.'

'Look, thanks.' He squeezed Singer's hand, quickly and awkwardly. 'I shouldn't allow myself to get like that, it's...' he tailed off, shaking his head.

'Go home and have a nice Christmas dinner, take it easy and relax. Nobody here thinks any the less of you.'

Manus gave a wry smile, patted Singer's shoulder, then pulled his oilskin tight and left. Singer watched him walk away, across the writhing sea-grass. The man had told them plenty about Sophia Clements, but Singer sensed that now was not the time to be asking about someone called Declan.

Ronan grunted, carrying a heavily tarnished artillery shell case through the kitchen. Singer and Melissa glanced up from chopping the vegetables. Both had sizeable glasses of white wine poised on the table in front of them.

'Where did you get that?' Singer's voice had the tone of a child who wanted one too.

'You wouldn't believe some of the stuff that's in those outhouses,' Ronan panted, pushing his way through the hallway door.

'Would it be rude to ask...'

'Gonna start a war in the living room. Merry fucking Christmas,' Ronan's voice echoed from the hallway. Singer and Melissa shared a look, then resumed chopping the vegetables.

'All we need is a fairy for the top.' Dionne contemplated Ronan's piece of driftwood stuck upright in the artillery shell case in the living room bay window. Outside, it was darkening, and the storm still blew with vigour, if not quite with the same feral ferocity of the morning.

'But I shall never fit up there.' Ronan struck an Eros-style pose, clutching a wine glass instead of a bow, and grinning fixedly. Dionne and Oona got the giggles.

The jutting, flayed branches of the tree were hung with an interesting assortment of *objets trouves*. Dionne had shown considerable skill in fashioning shiny stars out of tinfoil and had tied the hundred-year-old ribbons formerly used as bookmarks into tasteful bows. Oona had contributed several pieces of cheap but colourful jewellery culled from her and Dionne's bedrooms, and Ronan had pierced numerous apples, oranges and even onions with string, then strung them where the wood could take the weight.

'You realise those will stink after a few days,' Oona had pointed out.

'*Sic transit gloria mundi.*' Ronan lifted a bottle of red wine from the occasional table and topped himself up generously. 'To the tree!' he declared, raising his glass.

Dionne put on a mock-shrewish voice. 'Ronan Doherty, did your mother teach you no manners at all?' She and Oona held their empty glasses out. He filled them and the three repeated the toast. As soon as they did, one of Ronan's onions fell off and rolled across the floor.

They were halfway through the main course of salmon, potatoes and peas, and halfway through a conversation about how much they all hated turkey and what a pleasant change salmon was for Christmas dinner, when a knock came to the front door. It wasn't a loud, doom-laden knock – if anything, it was uncertain and tentative. Still, it was a knock nonetheless, and all five froze, glancing around the table at one another, then peering in unison towards the kitchen window. The knock came again, although this time it was more of a rapping, a politely urgent appeal to please be allowed in out of this dreadful weather. Singer jumped up.

'Manus. Has to be. I mean, who else would...' He lifted an oil lamp and started towards the hallway, sensing in his stomach that the knock was far too light to have emanated from any publican's fist. The girls followed Singer to the porch. Only Ronan remained seated. He emptied his glass in one gulp and reached for the bottle.

Singer opened the front door. Rain and wind swirled from his feet up to his face, causing the lamp to flicker and burn blue. Outside, barely visible, a figure stood in a sopping belted raincoat. It wore neither hat nor hood, but stooped under the weight of a suitcase in one hand and a smaller, but seemingly heavy, plastic box in the other.

'I say,' the figure enquired, in a cut-crystal English accent, 'I was wondering perhaps if you hev a Ronan Dockerty staying heah.'

'What?' Singer had heard the figure's words, but his conscious mind refused to accept that it could have any possible entrée into their circle.

'Ro-nan *Dock*-er-tee?' the figure enunciated in that devastatingly polite tone a certain class of Englishman deploys when addressing foreigners, morons and three-year-old children.

'Ronan? Uh…yes, Ronan's here. Ronan!' Singer bawled into the house. 'It's for you!' After a short delay, Ronan emerged from the kitchen and slunk, head bent, down the hall. The girls and Singer stood aside for him, but stayed to see what might happen next.

'Jay!' The inflection of airy delight in Ronan's voice was deeply unconvincing. 'Come in!'

The figure set down its suitcase, turned and waved in the general direction of the sea. It was then that the others noticed a pair of car headlights on the pier, which flashed, moved as if reversing, then drove away.

'Lovely chap,' the figure declared, lifting its suitcase and shuffling through the front door, 'but he cost me a hundred bloody quid and I couldn't understand a single word he said!'

Ronan led the newcomer through the gloom of the hallway and into the shadowy end of the living room. The others followed, agog. He dropped his suitcase on the floor, and, much more carefully, deposited his other piece of luggage, the plastic box, on top of the occasional table.

'Tried to phone ahead to say I was on me way,' he lifted a large handset attached to the box by a wire, 'but dashed if I could get a signal, let alone find your numbah. Fect, I can't get any signal heah at all.' He held the handset to his ear and tapped impatiently at a metal lever on top of the box.

'Signal? What signal? What is that thing?' Singer demanded.

'Mobile phone.'

'A mobile *what*?'

'Telephone – you know, ring ring. Nevah go anywhere without it. Bloody expensive, but damned convenient.'

'Doesn't look very mobile to me,' Singer muttered, holding his lamp aloft to shed some light on its owner. The newcomer was, like Ronan, of slender build, but a head shorter, making him smaller than Melissa, and about the same height as Oona and Dionne. He was fresh-faced in what is universally imagined to be the English way, with clear blue eyes, a slightly weak chin, a small nose, a long fore-head and straight hair, which was short at the back and floppily fringed at the front, dirty blond but dark at the roots.

'Frisby,' he announced, shaking each of the girls, then Singer, by the hand. 'Jay Frisby.' He had a direct gaze and unleashed a confident, full-toothed smile every time he spoke. Singer inflicted a Manus-type squeeze on the slender, cold fingers proffered to him.

'*Frisby?*' he echoed.

'Yah. Danish, I'm told. Ancestors must have been Vikings, what – rape and pillage and all that. But these days, we hail from Leamington Spa. Neah Warwick. Chunders is three miles from Leamington.'

'Chunders?'

'Chunsborough – family home. Five hundred acres and no bloody good to anybody, at least not until the old man pops it!' Frisby laughed out loud. Singer did too, but his was a different sort of laughter.

Ronan seemed to snap out of a semi-trance and coughed. 'I, errrm, know Jay from the magazine business in London. I did a special edition on luxury yachts, and, er, we became social, you know, contacts…that way,' he finished lamely.

'You're in the luxury yacht business? What a marvellous way to make a living!' Frisby either did not notice the leaden sarcasm in Singer's voice, or else chose to ignore it.

'Yah. It is, actually. Had a cracking summer, shifted seven big units and umpteen smaller chaps. Goes a bit quiet in the winter, but still, I always carry this,' and he patted the plastic box, "cos you never know when some squillionaire might need a new toy, what?'

'Bet you can't wait for that thing to tinkle,' Singer practically sneered.

'Well, yah. Absolutely.'

'But it won't, here.'

'Well, yah. So it seems, eh? Blasted signal…'

There was a short, awkward silence. Oona broke it. 'We were having dinner – are you hungry?'

'Femished!' Frisby cried, so the girls showed him towards the kitchen. Ronan made to follow, but Singer restrained him with a hand around the upper arm, waited until the door had swung shut, then snarled, 'Ronan – what the fuck?'

He feigned incomprehension. 'Er…what the fuck what?'

'What the fuck,' Singer kept his voice down, but his fury was unmistakable, 'is that guy doing here?'

'I invited him.' Ronan tried to keep his tone casual.

'You *invited* him?'

140

He nodded.

'To visit or to stay?'

'To stay – we still have plenty of—'

'What the fuck for?'

He shrugged, although a hint of defiance showed through his uncertainty. 'Because I thought it was okay to invite anyone we wanted here.'

'*Did* you? When did you invite him?'

Ronan frowned at the dark beyond the bay window. 'Umm, uh, let me think now…we'd been here a couple of days. I rang him from McFall's.'

'So, all of a sudden, you took a notion into your head to ask little Lord Fauntleroy over for a spiffing Crimbo?'

'Look, he's not—'

'You said nothing to me.'

'Excuse me, *you* invited three people without telling me!'

Singer gestured impatiently around the room. 'Let's just forget for a second that I organised and paid for this place, not you. I told you what happened over the girls. And I must say I've noticed, in spite of your hissy fit, that you seem to have no problems with their company.'

'What's that supposed to mean?'

'Your tongue hangs out of your mouth like a wet towel on a washing line every time Dionne walks into the room.'

'Hey! Fuck you!'

'But that's okay – everybody likes everybody, and we have a nice atmosphere going here. So why bring this guy into it? He's gonna wreck everything!'

'How do you know?'

'Because he's like something out of *Brideshead Revisited*, that's how! I mean, any minute now he's going to whip out his teddy bear and start prattling on about Oxbridge and Marmite and thrashing the Windies at cricket! Where did you *get* him?'

'He's a friend of mine!'

'Really? How come I've never heard you mention him before?'

Ronan bristled. 'What are you, some sort of expert on the subject of me? I don't need your permission to be friends with anybody!'

Singer's voice took on a menacing edge. 'How long have you known Gatsby? Be honest.'

'Frisby. Since September, when I did the special edition on boats. I mean, yachts.'

'So you've known this idiot for three whole months, and suddenly you feel compelled to invite him into *my* life?'

'You fucking hypocrite! You didn't know those women at all before you invited them into mine!'

'I didn't invite…' Singer began, but at that very instant, Oona popped her head around the door.

'Is everything all right in here?' she asked, a shade too brightly. Both Singer and Ronan made a hopeless job of pretending that everything was.

'Yes, yes, uh, fine, of course, yes…' they jointly stuttered.

'Good,' she continued, with now-obvious artifice, 'because we're patiently waiting for you, to restart dinner.' She closed the door again, more firmly than necessary. Singer opened his mouth as if to pick up where he left off, but thought better of it and followed her, with Ronan meandering sulkily behind. They resumed their places at the kitchen table. Frisby seemed blithely unaware of any tension in the air and waved a lump of salmon around on a fork, regaling Dionne and Melissa about the fearsome difficulties he'd had 'finding this blasted place'. However, they both eyed Singer and Ronan as the pair sat down.

'How far have you travelled today?' Singer asked Frisby, with forced politeness. From the additional light given off by the candles on the table, he could see that Frisby wore a beige V-necked Pringle sweater with a lemon shirt underneath.

'London, old boy. Only one flight to Dublin this morning, so on I hopped. But I arrived to find no buses or trains running. Frisby comes to Ireland – Ireland is closed!'

'So how did you make it all the way up here?'

'Waved a bit of cash around at the airport, security chap said his brother was a taxi driver and would do the trip for a ton. Five hours later, and Frisby is in the building!' He held his hands wide, as if expecting applause. When he received none, he poked an index finger into his right ear. 'Still, I think I've gone deaf on this side, 'cos the blighter blathered all the way here. Heaven knows what about.'

'What company do you work for?'

'What?'

Singer repeated the question. Ronan threw him a furious look.

'Oh, er, outfit called Excelsior Marine. Madly exclusive, top-end stuff.'

'Why didn't you come over in one of your boats?' Dionne piped up. 'We have parking out front.'

'Well now,' Frisby turned to her, reaching his arm across the back of her chair. She did not flinch or move away. 'If Dockerty here had told me he had a harbour to hand and such lovely ladies knocking about the place, I would surely have shown up in the biggest cabin cruiser I could find, and treated you to a champagne reception on board!' He clinked his glass off Dionne's.

Singer stood, lunged for the centre of the table, grabbed a wine bottle by the neck and stormed off to the living room, where he pulled an armchair up to the fire. He stared into the smouldering turf, drinking directly from the bottle.

The following morning, St Stephen's Day, found Singer staring into heaving white waves instead of iridescent red embers. He sat on the pinnacle overlooking the gorge, dangling his legs over the unbroken hundred-foot drop. His head hurt. The storm had blown over, and although it was still breezy, sunshine pierced the clouds as they ran before the wind. The island looked like God had just made it, while the ocean was a map of shadows racing over a vast plain of aerated green water and restless foam crests.

'There you are, you silly moo.' Oona's voice made him jump. He'd been so lost in thought he hadn't heard her climb the pinnacle behind him. He pressed both palms against the rough, damp rock and pushed himself back from the edge. 'Is your arse not soaking wet, sitting up here?' She stood with only her head and shoulders in view, like a submariner peering over the conning tower of his vessel. Her hair, Singer noticed, had grown in the ten days – Christ, was that all it was? – he had known her. It blew sideways across her face, emphasising her grey eyes, slightly upturned nose and boyish smile. Singer knew he was being an idiot, huffing up at the gorge all by himself. But like an offended child, he had secretly hoped that someone would follow him.

She pulled herself onto the summit, staying well back from the edge. Remaining seated, Singer pushed himself over beside her. Never, ever stand suddenly upright beside a drop – everyone knows that.

'We're all a bit lost without you down there. We don't know what to do without our leader. So I was sent up to fetch you.'

143

'Bollocks. Get Frisby to summon one of his yachts, that'll keep everyone happy.'

She giggled. 'You should see him, actually. I left him walking up and down the beach, trying to get a signal on that stupid phone thingy of his.'

In spite of himself, Singer laughed. 'He's like a graduate from some academy for yuppie arseholes. There *are* no mobile phone networks in Ireland – doesn't he know that? I mean, can you ever see mobile phones catching on in a country like this?'

'Are you sure you don't dislike him because he's English?'

'Gimme a break – I lived in London for four years. Frisby represents the English like a hod-carrying, wife-beating alcoholic represents the Irish – he's more of a parody than a real person.'

'Is it because he's rich?'

'How do you know he's rich?'

'Is it because he's good looking?'

'It's because he's here.' Singer felt the irritation that had been washing out of him with every wave come flooding back again.

'Look, if it's any comfort, I've just been speaking to Ronan. It's really none of my business, but I get the feeling he invited Frisby because he felt outnumbered.'

'He did it purely to annoy me.'

Oona looked down, smiling slightly. 'Then it's definitely working.'

'It's just that I...'

'Listen, Frisby may be a bit of an eejit, but I think he's harmless underneath it all. He's just a boy – certainly no challenge to someone like you.' She glanced up to see whether her flattery was working, but Singer's stern mask lent no clues, so she looked down again. 'But if you're right, and Ronan asked him here to piss you off, then Frisby is as much a victim of Ronan's sneakiness as you are.'

'So I should be nice to him?'

'I think what's happening at the Pier House is far too special to be wasted over some silly tiff.'

'What's happening at the Pier House?'

'Like you need me to explain.' This time, when she raised her face, her gaze was more than a match for Singer's. 'I want the feeling back. I want this to last, at least a few weeks longer. But you're spoiling it.'

'No, Ronan's spoiling it.'

'Listen to you, like a kid. Don't be angry, you're causing a bad vibe.'

Singer lay on his back, with his arms behind his head. His eyes followed a rag of white-grey cloud, scudding close overhead. 'I think you're the only other person who fully understands the Pier House,' he said eventually. 'Ronan certainly doesn't.'

Internally, Oona sighed with relief. 'Melissa gets it, big time. But she gets it in her own way – different from us, although possibly even stronger.'

'Why is that, do you think?'

'I've known Melissa for most of my life, and I still have no idea who she really is. But maybe,' at this, she reached into her raincoat pocket, 'she's different because she doesn't drink as much as we do.' She produced a tiny silver hip flask, and waved it in Singer's sightline. He sat up, abruptly.

'Oh, good girl.'

'Aren't I, though?' She unscrewed the cap and handed it over.

'Ladies first.'

'Big fuckin' pansies before.'

Singer took a sip and pulled a face. 'Yuk! What have you done to this whiskey? There's...*bits* in it.'

'Oh, I dropped a handful of Potter's Asthma Remedy into the mix.'

'You *what*?'

'You know that stuff Ronan takes? I stole some.'

'Why?'

'To give it a kick.' She took the flask back, put her thumb over the opening, shook it, and swigged. 'Ahhh...think of it as a rather interesting cocktail.' He accepted the concoction and swallowed, pulling a face.

'What will happen to me?'

'On an empty stomach? Very mild hallucinations, sometime in the next fifteen minutes.'

'Cool.' The pair polished off the contents, then lay on their backs, side by side, staring up at the sky. 'Shouldn't we go somewhere safer?' he wondered.

'Not a bit of it. We're like corpses the Red Indians used to leave out to be eaten by the eagles. This is the most special spot, in a very special place.'

'Is this why you suffer from depression, from taking drugs?'

Oona did not answer right away. Eventually she said, 'What makes you think that I suffer from depression?'

'Because Dionne told me that you do.'

'When did she tell you that?'

'The day you arrived.'

'Doesn't waste time, our Dee. She had no fucking business.'

'So it's true?'

Again, after a bit of a silence, 'I'll answer your question if you answer one for me.'

'Go on.'

'The last time we lay up here – do you remember that?'

'How could I forget? The skin still hasn't grown back on my elbows, knees or my arse.'

'The last time we lay up here, you said something about inviting Dee because you knew she wouldn't come alone.'

'Dionne invited herself. I said I *encouraged* her, because I was hoping she wouldn't come alone.'

'Pedant. Okay, what did you mean when you said that? You dropped that little remark, then blanked me when I tried to take you up about it. You shouldn't say things like that unless you're prepared to explain what you mean.'

'I meant I hoped Dionne would come here and bring you with her.'

'Fuck. I thought it was Melissa.'

'Melissa what?'

'I can see you're not into Dionne, that much is clear. But I was pretty sure you were clicking with Melissa. The two of you are very alike – self-contained and cryptic to the point of arrogance.'

'Thanks. But I had no idea Melissa even existed until the night you arrived.'

'You mean you sat in that Dublin pub, you spent the entire evening talking to Dee, then you shifted her outside, all because you fancied *me*?'

'Well, you weren't saying very much. In fact, you didn't say anything at all. You cried into your drink for about three and a half hours – so I figured a blow job was out of the question.'

'Don't be vile!'

'Sorry.'

'It's the Surmontil, it makes me weepy.'

'Sur-what?'

'Anti-depressant. But I've stopped taking it – I don't need it, when I'm here.'

'Cool.'

'No, not cool. I'm headed for a frightful crash when I leave. I'm meant to take one every day.'

'Oh dear.'

'Something else is not so cool. I'm not cool about you fancying me.'

'What makes you think I fancy you?'

'Uhhh…okay…that Potter's Remedy must be working already. Either that, or I've got completely the wrong end of the stick.'

'All I've admitted is that I cunningly manipulated Dionne into bringing you here.'

'You've admitted to being a scheming shite.'

'I liked you when I met you. I liked you as a person. I thought you were interesting.'

'Huh?'

'I'd never seen anyone cry and drink so much at the same time. I felt I had to get to know you better.'

'You're a Jesuitical swine. So you *do* fancy me?'

'Can we go somewhere a bit more private and find out for sure?'

She rolled on her side, and slapped him hard on the shoulder. 'Stop that! If I have to spend the next two weeks thinking you want to put your…*thing* inside me, it will wreck my head. Please. Shag Dionne instead – she wants you to.'

'Ah. But maybe I don't want to put my *thing* inside her – as you so elegantly put it.'

'Then shag Melissa – if you can. But you have to promise to tell me what she's like, because I don't know anyone else who has.'

'You've got sex on the brain.'

'Take the words "pot", "kettle" and "black" and form a popular cliché.'

'Look, I just wanted to get to know you better, and I'm really glad you're here. Let's just leave it at that, shall we?'

'You're even sneakier than Ronan – you *prostituted* yourself with my friend!'

'I hope it was worth it.'

'Well, now that you know me a tiny bit better – was it?'

'Actually, I think I'll go and make friends with Jay Frisby. He's more of a lady than you are.' Oona lunged and sank her teeth into Singer's bicep, mainly taking a mouthful of combat jacket, but inflicting a nip nonetheless. 'Oww!' he roared, but then chortled, 'Do that again, only lower down.'

'You pig!' she shrieked, battering at his chest with both hands. He laughed all the more, and so did she.

'I'm serious,' she gasped. 'Please don't think of me that way, it will ruin everything. And Dionne will fucking *kill* me, you have no idea how single-minded she can be when she gets an idea into her head. You're hers, sweetheart, whether you like it or not.'

'She can't make me.'

'I wouldn't count on that.'

'Speaking of Dionne – if you take anti-depressants, then what she said must be true.' Oona flopped on her back, and fell quiet again. 'Come on,' he insisted. 'I've confessed to being a manipulative bastard. Now you have to tell me whether you're mad or not. Dionne says you were found naked in Berlin. I just want to know what the chances are of a repeat performance.'

She slapped at him again, but only half-heartedly, and sighed, staring upward. 'I still had my knickers on when they found me, thank Christ, but otherwise, yes, I was naked.'

'Why?'

'I was looking for a *Flakturm*.'

'You were looking for what?'

'*Flakturm*. It means "flak tower". There were three of them, built during the Second World War. They were huge concrete fortresses, mainly anti-aircraft positions, but civilians sheltered there too. When the Russians encircled Berlin, some of the fiercest fighting took place around the *Flakturme*, yet they were so strong, they were still standing when the rest of the city was reduced to rubble.'

'How come you know, or care, about that sort of shit?'

'I've read tons of books about the war. I wish I could have been alive then.'

'God, why?'

'I don't know. I just feel I should have been. I feel like I missed my proper time – I can't explain it.'

'But it must have been brutal back then. I mean, do you have any idea how many people died in the Second World War, all of them horribly?'

'Sixty-two million. They reckon a quarter of a million in the last three weeks alone, mostly in Berlin.'

'So what makes you think you wouldn't have been one of them?'

'I suppose when one fantasises about the past, it's never as a victim. I imagine myself as part of some women's regiment, repairing trucks or aeroplanes. Not as a nurse – I'd be crap at that.'

'If you can't look at blood, then you shouldn't wish for war.'

'But you're a photojournalist – you must understand the romance of it, being swept along by the tide of events, and making a big adventure out of it, like Robert Capa or Lee Miller?'

'Robert Capa stepped on a landmine and Lee Miller died a lonely alcoholic. Yes, I understand the romance of that era, and I love their photographs. I think every man who picks up a camera wants to be Robert Capa, even if only because he got to sleep with Ingrid Bergman. But there's nothing like a bit of reality to turn you right off people killing each other. I'm quitting photojournalism – when I leave here, I'm not going back to it.'

'But war is a story that needs to be told.'

'I agree whole-heartedly. By other people, from now on.'

'Are you afraid?'

'No.'

'Is it because of something that happened when you were young?'

Singer fell briefly silent. Then, 'You're right, Dionne doesn't waste time, does she? No, what happened when I was young was the reason I got into photojournalism. But something else happened, earlier this year – and that's the reason I want out.'

'What happened?'

'I'll tell you some other time.'

'But it was horrible?'

'It was wretched. The people who did it would tell you they were fighting a war, but to me, it looked like cruel, pointless murder.'

'You saw people being killed?'

'Two corporals, beaten to death by a mob.'

'I saw that on the news, it was evil. So you were there?'

'Unfortunately, yes. Or maybe it was the best thing that ever happened to me, I haven't decided yet.'

'Okay – so what will you do, if not photojournalism?'

'I don't know, but you're very good at turning the conversation away from yourself.'

'Drat. Spotted my little ploy, huh?'

'Very much so. Did you find what you were looking for in Berlin?'

'Yes, I did. One of the flak towers is still standing – you can even admire the view from the top of it. Another is in East Berlin – you can't go there, but anyway it was demolished and turned into a hill, so there's not much to see. And the third was in the Tiergarten – that's the one I was looking for when I, uh, messed up slightly. I knew it had been demolished, but I thought there'd be some trace of it.'

'And do you often travel in the nude?'

Oona put a hand over her eyes. 'That's the bad bit. I went to the Tiergarten around teatime, and fell in with a bunch of punks drinking cider on a park bench.'

'Classy.'

'They were very sweet, actually. Young guys, just smoking dope and drinking cider in the sunshine. Berlin's like that, people just hang out. I asked them about the tower, and they hadn't a clue but they offered me a drink. I stayed with them a while, they spoke good English. But one of them had magic mushrooms, and I very foolishly took some, before I continued on my merry way.'

'Ah.'

'Yes – "ah". I should have stayed with the punks or else had the sense to jump in a taxi back to the hotel. The mushrooms were much stronger than I thought they'd be, and I ended up wandering alone in the dark. The Tiergarten is massive, and I remember it being very peaceful and beautiful. Then, I walked into a grove of white birch trees, and the moon came out. I'd never seen anything like it. The trees glowed like the moon, the same luminous, shimmering white. It was as if I'd discovered a palace, made of moonbeams. Of course, I was tripping off my head. I took my clothes off in the birch grove, I'm not sure why, except, as they say, it seemed like a good idea at the time. Perhaps I thought I was a wood nypmh. I don't know how long I walked around like that, maybe a couple of hours, before the park police found me.'

'You were extremely lucky they found you before anybody else did.'

'Yes, I was.'

'Well, congratulations – that's pretty fucking nuts. But in my book, it doesn't make you mad. Crazy, but not mad.'

'When they finally got me home, my mum had me locked away for six weeks. You see, I pretended not to remember anything, which probably didn't help. But it was one of the most wonderful experiences I've ever had. It was pure magic, like being here is pure magic. But I haven't told you the ending.'

'Go on.'

'The police took real good care of me – they were very nice, gave me clothes and coffee and cigarettes. When I came down and explained what I'd been looking for, the duty sergeant told me that every last trace of the flak tower was gone. He said that after the war, the British blew it up and took all the rubble away. His father had fought and died in the Tiergarten *Flakturm*, that's how he knew about it. He even showed me photographs – it was an awesome building. Ugly, but awesome. He said it had been a hospital and they'd stored valuable artworks there, too. So I could have searched forever, naked in the moonlight, and never found what I was looking for. Because this amazing place where people killed, kept art, hid from bombs and tended each other's wounds was gone, every last bit.' She propped herself up one arm, and smiled at him. 'Now, isn't that a great metaphor for life, or what – me searching for a thing like that, but it doesn't exist?'

'I'm sure I'll think it's a fantastic metaphor, once I work it out. But right now, I feel unusual.'

'That'll be the Potter's. Don't worry, it shouldn't last for long.'

'How long?'

'Oh, about an hour or so.'

'Great. So what was it like, being sent to the looney bin?'

'Like *One Flew over the Cuckoo's Nest*, actually. Very similar.'

'Your mum must have been seriously pissed off at you. Is it true that you stole her money?'

'Dionne told you that too?'

Singer nodded.

'The bitch!'

'I think she was warning me off you. She said that terrible things would happen if I became friendly with you.'

'Fucking *cow*…'.

'I'm afraid she only succeeded in making me even more curious.'

'So, what you really want to know is – am I mad or not?'

'Yes.'

'Well, I suffer from depression, that much is official.'

'How badly?'

'It depends. I get very up, but also very down. The two extremes. Right now, I'm up, because I'm happy here. I'm supposed to take the Surmontil to keep a balance, but I'm not convinced that it works. One of the symptoms is, I can get a bit…manic. At least, that's what they call it, but I prefer to think of it as mildly obsessive. Yes, I stole money from my mother, but at the time, it didn't seem like stealing. It's not like I spent it on heroin. I needed the money, to go and do something I knew I had to do.'

'What, see a few demolished buildings?'

'I read about the *Flakturme*, and I knew I'd feel something when I saw them.'

'Feel what?'

'Connected to a different time, to another era.'

'Could you not just go to a museum for that?'

'You risked your life in a storm to feel something special instead of going to a church.'

After a pause, he said, 'Good answer.'

'Damn right it's a good answer. And part of the magic of the Pier House is it makes us feel like we're living in another era. Do you agree?'

'Of course.'

'But it only feels that way because it's not what we're used to. It's not really like living in another era, because we don't have head lice, there's a flushing toilet and you can drive your car to Letterkenny and buy wine from all over the world.'

'So?'

'So time is tricky. It's not to be trusted.'

'What the hell are you on about?'

Oona suddenly sat upright. 'Sit up,' she ordered.

'I'm much happier lying down, thank you.'

'Sit up – this is important.'

Muttering, Singer obeyed. 'Grr...yuk. I feel dizzy. Wow. Look at that.' He pointed at the grain in the rock. To his eyes, it seemed alive with colour, with pinks, blacks, greys and silvers.

'Silica. Feldspar. This used to be sand, at the bottom of a seabed.'

'But the seabed's away down there.'

'No, that's a new sea. The sea that caused this rock is gone.'

'Gone where?'

'Gone away. Mountains, continents, oceans, all gone. Look around you.'

He obeyed. The stone, the sea and the sky all stood out with a clarity he'd never experienced before – he didn't feel high, just unsteady, but able to see much more sharply than usual. He wondered why he couldn't see like this all the time – that way, he'd be a better photographer.

She patted the rock. 'One of the first things I learned when I started studying geology was that these rocks we're sitting on exist because, eighteen hundred million years ago, there was a huge super-continent down by the equator. You got that?'

'Super-continent, equator, long time ago – got it.'

'Okay, that super-continent tore itself apart, through tectonic movement. When it split, it formed a basin, and in that basin was an ocean, called Iapetus. The rock beneath your bum used to be sand, at the bottom of Iapetus. You got that?'

'Bum. Sand. Iapa-thingy.'

'After many millions of years – we're not sure how many – the earth's crust closed up again over the ocean, compressing the sediment, and creating the rock you're sitting on. There was a lot of volcanic activity too. You still with me?'

'Barely.' Singer lay down again, rubbing his face.

'Try to keep up. Around that time, England, Wales and most of Ireland travelled north and crashed into Scotland, which was travelling south.' Oona pointed to the edge of the pinnacle. 'The gorge below us is part of a fault in the earth's crust which marks the spot where that happened. Literally, you and me are sitting where worlds collided.'

'See, I told you we were meant for one another.'

'Shut up. After this collision, a huge mountain range, much bigger than the Himalayas, sprung up roughly where the Atlantic Ocean is now. But since then, it's been washed away, and now there's only water there instead.'

'My head feels funny.'

'Funny? Do you want to know what's funny?'

'No. I don't want to know what's funny.'

'What's funny is, we know these things to be true, but because we can't nail down precisely when everything happened, there is, in geology, a phenomenon known as "missing time".'

'Missing time?'

'Yes. Whole chunks of time go missing, as easy as losing money when you're drunk. Hundreds of millions of years lost here, tens of millions mislaid there. The loose change of the ages.'

'That could be awkward.'

'Missing time is very awkward, if you consider that the entire existence of mankind only spans about two hundred thousand years. In terms of missing time, we are nothing. We're so insignificant, we don't even qualify as loose change.'

'Stop this, you're bending my mind.'

'No. You asked me about my depression, and now I'm telling you what I think triggered it. I've always felt a bit wrong in myself, but my head didn't start to feel really out of place until I read about missing time. We are microbes, clinging to a ball of rock, hurtling through infinite space at sixty-seven thousand miles per hour, able to survive because of a tiny layer of gas. And from what I read, we're destroying the gas that keeps us alive. But fair enough, we all know that. But the ball of rock we're standing on has been rearranging itself for so long, even the missing pieces beneath our feet were around for ten times longer than us. If that's not enough to make you feel small, I don't know what is.'

'Please stop.'

'One day, we're going to look back on the Pier House, and that's how it's going to feel – like missing time. Lost and gone forever.'

'Please stop talking.'

'No. You climbed this pinnacle in a storm because you said the waves made you feel small before – what was it? Oh yes, "the goddess nature". You don't know the meaning of "small". Nature isn't a goddess, it's an eternity, where mankind doesn't even register. Never mind the Pier House – one day, the entire history of humanity will be just another slice of missing time, with nobody around to count it.'

Still flat on his back, he reached an arm out, grabbed her around the shoulders and pulled her head down onto his chest. She smelled of fresh air and that funny stuff, tiger paste, or whatever it was called.

'Hey!' she protested.

'Lie still!' he commanded.

'Stop that!' she yelped, but he held her fast.

'This rock is spinning around – any second now, it's gonna collapse, and tip us into the sea.' He used his free hand to cover his eyes. 'So please stop talking, and just lie still.'

Oona tried half-heartedly to pull away, but he only squeezed her closer, so she gave up and lay on top of him, listening to his heart with one ear, and with the other, to the echo of the waves pouring through the gorge below, like the rush of blood along a giant artery.

'Frisby, old chap! How the hell are you?'

Singer strode down the last leg of the hairpin path, with Oona straggling along behind. Frisby, Ronan and Dionne stood amongst

154

the maze of propped-up fishing boats. From high above, Singer and Oona had spied Frisby tapping the sides of the vessels and gesticulating, obviously imparting his professional expertise. Frisby wore a blue blazer with brass buttons and a red paisley cravatte, cream slacks and brown loafers. He held his cumbersome plastic box tucked under one arm. Ronan was wrapped in his grey overcoat and purple scarf, and Dionne had her black PVC coat on, with matching boots, and her white, snowball-shaped fur hat. With their anoraks crumpled and streaked with dirt, Singer and Oona looked positively scruffy in comparison with the dandy little gathering.

'What have you two been up to?' Dionne enquired.

'You asked me to find Singer, and here he is,' Oona replied.

'You've been gone for ages.'

'He was very far away, striding the cliff-tops like something out of a Caspar Friedrich painting.'

'Pardon?'

'Where's Melissa?'

'She went off walking up to the village.'

'Frisby!' Singer repeated, with exaggerated bonhomie. He took Frisby's free hand and pumped it. 'How utterly spiffing to see you. Well,' and he gestured at the rotten, rusting boats, stinking of dead fish and diesel, 'have you purchased the entire fleet?'

Ronan eyed Singer with suspicion, but Frisby seemed pleased at the greeting.

'Fraid I'd have terrible diffs shifting this lot – so no sale.'

'What about your gizmo there? Bloody thing working yet?' Singer grabbed the handset from the box under Frisby's arm. 'Hellooo?' he called into it. 'Can I have Kensington one-five-four, please? Yes, am I through to Harrod's? Now see here my good man, please send fifteen crates of your finest champers around to Dunaldragh straight away. And a tin of duck pâté. No, actually – just send me the duck, and a four-pound lump hammer, and I'll turn the blighter into pâté meself.'

'Have you been drinking?' Ronan asked him.

'All my life,' Singer affirmed. 'Still no signal?' he asked Frisby.

'No, perhaps I should take it up that hill...'

'There's nothing up there, except for some frightfully old rocks. I'll show you the best place for this thing.' Still holding the handset to his ear, he began walking up the road, so that the flex stretched and Frisby had no choice but to follow. 'I'm taking it to a fine establishment known locally as McFall's, where it will be perfectly at home amongst their stupendous collection of useless objects.' He did a poor Richard Burton into the mouthpiece. 'Broadsword calling Danny Boy. Broadsword calling Danny Boy. Come in, Danny Boy.'

Smiling, Oona stepped after Singer and Frisby. Dionne and Ronan exchanged puzzled glances, then fell in behind.

A huge surprise awaited the party upon reaching McFall's – the bar had people drinking in it. A dozen or so fishermen, dressed in an assortment of blue boiler suits, Wellingtons, jumpers and jeans crowded the small space out rightly. They had obviously been at it from quite early on, because the air reeked of Guinness and tobacco. It was as if the passing of Christmas had brought the end of an embargo. A grinning, red-faced Manus held court from behind the counter, and Singer struck up conversations with the clientele as easily as if he had lived in Dunaldragh all his life. When Frisby requested a gin and tonic, Singer ordered him a double, and thereafter kept the refills coming fast. Ronan and Dionne sat hunched behind the corner table, peering about them in shy bewilderment, while Oona, perched on a barstool, soon found herself fending off competing marriage proposals from two jolly, overweight, middle-aged brothers by the name of O'Geary. Singer introduced Frisby first to Manus, then to several others, as 'a British boat dealer', with the result that he was immediately swamped with enquiries about the cost of navigation equipment and refurbished engines.

A few hours and quite a few drinks later, Singer sat in the corner against the bar counter. Michael lay at his feet, and Singer bent occasionally to pat him. Frisby, by this time, had escaped his interrogators and squeezed in beside Ronan and Dionne at the table. He was talking very animatedly to the latter, while Ronan looked on peevishly. Mrs McFall emerged from the back hallway carrying two platters of neatly cut sandwiches, which she placed on the counter before retreating, without bidding any of her customers the time of day. Still, burly arms with hands like gravel-packed rubber gloves reached out and made short work of her offerings. Manus then appeared, bearing a plate with white, shredded meat upon it and a dollop of mayonnaise. He placed it on the table before Frisby, Ronan and Dionne.

'Have a go at that, and see what you think of it.'

'What is it – chicken?' Ronan asked.

'Try it and see.' Reluctantly, all three lifted pieces of the meat and nibbled.

'Mmm – delicious!' Dionne declared, reaching for more, this time dipping it in the mayonnaise. Ronan chewed his morsel thoughtfully, and Frisby pulled a face and washed his down with gin.

'Some sort of fish, what?'

'Crab's toes,' Manus informed him.

Frisby guffawed. 'Don't be silly, crebs don't have toes!'

'Do you hear that, boys?' Manus addressed the well-oiled clientele. 'The boat expert here says that crabs don't have toes!' He scurried off behind the counter again, and, to general laughter, returned waving a large brown object tipped with a pair of black pincers. Frisby's eyes opened wide with disgust, Ronan's with horror. Manus waved the crab in Frisby's face, then cracked it open with his bare hands, revealing a lump of the pale, moist flesh within.

'There you go – crab's toes!'

'That's not a toe, old boy – it's a claw. Crebs have claws!'

'Excuse me, can I have that?' Dionne took the claw, scooped the flesh out with her fingers, dipped in the mayonnaise, and stuffed it in her mouth.

'Mmmff…that's the nicest thing I've tasted since I got here. Do you have any more?'

'I might be able to fetch you some tomorrow morning.' Then, as he walked past Singer, Manus muttered to him, in an aside, 'Do you see that dog there?' he nodded down at Michael. 'I'd say he's forgotten more about boats than your friend with the fancy jacket ever learned.'

'Somehow, that doesn't surprise me.' Singer dragged on his cigarette. 'What's the best whiskey you have back there?'

'That would be the Crested Ten.'

'A large one, please, and I'd be honoured if you'd join me.'

10

'Rub there. No, there – between the eyes. Aow! Careful, your nails are too long!'

Dionne pushed a reclining Oona off her knee. 'Rub your own silly head. Anyway, mine feels worse.' Dionne raised her hand to her temples and massaged gently. With more than her usual faint amusement, Melissa sat on the living room floor in her leotard, watching her two friends sprawled on the sofa, pale-faced, dressing gowns wrapped tightly about them.

'I can't believe we don't have a single headache tablet between us,' Oona moaned.

Dionne snorted. 'I can. There's nothing else from the twentieth century here, so why do you think there would be headache tablets?'

'Does Singer have any? He drinks – he's bound to have some.'

'I already thought of that. He's not in his room.'

'Where is he?'

'How the feck should I know? Probably up wherever you found him yesterday, communing with nature. Anyway, I've been through his luggage and he has none – tons of cameras and shite, but no Paracetamol.'

Oona scooped a fingertip of Tiger Balm from the tin in her hand and offered it up. 'You can have some of this if you want. It sort of helps.'

'Keep that muck away from me.'

Oona pouted and spread the goo beneath her ears.

'What time did you come home?' Melissa asked from the floor.

'God knows,' Dionne answered, 'but it was late. Jay couldn't walk, so Singer carried him all the way down here over his shoulder – and Jay puked on his back!' She caught a fit of the giggles.

'The poor little fella, he's so sweet.' Oona giggled, too.

'Yes, I like him.'

'But I thought you liked Singer?'

'I do, but you have to admit Jay's quite tasty.'

'He's a little pretty boy.'

'Who happens to be worth a few quid. I don't think Ronan likes me paying attention to him, he was ever so narky up in the pub.'

'That's because he fancies you, but you were flirting with Frisby.'

'You think Ronan fancies me?'

'You know fine rightly he does.'

'I think Jay fancies me, too.'

'Yes, but he likes Melissa more.'

'*Excuse* me?' Melissa yelped.

'Oh, come on. You must have noticed, the way he stares at you.'

'I can't say I have,' Melissa replied, primly. Footsteps sounded above the ceiling, and the three looked up.

'Well, you'd better go and put some clothes on, because if he comes down and sees you like that, he might try to jump you.' Oona nudged Dionne in the ribs and put on a Frisby voice. 'I say, dashing filly, what? Fancy a jolly good brushing-down?'

Dionne caught the giggles again. 'Oohh, stop it, this isn't helping my head.'

'I have a plan,' Oona announced, 'whoever's first down the stairs, Ronan or Frisby, we send them up to McFall's to fetch headache tablets. And while they're at it, they can also buy the makings of a fry, and cook it for us!'

'I don't want a fry, I want crab.'

'Have sex with Ronan, then – you're bound to catch them. Ugh! Ginger pubes!'

Dionne squawked with horror. Even Melissa laughed. 'No,' Dionne panted, 'I meant Manus's crabs!' The three shook their hands and squealed all the more. 'No really,' Dionne whimpered, 'sea crab, with mayonnaise. Perfect hangover food, instead of a big, fattening fry.'

'Oh, like mayonnaise isn't fattening.'

'The crab would make up for it. It's yummy – I've never tasted anything like it. I shall marry Frisby for his money and live on a yacht and eat crab forever after. And have sex with Singer behind his back.'

'Good luck to you.'

The door opened at the far end of the room, and Ronan and Frisby came through it. Both looked extremely hungover.

'What's all the screeching about?' Ronan scratched his head.

'We were laughing at you behind your back. Come over here – we have a job for you!' Dionne ordered.

Frisby strode in a straight line towards the back of the sofa and toppled over it, landing between Oona and Dionne. Only then did he notice Melissa, sitting cross-legged before the fireplace. He slid off the sofa onto his knees, crawled over to her and tried to put his head in her lap. She, however, nimbly stood up and sped towards the door.

'I have to change,' she announced as she passed the gawping Ronan. Frisby lay on the carpet, like a dead dog.

'Ohh…I feel woeful,' he whined. Oona and Dionne exchanged glances.

'Now, which of you is going to be a perfect gentleman, and go to the shop for us?' Dionne asked.

'Get Singer to do it.' Ronan collapsed into one of the armchairs.

'Singer's not here.'

'Where is he? No – don't tell me. He'll be hanging off a cliff somewhere. What do you want from the shop?'

Dionne smiled sweetly. 'We want headache tablets, and we want crabs for breakfast.' She giggled slightly.

'Crebs?' Frisby enquired, his face in the carpet.

'We want anything for breakfast, you decide – bacon, eggs, what-ever. Please, will you make us breakfast, Ro, please?' Dionne whee-dled. 'We're two ladies in distress, and this morning we require that men do things for us and generally be our slaves.'

'Right, Frisby.' Ronan poked the prostrate form with his foot. 'Let's go.'

'Can't you go on your ownio, old boy?'

'No, you piece of upper-class sludge. I thought you people were supposed to be officer material – on your feet!' He tried to pull Frisby upright by the arm.

'I've just remembered, where's my phone?'

'You left it in the pub. Manus hung it from the ceiling in a net – don't you remember?'

'No – why did he do that?'

'Because Singer told him to, probably.'

'S'long as it's safe. You know, now that I think about it, I do believe I might have been sick all over Singer last night, too.'

Ronan laughed. 'You're lucky he didn't beat the shit out of you.'

'Rather.'

'He had sex with you instead.'

'Really?' Frisby looked alarmed and felt between his buttocks. The girls laughed filthy laughs.

'What makes you think he had sex with you there?' Ronan hauled him towards the door.

'Result.' Oona held her hand up and Dionne feebly high-fived it.

However, they heard the pair clatter out through the porch, then, moments later, Ronan returned to the living room.

'I think you'd better come and see this.' His face was solemn.

'Do we have to?' Dionne groaned. 'I want to stay on my cosy sofa.'

'Really, I'd prefer if you came and saw what's outside.'

Grumbling, the two women followed Ronan to the doorstep. A sack stood propped against the sundial. The bottom half of it was sopping wet. Frisby had opened it, and was peering inside.

'This was tied to the top.' Ronan passed Dionne a crumpled, handwritten note, black marker on a piece of oil-stained brown paper. It read, *Remove claws, then boil for fifteen minutes.*

'Crebs,' Frisby announced. 'Blasted beg is full of facking crebs.'

Dionne dashed forward, and looked into the sack to see an impenetrable heap of brown carapaces, some of them bigger than a man's hand. Here and there, a leg or a feeler twitched, but mostly, the contents of the bag were still.

'Breakfast!' she announced, delightedly.

Oona looked towards the harbour – sure enough, several of the boats were tied up inside it, rising gently on the swell. 'Manus must have been out checking his pots this morning. But Dee – you can't eat crabs for breakfast.'

'Damn right.' Frisby looked as if he might be sick again.

'Why ever not?' Dionne demanded. 'They're scrummy! Wait here!' She dashed off into the house, and returned moments later carrying a bottle of white wine, a jar of mayonnaise and a sizeable wheel of

Singer's soda bread – baked, on this occasion, without Ronan's help. 'There! We have the makings of a perfectly good brunch! All we need now is to cook those things.' She opened her eyes wide and touched Ronan's hand. 'How hard could that be?'

'No idea.' Ronan rubbed his chin, looking somewhat concerned. Oona watched, grining on the inside, as Dionne stepped up to Frisby and kissed him on the cheek. Frisby looked as if she'd hit him with the wine bottle. She spun around, and hugged Ronan in such a way that the top half of her chest and most of one shoulder emerged, quite beautifully and naturally, from underneath her dressing gown. Ronan returned the embrace awkwardly, then pushed his glasses up onto his nose. 'But I'm sure we can give it a go – right, Frisby?'

'Oh, thank you, thank you – I can't wait. Come on, Oons,' Dionne trilled, 'let's go get dressed for brunch.'

'But I don't want crab for brunch.'

'Good – all the more for me.'

Alone, Ronan and Frisby pondered the sack.

'Well, I suppose,' Ronan frowned, 'the thing to do is get this lot onto the kitchen table, and take it from there.' He was trying very hard not to think of the big blue crab he'd seen in London's Natural History Museum, feeding morsels through its gaping mandible with a delicate pair of feelers. Kraken.

'See here, bollocks to this, Dockerty, I don't want—' Frisby began.

'Shut up and grab the bottom.' Ronan seized the top of the sack, and between them they wrestled it into the kitchen and dumped it onto the big oak table. Out tumbled about two dozen inert crabs, tannish-red on top, creamy white on their ribbed bottoms. Ronan took an iron pot from a cupboard and plonked it down beside them. 'Right, off with their claws.' Neither made a move. Frisby looked as if he'd been asked to perform an execution. Ronan didn't feel much better.

'How the fack do we…I mean, I've nevah…'

Ronan picked up the nearest crustacean, which was lying motionless on its back, apprently dead – therefore beyond pain, and more importantly, beyond causing him any. He took a hold of one claw, pulled gingerly, then shrieked and threw the crab from him.

'Ahh! Bastard bit me!' The guilty party rocked on its back in the middle of the table, legs nervelessly splayed, as lifeless as before.

'This is a total nightmare – it's like something from facking *Alien*!' Frisby hugged himself. He looked genuinely frightened.

'How the hell did you people win two world wars?'

'But it bit you!' Frisby protested. 'You're the one screaming like a girl, chum!'

'Actually, uh, I don't think it bit me as such – perhaps it just twitched, a sort of reflex action.'

'I value me fingers, old chap.'

'They're only a bunch of dead crabs – come on!' Ronan seized the corpse that had offended him and, with a crunching noise, tore a claw off it, which he dropped into the pot with a clunk. 'There! Now, give me a hand, or you have to do all the washing up by yourself for the rest of the week.'

Frisby pulled a face, picked up the smallest crab on the table and tugged. The two worked in grim silence, but gradually, the pot began to fill. Ronan lifted it and turned to carry it to the sink, to top it up with water. He heard a 'Fack!' and turned to see Frisby frozen in mid-declaw. He was staring at the sack in alarm.

'The facking beg – there's something in there, Dockerty. Facker just moved.'

As the words left Frisby's lips, the lip of the sack twitched and, sideways, facing him, out crept the biggest crab Ronan had ever seen beyond the confines of the Natural History Museum. Its body was the size of a large dinner plate, and its claws, raised and open as they were, looked wide enough to lop a child's arm off, let alone a man's finger.

'Aahhhh!' Ronan dropped the pot, spilling the fruits of their labour over the stone floor. He backed across the kitchen, then howled again when his backside made contact with the blazing-hot range.

Kraken!

Frisby dropped the crab he'd been working on, and alerted by the movement, the monster swivelled rapidly around towards him, claws still held high. It advanced slowly.

'Dockerty – help! Help!'

'What do you want me to do? Get out of its way!'

Frisby stepped back, but bumped into a chair and sat heavily down upon it. The giant was now level with his face. Trembling, he stuck a hand into his pocket and came up with a small bone-handled penknife, which he opened and poked at the creature.

'Get away from me!'

The crab lunged. There was a brief struggle, during which Frisby fell off the chair, then the crab scuttled sideways, clutching Frisby's pen knife in its right claw. It stopped and waved the knife threateningly at the empty space around the table.

Ronan howled. 'You've been disarmed by a crustacean! What kind of man are you?'

Frisby crawled across the floor, reached for the sink and pulled himself up. 'You're one to talk, you bloody bastard, you, leaving me to sort the bleedin' thing out on my own!' Frisby's upper-crust twang seemed to have completely deserted him, to be replaced by a pure southern English staccato. Ronan noticed this in spite of their mutual panic, but at that moment, the kitchen door opened and Dionne and Oona stepped through it, fully clothed, although minus make-up.

'What the feck is going on?' Dionne started, then took in the crab on the table and the claws all over the floor. 'Jesus…'

Oona burst out laughing. 'Did the creature from the deep get the better of you, boys?' She moved to the table for a closer look and the crab turned towards her, brandishing its weapon. 'Did these bad men want to eat you, honey?'

Dionne seemed uncertain what to say. Seeing Oona stand so close to the table, Ronan and Frisby felt embarrassed about cringing down the far end of the kitchen and tentatively stepped forward. Something crunched beneath Ronan's feet – one claw less for lunch.

'Fuckah got me knife,' Frisby pointed out, somewhat superfluously, unless it was to demonstrate that his Oxbridge modulation, after a momentary lapse, was now fully restored.

'So what are you going to do about it?' Oona did not disguise her amusement.

'We managed to, uh, overcome all the others.'

'But what about this one?'

'Yes, Ronan, what about this one?' Dionne added. The monster crab crept around the edge of the table, as if looking for a way off.

Oona walked over to the cutlery drawer, selected a fork, and carefully offered it handle-first to the crab's empty claw. It nipped hard, then waved both knife and fork around before its black, beady eyes. 'Watch out!' she warned. 'It's hungry!'

Melissa arrived and her habitual composure slipped as she surveyed the scene with patent disapproval.

'What have you lot been doing to those poor animals?' she demanded crossly.

Everyone looked at Ronan. 'I, uh, er – Dionne wanted crab for lunch, and I, that is, me and Frisby, we…'

'Children,' she tutted. 'All of you – children.' Abruptly, she lifted the menacing crab from behind so that, in spite of much waving of its weaponry and scrabbling of its legs, it couldn't reach her. Holding it at arm's length, she marched out the front door, across the sea-grass and onto the pebble beach. The others followed. The tide was low, so she walked to the water's edge and set the creature down. It scuttled sideways, then stopped, brandishing its battle trophies. Then a wavelet washed over it and it lumbered off after the receding water. A larger wave came and claimed it, and it was gone.

'Damn shame,' Frisby frowned. 'Bloody good pen knife, that.'

Across in the harbour, Singer and Manus tried hard to stifle their laughter, lest it be carried shoreward on the breeze. The pair stood crushed into the tiny cabin of Manus's boat, each holding a pair of binoculars to their eyes. Singer wore Wellingtons, an old pair of oilskin trousers and a jumper, rolled up at the sleeves. He caught his breath.

'Good morning's fishing, Manus, thanks for taking me out.'

Manus chortled, 'No problem. Didn't I tell you it would get rid of your hangover?'

'By god, you were right – I've never felt better.'

During the week before New Year's Eve, the weather turned stormy again. Ronan, Dionne and Frisby didn't venture much outside, preferring the perpetual warmth of the living room fire, where they could drink, read and chat in comfort. Oona and Melissa still took daily walks together – sometimes with Singer, sometimes without. Both Melissa and Singer would often disappear for hours at a time, but rarely together – she did her exploring first thing in the morning, Singer did his whenever the waves were high, or whenever he was thirsty. All six went to the pub every evening at ten and stayed there until around one, before walking home, laughing and joking, by torchlight. Some nights, there'd be a few fishermen propping up the bar, other nights, they were the only customers. Frisby taught Oona, Singer and Melissa how to play whist, and this they did upon return-ing from the pub every morning at least until two, more likely three or four. Melissa began to sleep a bit later, but still did her exercise upon rising, no matter who was present in the living room – Frisby tried desperately to scrape himself out of bed for this daily ritual, but only managed to do so twice.

Oona began to collect semi-precious pebbles from the beach, and samples from the rocks all around. She drafted rough sketches for a geological map of the area, and regretted not having brought some of her long-ignored textbooks on holiday with her. Every afternoon, Ronan would spend an hour or two alone at the kitchen table, pen, paper and wine glass laid out in front of him. Given the surroundings, he felt he ought to be inspired, but at first, all that came out were vague verses about the sea. Then he began to tinker with a theme that he'd always considered a tad beneath him – that of love. Lines and imagery tumbled into his mind, but he refused to show anybody the results.

Singer, meanwhile, when he wasn't clinging to a cliff or a barstool, took to shutting himself in the pantry, where he had set up his darkroom equipment. Towards the middle of that week, black-and-white photographs started to appear in the kitchen. When they had covered most of the available surfaces there, they began spreading to the hallway, hung from string tied between the hooks. Then the table in the living room disappeared under images of the sea, the house, the cliffs, the island, the pub and, of most interest to the others, portraits of all five taken, more often than not, unawares. Ronan, leaning up against the tower, the sunlight on his glasses turning his eyes into blank, white discs. Dionne doing her make-up in the bathroom mirror, face framed fabulously by her hair. Melissa on the island, staring out to sea. Frisby strutting far away along the beach, handset to his ear, box under one arm, trying to get a signal. Oona's favourite, naturally, was an image of herself – Singer had caught her curled up on an armchair, her face illuminated by an oil lamp, absorbed in a heavy volume of *The Illustrated London News*. So that's how I look, she thought, when I'm outside of me.

'Singah? Ken I come in?' Frisby's voice was muffled by the pantry door.

'No! If you let the light in, you'll ruin everything!'

'Please, Singah – we need to talk, old chap.'

'What about?'

'I've gathered from Dockerty that my arrival heah was a bit unexpected.'

'Really?'

'And that you may not have been best pleased.'

'Rubbish.'

'I'm frightfully relieved to heah you say that.'

'Whatever. Look, I'm quite—'

'No, heah me out, old boy, because I have a bit of a confession to make.'

'Frisby, I'm at a delicate stage here, and I need to concentrate.'

'Sorry, old chap. Can't wait – it's bursting out of me. I positively, absolutely have to tell you how I feel about you.' Inside the pantry, something heavy smashed – a glass ashtray, by the sound of it. 'I say, are you all right in there, deah heart?' There was a long pause. 'Singah. Please don't shut me out like this. You can't deny that you feel the same way about me.' Singer wrenched the door open, a cigarette hanging from his mouth.

'You are so big and rough and macho, Singah,' Melissa enunciated in a perfect Frisby voice. 'Please. Bend poor old Frisby ovah the kitchen table and give him a right good seeing-to.' She reverted to her own voice. 'Then he'd know how I feel every time he looks at me.'

'Jesus!' Singer exploded. 'You almost had me going, for a moment!'

'I did have you going, for a moment.' She looked over his shoulder and saw the bottle of whiskey and a glass. 'What have you got in there, your own private pub?'

'I'm, uh, just waiting for some prints to dry.'

'Good. They can dry by themselves. I want you to come for a walk with me.'

'Now?'

'No, last Thursday.'

'What's the weather like?'

'Strangely enough, it's wet. Get your coat.'

The two trudged in silence through the sea-grass. The wind had eased, but the air was soft with rain so they kept hoods up over their woolly hats. When Singer saw that she was leading him up towards the spinney in front of the pub, he strode with an extra spring in his step, but when she turned left out of the rusty gate and kept on going, he stopped in the middle of the road like a child whose mother has passed a display of sweets, deliberately ignoring it.

'Hey!' he called. But Melissa obviously had no immediate intention of bestowing her custom on McFall's, and she marched on, up the rise. Grumbling, he jogged after her.

After another ten minutes of soaking silence and steady uphill walking, they reached the top of the valley. The road crested, leaving the sea behind, dipped into a forest of gloomy, impenetrable pines, then ran for the hills through an open, striped pattern of fields. Beyond the fields, the occasional nondescript bungalow cringed beneath the rain – Dunaldragh village seemed to consist of a random, mile-long scattering of such properties, rather than a community of buildings with any recognisable heart or centre. From some of the dwellings' chimneys, plumes of smoke mingled with the rain, leaving the smell of burnt turf in the air. Singer blinked with curiosity, this being the first occasion he had travelled the road in daylight.

Set slightly back from the road, an ugly shack built from green-painted corrugated tin bore the legend 'An Post' – Post Office. Its grimy window displayed random commodities such as brass polish, bootlaces and plastic combs, and a closed sign. At this unedifying edifice, Melissa turned right off the road into a lane, which passed a small concrete primary school of utilitarian 1950s design, then ended outside a set of well-maintained, white-painted metal gates. Beyond the gates, up a gravel driveway bordered by yews, stood a plain church, with a louvred belltower but no steeple, built of the same dark stone as the Pier House. Like the Pier House, its architecture was simple but pleasing, with lancet windows the only genuflection towards some higher purpose. Melissa walked confidently up towards the entrance, which, like everything else in Dunaldragh village, was not open for business. The gravel drive split into two paths, running each side of the church. Melissa chose the left one, and Singer saw that it led into a graveyard, very different from the extravagant theme parks of sentimental sculpture he'd so enjoyed documenting in London. Nonetheless, he took several photographs. The headstones here were straightforward and austere – name, date and occasionally some pithy, one-line petition. Some were tall and plainly quite old, others smaller and more modern.

She made her way through the stones towards the back of the burial ground, where Singer saw one that stood out from the rest. It was a cot grave, with crumbling iron railings around it and a flat stone within. She stopped beside it. In spite of the mizzle, she removed her hood and hat. The stone was slate, and therefore as clear to read as the day it was laid. It said,

Sophia Clements

1844–1909

Tempora mutantur,
nos et mutamur in illis.

'It's her. What is it again? "Times change, and..."?'
'"We change with them."'
He walked around the tomb, looking for further inscriptions, but there were none. 'She didn't leave much in the way of clues, did she? But at least this proves that she existed.'
'You doubted that?'
'No, but there's always something reassuring about conclusive proof. Rather pisses on your theory, though.' His eyes widened and he clapped his hand to his mouth. 'Sorry, I know I shouldn't say bad words here. I meant, that's your theory screwed...' He clapped his hand to his mouth again.
'Swearing is the refuge of the inarticulate, and it's interesting to note how infrequently you leave it.'
'Your theory was that Sophia's evil father placed the sundial in front of the Pier House. Well, she would hardly have wanted his words carved on her grave, if that were the case.'
'I was merely surmising. Who knows, she may have had the sundial made herself, after she inherited. Perhaps the quote was personal to her, not her father. Or, perhaps her father did build the sundial, and whoever buried her – her family, the locals – may have copied the inscription onto her tombstone without her consent. Or perhaps Sophia came to treasure the quote because ultimately, her father's hope came true – she did change, from a tortured teenager driven mad by disgust, to the wise, kindly woman Manus says she matured into. Perhaps taking these words literally to her grave was Sophia's final act of forgiveness.'

'Which version do you believe?'

'How can I believe, when I have no way of knowing? But the first thing I will do when I get back to Dublin is unearth the provenance of that quote.'

'I can do better than that. I'll ring my Uncle Lucius tonight. He's a university professor – he can go and look it up for us. Might even know off the top of his head, he's that sort of fellow.'

'No, don't. Please, leave this to me. I promise I'll write to you with whatever I find.' She reached across and pulled his woollen hat off.

'Hey!'

'The least we can do is give Sophia a moment of silent respect, to thank her for the house, if nothing else.'

'What, like she's sitting on some cloud, watching us?'

'I'm not religious, if that's what you're asking. But you know that feeling you get, when you're in the Pier House, and everything's quiet, and you look out the window at the sea – you know that feeling, don't you?'

He paused before answering. 'Yes, I do.'

'Well, Sophia must have looked out those windows, and felt like that too. In my mind's eye, I can see her, looking through the barred windows of her bedroom as a lonely, frightened girl, then through the living room window as a much older, perhaps happier woman.'

'You think about her quite a lot, don't you?'

'Yes. Why didn't she leave when she inherited her share of the estate? Imagine you'd been banished somewhere remote, young and sick, with a dirty disease you'd been given by god knows who – by your father, maybe. You'd think the first thing you'd want to do is leave, whenever you could. But Sophia got better, and when Leitrim died she not only got her freedom back, but came into money. Yet she stayed – why?'

'Maybe she had nowhere else to go. Or maybe because, for better or worse, the Pier House was her home, and she grew to love it.'

'"Times change, and we change with them."'

The two stood before the grave, with their heads bowed in the rain, for quite some time.

On the day before New Year's Eve, the girls asked Singer for a lift into Letterkenny. Arriving in town, they arranged to meet him at a designated bar and bustled quickly off, smirking amongst themselves. Singer assumed that, as females, they'd simply been away from shops for too long, and went off in search of booze and photographic paper. Once again, the crowds made him claustrophobic and he completed his errands as quickly as possible, then curled up in a dark corner of the designated bar with a copy of Fitzgerald's *The Love of the Last Tycoon* that he kept in his glove compartment. He read for a couple of hours before the girls returned, laden with mysterious parcels and bags.

Back at the Pier House, Singer, Ronan and Frisby were dispatched off to the pub, so it was plain, if it wasn't plain already, that something was up. However, as males, the trio didn't waste much time in speculation and passed a very pleasant evening drinking and playing poker for bottle-tops with Manus.

On New Year's Eve, in the afternoon, Melissa ordered that all the furniture in the living room be shifted around and directed Ronan and Singer in lifting and heaving until a large open space was created in the middle of the floor. Oona, noting that some of the oil lamps were out of fuel, wondered what to do. Ronan remembered the drum of paraffin in the outhouse, and the pair carried two lamps apiece to refill them. Oona set hers down beside the drum and peered around the dusty shelves.

'This place looks bigger from the inside – what a lot of junk.' She lifted one corner of the filthy tarpaulin draped over the bulky object in the middle of the floor. 'What's under here?'

'No idea. Holy…' Ronan's eyes widened. 'Is that what I think it is?'

Oona pulled the tarpaulin further back. 'Yes, it is. I think you should go and fetch the others.'

'This had better not be another facking beg of crebs, Dockerty,' Frisby warned as Ronan showed him, Singer, Melissa and Dionne to the outhouse. As each of the four stepped through the door, they gasped. An old hearse took up most of the available space, its black coachwork dusty and the generous chrome trim around its nose and rear compartment gone green and pitted with age. Its tyres were hopelessly flat, and the lace curtains strung around the rear compartment had the colour and quality of dried seaweed. But what took them aback was the sight of Oona, lying flat on her back inside, eyes closed, hands at prayer on her chest.

'Oona Tyler!' Dionne squawked. 'Get out of there! That is *extremely* bad luck!'

'Actually, it's quite comfortable.' Oona's voice was muffled. 'A bit smelly, but I might sleep here some night.'

'You are *so* tempting fate, don't say I didn't warn you!'

Frisby heaved open the driver's door and climbed behind the big steering wheel. 'Where to, madame?' He didn't have to try very hard to assume a Jeevesian demeanour.

'To Hell, my good man – it's the only place that will take me.'

Once again, the boys were ordered off to the pub, only this time with strict instructions to return at nine – no earlier, no later. By some minor miracle, this they managed to do, returning to find a note pinned to the front door, in Melissa's handwriting.

> *Please change into the clothes provided for you in the hallway.*
> *Then you may proceed to the living room and help yourselves*
> *to refreshments. But you MUST wear the clothes!*

On three hooks in the hallway hung three black suits, complete with white shirts and bow-ties. Singer muttered because his jacket pinched his shoulders, and Ronan, once dressed, looked ready for a career walking five paces behind the hearse in the outhouse. All he lacked was a top hat. Frisby, the only one who seemed at home in a formal suit, had to do up both their bow-ties.

'Why do we have to dress like Victorian capitalists?' Singer snorted.

Still, curiosity got the better of disgruntlement, and when they opened the living room door, the light poured out of it. The walls had been decorated with festoons of tinsel and coloured crêpe paper, interspersed with brightly glowing oil lamps and red candles stuck in wine bottles. The old valve radio wafted a Chopin waltz around six glasses of varying shapes that stood on top of it, while beside it on the floor, four bottles of sparkling wine chilled in a big iron cooking pot filled with ice.

'What, ho!' Frisby rubbed his hands together and made short work of one of the corks. 'I feel refreshed already!'

They stood around the fireplace, sipping the sparkling wine and eyeing the transformation of the room in quiet wonderment. Then the door flew open and in swept the girls. All three wore Edwardian-style dresses, with low-cut chests and high belted sashes. Dionne's was particularly stunning, a flowing white lace affair, almost as translucent as her skin, with matching fingerless gloves, and her hair tied up in ringlets. Melissa's costume was more conservative, in navy velvet with a pale blue sash, lace at the chest and a subtle art-nouveau pattern down the front. Oona wore a plainly cut green cotton gown with a russet-brown sash and a bow at the back. Singer led a round of applause as the arrivals twirled and curtsied.

'Why, it's the Three Graces! What is it – beauty, charm and…'

'Dis-grace?' Oona suggested, fluttering her heavily mascaraed lashes.

'Let's hope so,' he stepped forward, took her hand, bowed, and kissed it.

'No sex before alcohol, please. We're ladies.'

'Sorry, madame, I'll call the wine waiter right away. Boy!' Singer clicked his fingers at Frisby. 'Get these women drunk as quickly as you can.' Frisby leapt for the ice bucket as if electrocuted.

Ronan pushed his glasses up onto his nose. If he could have eaten Dionne with his eyes, he would have. 'Where did you get those dresses? They're, uh, rather stupendous.'

'Well, a trawl of Letterkenny's second-hand shops provided the raw materials, but mainly we have to thank Mrs Beeton here, who is a veritable goddess with the old needle and thread,' Oona gestured at Dionne, 'which is just as well, because neither Melissa nor I can sew for shit. Mine,' Oona looked down at her outfit, 'used to be a night-dress, and Melissa's started life as a pair of curtains. Your suits are hired – I hope we guessed the sizes correctly.'

'One of the few benefits of being from a very large family,' Dionne curtsied again, 'is learning how to make do.'

'Make do?' Singer laughed. 'You'd make someone a wonderful wife, that's what you'd do!' Dionne blushed from her elbows up, but Singer appeared not to notice. He moved on to Melissa, tapped his heels together and gave her a curt bow. She nodded and accepted a glass from Frisby, who practically jumped forward and drew himself up before her, trying to appear taller than he was. Melissa's dress accentuated her neck, which, Singer thought, would have made a swan jealous.

'So, who knows how to waltz?' Dionne asked. The three men looked at one another. 'I thought not. Fortunately, Miss Montgomery here does, and she has instructed Miss Tyler and myself in some of the basic steps. The rules are quite simple.' She deftly stole Singer's glass from his fingers, placed it on top of the radio, then took his hands, holding one of them and pulling the other around her waist. 'If you don't dance with us, you don't drink our Asti Spumante. We have another four bottles chilling in the kitchen sink, by the way. The second rule is, you must change partners after each dance. We've discovered that if you turn the radio dial to Moscow, it will play Chopin, Brahms and Strauss all night. The third and final rule is, no smooching. We are ladies, and we won't stand for it. Now, Miss Tyler, if you will?' She nodded at the radio.

'Yes, Miss Brady.' Oona stepped forward and turned the volume up.

'Thank you. Now after me, Mister Singer, and for goodness sake try to pay attention, you bloody great lump...a one-two-three, one-two-three...'

Casual passers-by were virtually unheard of in Dunaldragh Bay, and certainly there were none at dawn on New Year's Day, 1989. Which was probably just as well, for they would have been deeply baffed by the sight of six partygoers tottering around on the harbour in Edwardian attire, swigging from wine bottles, like ghosts from a long-gone era waiting for a boat to take them home to Hades.

'Let's do this every year,' Oona sighed, half-sitting, half-slumping onto a pile of fishing nets. 'I've never been happier in my life, and I shall spend all year looking forward to next Christmas. I mean, normally I hate Christmas, but this...this has been...' She lay back on the nets, arms apart.

'Hear, hear!' Frisby raised the bottle he was holding. 'I agree with this woman, whatever she says. What did she say?' he enquired of Ronan.

'She says we should cut you up into little pieces and use you as crab bait.'

'You leave him alone,' Oona admonished, skyward, 'because he's very cute and he agrees with me. You agree with me too, don't you, Singer? That we should come here every year?'

'Til death us do part.' Singer raised his bottle in a toast, but before he could drink from it, Dionne snatched it off him and plonked herself down beside Oona. Melissa sat carefully beside Dionne, who immediately availed of the available lap to put her head down and have it cradled.

'Are you chaps not freezing?' Frisby asked the girls, as Singer, in turn, snatched his bottle from him.

'Probably,' Dionne reflected, 'but we're too drunk to feel it.'

'Have to say, nevah met girlies who can hold the jolly old vino like you three.'

'Then obviously,' Dionne swallowed from her bottle, 'you've never been to Dublin. And what the feck's a girlie, while we're at it?'

'I think he means those fellows with bumps on their chests,' Ronan suggested.

'Couldn'a put it better meself!' Frisby aimed a punch at Ronan's shoulder, and missed by several inches.

Oona wheedled, 'We should come here every year, shouldn't we, Dee?'

'Absolutely, babes. Here, have another drink.'

Oona sat up and swigged. 'Ronan, do you agree?'

'I'm rather hoping to be invited to Buckingham Palace next Christmas, actually.'

'You ninny.' Frisby slapped Ronan's shoulder, making contact this time. 'Everyone knows the Queen winters at Sandringham.'

'Then I'll have the place to myself, you English ponce.'

'Whoever loves me the most,' Oona commanded, 'take one step forward. I have a mission for you.' Singer and Ronan both took a step backward. Frisby swayed on the spot, befuddled.

'Jay, I need you to be a very sweet boy and trot up to the house. I want you to fetch me a fountain pen, a teacup, the sharpest knife in the kitchen and *Chambers's Miscellany*. That's a very old poetry book, you'll find it on the kitchen dresser.'

'Oons, what are you—' Melissa began, but Oona shushed her.

'Come again?' Frisby stared at her with a look of exaggerated enquiry.

'Would you like me to carve a list on his forehead?' Ronan asked. 'In mirror writing?'

'You shut up, ginger-baps. Jay – a fountain pen, a teacup, a sharp knife and *Chamber's Miscellany* – got that?' Frisby nodded and staggered off in the direction of the house, which loomed like a mausoleum in the morning mist.

'And bring more booze!' Oona hollered after him.

Singer stood on the harbour lip. 'Really,' he addressed Ronan, 'we should have made him swim across.'

'When he comes back, we'll strip him naked,' Ronan leered, 'push him in the sea, and throw stones at him.'

'Why are you two so horrible to that lovely young man?' Dionne demanded.

'Because he's small,' Singer answered.

'And foreign,' Ronan added.

When Frisby returned from his mission, Oona put the book and pen in her lap, then held the knife and teacup aloft.

'One more time,' she announced, 'does everybody agree that we should always come back here, every Christmas, for ever and ever, amen?'

'Yes,' the others chorused raggedly.

Oona cut her left thumb open with the knife and held it into the teacup. Melissa tried to reach over to stop her, but was impeded by Dionne's head on her lap. The ragged slit dripped gobbets of dark blood onto the white porcelain. Singer, Ronan and Frisby just stood and gawped.

'Oona! What in heavens are you—'

'If Sophia Clements can do it, then so can I.'

With her free hand, Oona opened the poetry book at the flyleaf, then lifted the fountain pen and dipped it in the teacup, which she grasped in her left hand so her thumb could bleed into it.

'Everybody is allowed to suggest one club rule. It has to be within reason and enjoy universal consent, so Dee, you can't make it a rule that Singer has to have sex with you every night, and Ronan, you can't make it a rule that Dee has to have sex with you, and Jay, you can't make it a rule that Melissa has to have sex with you.' She sniggered. 'And I can't make it a rule that Manus and all those big rough fisherman up in the bar have to have sex with me, all at once.'

'Oona Tyler!' Dionne squealed and slapped her on the back.

'If you make me spill my blood, I'm going to use yours,' Oona threatened. She dipped the pen in the cup. 'Okay, I'm writing the first rule, so be ready with yours when I come to you. If you take too long, I'll coagulate.' She scratched for a minute, while the others watched, drunkenly fascinated. 'Okay, Dee, shoot.'

'Well, in spite of your total foulness, I've enjoyed tonight more than anything, so I always want us to throw a formal ball on New Year's Eve.'

'Seems perfectly reasonable,' Oona dipped and wrote, 'provided you make the dresses — Melissa?'

'That cut is deep — do you realise it will probably scar?'

'Then it shall be a noble scar, and nothing compared to some of the samples I've seen elsewhere, believe me. Your rule, please.'

'Oh…this is silly. I suppose I want us to always respect the house, and its memories.'

'I think that goes without saying, but in the interests of not bleeding to death, your motion is passed.' She scribbled. 'Frisby?'

'Well, we should absolutely, positively never forget how beautiful you ladies are on this very fine morning.'

'You utter kiss-ass!' Ronan interjected.

'Be quiet!' Dionne intervened. 'I think that's a great rule!'

'It's a bit slurpy, but I can totally see where you're coming from and therefore declare your submission admissible. Ronan?'

'You women should never forget how handsome and virile I am every morning, and that my room is the first door on the right along the corridor.'

'Yes, we'd better make your manliness a club rule, because otherwise it shall certainly be overloooked.'

'You cruel bitch, you won't say that when I'm rich and famous.'

'Especially if you're rich enough to afford a lock on your bathroom door.' Everyone except Ronan sniggered. 'Singer?'

Singer studied his bottle. 'Pass. I'm not a rules sort of guy.'

'Oh, stop being such a poser and play the game. A rule! Everybody — Singer has to have a rule!' The others cawed at Singer until he held a hand up.

'All right, if you insist. I vote for world peace.'

'No! It has to be something within our power to do!'

'Okay. I want us always to be friends, and not allow anything to screw that up. There, is that mushy enough for you?'

'What's that supposed to mean?' Dionne queried. 'That we have to be *just* friends?'

'I want everybody to do whatever the bloody hell they want, without having to write it down like we're holed up in some Famous Five gang-hut.'

'The Famous Five didn't have a gang-hut,' Oona sighed. 'It was the Secret Seven.'

'So what are we – the Shiraz Six?'

'You're so big-headed,' Oona scribbled while she spoke, 'you never like anything that isn't your idea. You just want everyone to admire how big and clever you are, all of the time – don't you?'

'She's seen right through me!' Singer threw his head back and held his arms and wine bottle aloft. 'She's right! I can't stand the bitter shallowness of my existence any longer!' And with that, he stepped backwards off the lip of the harbour and was gone. The other five stared, open-mouthed, all the more so when they heard no splash. Ronan and Frisby staggered to the edge, closely followed by the girls. Singer looked up from below, bottle to his lips. His head was just below the level of their feet, as he stood on the deck of one of the fishing boats, a stack of nets beneath him.

'Idiot!' Oona pronounced.

'How's your thumb?' Singer asked.

'Sore, actually.'

He passed her up a cloth handkerchief from his pocket. 'Wrap that around it very tightly – idiot.'

Back at the house, as everyone yawned and made to retire, Oona used two candlesticks to prop *Chambers's Miscellany* open on the mantelpiece. The flyleaf opposite the title page now read,

The Christmas Club
Rules
Oona, Dee, Melissa, Singer, Ronan and Jay hereby agree to:
1. Always spend Christmas at the Pier House.
2. Always dance formally on New Year's Eve.
3. Always respect the Pier House and its memories.
4. Never forget how beautiful the girls are.
5. Never forget how virile Ronan is.
6. Never let anything screw it all up.

Signed – Oona Tyler, Club Secretary and Commodore-in-Chief, Sunday the 1st of January, 1989, in her very own blood.

N.B. The rest of the blood in this book isn't mine, but you have to be a member to know about that.

Dionne had to go to work on Monday and she stayed in her room the Sunday she was due to leave, crying so much that Melissa offered to return to Dublin with her. When Singer heard this news, he immediately asked Melissa to accompany him for a walk along the beach. As Dionne packed upstairs, she saw them through her window and cried all the more. Singer was talking earnestly, gesticulating at the house and out to sea. Melissa appeared to be listening and not saying very much. Ronan and Frisby both insisted on accompanying Dionne and Melissa to the bus, so the car was cramped to bursting on its journey to Letterkenny, its chassis scraping the road every time it went over a bump.

At the bus station, Dionne hugged Singer for a long time and kissed him on the face. She started crying again and he comforted her. When Ronan finally got his turn at Dionne, the bus was starting its engine, but he held her like he would never let her go. Singer embraced Melissa briefly and she embraced Frisby even more briefly. She turned to Ronan to say goodbye, but his face was buried in Dionne's shoulder.

'How soon can you come to Dublin?' Dionne asked Singer as she climbed the bus steps.

'I'll be down before you know it,' Singer promised.

'I'll come with him,' Ronan added. Dionne smiled wanly, but by the time she reached her seat she was sniffling again. Singer, Ronan and Frisby watched as the bus pulled out of the station and lumbered off, spewing clouds of black smoke.

Dionne cried quietly into her sleeve for a few miles, then Melissa offered her a tissue, so she dabbed her eyes and blew her nose.

'I must look really feckin' stupid.'

'Not at all. I brought some water – would you like some?'

'No. I don't mean I must look stupid because I'm crying. I mean I must look stupid to you.'

'What do you mean?'

'It's obvious that Singer likes you instead of me. All that going for walks, doing the cooking together, that private little world the two of you have built around some dead woman... I guess I was fooling myself. You're a damn sight better-looking than me, I don't even know why I'm surprised.'

Melissa's face was serious, her gaze direct. 'I don't think I'm better-looking than you.' Dionne laughed sarcastically, but there was a flat, unprotesting quality to Melissa's tone that sounded completely sincere. 'And I don't think Singer likes me in the way that you mean. I'm not sure that Singer likes anybody – not even himself.'

'I saw the two of you on the beach today. He was gutted when he heard you were leaving – he didn't care about me.'

'He invited me for a walk because wanted to ask me about something.'

'What?'

'I can't say.'

'I knew it – I'm right.'

'I can't say because he asked me not to tell anybody.'

'Well, that's completely reassuring, thanks a bunch.'

'Dionne. If I wanted to fuck Singer behind your back, do you think I'd be sitting on this bus with you now?'

In spite of her chagrin, Dionne's mouth fell open. This was the first time she'd ever heard Melissa use such coarse language. Melissa turned and looked ahead, as if she was watching a very faintly amusing film that nobody else could see. Dionne stared out at the dreary bogland, sad and perplexed.

The last day at the Pier House dawned stormy. Oona knew without having to look that Singer's coat and boots would be gone from the hallway when she rose, so she swallowed some tea as she dressed, took a camera from his bedroom and set out, up the hairpin path. Hunched against the wind and rain, she stood and watched him from the edge of the headland as he clung to the pinnacle while entire frothing pyramids of water collapsed all around him. She took some pictures – badly, she assumed, because of the rain on the lens. Finally, she summoned the nerve to climb down and join him. Her hands shook as she traversed the wet rock and pulled herself up the pinnacle. She tugged at the back of his trouser leg, and when he turned to her, his eyes shone with wild delight. He helped her up and showed her where to put her feet and hands, to share the ledge in such a way that she could see, yet not get swept away. Then it came, a wall of white-green water that looked and sounded like a liquid skyscraper falling over on top of them, and the greatest shock was not the explosive noise nor the sheer immeasurable power of it, but the fact that the sea level seemed to be so much higher than their heads. She had never looked upwards at the sea before. Somehow, at the last second, they were not consumed, the wave leaning over and falling instead into the gorge below. Her body, pressed to the stone, felt the impact as a deep oscillation of all the water inside her skin, then an outrageous plume of spray burst upward, falling back down on top of them like a hundred freezing cold bathtubs emptied all at once. The sheer weight of the plummeting water crushed her further into the stone, and she realised, when the naked shock of it finally passed, that Singer had one arm around her, to prevent her from falling backwards off the pinnacle. The salt stung her eyes and nose; she was sure she'd swallowed half the Atlantic. Singer's hair hung over his eyes. He swept it back, grinning.

Frisby announced that he would take the bus to Dublin with Oona, in order to fly back to London. Just as he had with Melissa, Singer invited Frisby for a stroll along the beach before he set off. Oona's last act before leaving the house was to return *Chambers's Miscellany* to the bookshelves. She poured four glasses of dry sherry and made the men stand by as she mock-ceremoniously replaced it.

'There. We're part of this house now,' she declared. 'Even if we all died, and none of us ever returned, someone else might open this book years from now, and weave us into the fabric of the place – just as we have, with Sophia. Gentlemen – to the Pier House.'

'To the house!' They clinked their glasses and drank.

'To missing time,' Singer then added.

Oona smiled and downed the rest of her sherry in one.

With the other two delivered to the bus, Singer and Ronan spent their last evening in the pub, chatting to Manus. The following morning, they packed the car, then walked around the house, surprising themselves at its sudden emptiness. It was if they somehow expected to see Melissa exercising on the living room carpet, Oona holding court at the kitchen table, or Dionne flouncing down the stairs in her faux-fur coat. They locked the heavy front door and the secret life that buildings have when nobody occupies them silently resumed. They dropped the iron key off with Manus – there was no sign of Mrs McFall – and, after quite a few finger-crushing hand-shakes, set out on the long road back to Belfast.

11

Ronan asked to be dropped at his parents' house in the south of the city, but when Singer stopped at the garden gate of the anonymous, seventies-style bungalow, he seemed reluctant to step out of the car.

'It's not that I don't enjoy staying at your place,' Ronan lied, squinting along the street at all the other anonymous, seventies-style bungalows with their viciously pruned gardens.

'Of course not.' Singer tapped a tattoo on the steering wheel with his fingernails as the engine ticked over.

'It's just that…well, I've no money left, not a bean, and I suppose I'm going to have to face the music sometime.'

'You're twenty-seven. Tell your da to piss off.'

'If I do that, you can expect me back on your doorstep within the hour.'

'No probs.'

Ronan studied a freckle on the back of his hand. 'So, um, what's the story with Dionne?'

'What about her?'

'Will you be going down to Dublin to see her soon?'

'I'll be in Dublin at some point, I don't know when.'

'Yes. Well, I wouldn't mind heading down there myself – there's a few things I need to take care of.'

'Yeah? Like?' Singer knew that Ronan had about as much business in Dublin as he had in Beirut.

Ronan frowned. 'Oh, you know...stuff.' He patted his overcoat pocket. 'I suppose I could look Dionne up if I'm in town. The thing is, I could have sworn I had her phone number somewhere, but I don't know what I've done with it.'

'I hate that. I'm always losing people's numbers. Here.' Smiling slightly, Singer reached across Ronan's knees to the glove compartment, from which he extracted his copy of *The Love of the Last Tycoon*. Ronan saw Dionne's large, rounded handwriting on a scrap of paper sticking out of it. Singer copied the number onto a corner of the paper, tore it off and handed it to him.

'Thanks. And thanks for the holiday and for putting me up and all that.'

'Don't be silly, it was fun. Listen, good luck in there. Ring me, we'll go for a pint.'

Ronan watched from the garden gate as Singer's car roared off up the street. He gathered himself, hauled his leather suitcase up the path and rang the doorbell. As he waited for the door to open, he wondered if he could take his father on if it came to fisticuffs. Probably not. At the very least, he was in for a furious two-day lecture, extended across every mealtime for the foreseeable future, as long as he sought sanctuary in this place. But he had no other choice.

His mother, a little mouse of a woman, answered the door. Her face was red and puffy – she looked like she'd been peeling onions with her eyelids. She wore a brown trouser suit with a beige polo neck underneath it. Her hair was that indeterminate shape women's hair assumes in their mid-fifties, and she wore brown plastic earrings that easily predated the moon landings. Ronan was profoundly shocked when she stepped forward and threw her arms around him. She hadn't hugged him since he'd grown out of short trousers.

'You're here! You got my message! Oh, when I couldn't reach you in London, I rang Linda's parents in Maidstone, I hope you don't mind, but they said you'd...they said the two of you had...well, you know. And then I didn't know whether you were alive or dead! I thought maybe you'd thrown yourself off a bridge – nobody seemed to know where you were!'

'Relax, Mum, I was, uh, busy over Christmas. I'm thinking of changing jobs, and...'

'Linda's father said you no longer worked for him. He was quite adamant about that.'

'Yes, well, that's something I've been meaning to discuss with you and, ah, Alan. Is he here, by the way? Still at work?'

Ronan's mother took him by the sleeve. He dropped his suitcase in the hallway and she led him into the good room, the one he'd never been allowed into as a child. It was stuffed with disgusting ornaments of shepherdesses clutching lambs and roses, and the chairs and sofa still had clear plastic wrap on the cushions from the factory, his father having insisted on this to keep them clean. Ronan's mother guided him to the sofa, gestured for him to sit, then pulled a chair up close and poised on the edge of it, her back rigid, hands pressed together.

'Ronan, I'm afraid I have some very bad news for you.' She pursed her lips and her eyes filled with water. 'You're not the only one to have had the rug pulled out from under you in recent weeks.' Ronan felt a knot in his stomach. He pushed his glasses back on his nose. 'Your father...your father has left me,' her voice faded into a pitiful squeak, 'for another woman. Some...Jezebel in his place of work. A youngster, not even half his age.' She put her hands to her face and whimpered into them.

'Thank fuck for that,' Ronan exhaled and flopped backwards into the sofa. He gave a short but joyous laugh. 'That's the best news I've had in ages.' For the first time ever, he put his feet up on the coffee table.

The new dispensation in Ronan's parental home began immediately. Whereas he had been expecting to have to skulk in the shadows and spend his days in the local library while pretending to look for work, instead he was able to relax and take possession of the place. He tore all the industrial plastic off the sofa in the good room and spent a lot of time lying on it, with his feet up, reading. His mother, expanding outward from her bedroom now that the ogre was gone, put a picture of Audrey Hepburn on top of the television, and it reminded him of Melissa. She also waited on him hand and foot, cooking far too much food, glad to have him about the place, but perhaps more fundamentally, indulging her only son in ways that had been strictly forbidden up until that point. Ronan took full advantage, finding that his unexpected privileges even extended to being able to borrow his mother's car and, more importantly, her money.

His father eventually learned of his return, but Ronan was tickled when, instead of having to endure a self-righteous harangue, the man humbly invited him on the phone to meet in a city centre café. More out of curiosity than filial love, Ronan agreed, arriving to find his previously ultra-conservative progenitor wearing a black leather jacket with a Hawaiian shirt, his balding hair dyed reddish-purple with henna. The man looked ridiculous, even more so when his new squeeze showed up laden with shopping bags. She was young all right, but plump and very plain – in fact, she reminded Ronan of Linda, and he found himself averting his eyes when she ate a Danish pastry, using a knife and fork. His father, whom he had never, growing up, seen without a censorious frown on his face, fawned over the girl like a lovesick dog, grinning from ear to ear, even – yeech – holding hands in public. Ronan felt quite nauseated. However, upon parting, his father wrote him a cheque for three hundred pounds, and Ronan didn't care whether he was showing off or merely purchasing a salve for his conscience – he subconsciously filed the gesture away as yet another way his parents' realigned situation could be fruitfully exploited, for his father was a notorious tightwad, and obviously not in control of his actions. When the cheque cleared, Ronan went back into town and bought a whole new wardrobe, including two pairs of shiny brown leather brogues, a cream belted overcoat, a few lavender-coloured shirts and a nicely cut brown serge suit. For a plan was forming in his mind, and he would need to look the part.

When Oona returned to Dublin, she felt as if she were flying off the rails, only in very slow motion. Time moved as gradually as it had at Dunaldragh – every day seemed to last forever. But whereas in north Donegal the sensation had been delicious, like sweet liquid running down the side of a glass, back home in the city the hours seeped sourly. Her first instinct was to shut herself away in her mother's flat and not go out. Reluctantly, she began taking her Surmontil again and, after a few days, although she still felt detached and even a bit afraid, time sped up again and seemed to pass at something approaching a normal rate. She tried not to succumb to the creeping sensation that some godly hammer was about to be brought crashing down on her head. Bouts of nameless dread alternated with long periods of lassitude, when all around her seemed insufferably dull and her future inconsequential.

She forced herself to take long walks. These helped and gave her an excuse to call on Melissa, who was, unusually, not always home. Dunaldragh, Oona realised, had jerked Melissa out of her previously hermetic existence. On the occasions when Oona did find her home, the two sipped tea in the preternatural calm of the Ranelagh house and invariably agreed that neither had seen anything of Dionne, who seemed to have thrown herself into her work with a vengeance. During one visit, Oona noticed through an open door that Melissa had emptied an entire downstairs room of furniture, with the exception of a full-length mirror up against one wall. The floor was messy with what looked like old clothes, and mess of any sort was not something one associated with Melissa Montgomery. However, her host had casually closed the door and shown Oona upstairs without commenting. She then mentioned that she'd written to Singer – she explained that she'd been out researching the provenance of the Pier House sundial quote, and had uncovered much more than she'd bargained for. That conversation was the high point of Oona's January, and reinforced her determination to return, as soon as possible, to Dunaldragh.

Walking home from Ranelagh that night, inspiration struck. The following morning, Oona took a bus into town and walked through the entrance arch of Trinity College, her alma mater. She made her way through Parliament Square to the Museum Building, where she applied to undertake postgraduate research in Geology, her specific suggested area being the intense brittle deformations surrounding the Leannan Fault in north Donegal. She left uplifted, and a good-natured chat with one of her former tutors gave her the impression that acceptance would be a mere formality. So, the train may have wobbled, but for now, it stayed on the tracks.

1989 began bloodily in Northern Ireland, with five people murdered in January and ten in February, including a prominent solicitor, whose brutal execution while eating a family meal generated international headlines. Singer's phone rang every ten minutes with clients looking for pictures, but he ignored it, eventually leaving the receiver off the hook. He felt bad about being so unprofessional, but was afraid that if he talked to anybody, he might be persuaded into taking one more job, and like a man trying to give up drink or cigarettes, a single fall from the wagon might put him back where he started, photographing victims of violence full time. Not that there was any question of Singer giving up drink or cigarettes. However, these two luxuries apart, he lived frugally off the remains of the compensation money his Uncle Lucius had given him on his twenty-first birthday, awarded in trust over a decade previously, after Justice Ambrose Singer, his wife Betty and his eight-year-old daughter Carmen – along with a police bodyguard called John McClelland – were killed in an IRA car bomb close to the judge's home near Cultra, County Down.

Towards the end of January, he received a letter from Melissa. It read,

The Garden
Mornington Road
Ranelagh
Dublin 6

23 January 1989

Dear Gareth,

I hope you don't mind me using your Christian name. Somehow, it seems okay to call you Singer to your face, but starting a letter with someone's surname, even if it is their preferred one, seems intolerably formal. Anyway, I promised to write once I found out about the 'Clements' quote. I've spent quite a bit of time at the National Library – this is such an interesting topic, it requires more research. In the interim, I think you'll agree that what I've found raises more questions than it answers.

Firstly, the quote is from one John Owen, a Welsh poet and 'epigrammist' (now wouldn't that be a wonderful profession in this day and age), who lived from 1560 to 1622. The meaning I gave you is, I'm glad to say, correct. 'Times change and we

change with them.' Owen, in turn, seems to have borrowed the phrase from a much older source – 'Omnia mutantur, nos et mutamur in illis' *was the motto of Lothaire the First, a ninth-century descendant of Charlemagne. Can you imagine how complicated this could get if I allowed it?*

The bad news is, I'm afraid I can find absolutely no connection between John Owen the epigrammist and the Clements family, except that Owen was a devout Protestant and the Lord Leitrim branch of the Clements family first surfaces in Ireland in the early 1600s, fighting for our much-loved puritan invader, Oliver Cromwell. This could just be a wild shot, but the 'Tempus' quote is sometimes wrongly attributed to another John Owen, an English theologian who was Cromwell's chaplain in Ireland – this false path had me very excited for a day, conjuring up all sorts of nefarious connections between the hated Cromwell and the equally hated third Earl of Leitrim.

Leitrim's house, Lough Rynn, still stands near Mohill in County Leitrim – but the Clements family are long gone, and it was recently bought by an American. In the mid-1800s, the third Earl owned over 90,000 acres – four whole counties. His reputation as a ruthless landlord seems to be in no doubt, and various tracts from the time, most of them deeply partisan, imply or directly state that he had a horrendous attitude towards women. Droit de seigneur *and all that. However, this may have been a means of further blackening his name. His assassination in 1878 was a notorious event in this country. He's buried in Dublin, in the vault of St Michan's of all places, where the bodies mummify in the dry conditions. Have you ever been there? You can shake hands with one of the dead bodies (not Leitrim's). He was lucky to have made it that far – apparently there was a riot at his funeral, and they tried to throw his coffin into the Liffey!*

But here's the rub: the third Earl never married. He had no wife, and no children – however, in keeping with his vile reputation, Mohill is supposed to be peppered with his unacknowledged descendants. He seems to have been such a bad-tempered old coot that he fell out with his immediate family. He disinherited his nephew, his brother and two sisters, although he was supposedly kind to another sister, Caroline. He gave the bulk of his estate to a male second cousin, which must have seriously irritated the rest of them.

There's lots, lots more — detailed, eyewitness accounts of Leitrim's murder exist and they alone make fascinating reading. I could go on all day, but it's a matter of filtering all the information and trying to keep some focus on what's relevant. Of Sophia, there is absolutely no mention whatsoever. Was she one of his illegitimate children? A young mistress? Manus said the Pier House was built in 1861 and Sophia sent there the following year — that would have made her 17, and Leitrim 55. Personally, I'm inclined towards the illegitimate child theory, if only because Sophia refers, if you remember, to 'my father' in the coded poem.

Before you dismiss my theories as speculation, believe me, they're nothing compared to some of the stuff in the National Library. One of the newspaper stories published in the wake of Leitrim's murder claims that he had 'debauched' a young servant girl, the daughter of one of the killers. Yet another has a young servant girl turning up dead in the lake by his house, two days before he was done in! So you see, Gareth Singer, you have some way to go before you can even begin to live up to the reputation of this most eminent Victorian.

Finally, to other matters: I've thought carefully about your idea, and the answer is yes, I believe that I can do it. How well I'll do it is another matter entirely, but get in touch when you settle on a date. The more notice for me, the better. I trust all is well with you, and that your plans are proceeding apace. I have not heard from Dionne, but I do see Oona. She has been rather down since returning to Dublin, but leaving Dunaldragh wasn't easy for her.

Regards,

Melissa

Singer spent a morning at the table in his tiny living room, pondering Melissa's letter and scribbling notes, sipping whiskey from a teacup. Then he tore all the remaining photographs of rioters, soldiers and paramilitary funerals from his wall. He pinned up

Melissa's letter and dozens of pictures taken around Dunaldragh Bay. For the next two days, he didn't leave the house except to buy cigarettes as he elaborated his montage. He reprinted some photographs with darker exposures. Others he enlarged, to create different images – it was as if he was trying to project something from inside his head onto the peeling wallpaper. While enlarging the shots he'd taken in Dunaldragh churchyard, he noticed a detail in one that caused him to pause, reach for his magnifying glass, then rummage for the negative to blow the detail up further. He hung this particular print separately from the rest upstairs in his bedroom, so that he would see it every morning and remember to do something about it when the time came.

He bought a portable electric typewriter from an office supply shop downtown, which earned immediate pride of place on the living room table, alongside a ream of fresh A4 paper, a whiskey glass and an ashtray. Most nights he sat drinking, smoking and typing until late. Once, lost in thought, an unexpected image of Stacey Edwards slaving over her thesis at the same table popped into his mind, but he immediately banished it as an unnecessary distraction.

Towards the end of February, he sat in the café of the National Gallery in Dublin, waiting for Dionne to show up. Tearing himself away from his typewriter, Singer had travelled to the city that morning on impulse, to a see a painting. Just before setting out, he'd telephoned Melissa because he wanted her to see the painting, too. But when she hadn't answered, he'd chewed his lip for a minute, then rung Dionne at work. Now, he was beginning to regret having done so. She was half an hour late, he'd drunk three cups of coffee and he wanted to go to the toilet, then back upstairs to look at the painting some more. He'd already sat staring at it for over an hour. But he was afraid that if he left the café now, he'd miss Dionne, then there'd be a fuss. He was rereading his brochure for the fifth time when he glanced up and saw Melissa coming down the corridor towards the café. He was pleased, but confused. She entered the café and looked around. Then he realised that he'd been mistaken – the woman looked like Melissa, but was slightly shorter, and her face…the woman smiled and came towards him. When she reached the table, she bent forward, kissed his cheek and sat down.

'Sorry I'm late – I'm hanging for a coffee, is it any good in here?'

'Dionne. Jesus. What have you done to your hair?'

She patted the back of her black-dyed elfin cut, complete with heavy fringe. 'Do you like it? It's my new look.'

'I suppose. But you had such long, blonde...wow. You know, for a minute, I thought you were Melissa.'

Dionne frowned. 'I had it done in a much better place than the one she goes to. I'm sorry you don't like it.'

'Christ, no, I do like it, it's just that I thought you were...look, never mind – how the hell are you?' They exchanged pleasantries while Dionne had a coffee and Singer, after a hurried visit to the toilets, drank his fourth. Returning to the table, Singer noticed that Dionne had gotten quite skinny and that her clothes – black pedal pushers, a plain grey jumper...no, best not say anything about the clothes.

'So you're here to see a painting?' Dionne asked brightly. 'Which one?'

'It's a Böcklin, it's part of that nineteenth-century landscape exhibition they have upstairs.'

'You came all the way to Dublin to see one painting?' she asked, this time a bit too brightly.

'Yes. Well, no – to see you too, of course. It's on loan from the Metropolitan in New York, but the exhibition closes tomorrow and it's a damn sight easier to drive to Dublin than it is to fly to...look, do you want to come upstairs and I'll show it to you?'

'I'd be delighted,' she smiled. 'What are you thinking of doing afterwards?' As they climbed the stairs, Singer understood why he was feeling somewhat unnerved. Intellectually, he knew the woman at his side was Dionne, but the way she looked, talked and acted was nothing like the relaxed, self-confident person he remembered from Dunaldragh. Rather, she was stiff, more formal, yet with her mouth fixed in a strange little smile.

Singer stopped before a very dark oil painting, which depicted a curious-looking island, the colour and shape of a corrupted wedding cake, under a threatening sky. The island had a slice cut out of it, and a tall clump of black cypress trees grew at its impenetrable heart. Looking closely, Dionne could see a tiny, shrouded figure being ferried across the glassy water into the frightening, final embrace of the blackness.

'Yeech!' she recoiled. 'What is it?'

'It's called *The Isle of the Dead*. Böcklin was so obsessed by this image that he painted five versions of it in six years. They say he was inspired by San Michele, the cemetery island near Venice. It's one of the most beautiful images I've ever seen.'

'It's one of the most depressing!' Dionne, at last, was starting to sound like herself again. 'Why would anyone want to hang that shaggin' thing on their wall?'

'It makes me hope for a peaceful death. I don't mean that I want to die, but this picture represents the soul, on the very verge of understanding death's mystery. In my last hours, I would like to think that I'd achieve the same understanding, rather than fighting death or having my life ripped away from me.'

'Jesus, have you not been getting out much lately?'

'Now that you mention it, I haven't – I've been working very hard.'

'I thought you were giving up the photojournalism?'

'I have given it up. I'm working on something completely different.'

'What, taxidermy? Embalming, maybe? No, don't answer that. Look, we've seen the painting – let's go for a drink. I was rather hoping you'd take me to dinner.'

'Actually, I'd like to stay a little while – I want to look at this a bit longer. I'll probably never see it again.' Singer sat on a red leather bench in the middle of the floor. 'I could meet you again in a couple of hours, if you don't want to stay.'

Dionne swallowed. 'Never mind. Actually, I have something to do later. Enjoy yourself with your lovely painting.' She turned on her heel and walked for the door.

'Dionne!' Singer called after her. An elderly couple at a Turner peered over towards him, as did the gallery attendant. Dionne didn't hear Singer's footsteps in pursuit, so she kept on going down the stairs and out onto Merrion Square. By that time, she was crying. She stopped, pulled out a compact, dabbed her eyes and tried to fix her make-up. She caught sight of her new haircut in the mirror and flung her compact onto the road, where it was promptly crushed under the wheels of a passing car.

'You say you want to move to Dublin to do what?' Ronan's mother served him cream of celery soup with a ladle from a pot in the middle of the table. Ronan sat back a bit and shielded himself with his napkin, lest the woman splash any on his new trousers.

'I've done quite a bit of market research,' he announced loftily, 'and I'm convinced that there's an opening in the market for an arts magazine in Dublin.'

'A what?'

'An arts magazine,' Ronan repeated, before adding, with a touch of snideness, 'a bit like your *Woman's Own*, only with poetry, arts and culture, instead of recipes and knitting patterns.'

'That sounds nice.' She served herself soup and sat opposite.

'Yes. Well the thing is, you see, I'd need a few quid to get it going.'

'Oh.'

'Then there's the question of a flat. That would cost extra, but not too much. There are so many unemployed people in Dublin these days, property is dirt cheap. I would rent at first, of course – no need to buy straight away, but I would need somewhere decent.'

'I've never been to Dublin.'

'No, you haven't. So what do you think?'

'What do I think of what, dear?'

'Of investing in my new magazine?'

'Investing?'

'Yes. You lend me some money, and I pay you back with interest, later.'

'Would it be expensive?'

'A couple of thousand should get me going.'

'Oh dear, that's a lot.'

'Yes, but you're guaranteed a return in a few years. I mean, if I sit around here doing nothing, I'll be living off you and you'll never get anything back.'

'But at least I'd have you. I like you being here, Ronan – especially with your father gone. At last, we can finally do all the things we never got to do together. When I think what I put up with, for all those years…'

Ronan looked around at the kitchen, which had been the last word in culinary design – in 1970.

'But I'd be in Belfast quite often, covering exhibitions, and of course I'd come and stay. Then, when I have employees, I could take a back seat at the magazine and come and stay more often.'

'But if there are so many unemployed people in Dublin, why do they need an arts magazine?'

'Mum. Artists are always unemployed. Everyone knows that.'

'But could you not start an arts magazine here in Belfast?'

Ronan paused with his spoon halfway to his mouth. 'Yes, if I only wanted it to be two pages thick.'

'Why did I do it? Why the fuck did I do it?'

Dionne and Oona sat in the lounge of Wynn's Hotel. This time, they both cradled gin and tonics – large ones.

'Um, it's pretty radical all right.' Oona frowned at Dionne's hair. 'But I don't think it's you.'

'I'm not talking about my hair.'

'Oh. What are you talking about?'

'Well, I *am* talking about my hair, but why did I think he'd like me any better if I looked like Melissa? I am so…fucking…embarrassed. I've never done anything like this in my life.'

'No, you haven't.'

'I mean, usually I'm the one who's beating them off with a stick, you know? But nothing seems to work with this guy. I've tried everything, and I'm at that stage now where I…' Dionne looked away, her eyes filling. 'Fuck him. Just fuck him.'

'Dee, you are a very beautiful woman. I'd ride that oul' fella over there in exchange for half your looks.' She nodded at an elderly priest half-asleep over a thimble of port in the corner.

In spite of herself, Dionne laughed. 'Jesus, you'd kill him if you did.'

'Well he's about all I'm fit for. I haven't been too good myself lately.'

Dionne starting whining again, as if Oona hadn't spoken. 'Seriously, I don't know what to do.'

Oona sighed. 'Grow your hair back, is the first thing.'

'Thanks for the advice.'

'No, really, I'm growing mine.'

'Then what am I waiting for?'

'I don't mind you being self-centred, but there's no need to be nasty.'

'Sorry. I'm just annoyed at myself.'

'Look, can I say something?'

'What?'

'To be honest, I don't see what all the fuss is about. Singer is an okay guy, but he's no oil painting…'

'Please, can we not talk about oil paintings.'

'Whatever. Look, we went to Donegal, we had a ripping good time, now here we are back in dirty old Dublin, where you can have the pick of the crop.' Oona was lying, by dismissing her stay at the Pier House so casually, so she tried to sound more blasé than she felt. Now was probably not a good time to tell Dionne that she was hoping to work in Dunaldragh next winter.

'I don't want the pick of the crop, I want him.'

'Do you really want him that badly, or is he just unfinished business? Is this love, lust or plain old pride?'

Dionne pouted, and wolfed her G & T. 'Another drink, I think.' She waved her glass at the waiter.

12

Singer returned to the Pier House in July, when the forecast was for a week of good weather. His heart lifted as he drove through the forest at the top of the valley and down the hill, past McFall's, on down to the harbour then along the lane through the rocks, onto the sea-grass. He parked beside the sundial. The windows of the house had been lifted open and the building inhaled the fresh air as gladly as he. A slight zephyr blew onshore, the harbour was full of boats, the grass dunes wore a summer dress of sea-pinks and a high sun baked the bay and cliffs. The sea was a dark, imperial blue, settled but still powerful, sending in bright white waves that buffeted the beach in jest.

'Tell the director that I'm ready for my close-up.' Manus stood in the doorway of the house. His normal reddish hue had turned darker than nicotine. He wore jeans and a grimy white shirt with the sleeves rolled up. Singer stepped eagerly over to have his fingers mangled.

'Listen, thanks for everything you're doing, I'll make it worth your while.'

'I've never acted before, this should be interesting.'

'Well I've never directed before, so it could be very interesting.'

'How many did you say you have coming?'

'Seven more, apart from me. Five crew, two actors. You remember Melissa, don't you?'

'The tall, good-lookin' cutty?' Manus showed all his teeth. 'What kind of film is it you're makin' here?'

'Not quite what you have in mind,' Singer smiled, 'although there'll be a small bit of tasteful nudity all right.'

'Jayz, in my day, we were hard put to get a girl out to dance.' Manus grinned all the more, shaking his head.

'It's not that kind of film, you dirty old git.'

Manus roared and jerked his thumb at the house. 'I have the rooms ready, the place is dusted and cleaned. When do the others get here?'

'I pick herself up in Letterkenny tonight, the rest should be here tomorrow afternoon.'

'Then be sure and stop up for a pint later, won't you?'

When he was alone, Singer unpacked his car and spread a sequence of large black-and-white photographs on the kitchen table, showing the house and the island. One of the photographs didn't belong to the sequence – this one had hung in his bedroom for five months, waiting for what he did next, which was to climb into his car and drive back up the valley to the church. He walked around the little graveyard, referring to the photograph to establish exactly where it had been taken. The image had been blown up and it centred on a headstone half-hidden by another. On the half-hidden headstone was the word 'FALL'.

Singer quickly found the grave. The stone was a modest, modern, pink granite affair. When he saw what was engraved on it, he nodded with satisfaction, then returned to his car, where he put the photograph in the glove compartment. He lit a cigarette, and drove to Letterkenny to wait for Melissa.

The following morning, the air stopped moving and the land and the sea stood still, as if the entire world had been arrested by the sun's heat. Melissa had already been out for a walk by the time Singer woke, and he came down to the kitchen to find her packing a shoulder bag with sandwiches and apples. She wore sandals with thin leather ankle-straps, a pair of ragged denim shorts and a black vest. The outfit made her look even taller than he remembered her. Her legs seemed to go on forever.

'What's the story?' he yawned, his head fuzzy. He lifted a litre bottle of cheap white wine from beside the shoulder bag. 'Yummy – chilled. Good of you to fetch breakfast.'

'Give.' She took the bottle from him and wrapped it in newspaper before stuffing it into the bag. 'I bought it from Manus this morning, but it's for lunch, not breakfast.'

'Shucks.'

'He has a headache too, if that's any comfort to you.'

'It is, actually.'

'You said you wanted to spend today going over the script?'

'I think it would be very useful for both of us.'

'Then why did you drink so much last night?'

'Because I guess I'm just happy to be back here, and anyway, I work much better with a hangover.'

'Now isn't that a happy coincidence. Well, I'll be glad to co-operate, provided we can work outdoors. It would be a shame to waste that sunshine, so I've made us a picnic. But I have to warn you...'

'What?'

'I freckle very easily – is that a problem?'

'No, I'm told that our wardrobe lady is a total pro. She'll be whitening your face for some scenes, but for the flashbacks you're a healthy, outdoors type, so freckles are permitted.'

'And on the table here,' she indicated his photographs, 'is this a storyboard?'

'It's more of a guide to some of the principal shots.'

'But what we need to do now is fill in the detail?'

'Exactly.'

'Okay, let's go.'

'But I'm only just up.'

'You're dressed, aren't you? We're wasting sunshine standing here, so grab your scripts, Scorsese, and get a move on.'

They climbed the hairpin path to the tower and saw how, in the distance, the cliffs and coastline had dissolved in a heat haze rising from the flaccid sea. The island was like a hallucinatory purple blot, hovering under the ivory dome of the sky. It really was extraordinarily hot. By mutual, wordless consent, they climbed down the nose of the headland, past the base of the pinnacle overlooking the gorge, and down, further down, through a shattered temple of rocks not even

Singer would have dared attempt in the winter. But in this weather, the tortured grey shapes were warm to the touch, and the ocean no threat, so they descended to the water's edge, where they found a large tidal pool, enclosed on three sides by glistening, irradiated walls. The fourth side opened onto the sea, which rose and sank lazily and noiselessly.

Melissa set down the bag and removed her sandals, shorts and vest to reveal a simple black bikini. Her body was so long and pale, and her breasts so small, that only her hips gave it away as female. Singer tried desperately not to stare. Without a word, she dived neatly into the pool and swam to the bottom. She stayed under for some time, writhing through curtains of bright green seaweed like some giant, albino eel. He was indeed beginning to wonder whether she was blessed with gills when she surfaced on the far side and nimbly lifted herself out onto a boulder.

'Freshen up,' she commanded, gesturing at the water, 'then we'll get started.'

'But I didn't bring any swimming trunks.'

'So who's going to see you here?'

He looked around. Their private suntrap would have been visible only to a boat passing close to the tip of the headland, and even then, not for long. 'Have you ever seen a grown man naked?' he asked, kicking off his trainers. But she had already slipped back beneath the surface.

Just before she settled against a rock to read her script, Melissa removed her bikini top and donned a pair of sunglasses. Again, Singer hoped that his face betrayed nothing but supreme nonchalance as he redonned his T-shirt and boxer shorts. He hadn't dried, so they stained with patches of wet. He rummaged in his jeans for his sunglasses, which he then dropped in the pool and had to dart out an arm to catch them as they drifted downward in slow motion.

'*Sophia's Leaving*,' she read the title. 'It's nice that you kept her name.'

'The character isn't her, but she kind of gave me the idea for it. Actually, you gave me the idea for it.'

'Did I?'

'That time you talked about Sophia looking out of the windows of the Pier House. Sort of a timeless image – it came from there.'

For the next two hours, they read through the script, Singer taking the part of the other principal player, and Melissa standing, walking and striking poses, rehearsing expressions and emotions. He saw the pictures he'd nurtured in his mind for six months come alive as she made suggestions that improved on his work. Sharing the only pen he'd thought to bring, they scribbled on their respective copies of the script, and if he had been given a penny for the number of times he said 'That's exactly how I want you to do it tomorrow', he'd have been rich by the time they grew hungry for lunch. They swam again, then ate their sandwiches and passed the bottle of white wine back and forth. She offered him an apple, which he accepted.

'Do you mind me asking – how did you arrange the funding for this so quickly? I've never heard of anyone get money from a film board for making anything.'

'There is no funding - I'm paying for all this myself. I have a bit put by, and when I was here at Christmas, I couldn't stop thinking what a fine place it would be to set a film. So empty, so beautiful. By the time I left, I knew what I wanted to do next.'

'Very noble, and I'm all for artists pursuing their art, but why are you putting your life savings into a fifteen-minute film that will probably never make any money?'

'It's not my life savings. It's money I was given for other people's lives.'

'When your family was killed?'

'Ronan Doherty has an even bigger mouth than I thought.'

'Dionne told me, not Ronan. What happened?'

'There's no need to discuss it – I shouldn't have mentioned it.' Singer tossed a pebble into the pool and watched it sink.

'So we're going to have the classic actor–director relationship, are we?'

'What do you mean?'

'I'm supposed to bare everything of myself, while you remain smugly covered up.'

'I just don't think my family history is relevant.'

'Subconsciously, you obviously do.'

'Forget I said anything.'

'No. I grew up without a mother. Try me.'

He sighed. 'My father was a High Court judge. During the early years of the Troubles, he had a lot of people locked away. The police gave him a permanent armed guard – nearly all the judiciary had police guards back then, many still do. The IRA couldn't easily get at him, so they planted a roadside bomb, a very powerful one, close to where we lived in the country. The policeman was driving my mum, dad and little sister into Belfast, and brave men blew them up.'

'Jesus. Where were you?'

'Why does it matter?'

'*Quid pro quo.* You want me to take my clothes off for your camera, yet I know next to nothing about you.'

'I was locked in my room, for being bold. I was ten years old. I found a pot of white paint in the stable and told my little sister it was fairy dust. I guess my mum didn't appreciate me painting my little sister's clothes white, just before a trip into town. So they cleaned her up and went off without me, as a punishment.'

'So how long were you left locked in your room?'

'No time at all. The bomb was close to the house, and the blast so big it broke my bedroom window. In fact, that's what I remember of the actual explosion, crying into my pillow and feeling sorry for myself and all this stuff landing on my back and legs, and I looked around and it was glass. I went to the window and saw black smoke coming from behind the trees, so I climbed out onto the porch roof, jumped to the ground and ran up the road. I knew it was them.'

'Did you...see them?'

'The road where it happened was just one big hole. My dad's car had been thrown into a field. It was upside down, and on fire. Something I'll never forget – the field was ploughed, and I kept tripping over the furrows as I ran towards the car. They were still inside, what was left of them. The driver and my father had taken most of the blast. My mum was dead, but recognisable, and my little sister was pressed up against one of the windows, covered in blood. Her eyes were open, she could see me, and she...she was screaming. I wanted to open the car door to pull her out, but I couldn't get close enough, the heat was so awful, so I jumped up and down, I ran in circles and I threw myself on the soil and cried. After a while, she stopped screaming.'

In spite of the sun, Melissa had visibly paled. 'Did no one come to help?'

'After about ten minutes, a neighbouring farmer arrived. He tried to drag me away from the car, and I'm afraid to say that I bit him.'

The pair of them stared into the pool for quite some time, Melissa trying to imagine what Singer could see in it.

'Is this why you're intent on drinking yourself to death, because you want to join them? Because you feel guilty about your sister?'

Singer was taken aback. 'I don't drink that much.'

'Nobody else I know drinks whiskey for breakfast.'

'Hey! Go to Spain, and you'll see people drink a brandy with their morning coffee, it's no big deal.'

'This isn't Spain.'

'Today, it sure as hell feels like it. So what was it like for you?'

'What?'

'Growing up without a mother?'

'Oh. She died having me, so I never knew her.'

'That's tough. At least I have memories of mine.'

'I know you're deliberately changing the subject, but no, it wasn't that difficult. I had the best father a child could ever want, and I had him all to myself. It didn't occur to me until I went to school that things could be any different, and I loved my father so much, by that time I didn't care.'

'He must have been a great guy.'

'He was. He was quite a big stage actor in his day, but gave it all up to look after me. My mother's death hit him hard, but of course I didn't understand any of that until much later, after he fell ill.'

'Ill?'

'MS – multiple sclerosis. To anyone else apart from you, I'd say pray to whatever god you pray to that you never have to watch someone die from MS. It takes forever.'

'I'm sorry…'

'By the time he was really sick, I was old enough to take care of him, so we agreed he should stay at home – you know, instead of going into hospital. We had a nurse come over every day, so it wasn't too bad, I was able to do my studies. My father had a great take on life, he never stopped teaching me, reading to me, talking to me, encouraging me – I was very lucky to have such a person to myself for so long. He was an Epicurean.'

'You mean he liked food and wine and stuff?'

'That's a common misconception and an interesting reflection on the human condition – Epicurus was a Greek philosopher who laid down the rules of being happy, so everyone assumes he was either a gourmet, an alcoholic, a degenerate or all three. Far from it, he and his followers lived a very simple life in Athens, in a place called The Garden.'

'That's the name of your house, isn't it?'

She smiled. 'Daddy's little joke.'

'So what are the rules of being happy – be physically beautiful and speak as seldom as possible?'

'Reality springs from sensation, from your own experience, from nothing else. I prefer to watch, feel and think, instead of talk. I talk only when I want to, and never for the sake of it, which most people do, because they're terrified of silence. But I talk an awful lot to you, for some reason.'

'I'm flattered.'

'You should be. But I want to stop talking now, I'm sleepy.'

'So, do you feel better about undressing for the camera now?'

Melissa stretched her long body out flat beside the pool, rolling the one small towel she'd brought underneath her neck.

'I'll try to overcome my inhibitions.'

Singer smiled, and then yawned. He, too, had grown woozy. The sun had passed its zenith and cast shade into their roasting room in the rock. He sat with his back to her, staring out at the glassy sea. When he thought she might have dozed off, he rested down on one elbow. As he did, he felt a hand on his shoulder. It guided him lightly backward, until his head lay on her stomach. The hand stroked his cheek, then fluttered away, coming to rest half in, half out of the pool. He turned sideways, away from her ribs, and felt her stomach against his cheek, firmer yet softer than any pillow. The rhythm of her breathing sped up, then gradually slowed again. He tried to lie perfectly still, even closing his eyes and pretending to sleep, but he felt his arm beneath his body go to sleep instead, so he adjusted it, and in doing so brought his lips against her skin. He half-kissed it, more of a lazy nibble than a kiss. She stopped breathing. He raised his head, thinking he'd done the wrong thing, but her hand sprung from the pool and gently pressed him down again. He obeyed, and wisp-like fingers played with his hair. So he kissed her lower stomach again, this time with more purpose, licking lightly at the skin, and the hand quit his hair and tugged at his T-shirt. He was on top of her, pulling her bikini bottoms to one side. With sudden force, she threw an arm around his neck, heaving his face down to hers. They kissed, ever harder as he joined her. Her tongue was cold and tasted, for some reason, of cranberry. They writhed and pressed, then she bucked and he lost balance, and together they rolled over into the water. Their pelts screamed with the sudden cold, and he instinctively tried to tear away, but she wrapped her legs around him and held fast as they sank, bodies locked, mouths and nostrils bubbling. He closed his eyes against the salt water and came without really knowing what he was doing, but still she clutched him to her, even as the rocks at the bottom scraped his back, and ground her hips until she, too, had finished. Only then did she release him, and they surfaced, gasping and spitting. He splashed to the side, but, treading water, she kicked off her bikini bottoms and swam over to him, throwing an arm around his neck and wrapping her legs around him again.

Singer's mouth tasted of salt and blood. 'Are you taking…I mean, are you on the, uh, Pill, or anything?' He lay on the rock, staring at the sky. 'Because we just did…or I mean, I did, you know…twice.'

'No,' Melissa answered, as casually as if he'd asked whether she took sugar in tea. She slid into the pool, climbed out on the boulder opposite and stood, naked as a statue. 'But it's my safe time, I'm pretty sure we'll be fine.' She dived over the rock, into the open ocean.

'Well that's all right then,' he panted, 'I suppose.' When he realised where she'd gone, he dived in after her. The ocean was much colder than the pool, a chill current running up the underwater cliff. He felt the depths beneath him, as if he'd stepped out of an aeroplane and hung suspended in mid-air. In winter, these waters would have dashed them off the headland, filled their lungs full of foam, then swallowed them whole. Melissa trod water further out. He swam to join her.

'Look,' she nodded. The mouth of the gorge opened off to their right, and she sidestroked towards it. Reluctantly, he followed. The contrast between the gargantuan throat and the sunny little niche they'd just left was stark, and frightening. 'Shall we swim into it?' she asked. 'The water's calm enough.' Almost in response, a surge carried them to the entrance. As the dripping walls closed above, all turned to gloom, the only light a high, uneven strip of sky. Singer thought he could see a finger of rock where the pinnacle might be. Their eyes adjusted, and they made out a cave at the back of the gorge, choked with misshapen, dark-green boulders. 'We could make it,' Melissa whispered, as a wave lifted them, then rolled onward, breaking into the cave. 'I know I could,' she added.

But Singer was acutely aware of the cold darkness, and of a void beneath his feet, as if the gorge went down forever. 'No. What if one of us got a cramp?'

'Are you afraid?' she mocked. Before he could admit that he was, she put her head underwater and swam with neat strokes to the green rocks at the lip of the cave. She hauled herself out on one, where she sat like some parody of a mermaid, preening at the gates of Hell. He swam over to her, but stayed in the water, peering into the cave. All he could see were more boulders, disappearing into blackness. Then the cave exhaled, a freezing breath of air that smelled of seaweed and decay. Melissa trembled and stood on the rock.

'I think we've seen enough, don't you?' She dived over his head, and gratefully, he swam after her, back to the sun.

'I can't believe I've agreed to do a sex scene with that guy.' Descending the hairpin path, they could see the diminutive figure of Frisby, strutting around on the harbour. Singer had offered his hand to Melissa two or three times on the climb back over the headland, but she hadn't taken it. Now, they walked side by side, as casually as if they'd been for an afternoon stroll.

'It's not a sex scene, exactly.'

'Excuse me, I have to take off my clothes, get into bed with him, straddle him and fake an orgasm. I call that a sex scene.'

He laughed. 'It's a dream sequence, and it will be ever so elegantly shot, I promise you. And you won't be on top of him when you fake the orgasm, you'll be sitting on a bench with a fifty-four-year-old cameraman looking up at you.'

She snorted. 'Why did you pick Frisby, of all people? What makes you think he can act?'

'I don't think he can act, not in the same way you can. But in another sense, I think he's a very good actor, and his looks are perfect for the sort of handsome, foppish type I need for the part.'

'Sorry, you've lost me. You don't think he can act, but you think he's a very good actor?'

'When I went home after Christmas, I rang a newspaper contact in Warwick. There's no such thing as a country estate or even a farm called Chunsborough within a hundred miles of Leamington Spa. If there is, it's a damn sight smaller than five hundred acres. My contact also checked the companies register, and he spoke to a guy who runs a marine trade rag. Excelsior Yachts doesn't exist either. Listen to the names – "Chunsborough", "Excelsior" – they even sound made-up. Turns out they are. I think the little Lord Fauntleroy act is precisely that – an act.'

'You have a hard, suspicious mind, Gareth Singer. Who else have you been checking up on?'

'Nobody. But what was it you said, about all our perceptions coming from sensations? I sensed when I met Frisby that something was off. I knew a few genuine Hooray Henrys when I was a student in London, and it was as if he was trying too hard to be one, a sort of indentikit posh boy. Millions of wannabe yuppies have reinvented themselves in the eighties – I'd say our little friend is one of them.'

'So who is he, really?'

'What does it matter? Who are you? Who am I? Who is anybody, other than the face we present to the world? As long as he can keep up his act for the duration of my film, that's all I care about.'

'What, ho!' Frisby hollered. He'd spotted them on the path, and trotted up towards them like a terrier. He threw himself at Melissa, who returned his hug politely, then he pumped Singer's hand. He wore a pink shirt, brown loafers, pale slacks and a cricket jumper tied around his shoulders. 'So how are you crazy kids?' he cried.

'All the better for seeing you,' Singer smiled. 'How's the yacht business?'

'No idea, old chap, I was headhunted by a merchant bank. I'm in the City now, working on flotations.'

Singer laughed, slapped him on the back and walked on. He'd spotted a large grey van that had stopped where the road ended, too big to fit up the lane to the Pier House, where Frisby had parked his hire car. Three men and two women stood around it, smoking. 'I think our crew has arrived.'

'You weren't joking when you said you had a ready-made film set.' Vaughan, a cameraman with big grizzled sideburns and a pot belly, sat by the range, peering up at the high ceiling. 'This kitchen alone is bigger than my entire bloody house.'

'And I wasn't joking when I said there's no electricity – you brought a generator for the lights, right?'

'It's all in the van.' Sears, Vaughan's assistant, was a slight, sharp-faced man, whose one lazy eye and permanently fixed baseball cap – presumably intended to mask the lazy eye – made him resemble an extra from *Deliverance*.

'Well, I want to get to work on this lovely lady straight away.' Charlie Pine, a maternally plump woman with big earrings and a permanent grin, stroked Melissa's hand, who sat beside her at the table. 'I want to check that dress for size, and try on some wigs, so we find one that sits on your pretty head just right.' Melissa retreated behind her faint smile. Singer felt hypersensitive towards her, in a way that he'd never felt before, but he betrayed nothing, instead handing out sheets of paper to the assembled group, which also included Frisby, Brian the soundman, Manus and Vaughan's daughter, a young, robust woman called Mandy, whom Vaughan had suggested as a runner. Diplomatically, Singer had agreed. He coughed, and addressed them.

'I have a shooting schedule worked out, starting early tomorrow. We sleep here in the house – it's big, but basic, although you'll learn to love it. The nearest hotel is thirty miles away, which is impractical, given that all our locations are around the house or on the island. Manus, who plays our boatman both on and off camera…'

Frisby shouted 'Yayyyy!' and clapped. Everyone else stared at him in silence.

'…Manus is also our caterer, and has kindly agreed to come down and cook us breakfast every morning. But the really good news is that he also owns the only pub around here, so not only will he do us a hot dinner in the evenings, I'm also running a nightly tab for cast and crew.' This latter statement drew noises of approval from the newcomers. Manus beamed like the sun. 'This is the script.' Singer handed out copies from a pile on the table. 'For those of you who haven't read it yet, I'll run through the storyline. Harry Benson here,' he gestured towards Frisby, who bowed, 'has arranged to meet his girlfriend Sophia,' he nodded at Melissa, 'for a trip to a lonely island to stay in a big, empty old house. We first see Harry at the harbour, pacing up and down, waiting for Sophia to arrive, but she doesn't. The boatman tells Harry that he must make the round trip before nightfall, so Harry decides to go to the island, after making the boatman promise to watch out for Sophia, and bring her first thing in the morning. We shoot this to make it seem as if the Pier House is in fact out on the island. Harry arrives, explores the house and the island, which is abandoned. As he explores, he wonders where Sophia is, so we see flashbacks of him and Sophia doing routine stuff together, every inch the healthy, happy, outdoors-loving couple. He's puzzled, but resigns himself to a night alone in the spooky house. He drinks whiskey in the darkening kitchen and imagines that he hears Sophia's voice, coming from somewhere in the house. He runs from room to room and does a pretty good job of scaring himself. But eventually he goes to bed – we even have a four-poster upstairs for this – and during the night, he awakes to find Sophia standing in his room, looking out the window. But this isn't quite his Sophia, she's wearing a black Victorian dress, and her hair is much longer, tied up in an old-fashioned bun. This sequence is shot in a way that implies Harry is dreaming. Sophia doesn't speak when he asks her questions, it's almost as if she can't hear him, but instead she turns around, lets her hair down and undresses, so he plays along.'

'Yayyyy!' Frisby repeated – this time nobody bothered to look up.

'Sophia makes love to Harry, and he falls asleep. He wakes in the morning alone in bed, and, after looking for her around the house, assumes she has gone for a walk. So he steps out for a look-see, but starts to panic when he can't find her. He runs around the island, calling her name – nothing. But he spots the boat returning, and when it arrives, he interrogates the boatman, who denies bringing anybody to the island the night before. Harry insists that Sophia must have travelled out by other means, and fears that she went for a morning swim and is in trouble. So the boatman takes him all around the shore, but still they find nothing. Completely bewildered, Harry gives up, but jumps off the boat as soon as it reaches the mainland, runs to the pub and uses the pay phone to ring Sophia. No reply. So he rings her mother, who sounds awful, and she tells him that Sophia was killed in a car crash driving up to meet him. Cue tearful devastation on his part, and a final shot of the island. Cut to the front of the Pier House, where we see Sophia standing at an upstairs window, wearing her Victorian outfit. Camera pulls in, she turns away from the window, fade to black. It's your basic, straightforward ghost story, so plenty of dramatic lighting, minimal dialogue, lots of atmospheric shots. Any questions?'

'Yes.' Charlie Pine raised her hand, smiling sweetly. 'Do you know you have a very large hickey on your neck?'

'What's a hickey?' asked Frisby.

'Jump in the car, I want to show you something.'

'I don't think that's a very good idea. That wardrobe woman *knows*, she can smell it off us. Go and put a shirt on, she's right – I must have savaged your neck.' Singer and Melissa had been left alone in the kitchen while Frisby and the crew creaked around upstairs, haggling over bedrooms and unpacking bags.

'You have to see something,' Singer insisted. 'It has nothing to do with what happened today.' Reluctantly, she followed him to the car. But as they set off down the track, she reprised her theme.

'Listen, I think what happened today, to borrow your euphemism, was good for both of us. I enjoyed it, and I hope you did too.' Singer stared at the road ahead. 'But I don't want that crew to think that your film is some vanity project for your girlfriend. I want them to take me seriously. So, no holding hands, and separate beds – are you okay with that?'

'Sure.' Singer tried to sound diffident, partly because of Melissa's intimidating self-certainty, but partly because he wasn't sure what he really was feeling – a combination of elation and fear, probably. Nonetheless, he enjoyed the puzzlement on Melissa's face when he pulled up outside the old church. He killed the engine, reached across her into the glove compartment, extracted the graveyard photograph and handed it to her.

She frowned.

'What is this?'

'It's a blow-up of a shot I took for no particular reason, the day you brought me to Sophia's grave. When I developed it, in the background, I noticed the word 'FALL' on one of the headstones, so yesterday, I came back for a second look. Come and see for yourself.'

They walked around the side of the church and he led her to the granite headstone. It read,

Here lies DECLAN MCFALL

Of Dunaldragh, drowned

24th December, 1978,
aged 24 years old

*'For I will go down into the grave
unto my son mourning.'* GEN. 37:35

Melissa held a hand to her mouth, then gently leaned her head
against Singer's chest. 'Forget everything I said in the car,' she whispered. 'Please, hold me.'

It was the last day of the shoot, the final scene. Everyone was tired
after a week of work and drink. Melissa's magic, the sheer presence
she kept hidden and that seemed to come from nowhere the second
the camera starting rolling, had lifted what Singer knew to be a pretty
mundane story into something much better than it should have been.
Even Frisby had been passable, although Singer had run him ragged,
making him do take after take, to be sure of having something useful.
But now, they had set up in the hallway of McFall's, for the scene
where Frisby's character learns on the phone that his girlfriend is, in
fact, dead – and Frisby was unable to look suitably shocked. Singer
had tried everything.
    'Imagine your parents have been murdered by a knife-wielding
maniac. Imagine someone has emptied your bank account. Imagine
England have lost at cricket.'
    But nothing worked. So he called a break and offered the crew a
lunchtime drink. He sent Mandy the runner down to the Pier House
to fetch Melissa, who had finished all her scenes and was sunbathing
on the pebble beach. He ordered Frisby a large gin and tonic, then
two more in quick succession. Mandy returned with Melissa, who
wore her black bikini with a blue sari skirt, sandals, sunglasses and a
floppy straw hat.
    'Yes?' she enquired of Singer. He offered her an empty chair,
carried out from the pub into the sunshine.
    'I thought you'd care to join us for a drink.'
    'But I was perfectly...'
    'A nice iced Martini and soda, perhaps?'
    'Yes, but...' He disappeared into the narrow hallway, which was
stuffed with tripods, lights and cameras. Cables trickled about like

black snakes. When he re-emerged, Melissa had settled. The men pretended to chat idly, but all of them, especially Frisby, feasted on her flawless now-brown skin, endless legs and elfin face. After a few more drinks, Singer asked Frisby and the crew to get back into position, which they all did, grumbling. Melissa made to leave, but Singer asked her to sit and watch, from the chair that he had surreptitiously positioned to be visible from the pay phone. Frisby found his mark and held the receiver to his ear, swaying slightly. Singer asked Vaughan if he was rolling, and when he got the nod, he stepped forward and bent his head to Frisby's, whispering in his ear. Frisby peered down the hallway, but as Singer whispered, his eyes widened with surprise. Singer stepped out of shot and, as Frisby held the phone, his eyes filled with tears. He tried to wipe them away, but they filled faster than he could wipe. He rested his head against the body of the pay phone, and gave Singer a hurt, bitter look.

'You bastard!' he hissed through clenched teeth. He flung the receiver against the wall, and stormed off up the hall. Singer told Vaughan to cut. Melissa, pleasantly surprised, rushed forward to congratulate Frisby on his performance, but he brushed her off and stalked down the road towards the Pier House. She watched him go, then beckoned Singer across the road into the shade of the trees. It took all of her skill to let him hear the anger in her voice, without showing it in her stance.

'I thought he was acting, but he wasn't, was he?'

'What do you mean?'

'You told him, didn't you? You told him about us!'

'I gave him a bit of necessary direction.'

'You think you're so fucking smart, Gareth, but you don't give a shit about anyone's feelings.'

'Without that final shot, I had no film. Sorry.'

For a moment, she looked as if she might lift her hand and slap his face. But she visibly brought herself under control and pushed past him, through the rusty gate that led down onto the sea-grass.

13

'So, how's your magazine going?'

Ronan had invited Dionne for a drink after work. Having put him off three times in as many months, citing deadlines, she'd finally caved in and he had suggested the front lounge of the Shelbourne Hotel. She'd arrived, dressed in a sharp cream suit with a knee-length skirt and padded shoulders, a striking slice of feminine modernity against the dowdy Victorian décor of the lobby. She peeled off a pair of red leather gloves and hung a dainty umbrella over the side of her chair. It dripped a September shower onto the carpet.

'First issue's just out.' Ronan reached inside his briefcase and slid a copy across the table. 'So I brought you one.'

'It's funny to see you wearing a suit and tie.'

He pushed his glasses back on his nose, blushing. 'You've, uh, really changed your hair.'

'Do you like it?' She turned her head from side to side, displaying a geometric cut and a pair of red, triangular earrings. 'I've gone blonde again – I tried dark, and it seriously didn't suit me. I'm thinking of growing it back long, actually.'

'I liked it long.' He poured himself coffee from a silver pot.

She smiled thinly and, without lifting it, made a cursory study of the magazine. '*Avalon?*' she read the title. 'What's Avalon? I used to own a farm, now I only 'ave a lawn?' She tittered at her own wit.

'It's a reference to Yeats,' he sniffed. 'Most people involved in the Irish arts scene would spot that…'

'Oh, sorr-eee.'

'…but it's also a nod towards Arthurian myth, obviously, which is the foundation of so much literary and…'

'It was a Roxy Music album! No, wait, it was a single, wasn't it?' She sang the next word, 'Av-a-lon…hold on, maybe it was both? God, whatever happened to Roxy Music, eh?'

'I shall make urgent enquiries for the next issue.' She feigned not to notice the sarcasm in his tone.

'I used to have such a huge crush on Bryan Ferry – mad, isn't it?'

'Speaking of which,' Ronan blushed, and coughed, 'I'd like you to read something on page twenty-three.' Dionne raised an eyebrow, but lifted the magazine and flicked through it. 'Top left-hand corner,' he instructed. The top left-hand corner of page twenty-three was occupied by a short poem. It read,

Girl, by the sea

Her skin is the sea, lucent.
Her arms are the waves, all-enfolding.
Her thighs are the beach, white as quartz,
And her eyes are bright stones – agate,
Cornelian,
Drifting on the laughter of the gulls.
Clouds pass – her hair.
I could stay amongst her, linger,
And let the tides of her existence wash over me.

The poem was signed *R.C. Doherty, for D.B.* It took a couple of seconds to dawn on Dionne who D.B. might be, but when it did, she felt her cheeks burn and turn as red as her earrings. Her sophisticated, girl-about-town façade crumbled in that instant, and she flailed around for something to say while she tried to rebuild it. The best she could manage was, 'Uh, umm…what does the C stand for?'

'Well, I'm using the sea as a metaphor, for a woman's—'

'No, I meant the C in your name. As in R.C.'

'Oh. That. My middle name is Colum.'

'Colum.'

'I don't use it, except in my signature.'

Dionne babbled. 'Well now there's a funny thing – middle names, huh? My middle name is Ursula, so I never use it, especially not as an initial.'

Ronan frowned. 'Yes. Dub. How quaint.'

'So, how long are you in Dublin for?' She decided that the best way to deal with the excruciating embarrassment of the so-called poem was not to deal with it at all. She closed the magazine and placed it back on the table, then moved her hands away from it, as if it had nothing to with her – which indeed it hadn't.

'I'm here for the foreseeable future. I have a lot of confidence in *Avalon*, and I need to be Dublin based, so I've found a nice big flat on Herbert Street, just five minutes' walk from here, actually. You should come over and see it some time.'

'You bought a flat?' Dionne gratefully seized on the change of subject.

'No, just renting for the present.'

'If they offer you the chance, buy it.'

'I should hardly think so, it's very old. If I was going to buy, I'd want something vastly superior. But perhaps it has potential – I'd love you to give me your professional opinion. I'd cook you dinner.'

'Trust me – if it has walls, buy it, no matter what condition it's in. Dublin is on the verge of going mental.'

'How do you know?'

'Number one, I work for a firm of architects, and I'm getting very familiar with the whole property scene. There's a lot of interesting things happening out there,' she winked, 'if you know what I mean. Number two, Dublin is so decrepit, things can only get better. It's way under-priced for a European capital. I've already put all my wages into a house in Donnybrook, along with a girl from work. As soon as I can afford to, I'm buying her out.'

'Oh. So you're not living at home any more?' Ronan's privately nurtured co-habitation fantasy dissolved to dust. He could have edited his magazine and written her more poems, while she went to work then hurried home every day to their comfy flat in Herbert Street, for all the treats he'd have in store for a wonderful girl like her.

'God, no. I just had to get away from my family. At long last, my very own bedroom, and no sneaky sisters to steal my knickers.' She cocked an eyebrow. 'Or maybe it was my brothers, come to think of it.'

'Will you be going to Dunaldragh this Christmas?'

Dionne studied her nails, the red of which matched her earrings, gloves and umbrella, but thankfully, no longer her cheeks. 'I don't know. I haven't thought about it. You see, I kind of like stuff like central heating, telephones and light bulbs.'

'Haven't really thought about it myself,' Ronan interjected. 'I might be busy with the magazine, and sure, if we're both in Dublin for Christmas, we could always spend some time together and...'

'Is Singer going?' She looked at him, bluntly and directly.

He paused. 'I believe so. I haven't seen much of him – you know he was back up there in the summer, making a film with Melissa and Jay?'

'No, I didn't! When?'

'July, I think.'

'Why did nobody tell me?'

'I've been ringing you since I moved down, trying to get you out, and since this is the first...'

She waved her hand. 'Never mind, tell me more about this film.'

'Well, Jay merely informed me that it was happening, and that was back in June. I never particularly thought of Singer as the creative type, and I've been up to my eyes with the magazine – which I'm very excited about, by the way. For the next edition, I'm hoping to—'

'What's the film about?'

Ronan frowned and took a long sip of coffee. 'I saw Singer about a fortnight ago, but you know what he's like when it comes to explaining anything. And since I don't have contact numbers for either Melissa or even Oona...'

'Melissa's gone totally quiet, but then, I've been insanely busy at work, as you know. I saw Oona last week, she's going back to the Pier House in November.'

'You mean December.'

'No, in early November. She's started studying again, and she wants to go look at rocks and stuff.'

Just then, a tall man with thick black hair and brown eyes walked up behind Dionne and put his hands over her eyes.

'Guess who?' he grinned.

Dionne leapt up and hugged him. 'Greg! This is Ronan Doherty, d'you remember, I told you how I spent Christmas at that mad place in Donegal...' Greg smiled winningly and shot out a dry, manly yet well-tended hand, which made Ronan's feel wet and limp in comparison.

'Pleased to meet you. Gregory Fielding – but everyone calls me Greg.'

'I'm sure they do,' Ronan responded, without quite knowing why.

'Ronan met me for a drink after work, and do you know,' she looked around, 'I haven't even got around to ordering one! What will you have?'

'Table's booked for seven.' Greg consulted a wafer-thin watch with a black leather strap.

'Oh god, I had no idea it was so late. Ronan,' she pulled on her gloves, 'we have to do this again real soon, okay?' Ronan nodded dumbly. Dionne took Greg's arm and made a telephone receiver out of her free hand. 'Stay in touch!' The couple stepped away, then she realised she'd forgotten her umbrella, so she swung around, snatched it, mouthed 'Bye!' and they were off, out the revolving doors.

Ronan saw that she'd also forgotten her copy of edition one, volume one of *Avalon*. He jumped up to pursue her, but knocked his coffee pot over, which emptied itself all over the magazine. Seamus Heaney's kindly yet pensive visage turned dark brown, as he pondered potatoes and the problems of mankind. Ronan slumped back into his armchair.

'Bugger!' he announced to the middle-aged ladies sipping tea on the sofa opposite.

When Trinity College accepted Oona as a research student, she stopped drinking and cut down on her smoking, which for two months was sheer hell, the only salvation a fine Dublin summer that allowed her to bathe at the Forty Foot in Dun Laoghaire every day. This started off as a penance, a sort of mortification of the flesh, but she quickly grew addicted and supposed that the morning plunge into the freezing-cold sea must be releasing endorphins, because she always felt great afterwards. The old men who clustered at the bathing spot jokingly chatted her up, making her laugh and feel welcome. She ate more healthily, and by September she could bear the sight of herself in a mirror. She allowed her hair to grow and bought clothes with the money she saved on alcohol. She got on much better with her mother, a dotty if kindly former air hostess who lived off a generous pension. Significantly, her mother stopped hinting about her finding a place of her own, although this remained, in her own head, a medium-term priority. She even weaned herself off her anti-depression tablets without any apparent ill effect.

Still, by the time the Trinity term commenced in September, she was incredibly lonely. She had seen Dionne precisely twice in four months. Her friend seemed to be doing well for herself, and made sure on both occasions that Oona knew it. But strangely – very strangely – Oona didn't feel jealous. Melissa had returned from her film-making debut in July looking more stunning than ever. Without being able to articulate quite why, Oona was peeved that Singer hadn't invited her to participate, but upon analysing her peevedness, decided it probably had more to do with Singer, Melissa and Frisby having an adventure in Dunaldragh without her, for certainly she knew absolutely nothing about film-making. Melissa didn't have much to say about the experience, except that Dunaldragh had been very pretty but the film hard work. In August, she had disappeared off to Manchester, to understudy Helena in some regional production of *A Midsummer Night's Dream*, so that by the autumn, Oona felt starved of company.

However, the day came when she found herself packing for her field trip to Dunaldragh, and suddenly her months of self-denial all seemed worthwhile. Here she was, returning to a place that made her happy, healthy in mind and body, with a sense of professional purpose and a very merry Christmas to look forward to, when she would finally cut loose and laugh, drink and relax with the others – for there was no doubt in her mind that they would all come.

Manus arranged a taxi to drive her the thirty miles from the Letterkenny bus, and although she arrived in a pelting rainstorm, the sweet smell of burning turf mixed with salt in the air made it feel like she'd never been away. The Pier House itself seemed grey and huddled against the deluge, but Manus greeted her in the doorway and stayed for a mug of tea, a fag and a chat in the well-warmed kitchen. He asked her whether she'd seen Singer's film, and when she said that she had not, he grinned and told her that he'd been sent a copy, but had no video player to watch it on. He would borrow one and organise a screening up at the pub over Christmas, now would-n't that be a good night's craic? Oona agreed that it would. He carried her bags up to Sophia's bedroom, then hung the big iron front door key on a hook on the kitchen dresser and left. She unpacked her field equipment onto the kitchen table – her hammer, notebooks, maps, measuring tape, a compass-klinometre, a hand lens and a camera.

That night, she lit a fire in the living room, which, being empty apart from her, felt even bigger than she remembered it, but she curled up in her favourite armchair beneath an oil lamp and read the entries entitled Gems, Geneva, Genoa, Gentian, Geography, Geology, Geometry, England's Georges, Georgia and Geranium from *Cassell's Book of Knowledge*, Volume 4 – FLO to ISIS, no date given, but from the photographs and contents of the articles, published no later than the mid-1920s. This she had selected from one of several sets of old encyclopaedias that occupied the lower shelves. She fantasised about living in the Pier House forever and reading every last one of them, all the way through.

She grew sleepy and took a candle through to the kitchen to fetch a glass of water. As she turned from the sink, she saw that her field equipment had disappeared from the tabletop and instead there lay a motionless human form, covered entirely by a linen sheet, stained wet in places. She dropped the glass, which exploded with a sopping bang at her feet, and she nearly dropped the candle, too. She let out an involuntary yelp and her first thought, bizarrely, was for her field equipment – it was nowhere to be seen. The body on the table lay towards her head-first, and she wondered who could have put it there, because the house was deathly quiet, the only sound the wash of the waves. She approached the table, terrified, and reached for the sheet to pull it back and see who was under it, but a sudden impact made her jump, and she awoke pumping sweat in the armchair, the encyclopaedia having slipped off her knee onto the living room floor. She leapt up, seized the oil lamp and fled for the stairs. Halfway up, she stopped and walked slowly back down again, heart revving like an engine. Casting shadows away from her lamp, the coat-hooks made the hallway look like an abattoir. Reluctantly, she pushed at the kitchen door with her foot, holding the lamp high, not daring to enter. Her field equipment lay spread, waiting, across the big old table.

When the gathering seas permitted, Manus took her out in his boat to make observations along the eastern cliffs and also west around the headland. But he couldn't go too close to the gorge, as already the waves heaved, pitched and tugged at the vessel, seeking to do it a mischief. He told her that, as a lad, he'd taken a few friends in a rowboat all the way into the gorge on a still summer's day. He described a deep cave, ringed with boulders, that none of them had dared set foot in. The pair traded information, Oona pointing out different strata on the cliffs and explaining how they came to be there.

'A geologist thinks in four dimensions,' she explained, 'the fourth being time. Time is the tricky part. The earth's surface is a jigsaw that's constantly being pulled apart and then reassembled – understanding the "how" is much easier than working out the "when".'

In return, Manus had shown her promontories on the cliffs, which ancient people had converted into crude fortresses. He said that the name Dunaldragh was derived from such places, translating from the Irish as 'high fort'. He told her legends from the island, about cursing stones and early Christians, and explained that its name, Inistrahull, was open to interpretation – *Inis Tra Fola* meant 'Island of the Strand of Blood', *Inis Tra Thall* meant 'Island of the Distant Shore' and *Inis Tra Ulai* meant 'Island of the Tomb'. He also showed her where ships had struck rocks and pointed to a spot where several German submarines had been scuttled after the Second World War. When news of Germany's fall had come through on their radios, the U-boats had moored in Dunaldragh Bay, which during the war was in neutral territory. The crews had come ashore in dinghies, and the officers had bartered ceremonial swords and sidearms with his father in exchange for beer. These relics formed the basis of the collection that now graced the ceiling of the pub. The sailors had gotten mad drunk for two days, then taken their submarines on round into British waters to surrender. Oona wished she could have been there.

She broke her vow of abstinence gently, walking up to the pub of an evening, particularly if she'd spent the day alone. Sometimes, a few of the fishermen would be in, sipping pints at the bar, and she fell into easy conversation with them, enjoying their subtle, understated humour, while they in turn relished her bawdy wit and her cigarettes. Then, descending the hairpin path one afternoon in early December, her knapsack heavy with samples, she saw Singer's car parked beside the sundial.

He was sitting at the kitchen table, smoking and sipping whiskey from a teacup. Several bright yellow duty-free bags stood on the dresser. His clothes were casual, but much smarter than usual. He'd lost weight and he looked tired.

'Hi,' she laughed, hugging him, 'you're early! It's still three weeks to Christmas!'

'I know.' His voice was hoarse. 'I've come straight from Dublin Airport. I've been away for ages – I had no idea you were here. I hope I'm not intruding.'

'Where have you been?'

'Film festivals. I was in Toronto, then a couple in LA.'

'LA? Listen to you! It's Tuesday, so it must be LA! You don't hang around, Mister Big Shot!'

Singer smiled, and waved dismissively. 'It's not like that. I finished my little film pretty quickly and just jumped on a plane with it under my arm. I hadn't even entered it anywhere, but Toronto let me show it anyway, and I tell you what, I'm really bloody glad they did, 'cos I got a lot of interest.'

'What kind of interest?'

'There's something really weird happening in the outside world right now. All of a sudden, everyone's interested in everything Irish. I dunno, maybe it's U2, maybe it's just our turn to be fashionable, but that whole Celtic melarkey is hot, let me tell you.'

'It's the age of Aquarius,' Oona pronounced with a sneer. 'The Berlin Wall is down, the Cold War over, and the nineties are almost upon us. Hardnosed is out, cuddly is in. All the women's magazines are full of crap about crystals, aromatherapy, ethnic cookery and handmade hessian underwear. Every decade is a reaction against the one that went before, and the eighties were so brash and greedy, the marketing men need a new angle to sell us their shite. No wonder the Irish are fashionable,' she leaned against the dresser, grinning, 'we're so free-spirited and mystical, and unblemished by the modern world. The nineties will be Ireland's decade, just you wait and see.'

'Yes,' he nodded vigorously, stubbing his cigarette out and immediately lighting another, 'you're absolutely right. It's not a bad little film, but I'm a nobody, a beginner, yet I had all these top producers waving contracts and money under my nose.'

'What else did they wave under you nose?'

'What d'you mean?'

'You look fucked.'

'Um, yeah,' he chortled, 'there were quite a few late nights. It's crazy over there. I was hanging out with these two guys, mega-rich, they used to be music promoters, now they're totally into film. Big, fat, hard men, but they knew everybody. They dragged me to parties and said things like' – at this point he put on a crass American accent – 'hey, do ya know Tam Crews?' Oona laughed. 'And I'm like, how the fuck would I know Tom Cruise? I'm a scabby first-time film-maker from the back streets of Belfast! Of course, when I said that, they loved me even more.'

'You met Tom Cruise?

'For all of ninety seconds, yes.'

'What's he like?'

'Small, big teeth, dead eyes – pretty much what you'd expect.'

'You make it all sound so easy.'

'I'm a bit dizzy, to be honest. I went over there thinking nobody would give a shit, and instead they were crawling all over me.'

'So what's next?'

'That's a bloody good question, actually. What's next is I'm home, hiding from the madness, while I think about what's next. I've been offered serious money to direct a couple of small, B-list projects over there, kind of as a try-out, I suppose. But I'd rather do something of my own.'

'What do you mean by "serious money"?'

'I mean enough to finance me living out there for a few years, in quite some style.'

'You're joking. Most directors would kill for that sort of break. What are you doing back here?'

'Like I said, I need space to think. I don't know if I want to live in the States, particularly not LA. I gave them a treatment for some-thing I want to shoot here in Europe, it would cost them next to nothing. So, they want me to make their stuff, I want to make my stuff, and the way I look at it, that's a discussion we can have on the phone.' He stood, walked over and hugged her again, then held her at arm's length. 'Anyway, I seem to remember that I promised to be somewhere for Christmas.'

'I'm glad you remembered.'

'Well, I'm really, really glad to see you. You look fantastic – why is that?'

Oona blushed, then felt annoyed at herself for blushing. 'I've been taking care of myself, I suppose.'

'And what are you doing up here, all alone?'

'Oh, you know,' she smiled, 'just spending a bit of quality time with my rocks.'

'Rocks,' he repeated, nodding at the kitchen table, which was covered with samples. 'Great. I haven't slept properly for two months, so right now I'm going to, you know,' and he pointed his finger at the ceiling, 'but it's lovely that you're here.' With a final squeeze on her arm, he staggered out the kitchen door. As Oona listened to his creaks ascend the staircase, she bit her lip and stared through the front window at the sea.

Singer slept for eighteen hours, then reappeared looking even more tired, his hair a magpie's nest. But he had at least discarded his city clothes and donned the Dunaldragh uniform of jeans, thick socks and a scrappy woollen jumper. Oona had been writing up her notes at the kitchen table, waiting for the rain to blow over before heading out on her daily expedition. Singer asked whether he could join her, and the pair started up the mountain that dominated the eastern end of the bay, which, like many Donegal mountains, seemed like an easy enough climb until they were halfway up. It was particularly tricky keeping close to the cliff edge, which was more rugged and treacherous than it looked from below, but which Oona nonetheless wanted to study.

'I'm wrecked, and my ears are freezing.' Singer puffed, making for the shelter of a hollow in the mountainside, where he plonked himself down on a stone. 'Can we rest a bit?'

'You've been smoking too much, that's your problem.' She took a compass reading, made a note, then walked towards him. 'Hey. What's that you're sitting on?'

'My arse.'

'Ha ha. Get off. This is limestone.'

'So what?'

'There should be no limestone for miles around…and look, are those cupmarks?' She pointed to four circular, indented hollows in the side of the stone, which was large, and roughly cuboid in shape. 'Yes, they are,' she answered herself. 'Do you know what? Look about you.'

'What am I looking for?'

'Do you see how this stone is positioned? Smack bang in the centre of the hollow? It's almost like an altar, in a natural auditorium.

And this stone has been carried, and placed here – by humans. It definitely doesn't belong.'

'What are cupmarks?'

'Manmade holes, formed by rubbing another stone against the rock, over and over, for many years. They date from around five thousand BC.'

'Seriously? Why would anyone go to that sort of trouble?'

'No one knows, although the assumption is that cupmarks were a votive activity, some form of worship. This place was significant for the people who lived here, five millennia before Christ.'

'Well, I can see their point – it's a beautiful spot.' From this altitude, it almost seemed as if they were flying above the island and the bay in an aeroplane.

Oona jeered. 'Are you going all ethnic and tree-huggy on me? You gonna start waffling about nature as a goddess again?'

He laughed. 'We should wear sandals and kaftans and turn the Pier House into a hippy commune where free love and muesli prevail.'

'You wish.'

'Hey – seriously, though – it's good to see you back doing what you do best, missing time or no.'

She gave an ironic smile. 'I'm trying my best to feel positive about myself.'

As December wore on, the weather worsened and the pair spent more time indoors. Singer produced his electric typewriter from the boot of his car and carried it to the kitchen table, only to remember that he had nowhere to plug it in. Oona wrote up her notes and sketched maps while Singer sipped whiskey and settled for scribbling onto loose typing paper with a pen, poring over a pile of art history books, replete with big, glossy prints. He explained that he wanted to make his next film about the Scottish architect, Charles Rennie Mackintosh, and his wife, Margaret MacDonald. When Oona asked why, he said that Mackintosh was now recognised as a genius, but he'd been ignored in his own lifetime by all but a few tasteful patrons. He'd died in poverty, but his life story was fascinating – undiagnosed dyslexia, possibly autism, while Margaret was an amazing artist in her own right, and the two had been wonderful eccentrics. It was a love story, set in Edwardian Britain – all very Merchant Ivory. But he doubted very much if he'd get funding for it, because nobody in America had a clue who Mackintosh was.

'You don't strike me as the sort of person who'd be into love stories,' Oona remarked.

'All my favourite novels are basically love stories, but none of them have happy endings.'

On the evenings that they went to the pub, Singer would ask Manus for a huge pile of coins, then spend ages on the phone to his new contacts in America. At odd times, a breathless Manus would appear at the Pier House to inform Singer that his 'Yankee-doodles', as he called them, were waiting impatiently to speak to him.

'God damn that Frisby,' Singer remarked one day as he set out up the sea-grass in the rain. 'Maybe mobile phones aren't the dumbest idea in the world after all.' He told Oona that the Americans couldn't believe that he was living somewhere without electricity, let alone a telephone. Places like that didn't really *exist*, did they?

Evenings not spent in the pub were whiled away by the living room fire. Oona read *Cassell's Book of Knowledge* Volumes 6, NAV to SCA, and 7, SCA to ZWI, because she thought these combinations of letters seemed the most interesting. Singer, meanwhile, immersed himself in *The Illustrated London News*, concentrating on volumes from 1880 through to 1920, researching period details for his script.

'We're like an old married couple,' Oona remarked one night as she set off for the kitchen with a candle. 'Fancy a cup of tea, dearie?'

Singer put on an old man's voice. 'Ooh, I shall be running to the toilet all night if I do. Best make me another hot whiskey instead, love.'

On December twenty-first, they wandered up to the pub after dinner. Manus broke them news of two invasions; the US had gone into Panama, and Ronan had phoned to say that he, Dionne and Melissa would be driving up from Dublin the following day. Manus then proceeded to get quite drunk, and poured them several free-bies. At midnight, as they returned to the Pier House through the sea-grass, Singer's torch batteries ran out. He offered Oona his hand, which she accepted, and the pair giggled as they staggered through the dark, stumbling over hummocks and sliding on the wet grass. Finally, they made it to the front door. But Oona didn't release Singer's hand, rather she also took his free one, then pressed him up against the wall beside the door. He tried to hug her, but she resisted.

'You knew that I was staying here, didn't you?'

'Pardon?'

'The day you arrived, you pretended not to know I was here.' In the dark, she couldn't see his expression, but that also meant that he couldn't see hers. 'But you knew, probably from talking to Manus on the phone, and that's why you came here early.'

'Without admitting anything, would that make me such a bad person?'

'I've had a lovely time, and I wish it could go on forever, just you, me, and the house.'

'Then let's go inside and…'

'No. I want to have this conversation out here, where it's safe.'

'You don't trust me?'

'I don't trust myself, not after so much to drink. I've been trying to summon up the courage to ask you this for three weeks. I am right, aren't I? You knew I was here.'

Singer was quiet for a short time, and when he finally spoke, it was more softly than usual. 'I'm sorry. I've tried not to feel this way. It's just that when I first met you, it sort of hit me.'

'I will never, not if I live for a thousand years, understand why. I was a mess. A blubbering, red-eyed mess.'

'But the time we've spent together – it's been good, hasn't it?'

'Yes.'

'Then why would it be so wrong for us to…'

'Because you'd crush me. Because you'd chew me up and spit me out, and not even realise you were doing it.'

'How do you know?'

'Because I know. You're so used to getting your own way, in everything that you do.'

'Excuse me, but so are you.'

'Don't confuse impertinence with strength – I'm not as strong as you think I am. Dionne and Melissa – they're both strong inside, but I only pretend to be.'

'Everyone pretends to be stronger than they are, me included.'

'Listen, I have messy little flings with boys. Doomed from the start, and easy to manage. I don't do big and serious, because I can't, and you're big and serious.'

'I'm just me.'

'Ah. But you don't know the real me, the needy, weak, obsessive me, the me that gets very down – the me that I despise. I've made real progress this year, but it's been hard. If I got caught up with you, that could really set me back.'

'I like you enough to take the rough with the smooth. And what I like most about us is that we're honest with each other.'

'Fine – since we're being honest, what about Dionne?'

'That doesn't matter.'

'Maybe not to you, but it does to me. Dionne's my friend, but more to the point, she never forgets a slight. Never. It's the way she is.'

'What would she do, have us murdered?'

'If we copped off, she wouldn't blame you, she'd blame me.'

'All's fair in love and war.'

'And I can just see myself, sitting alone, with Dionne hating me, while you spend months at a time, off making movies.'

'That's highly unlikely.'

'Rubbish. You're about to go places, I can tell. The last thing you need is me, dragging you down.'

'But—'

'No, listen – I want this Christmas to be as beautiful, and as much fun as the last.'

'So?'

'So, do you think you can manage that, when the others arrive?'

'Ignore my feelings, in other words?'

'I have feelings, too.'

'But not for me.'

'I didn't say that.'

'Do you?'

'Yes.'

'So what's the problem? I don't understand.'

'Men never understand the things they don't want to understand. But please, for the moment, can we just enjoy each other's company?'

He pouted. 'I suppose so.'

'Thanks. This means a lot to me. Maybe when I'm stronger…' She kissed his cheek and released his hands. Singer fell quiet, so they went indoors. While he revived the living room fire, she went upstairs and fetched an armful of blankets and pillows.

'Tonight, we'll sleep on the sofa,' she announced. 'Fully clothed, and no naughtiness. But hugging is okay. We can pretend we're an old married couple. I'd quite like that, actually, if we could just clap our hands and have fifty years of missing time, and be old together, and cut out all the messy bits in between – stuff like sex, children and careers.' She sat and rubbed Tiger Balm under her ears from a tin in her hand. 'Do you want some?'

'No.'

'But it helps you breathe, and in the morning you'll feel less hungover. Here, hold still.' Singer wriggled, but Oona smeared some of the orange paste on his forehead.

'Ah! It burns!'

'Don't be a baby. Now lie down, and watch the fire.' They tucked themselves up on the sofa, his arms wrapped around her from behind. He would never forget the smell of the Tiger Balm, mingling with that of her hair, the old leather of the sofa, the turf smoke from the glowing fire and the reassuring smell of the house, solid all around them. For a long time, they savoured the greatest contentment of all, that of simply being together.

'I want to show you something tomorrow,' he eventually muttered, breaking the silence.

'Just as long as you don't show me anything right now,' she giggled. She stared at the fire a while, then asked, 'Go on then, what do you want to show me?'

But Singer had fallen asleep, his face buried in a pillow.

The pair stood before Declan McFall's grave.

'Have you asked Manus about this?'

'No.'

'Why not?'

'Because it's private.'

'Then what makes you so certain that Declan was his son? There might be other McFalls in the area.'

'Do you see the date he drowned – the twenty-fourth of December, 1978? Well, last Christmas Eve, me and Melissa found Manus lying drunk in Letterkenny. So bloody drunk, he didn't remember me driving him home. When I was trying to lift him into my car, he called me Declan.'

'Jesus.'

'Last year would have been Declan's tenth anniversary.'

'Poor, poor Manus. And poor Mrs McFall. No wonder she's so miserable, if she lost her only son.'

'It just goes to show you, you never really know what's going on in other people's lives.' They walked slowly from the graveyard, then gathered pace through the forest. 'I have a lot of time for Manus, he's one of the good guys. But it must be hard for him, trying to keep it all together. That pub couldn't make much money, and I'm sure what little it does must get gobbled up, trying to keep the Pier House from falling to pieces. Talk about a white elephant. He keeps that place for love, no other reason. Add to that a wife who's clearly lost the will to live – yet still he clings on, and keeps smiling.'

'He'd remind you of Sophia Clements, wouldn't he? Both staying in the same beautiful yet tragic place, unable to tear themselves away.'

'I never thought of it like that, but yes, you're right.'

'I'd like a grave like hers. Those iron railings – very classy.'

'Well, hopefully you won't be needing one for a while yet.'

They continued through the woods in silence, then started down the valley proper. When Oona next spoke, it was clear that she'd been mulling over something.

'How come you and Melissa never told the rest of us about finding Manus paralytic?'

'It just didn't seem right, at the time.'

'Do you and Melissa have any other little secrets you'd care to share with the group?'

'Secrets? Like what?'

'Well, they would hardly be secrets, now would they, if we already knew what they were? I thought we were honest with each other.'

Singer protested. 'We are.'

'There's such a thing as lying by omission, which I'd say you're very good at.'

'Look, I just felt sorry for Manus. Do you remember he came down last Christmas Day?'

'Yes.'

'Well, that was to apologise, but everybody was there, and I wanted to spare him the embarrassment. He's been more than good to me.'

'Bit of a Daddy figure for you, isn't he?'

'Why do you say that?'

'I've watched the way the two of you go on. He's the only person you genuinely look up to.'

'Don't you like him, too?'

'Oh god, yes. I mean, he's Bill, how could I not like him?'

'Bill?'

'From Enid Blyton. The kindly, paternal secret agent who somehow always had time to bring four profoundly irritating children and their parrot along with him whenever he was hunting dodgy foreigners. I loved Bill when I was little. So strong, yet so guaranteed to screw up in some way, so that the children had to step in and save the day. And yes, I love Manus too.'

'As much as you love me?'

'I thought we agreed to park that while the others were here?'

'Well, since they won't arrive for another few hours, why don't we park ourselves in this fine establishment and tell the owner how much we both love him?' They'd walked as far as McFall's. In the weak sunlight, the tortoise sign looked even more faded than ever.

'You just want a pint, don't you?'

'You see, this is why you and I should always be together – you can read my innermost thoughts.'

'Can I, indeed?' She followed him through the door.

'He's been very sweet, actually. Solicitous. Always there when I need him, happy to disappear when I don't.'

'How's his magazine doing?'

'No idea, ask him yourself. Poetry, shmoetry.'

'I thought it was arts in general?'

'You said it, babes. Arse in general. Er, no offence, Melissa.'

Oona, Dionne and Melissa sat glugging wine at the kitchen table. The latter two had arrived in the late afternoon, crammed into Ronan's mother's tiny hatchback, which he seemed to have permanently appropriated, and which was now parked outside, behind Singer's battered coupe. Traumatised by five hours of Dionne's backseat driving, Ronan had elected to refresh himself after the journey along with Singer up in the pub, while the girls stayed at the house to unpack. Thus far, they had managed to unpack two bottles of Sauvignon Blanc.

'What about your new man? How's all that going?'

'Absolutely nowhere. Mister Gregory bloody Fielding told his parents that I was from Tallaght, so my getting-to-know-you dinner at their big house in Foxrock turned into one of the most humiliating experiences of my life. A right pair of snobs. I broke it off the next morning.'

'I thought you liked him.'

'I did, until he failed miserably to stick up for me in front of his folks. I'm still quite upset about that, actually. Bastard. Mister Needs-a-New-Wardrobe Bastard.'

'What?'

'I stole his key from his desk in work and went round to his flat and cut holes in all his clothes with a pair of pinking scissors.'

'Dee! You total psycho!'

All three collapsed laughing, Dionne with malicious delight, Oona and Melissa with more surprised horror than Dionne probably recognised. When the laughter subsided, Oona asked, 'What about you, Melissa – how was Manchester? Emasculate any men when you were over there?'

'Quite the opposite. Spent most of my time lusting after a chap called Demetrius.'

'Oh? A new squeeze? Tell.'

Melissa smiled her faint smile. 'My love interest in the play. I understudied a big part, and believe it or not the actress actually managed to break her leg on the second night, so I ended up on stage every night for nine weeks. Now, I'm just tired. Very, very tired.'

'And what about this Demetrius?'

'After a lot of typically Shakespearian farting around, we finally get married.'

'No, I meant in real life.'

'Good-looking boy, but gayer than Christmas. Theatre, darling.'

Dionne piped up, 'Do you think Singer's gay?'

Oona looked at her. 'Who are you asking, me or Melissa?'

'Both of you.'

Oona and Melissa blinked at one another. 'I don't think so,' Oona answered.

Melissa looked Dionne directly in the eyes. 'I have to say, I don't get that feeling from him. Why, do you?'

'No. I'm just wondering why he doesn't seem to fancy any of us – there has to be a logical explanation. How did you get on with him when you were making that film?'

'Fine. It turned out okay. There were quite a lot of people here, during the shoot.'

'Oh, I wasn't implying anything,' Dionne said airily. 'I suppose I'm just weighing up my chances, now that Mister Gregory Arsewipe Fielding is Mister Ancient History.'

'What about Ronan?' Oona asked.

'Don't be soft,' Dionne snapped, then addressed Melissa again. 'Speaking of soft, what's the story with your most ardent admirer?'

'Excuse me?'

'Pretty-boy Frisby, is he coming this year?'

'I don't know. I haven't seen him since the film.'

'I heard he saw quite a lot of you, during the film.'

Melissa shrugged. 'It was in the script. I knew that before I agreed to do it.'

'Tongues hanging out, were there?'

'Actually, Singer put everyone out of the room apart from the cameraman for those shots, so it wasn't too intimidating.'

'I don't know how I feel about that – the man I think I still love, seeing one of my best friends naked.'

'Him, and hundreds of people in Toronto and Los Angeles. Thousands more at festivals all over the world by the end of next year, I should suppose.'

'The film's done very well, apparently,' Oona informed Dionne. 'Singer's been offered money to work in America.'

'Seriously? Why didn't you tell me that before?'

'I only just found out. As you know, Singer plays his cards pretty close to his chest.' At that, she threw a significant glance at Melissa, which Dionne didn't notice, and Melissa pretended not to.

Much later that night, to the horror of both Singer and Melissa, Oona got drunk and came straight out with it, in front of everyone. The girls had joined Singer and Ronan up at the pub. Everyone was tired, at that floppy stage of the evening where nicotine and alcohol just won't do it any more. The last pickled fisherman had winkled himself away from the bar and drifted out the door. Manus sat down at their table, carrying a bottle of whiskey and six glasses. Singer and Oona both accepted, the others did not. As Manus poured his own, Oona said, 'Tell us about Declan.'

'Oons!' Singer hissed. Melissa touched her shoulder, but Oona shrugged her off.

'From what I hear,' she persisted, 'it would do Manus good to talk about Declan.'

'Who's Declan?' Ronan and Dionne chorused in unison. Manus folded his arms and pursed his lips. His eyes turned hard in a way none of them had ever seen before, and for a few seconds, Singer was positive he would throw them out of the pub, and probably the Pier House as well. Mentally, he kicked himself for having told Oona anything at all.

'Declan was my son,' Manus answered slowly, 'and as some of you obviously are aware,' at this, he fixed Oona with a stare, 'Declan is no longer with us.'

'We're your friends, Manus.' She placed a hand on one of his forearms, like a white butterfly alighting on a joint of beef. 'We've only known you for a year, but it seems like much longer. Some of us,' she nodded at Singer and Ronan, 'have only known each other for a year, too, and in truth, we've spent very little time together, so perhaps we oughtn't to feel for one other the way we do. But that's the effect your house has had on us. This a good place, Manus, and we care about it, and that means we care for you. I'd never want you to think that the goodness only flows one way.'

Manus studied the wall above Oona's head, saying nothing. Singer shifted in his seat, but still, she ploughed onward. 'Is that why there's a hearse in our garage? Because of Declan?'

To Singer's immense surprise, Manus nodded. 'Yes. Declan was the last soul to ride in that thing. I bet you didn't know that about me, eh?' His eyes glittered.

'Know what?'

He gave a sharp laugh. 'I was the local undertaker, like my father before me. Now, wasn't that a great job to have?'

'But you're a publican.'

'Common enough, in Donegal, to be both.'

'You used to lay bodies out in the Pier House, didn't you? Declan, perhaps?'

'Oons!' Singer again. 'For Chrissakes…'

Manus held up a hand, smiling wryly. 'It's okay. You were bound to notice the hearse, one of the days. It's hard to miss. But what makes you think I used the Pier House for my business?'

Oona swallowed. 'I'm just guessing, is all.'

'Well, the answer is no, I didn't. I have a shed out the back of here where all that work was done. When I tidied them up, the loved ones would be taken to their homes, and waked there.'

'So why did you stop?'

'When I put my own son in a coffin, that was different.'

'How did he die?'

'Manus, you don't have to…'

'No. It's okay. I wish you all could have known him, you'd have liked him a lot, and he'd have liked you. You'd have been friends. He knew your Uncle Lucius,' Manus nodded at Singer, 'the two got on great. He never wanted to stay on at school, or move away – he was just a big, strong lad, who loved it here. All he cared about was the sea.' Manus drained his whiskey and poured himself another. 'When he was twenty-four, he went to Killybegs, and bought a boat, with his own money. Money that he'd saved, working for me. The boat was his Christmas present to himself, he said. Christmas, 1978. He had her towed around from Killybegs and took her out of the water, to rebuild the engine. That Christmas Eve, the water was calm, and I'd promised a few of the lads a crab or a lobster, so the two of us went out, to try his boat. That was my first time out in her, and it was to be my last.' He paused and drew breath, remembering.

'The boat sprung a leak, halfway out to the island. To this day, I could show you the exact spot. I don't know why she leaked, a gap in the planks from being lifted out at the harbour, or maybe Declan didn't fix something back properly, but she started filling up faster than the pump could empty her, so we swung around and tried to get back to the shore. But the engine compartment flooded and she stopped, and then she sank – only she didn't go to the bottom. She stayed herself, just below the water – there must have been a pocket of air trapped under the deck. So the two of us stood there, up to our armpits, balancing on the deck of this half-sunken boat, one at each end, facing each other, not daring to move in case we tipped her and lost her altogether. Two miles out from the cliffs, but still two miles from the island. And of course, not a life jacket between us.' Manus wiped an eye with the back of a huge hand, and stopped.

'It's all right,' Singer began, 'you don't have to explain…' Everyone except Oona, it seemed, felt that acute discomfort that children experience when they see a parent cry. Manus sighed.

'At this time of year, you can only stand in the water for ten minutes – twenty at the most – before you go numb. I could feel the cold robbing my strength away. The tide was on the turn, and pulling us east of the island, towards the open sea. "I can make it, Da – can you?" That's what he said to me. He knew if we stayed with the boat, we were finished. By that time, we were closer to the island than the shore, so we both struck out at the same time.' His eyes filled with tears again. 'Well, somehow I made it – I don't know how. Desperation, probably. I've never swum that far before or since. I didn't see him go under, I was so dog-tired, and my eyes ruined from the water. I must have swallowed half the bloody sea, but not as much as Declan did. By the time I touched the rocks, he wasn't with me. I broke into the lighthouse to use the radio, but I knew it was no good. We found him, two days later, ten miles up the coast. I blame myself in a thousand different ways – for not checking the boat, for not bringing life jackets, for not leaving the lobsters to enjoy their bloody Christmas in peace. He was my son, but he was also my friend, and now he's gone, and there's nothing anyone can do to ever bring him back.' Manus hid his face in his hands and rubbed his eyes as if he had smoke in them. Singer glared at Oona as much as to say, 'Are you happy now?', but she ignored him, moved to a stool beside Manus, put her arms around him and lay her head on his shoulder, while his barrel-like torso shook with sobs.

Melissa kicked Singer's foot beneath the table. She signalled with her eyes for him to look up. Mrs McFall stood in the shadows behind the counter, silent, her expression as bleak as an arctic storm.

14

Just as it had the previous year, the knock came to the door during Christmas dinner. Ronan nearly choked.

'Frisby – it has to be!'

Oona, who was seated nearest the kitchen window, pushed back her seat and reached for a candle.

'Are you expecting him?'

'No, I haven't heard from him for months.'

Singer snorted. 'Too busy trading in shares, I should imagine, or yachts, or castles made from clouds.'

'What do you mean?'

'Well, it's not Frisby,' Oona reported from the darkened glass. 'This guy is fat, bald and dressed like a biker.'

'A biker?' Dionne half-shrieked.

'Leather jacket, chains and stuff. Looks like a proper weirdo. Singer – you can go.'

Singer, still chewing a mouthful of food, took a gulp of wine, then grabbed an oil lamp, muttering, 'Better be a biker in serious distress, because if he isn't now, he soon will be.' He stomped off into the hallway. The others joined Oona at the kitchen window, where they could see the stranger from behind. Singer pulled the front door open, frowning, and held his lamp aloft. The others watched agog as Singer's face transformed from frown to disbelief to laughter, all in the space of a few seconds. He stepped back and gestured the stranger through the door.

'Must be someone he knows,' Ronan opined. The kitchen door flew open.

'Ladies and gentlemen,' Singer roared, 'may I announce, for your pleasure, all the way from god knows where, Master Jay Frisby!'

The creature that stepped into the room was indeed Frisby – yet it wasn't. His boyish features had bloated and he sported more hair on his chin than he did on his scalp, the former home to a straggling, Asiatic-style beard, tied at the end with a piece of red thread, the latter shaved into a pinkish-blue ball. His eyes stood out from the puffiness of his face, caked as they were with mascara and black eye shadow. His nose was pierced with a silver ring, and both ears had several similar adornments hanging from them. He wore a black T-shirt with a red, satanic ram's skull and a pentacle printed on the chest, beneath a black leather jacket festooned with chains and stapled with metal studs. The jacket seemed too small, unable to close over a nascent beer-belly. The look was completed by a pair of black jeans and an immense, clunking pair of black leather boots that made his legs seem plump and short. Having the astounded and undivided attention of the room, the apparition put its hands together as in prayer, and bowed.

'In a previous incarnation, some of you knew me as Jay Frisby. But Jay Frisby is dead. My rebirthed name is Balor, warlock of the Weald.'

Singer collapsed, screaming. The others stared, open-mouthed, not just at Frisby's appearance, but also because his introduction had been uttered in a flat, southern English accent, the Oxbridge twang nowhere to be heard. Ronan placed his forehead squarely in one palm.

'What's a warlock?' asked Oona.

'Where's the wheel?' asked Dionne. Melissa wore her faint smile.

'Weald, milady, *Weald*. It is the correct appellation for the part of Albion from which I hail. And a warlock is a wizard, usually a trainee.' Singer's howls arose even louder, from somewhere on the floor over by the range.

'I thought you were from Leamington Spa,' Oona countered.

'In a previous life, I may have bode a while in fair Leamington. But in truth, my birthplace is beside the iron spring, also known as Tunbridge Wells.'

Singer sounded as if he was about to choke. Even Frisby, who was obviously trying hard to ignore him, raised a patch of skin above one eye where an eyebrow had been shaved away.

'Jay, what's gotten into you?' Ronan lifted his head from his hand, his expression deeply pained.

'But is this any way to greet the reincarnation of an old soul?' Frisby bowed again, only this time more sweepingly. Oona and Melissa began to titter, infected by Singer's helpless laughter. 'In the Weald, we would welcome a traveller with wine, and with song! But the welcome of Hibernia is as cold,' he glanced over his shoulder at the shaking, prostrate Singer, 'and as loud, as her weather!'

'Stop…stop,' Singer moaned from the floor. 'Please, just be a carbon-copy upper-class twit again – my ribs can't take any more!'

'The one you speak of is dead,' Frisby pronounced, sitting heavily in Singer's empty chair and reaching for the wine. 'I help myself to mead, as none other lifts a hand to serve me. I, Balor, lived within the skin of the one you call Frisby for far too long. He was weak, a lost and lonely soul. I, on the other hand, am a student of Wicca.'

'Wicker?' Dionne piped up. 'You make furniture?'

'Nay, Wicca. The old art, older than mere furniture. Magick, to you, milady.'

'Jay, do you realise that Balor was the Celtic god of the dead?' Ronan was beginning to suspect that his friend's bizarre pretensions were not some elaborate joke. 'And that he lived on Tory Island, and had an evil eye?'

'Balor manifests himself in many different ways.'

'He was a giant, Frisby, not a tubby English dwarf.'

'Ronan!' Dionne intervened. 'Don't be rude! I mean, nobody is nasty to you about your silly magazine.'

'Eh?' Ronan paled. 'What's *Avalon* got to do with this?' He gestured at Frisby. 'At least I don't think I'm Aleister Crowley!'

'No, you think you're Oscar Wilde. How many copies did you sell last month, anyway?'

Ronan looked crushed. 'Dionne, that's hardly the point. *Avalon* is not a mainstream publication! Anyway, I thought you liked it!'

'Brothers,' Frisby intervened, 'and sisters. Let us not be at one another's throats. Saturnalia is a time for joy.'

'Satur…what?'

'Everyone knows that Christmas is mere propaganda, an historical replacement for the pagan festival of Saturnalia.'

'Everyone except me,' answered Oona.

'And me,' added Dionne.

237

'Never worry – call it what you will. I am overjoyed to see my friends, and happy to be back in this sacred place, where my true self was revealed to me.'

'Stop. Don't say anything more – I should be writing this down.' Singer pulled a spare chair up to the table, tears streaming down his cheeks. 'What was revealed to you?'

'My Celtic roots,' Frisby frowned solemnly. 'Jay Frisby understood that he had been summonsed here for a reason...'

'Yes, because I invited him,' Ronan interrupted. 'I mean, you. I invited you, last Christmas.'

'Ah, but the Frisby you knew has gone away, and Balor is awake. This place is rich in magick, and the magick wakened Balor, and set him free.'

'Have you swallowed some dodgy American self-help book?'

'Uh, Balor,' Oona spoke carefully, 'has it not occurred to you that you might have fallen victim to this emerging international trend for mystical, self-aggrandising bullshit? I mean, indulging the inner child is all very well, and I should know, but...'

'...but unfortunately there are no Celts native to the south-east of England,' Ronan finished Oona's point, dourly.

'Tolkien grew up in Birmingham,' Singer offered, 'and look what he came up with.'

'Fair friends,' Frisby stood, and took both Ronan and Oona by the hand. Ronan snatched his quickly away, but Oona let him hold hers. 'What does it matter where the body lies, so long as the soul knows its true nature?'

'He has a point there, you have to admit,' Singer agreed, grinning hugely. Oona stuck her tongue out at him.

'Your aura is strong, He-Who-Sings,' Frisby addressed him. 'I can see it.'

'You can see my what?'

'Your aura. Your chakra.'

Singer showed Oona his middle finger. 'The guru digs my chakra – so sit on it.' Oona lifted a fingerful of mashed potato from her plate and flung it at him as he erupted with laughter again.

'Actually, I don't think that the aura and the chakra are the same thing at all,' murmured Melissa, but nobody heard her.

'Stout friends! Let us drink, for at last the covenant is fulfilled, and we are one again!' Frisby raised his glass so violently that most of his wine sloshed into the air, and rained down across the table like a gush of dark blood. 'To the Christmas Club!' he exhorted, before swallowing what was left in his glass.

'To the Christmas Club!' Singer stood, and held his glass in the air, grinning.

'I thought you said it was Saturnalia?' Ronan tried to sound bored.

'Now,' Frisby ignored him, and plonked his plump body back in its seat, 'are there any vittles left? I could eat a Christian!'

'I have to say, I like the new Frisby – he's much more fun!'

Singer, Ronan, Oona and Melissa trudged up the hairpin path on their morning walk. Neither Dionne nor Frisby had emerged from their beds, and St Stephen's Day had dawned blowy, fresh and dry.

Ronan shook his head. 'I still think he's having us on. Nobody changes that much, not in the space of a few months.'

'Teenagers do,' Oona posited. 'Schizophrenics do. People in love do.'

'You yourself admitted,' Singer addressed Ronan, 'that you didn't know Frisby very well before you asked him here last Christmas. Maybe what we're seeing now is the true Frisby. Maybe the version we saw last year was the aberration. I checked him out, you know.'

'You what?'

'I checked him out. His stately home and his yacht company were figments of his imagination. The truth of the matter is, none of us have any idea who Jay Frisby is, or even if Jay Frisby is his real name.'

'How dare you do that to one of my friends?'

'Oh, behave!' Singer barked. 'You said you met him through work. How exactly did you meet him?'

'At a boat show. I was writing an article…'

'So, you were wandering around all these boats, yeah?'

'Yachts.'

'Whatever. You met Frisby wearing a shirt, tie and blazer, carrying that ludicrous mobile phone, and he told you he sold boats – was it something like that?'

'He knew a lot.'

'Compared to you.'

'He showed me around.'

'That's how easy it is, Ronan.'

'I don't believe it.'

'Apart from us, do you have any mutual friends?'

'No.'

'I rest my case.'

Melissa piped up. 'When somebody sends you a poem for your poetry magazine—'

'*Arts* magazine!' Ronan insisted.

'Sorry, arts – do you check whether that poem is their own work?'

'Well, usually I would recognise plagiarism, but if in doubt…'

'Exactly!' Singer leapt in, triumphantly. 'It's called checking your facts, and it's common journalistic practice. Well, I think Frisby's entire life is plagiarised. I think he latches onto something, and then becomes it. A chameleon, with no true personality of his own.'

Oona took Ronan's arm. 'I have a lot of, uh, experience with personality disorders, and much as I hate to inflate his already swollen ego by agreeing with him, I think Singer may be right.'

'I didn't approve of Singer running checks on Frisby either,' Melissa soothed, 'but it's hard to fault what he says.'

'Oh, so you two have already had this conversation?' Oona's tone was suspicious.

'During the film,' Melissa offered.

'You mean, you and Singer have known for ages that Manus had a dead son, and that Frisby was a fibber? You two have a right little cabal going on! Is there a password or a handshake we should learn to share your secret knowledge?'

'Wise up, Oona,' Singer sniffed. 'If you'd have been here at the time, I'd have told you too. It just slipped my mind, is all.'

'Hell of a thing to slip your mind.'

'You could say that I parked it.' There was a note of sarcasm in Singer's voice which Oona caught and understood, Melissa caught but didn't understand and which escaped Ronan altogether. But when they reached the watchtower, Singer immediately dropped over the edge of the headland and scrabbled his way down to the pinnacle overlooking the gorge without saying anything further. Oona snorted, studied the horizon for a bit, then slowly followed him.

'So tell me more about your magazine,' Melissa asked Ronan, out of politeness.

Ronan drew a deep breath. 'Well, it's an artistic journal, obviously, but we profile individual painters, writers and so on, as well as

reviewing exhibitions, books, plays and publishing original work –
the odd short story, but mainly poetry.'

'We?'

'Yes. Well. There's just me at present, but I'm thinking of hiring...'

'What's wrong?' Oona joined Singer at the top of the pinnacle. The
gorge was full of grey-green water.

'Me? Nothing – why?'

'You're being very tetchy.'

'You're the one who's tetchy.'

'Are you pissed off with me?'

'No, but I rather get the feeling that you're pissed off with me.'

'We could do this all day, couldn't we?'

'Yup.'

'Is it because I asked Manus about Declan? Because I wouldn't
shut up when you ordered me to?'

'No.'

'Sweetheart, you need to understand that we're not all extras in
one of your films.'

Singer laughed. 'Oh, but I'm well aware of that. Don't forget – you
already turned down the romantic lead.'

She dug him in the ribs with her elbow. 'Come on, you big softy!
I thought we'd agreed to—'

'Park that!' he interrupted. 'Do you know what?' He turned to
her, smiling. 'I have parked it. Let's not argue. Let's just sit back and
enjoy the show. *Pasa lo que pasa*, right?' He kissed her on the forehead,
took a step backwards, then threw himself forward and stood on his
hands, legs and feet kicking in the air. Cigarettes, a lighter, a pocket
camera and a hip flask all tumbled from his jacket pockets, bouncing
off the rock, as his heavy body swayed dangerously beside the precip-
itous drop.

'Get down!' she shrieked, throwing her arms around his thighs.
'You'll fall!'

'Of course, if you ever have any stories from the acting side of
things, or maybe you'd like to review the odd play, naturally our fees
wouldn't be all that great, but the prestige of being a critic is what

it's all about…' Ronan realised that Melissa wasn't listening to him, but staring transfixed at the pinnacle. He followed her gaze. 'What under God's name does that man think he's doing?'

When they returned to the house, they found Frisby sitting naked, apart from a pair of black Y-fronts, on the pediment of the sundial.

'Jay!' Oona laughed. 'Are you not freezing?'

'This is a place of great power,' he intoned, staring at the harbour. He had large brown nipples, a small tuft of hair on his chest, and his newly grown beer belly hung over his Y-fronts. 'Will you not meditate with Balor?'

Ronan gave a dry, cynical laugh and strode off into the house.

Singer crouched in front of the Englishman. 'Balor,' he began, solemnly. 'Great one.'

'I am not great, He-Who-Sings – yet.'

'The road to enlightenment is long, and pitted with many obstacles.'

'Stop it!' Oona yanked him by the back of his jacket, but Singer righted himself, ignoring her, and peered into Frisby's face.

'Do you see that mountain there?' he pointed towards the eastern end of the bay. 'Well, halfway up that mountain is a place of pagan worship.'

'You lie,' Frisby responded, with equanimity.

'Ask her if I do – Oons, there's this place, right, a hollow with a stone? The stone has cupmarks, Frisby – I mean, Balor. Ancient symbols carved by Druids, many millennia ago.'

'Truly?' Frisby met Singer's eyes, and for an instant, Singer saw a trace of the Frisby he'd met last year and gone on to make a film with – the shy, uncertain youth, a bluffer, but a boy with no real badness in him, trying be somebody in a world where the only true crime is being nobody.

'Stay close to the cliff top, but not too close. You can't miss it.' Frisby stood abruptly, and set off across the sea-grass. 'Hey! Hold on, dude! You'll be needing clothes, and boots!'

'But I am Balor of the Weald.'

'You'll be Balor of the Frostbite if you don't get dressed.' Frisby turned like an automaton and shuffled through the front door. Melissa followed Frisby inside, but Oona remained by the sundial. Singer gave her an 'after you' gesture, and put on his old man's voice.

'Come on then, dearie, and I'll make you a nice hot cup of tea.'

She looked away, as if she'd spotted something out to sea. 'No, thank you – I'll wait here for Jay. I think I'll go with him.'

'You're waiting for Godot?'

'He's still a human being, no matter how badly you treat him.'

'What? What have I done?'

She looked him in the eye. 'You can be very cruel to people who are weaker than you. Which is just about everybody.'

'But I didn't mean…'

'If I gave in to you, very soon you'd be treating me exactly the way you're treating Jay now. With contempt.'

Singer hesitated for an instant, flummoxed, then turned on his heel and marched indoors. But when he hung his coat up, while the others clattered around the kitchen, he snuck into the large, silent living room and crossed to the east-looking windows, where he was able to watch Oona and Frisby depart across the sea-grass. They weren't holding hands, and they weren't walking too close together. He laughed sourly at himself for spying like a jealous schoolboy. A yawn came from behind him.

'What are you doing?' Dionne lay on the sofa, half-asleep. She wore a skimpy T-shirt, a pair of pyjama pants and socks. 'Sorry,' she tossed her hair, which had grown back to half its previous length, and gone its natural wheaten blonde. 'I was dozing. I got up out of bed, and then realised I shouldn't have. What are you watching, out there?'

'I'll give you three guesses.'

'The little tree-hugger?'

'I shouldn't let him annoy me, but he does. He's such a fake.'

'He's harmless.'

'I wish he'd go and be harmless elsewhere.'

'Never mind about Frisby, c'mere and sit beside me,' Dionne patted the sofa. 'I haven't seen you for a year, and you never seem to have any time for me any more.' Singer sat, as invited. 'Well done, with your film. Are we ever likely to see it?'

'Not unless Santa brings us a telly, a video recorder and electricity.'

'I hear you're off to America. Will you still speak to me, when you're rich and famous?'

'I don't want to go to America. The next film I want to make is set in Glasgow, but I don't think they'll give me the money.' Now that

243

he was close to Dionne, he noticed that she had a warm, woman-fresh-out-of-bed aroma about her that was highly inviting. Her skimpy T-shirt reminded him that she had stunning breasts. He coughed and studied the carpet. 'What about you? Built any buildings lately?'

'Oh, architecture is very boring. But I've bought my own house, and I'm having that done up more or less for free, by our regular contractors. Then I'll sell it on and buy a bigger one. I like that side of things, it gives me a buzz.'

'My next film, if I ever get to make it, is about an architect.'

'Really? Who?'

'Mackintosh.'

'Oh, wow! His stuff is back in vogue again, isn't it? Art noveau and all that. Very good – well, if you're hiring any professional advisors…' Her smile, this time, showed all her teeth, which were very bright. Singer was about to ask her whether she'd had them whitened before he caught himself on.

'Listen, about that day in the National Gallery. I'm sorry if I…'

'Ah, don't be silly.' She put a hand on his leg. 'That was my fault. I was stressed out about some project in work.'

'I could have been more complimentary about your hair.'

'Men can never say the right thing about women's hair. If you're indifferent, we think you're bastards, and if you say that you like it, we think you're lying bastards. Forget all that, it's just nice to see you again.'

'It's nice to see you, too.'

Her hand left his leg, and settled on his shoulder. 'You owe me a kiss.'

'Do I?'

'From last year. I wanted to give you one, remember? And you put me off for what I thought would be a day or two, and now it's been a whole year.' She closed her eyes and puckered her lips, little-girl style. Singer leant over and pecked them chastely, but the hand on his shoulder moved to the back of his neck, and the kiss changed character immediately. He could have pulled back, but he didn't. Instead, he put a hand on her hip, and enjoyed the kiss. The living room door creaked. Both Dionne's and Singer's eyes shot open, she released him and he slid onto the floor with a bump, then sat upright with his back to her, as if he'd been sitting there all along.

'Yes, uh, I couldn't agree more, what you say about doing up your house, that must be a helluva lot of fun, having a house done up,' he babbled.

'Actually, it's a pain in the arse,' she replied, with humour in her voice. Ronan walked into view. The surprise on his face was palpable.

'Oh, hi, babes,' Dionne twittered easily, 'Singer and I were just saying, wouldn't it be lovely if some kind person came and offered us a cup of tea.'

'Really?' Ronan pushed his glasses up onto his nose and glared at Singer.

'Hi, Ro.' Singer knew he sounded overly casual. Ronan ignored his greeting and addressed Dionne, primly.

'I was looking for you, to ask whether you wanted breakfast.'

'You see, petal? Great minds do think alike! Will you serve it here, or are you going to make me walk all the way to that beastly kitchen?'

'I'd prefer if you came to the kitchen.'

'Cruel ginger pubes. Okay, coming now.'

'Yes. Well.' Ronan looked around as if he'd lost something, then, with a parting frown at Singer, stalked out again.

'Oh, fuck fuck fuck,' Singer whispered, 'I think he saw us!'

'Don't be daft, he couldn't possibly.' Dionne sounded delighted.

'Then he heard us.'

'Maybe. That was nice, let's do it again.' She hugged him from behind and kissed his ear. To the peal of her giggles, he sprung up like a kicked cat.

'But Ronan likes you!' he admonished.

'What, and you don't?' She stretched, showing her body off to its full advantage. He whimpered and flopped in an armchair, well away from the sofa. She stood up and stretched again. 'See ya around, big fella.' She turned, put her thumbs on her pyjama elastic and deftly flashed an immaculate backside. Singer's mouth fell open. She wiggled, then laughed merrily as she covered herself and exited with a conscious, stalking grace. Singer buried his head in his hands and whimpered some more.

15

For just under a week, it was almost as it had been before – a gentle rhythm of long walks by day and evenings by the fire, punctuated with good-natured sessions up at the pub, hangovers, conversations and card games. Frisby produced a Tarot deck and conducted readings in his ersatz Old English patter, that were baroque in their predicted outcomes. Occasionally, his newfound New Ageism would slip and he'd revert to near-normality – Oona watched him one day doing the dishes, and he looked for all the world like any young student, anywhere, just washing dishes. A sort of pudgy, little boy lost. However, Manus laughed at his mascara when they brought him to the pub. Declan's anniversary seemed to have passed without incident, and Mrs McFall even brought a tray of free sandwiches to their table, with what could have conceivably been a smile on her face, although Singer reckoned she just wanted an excuse to study the reconfigured Frisby up close.

It was hard to know how seriously he took it all, but there were days when Dunaldragh seemed like some mystic playpark for the young Englishman, with every rock, hummock and stream the supposed home of some obscure spirit, elf or sprite. He still slept late most mornings – Balor the warlock obviously shared Frisby the yacht salesman's attitude towards early starts. In the afternoons, he would roam through the sea-grass with a hazel rod, searching for the ley-lines that he vehemently assured the others must converge on the area. When asked precisely what a ley-line was, he was less vehement, saying that he'd know for certain when he found one. Once, from the living room window, he was observed sitting cross-legged on the beach, stripped to the waist, arms raised in the air. But his flesh was found weak, and he caught a cold. Refusing all medication bar alcohol, he asked Melissa to teach him some yoga as a cure, and she concurred, but the sight of him attempting the backward bridge with a runny nose set Singer off in hysterics again, so Frisby forewent the yoga moves and instead demonstrated what he claimed was tai chi. Singer had to be helped from the room.

One minor mystery solved itself almost immediately – that of Frisby's inordinate weight gain. He had abandoned gin and tonic as a tipple and instead drank beer in ferocious quantities, more even than Singer, who was almost twice his size. Then, his artificially convoluted speech became incomprehensible. He developed the habit, when returning from the pub, of bolting off into the darkness, declaring that he could see nymphs who wanted to commune with him.

'Who needs television,' Singer remarked, 'when you have a New Ager in the house?'

However, as the week wore on, the other five noticed a strained desperation just below the surface of Frisby's behaviour, as he seemed to contrive ever-more outrageous antics and outlandish claims, like a hyper child striving for attention. Melissa remained aloof – whatever narrow chance Frisby had ever had of winning her affection was comprehensively obliterated by this latest manifestation. Ronan overcame his exasperation and united with Singer in the sport of pulling Frisby's leg, devising stories designed to send the spiritual omnivore off on yet another quest. When Ronan told him that hawthorn trees were sacred to fairies, Frisby decided to map every one within a three-mile radius, convinced that the resulting blotches on a piece of graph paper would hold some crucial significance in his hunt for ley-lines. Singer preposterously hinted that Dunaldragh church might have been constructed by the Knights Templar, and Frisby spent two whole days taking crayon-rubbings from its stonework, in the hope of uncovering some hidden Masonic code that would reveal a holy secret of earth-shattering proportions. These wild goose chases, while amusing, and excellent for getting Frisby out of the house whenever his nonsense became overbearing, had, Singer noticed, the unintended side effect of driving Oona out with him. Blithely, she explained that she accompanied Frisby on his quests as it was as good a way as any of continuing her geological survey, but Singer began to suspect that she was making a point – about herself, and the kind of men she liked. It was almost as if she wanted to prove that she preferred Frisby's company to his, a possibility which he found impossible to accept. Yet there was nothing he could do, other than pretend not to care.

Meanwhile, to add to Singer's disquiet, Dionne flirted with him constantly, especially when Ronan was present. As a counter-measure, he dragged Ronan to McFall's for his daily lunchtime pint, attempting to reinforce their bond with tobacco, booze and simple man-talk. This appeared to work, until the day Ronan quaffed several large brandies, told Singer that he loved Dionne, then fell backwards off his stool. In between all of this, Singer worked on his script, Ronan devoured the poetry section of the library in search of forgotten gems for his organ and Oona's sample collection grew so large that it had to be transferred from the kitchen table into the pantry.

On the day before New Year's Eve, Manus arrived at dusk to tell Singer that his 'Yankee-doodles' wanted him on the pub pay phone. Singer grabbed his coat and set off, then returned over an hour later, ashen faced.

'What's wrong?' Melissa asked him as he poured himself a teacup of whiskey in the kitchen, still wearing his coat. He sat down at the table and stared into the cup. Melissa set down the dress she was working on and Dionne looked up from sewing a hem. This year's costumes were 1930s flapper-style, and even more elaborate than the previous ones. Singer's hand trembled as he lifted the cup to his lips. Neither of the women had ever seen him so shaken.

'Has someone died or something?'

He set his drink down. His voice was a whisper. 'They're going to give me two million dollars to make my next film.'

'Whaaat?' Melissa shrieked and leapt upright. She ran around the table and threw herself on top of him. 'Congratulations!' She ruffled his hair and dashed off into the house. 'Hey! Everybody! Guess what!'

Dionne smiled. 'Congratulations, honey. I knew you'd do it.'

'She didn't wait to hear the best bit.'

Oona, Ronan, Frisby and Melissa poured in through the kitchen door. Melissa was still jumping up and down, and the sight of Melissa Montgomery excited stirred yet more excitement still. Oona hugged Singer.

'I knew it. You're on your way, babes.' She kissed his cheek.

Ronan shook his hand. 'I'll expect an exclusive for the next edition of *Avalon*.'

Frisby stood quietly off to one side. To everyone's surprise, Singer stood and embraced him.

'Balor, old chap – our mutual friend Frisby helped me out big time during the summer, by acting in my film, and I never gave him the credit he was due. So, next time you see him, pass on my thanks, will you?' Frisby's eyes turned moist and he nodded, wordlessly.

'What was that you said about not hearing the best bit?' Dionne had returned to sewing her dress. He turned to Melissa.

'How well do you know Margaret MacDonald Mackintosh?'

'Who?'

'She died in 1933.'

'Oh, well, then I'd have to say we're very close. In fact, we see each other all the time.'

'You'll know her inside out by the time we start shooting.'

'What do you mean?'

'They're going to let me use you for the female lead. The producers liked you in our little short, but they've spent the past fortnight trying to bully me into using some starlet they're keen to promote. I refused, so I thought they were going to tell me to piss off. But now they've given me the go-ahead anyway.'

Melissa shook her head. 'I don't believe you.'

'Two million dollars isn't much to make a feature-length film, but considering I made my last one for five thousand pounds, we're going to have a bloody good go at it.' Melissa looked stunned. 'Okay – everyone get your coats.' He strode into the hallway, while the others stared after him.

'Where are we going?'

'Why, up to the pub, of course – Manus insists on hosting the party!'

Frisby tossed and turned in the four-poster bed. He was handsome, thin and floppy-haired again. Moonlight from the curtainless windows fell across his face. In the distance, the sea whispered a woman's name, over and over. Sophia…Sophia… The sea became a woman's voice and Frisby abruptly sat up. Accompanied by faint harp music, Melissa emerged from the shadows of the room, stepping into the beam of moonlight beside the bed.

'Sophia!' Frisby cried. 'How did you get here?'

Melissa untied a sash from her waist and let it fall to the floor.

'I waited ages for you at the harbour! What happened?'

She unbuttoned the stiff black collar of her dress and pulled her arms from its sleeves.

'I was worried sick! What kept you?'

She peeled the upper part of her dress away, and began to undo her skirt. Frisby slumped back onto his elbows, watching. The next shot showed Melissa from behind as she pulled down the skirt to reveal a long slip. She reached up to her hair, which was arranged in a bun, and undid a clasp. Her black hair billowed down her back, which was white in the moonlight. As a frontal shot showed her stepping out of the slip, she froze and the mysterious harp music stopped.

'That's my favourite part!' Manus cried. 'Can we play it again?'

Looking painfully out of place, a television set stood on the bar counter, wired up to a video recorder. The pub was empty, apart from the Christmas Club and Manus, all sat around the circular table. Manus squinted at the remote control in his hand, trying to find the rewind button with a thumb nearly as big as the control itself. From the wall, the big Victorian station clock chimed half-past two. Everyone was drunk. Singer had been buying rounds with wild abandon, then, when the locals had left, Manus had suggested showing the film.

'You're a dirty old man, Manus McFall,' Dionne squawked. 'And to think your wife is lying in her bed upstairs!'

'But Singer said this here is art. Does that not make it okay?'

'You've watched this bit fifty times! Now stoppit, you're embarrassing Melissa!'

'Seeing this reminds me, fair lady, of my one great regret.' The chubby, charcoal-eyed Frisby addressed Melissa, but stared at her frozen image on the screen.

'What, that you've put on so much weight?' Singer joshed him.

'Can we turn that off now, please?' Melissa sighed. 'I'm sick of looking at it.'

'That we consummated our union only in the imagination, and never in truth.'

'I think he means he's sorry he didn't really have sex with you,' Oona laughed. 'Is that what you're getting at, Balor the randy goat?' She leaned over and pinched his cheek.

'Milady's favours were not for me, but for another.' His reply might have passed Oona by, had Melissa not jabbed him in the ribs with her elbow. 'Aow! Milady! I have only ever wished you all the love of my soul, yet sorely do you bruise me! I merely said—'

'She heard what you said, Frisby, so shut up,' Singer warned.

'What did you say?' asked Oona.

'Nothing!' chorused Singer and Melissa, together.

'I'm not asking you two, I'm asking him.'

'I wish it could have been me, fair Melissa, owner of my heart,' Frisby rambled on, and Melissa's faint smile, which had served her well all evening, now failed her. She made a face at Singer, as much as to say, 'Do something!' Singer put an arm round Frisby's shoulder.

'You bested me,' he mumbled into Singer's face. 'You took the true prize, He-Who-Sings.'

'Frisby, leave it. Have a drink, okay?'

'What on earth are you talking about?' Oona persisted.

Frisby pushed Singer's arm away. 'He had her, didn't you know? Leaving me with ashes where my heart once dwelled.'

Melissa closed her eyes and leaned back against the wall, as if trying to merge with it. Singer jumped up, with the intention of hustling Frisby out the door before he said anything further.

'Balor, old boy, you're hammered. Come on, I'll get you home.'

'Wait a minute.' Oona put a hand on Frisby's arm. 'Who had who?'

Singer pulled Frisby to his feet, but he broke loose, sobbing and swaying. 'He,' he jerked a thumb over his shoulder at Singer, 'had her!' His other hand shot out dramatically, practically touching Melissa's forehead.

'How do you know?'

'Because he whispered it to Frisby, and made him cry!'

'Look, I only said that to get you to—' Singer began, but Ronan's pint of Guinness, aimed by Dionne, washed violently over him. She banged the emptied glass on the table, making everyone jump, then stormed out the door, leaving her coat behind. Manus and Ronan gawped. Singer, dripping, released Frisby and fetched a towel from behind the bar counter. Oona glared at him disdainfully.

'Bit of the old casting couch, eh, lover boy?'

'No!' Singer wiped black beer from his face, hair and clothes. 'And anyway, what business is it of anybody's whether I...'

'Poor old Frisby.' Oona stood up, and swaying tipsily, took him by the hand. 'Come on, we'll leave Bergman and Rossellini here to plot their brilliant careers together, while we find somewhere safe to – what was it?' she sneered in Singer's direction. 'Oh yes – somewhere safe to park you.' At that, she led Frisby out the door without looking back.

'I, uh, better go and see if Dionne is okay.' Ronan managed to look both embarrassed and relieved.

'Please, walk me home.' Melissa rose with him. Her face was pale and she wore a resigned expression.

Singer reached for his coat. 'I'll walk you home.'

Melissa's eyes were sad, but not unkind. 'I think it would be a good idea for you to stay up here, just for a while.'

'Hey, how come, all of a sudden I'm the bad guy?'

'You're not a bad guy,' she patted his shoulder, 'but as I warned you at the time, you should never have told Frisby about us. That was cheap and manipulative, and now it's backfired.' She nodded at the flickering, naked image of herself on the television screen. 'And please – turn that off.' She left and Ronan followed, with an apologetic shrug at Manus and Singer, who stood looking at one another. Singer took the remote control from Manus's hand and pressed the stop button. The screen went blank.

'I have a good mind to go down there and wring that little bastard's neck!' He snapped the remote control in half, sending bits of black plastic and batteries showering across the floor.

'If I were you,' Manus let himself behind the bar, 'I'd take the lady's advice, and hang back here for a bit.' He plonked a whiskey bottle and a pair of glasses down on the counter. 'And to think the evening started so well...'

A few hours later, Singer staggered through the front door of the Pier House. After several attempts, he lit a candle in the hallway and carried it into the kitchen, where he drank some water. The girls' half-finished costumes glittered in the candlelight, abandoned on the table. Regretfully, Singer lifted the fabric of one, wishing he could turn back time and escape the rotten sensation of wrong-doing that wrestled with whiskey-fuelled defiance for control of his heart. Chastened by the sad beauty of the forgotten dresses, he crept from the kitchen and went to climb the stairs, when he heard a snore from the living room. He decided to ignore it and grasped the banister when the snore sounded again, so he pushed open the living room door and stepped inside. The furniture had been rearranged around the wall, to clear space for the Christmas Club's New Year's Eve ball. This made the room seem even bigger, a void framed by four pallid oblongs that were the windows. The snoring came from the giant sofa, which had been pushed against the south wall, underneath the old framed photographs of steady, moustachioed lighthouse keepers. Someone lay covered by a blanket. From the rasp, it sounded like Frisby. Singer raised his candle, wondering whether he should check that the man had been laid on his side, in case he was sick – although choking on his own vomit was something he'd be sorely tempted to let Frisby get on with. But as he reached for the cover, it was pushed suddenly back from underneath and Oona sat up, blinking. She was naked, and so too was Frisby, who lay curled up beside her, mouth open, gurgling with each breath.

'Who's there? Oh, it's you. Have you got any cigarettes?' She made no attempt to cover herself, merely shielded her eyes against the candle.

'Sorry – smoked 'em all. What are you doing?'

Oona laughed. 'What do you mean, "what am I doing?" I'm doing what all consenting adults are permitted to do. Now, off you go to bed. Melissa's room is upstairs, left, then second door on the left.'

'Why are you doing this?'

She laughed again. 'Because I felt like a shag. Now that's something I know you'll understand without me having to explain.'

'There's no need for any of this. No need.'

'What's your problem? Do you find it so hard to believe that I'd sleep with Frisby, and not with you?'

'You're going to wreck everything.'

'Correction,' her voice turned harsh. 'You and Melissa wrecked everything, during the summer. It just took until now for the rest of us to find out. By the way, I'd avoid Dionne, if I were you. She's really pissed off with you for snogging her and leading her on again, and then as usual, doing nothing about it. She cried a lot before she went to bed.'

'It doesn't have to be like this.'

'Ah, but this is how it is.' She lay down and pulled the blanket up around her. 'Now, if you don't mind, a bit of privacy, please? Go park yourself elsewhere.'

Singer stomped from the room and slammed the door behind him, very hard.

'Wake up. Singer – wake up!' Ronan stood over him, shaking him. He knew as he opened his eyes that he was in for the hangover from hell. 'Singer! You have to wake up! Oona's disappeared!'

It all came flooding up to meet him, every last bit of the previous night's ugliness. He groaned and rubbed his eyes. 'What's the matter?' He tried to focus. Ronan was neatly dressed, washed and shaved, but his eyes were dead giveaway red, like anemones in a rockpool, behind those circular glasses.

'We can't find Oona. She's not in her room, and she's nowhere about the house.'

Singer snorted. 'I think you'll find her wrapped up warm and snug on the living room sofa.'

'No. Frisby's awake. He doesn't know where she's got to, either.'

'Oh well, if she's not attached to him, then she'll have gone for a nice big walk.' Singer rolled over. 'Case closed.'

'You don't understand. Her shoes, her boots, her coat, the clothes she was wearing last night – they're all here. But she's not.'

Singer sat up, his head spinning. For a moment, he thought he might be sick. 'I'll be down right away.'

'This is the kind of thing Oona does. You don't know her like we do.' Dionne sat at the kitchen table with an expression that somehow combined anger, indifference and wry triumph. Frisby sat opposite, head in hands, snivelling. His eye make-up ran in ghastly streaks down his face.

'You're not helping, Dee.' Melissa stood with one foot up on a kitchen chair, lacing her boot. 'Jay, neither are you. If you're so concerned, you should be helping us to look for her.'

'This isn't my mess.' Dionne reached for her cigarettes.

'You know she's not well.'

'And she'll probably turn up safe and sound, in Berlin or Timbuktu.'

Ronan came through the kitchen back door. 'She's not in the hearse – I've checked.'

'Good! Now that you've checked the hearse,' Dionne tittered nastily, 'would you mind driving me to Dublin?'

Ronan looked sheepish. 'Well, I just thought she might have crawled off and slept there...'

'Oh, who cares? I want away from this madhouse as soon as possible.'

'That's a bit cold, Dionne.' Melissa laced her second boot.

'Not half as bloody cold as this fucking ruin of a place, which I deeply regret ever having set foot in.'

'Well, I think we should help find Oona before we leave.' Ronan pushed his glasses back on his nose.

'You promised you'd get me out of here.'

'I will, but we can't just walk away with someone missing. She could be anywhere!' He and Melissa went to the hallway to fetch their coats, just as Singer came somewhat unsteadily down the stairs.

'It's all right. I know where she is.' He manoeuvred past them and left through the porch.

From the kitchen, Dionne's voice dripped with acid. 'Was that the knight in shining armour?'

'Come on – let's go.' Melissa ran for the door.

'That's odd, I can't find my overcoat,' Ronan muttered, rummaging through the garments in the hall.

She was wearing Ronan's overcoat, but nothing else. Her bare feet were cut from all the climbing, but she didn't appear to notice, as she sat, legs curled up beneath her, on top of the pinnacle overlooking the gorge. It was raining, and the rock was wet and treacherous. Singer pulled himself up beside her and sat cross-legged. His bum got wet, but somehow, that seemed part of the bargain. Her hair hung in dripping ringlets as she peered into the waters below with a distant look on her face. Her eyes were beyond tears. Eventually, she spoke.

'We've screwed it up rightly, haven't we?'

Singer held his face up to the rain. 'I'm not cross with you, if you're not cross with me.'

'I'm not talking about us. I mean "it". The whole thing. It's finished.'

'I never thought I'd hear myself say it, but that house is not a good place to be this morning. Although I'm sure we could get over it, if we tried.'

She picked idly at the rock with her fingernail. 'Always willing to take the lead, eh? Always ready to tell everyone else what they should do.'

'I don't mean it like that.'

'It was good, last year.' She gave a wry smile. 'It was better than good – it was amazing. But it was stupid to think that we could pull it off twice. Magical times like that, they only happen once, and always by accident. You can never repeat them. You can only tuck them away, and keep them in a safe place in your mind, because in every other way, they're lost and gone forever.'

Melissa watched from the tower as Singer helped Oona down from the pinnacle. By taking an elbow each, they managed to get her to the top of the path, but every step was reopening the cuts on her feet, so, in spite of her protests, Singer lifted her in his arms and carried her the rest of the way.

Dionne sat in Ronan's mother's car, staring stonily ahead, as if the car was already underway. Ronan packed the last of her bags into the overstuffed boot. Oona made Singer put her down on the sea-grass and she walked the last fifty paces to the sundial. Frisby rushed from the doorway and tried to embrace her, but she pushed him off and he stood, arms apart, in sorrowful confusion. Melissa leaned against the porch, expressionless. Ronan couldn't hide his astonishment at the bedraggled state of Oona, and his overcoat. Dionne's face was a study in contempt and her eyes carefully avoided Singer and Melissa as she watched Oona limp across to Ronan and hold him by the arms.

'Please,' she nodded at Frisby. 'Take him with you. I'd really, really appreciate it if you'd take him with you now.' She spoke into the car. 'Please, Dionne. There's space in the back.'

'It's not my car, and I don't care as long as I'm out of here some-time in the next sixty seconds.'

'He's your friend,' Oona begged Ronan, who sighed, walked over and guided Frisby into the house, holding him by the elbow.

'Come on, old man, time to go. Let's get your things.'

'Melissa,' Oona commanded, 'follow me to my room, and you can bring Ronan down his coat.'

Singer was left, standing uselessly at the sundial, as Dionne sat in the car, blatantly ignoring him. He wanted to say something, but had no idea what, so he said nothing.

'I think I should leave, too.' Melissa stood beside Singer at the sundial as they watched the chronically overloaded little hatchback creep away along the lane. 'Can you give me a lift to Letterkenny?'

Singer seemed to snap out of a trance. 'Of course. I'll drive you both.'

'Actually, Oona wants to stay, and for you and me to go. She told me to persuade you to leave. But obviously, you'll do whatever you want.' They turned and saw Oona standing at Sophia's bedroom window, looking down at them, brushing her hair. Singer waved, but she merely stared and brushed.

'We can't just walk away, not after what she did this morning. What if she'd thrown herself in?'

'Are you going to argue with her? Because I'm not.'

Oona stayed in her room as they packed their things. Just as they were about to leave, she came downstairs and ran out and hugged them both, with tears in her eyes.

'Here,' she placed a book in Singer's hand. 'You'd better look after this.' It was *Chambers's Miscellany*.

'You shouldn't be alone,' he protested.

'I told you I had my downside – well, now that you've seen it, I want you to leave. Go away, and forget about me.'

'You're such a bloody drama queen! What's the big deal?'

'The big deal is that you have a way of making people want to share secrets, it makes them feel special. But they only feel special until they realise that you do it with everyone you like.' She walked back inside the Pier House and closed the heavy front door. Moments later, they heard the noise of the lock turning – Oona was using the iron key to shut herself in. Melissa sighed, rolled her eyes and climbed into the car. Singer stood a few more moments, staring impotently at the façade of the Pier House.

He stopped at the pub, explained the situation to Manus, and paid him for their stay. Manus promised to keep an eye on Oona, which made Singer feel less terrible, but only marginally so.

'I'll come back and see you real soon – I promise.'

Manus crushed his hand, grinning. 'Be sure and do that.'

'By the way, I've borrowed one of your books.'

'Well then, you'll have to come back, won't you?'

Singer and Melissa drove to Letterkenny in silence. But when they reached the bus station, he didn't stop.

'I'll take you on to Dublin.'

'That's silly, you don't have to.'

'I'm not dumping my leading actress in the arse end of nowhere on New Year's Eve. One abandoned female per day is about as much guilt as I can handle.'

'She'll be all right – I hope.'

'Is she likely to do anything stupid?'

'Stupid? Possibly. Fatal? No. When she calms down, she'll realise that she's blown everything out of proportion. This is about her, not you.'

'Dionne was very angry with me.'

'That's the difference between Oona and Dionne – Oona will be ostentatiously annoyed with herself, Dionne will be quietly seething about us. I'd say we're both off her Christmas card list for the fore-seeable future.'

'Anyway, the journey will give us a chance to talk about the script.'

Melissa rubbed her head. 'Let's not – I have a brutal hangover. I hope you don't mind,' she yawned, 'but having taken advantage of your kind offer, I'm now going to be intolerably rude and sleep all the way home.' She reclined her seat and lay on her side, leaving Singer alone with his thoughts.

When they finally reached Ranelagh, it was well past dark and raining heavily.

'You'll stay the night,' Melissa instructed him as Singer carried the last of her bags into her hallway. 'It's too late to be driving to Belfast – you must be knackered.' She pushed her front door closed. 'And anyway,' she put her arms around his neck, 'may as well be hung for a sheep, eh?'

Later, around midnight, he woke up. At first, he thought he was in the Pier House, until he saw that the bedroom window was in the wrong place and that an orange streetlamp shone through it, not the moon. Melissa slept like a soft statue, her alabaster back turned towards him, and he remembered his whereabouts. He lay awake as rain slapped against the glass and wondered what Oona was doing. The more he wondered, the longer he lay awake.

Two hundred miles due north, Oona sat at the kitchen table in the Pier House, staring into an oil lamp, a glass of brandy and a half-empty bottle by her side. She stubbed out a cigarette, pushed her chair back and walked over to the dresser, where she took the old iron door key down from its hook. She returned to the table, sat, carefully lifted the glass off the lamp and rolled up the left sleeve of her cardigan. Using her right hand, she grasped the handle of the key with a tea towel and held its tooth in the lamp's flame. It took forever to turn red, time enough to smoke three cigarettes. When it was ready, she held the glowing end of the key over the tender skin of her inside left forearm, paused, then pressed down hard. The agony was sharp, instant, almost unbelievable, and she gasped. Her flesh sizzled, smelling of sweet bacon. With a shriek, she flung the hot iron from her and it bounced across the stone floor. The key-shaped burn was filthy white, with brown singeing around the edges. But as she slugged her brandy, Oona decided that the young waitress from Monaghan had been right – the results weren't pretty, but the pain sure as hell took your mind off things, and made you feel just that little bit better.

16

'How much are you paying for a place this big?'

Ronan's father walked slowly around the living room of his Dublin flat, hands rammed into the pockets of his Barbour coat. Ronan noted that the Hawaiian shirt, leather jacket and henna hair dye of his dirty little fling had all vanished, and that once again, his appearance was that of an angry, mean-minded, self-regarding nobody of a civil servant. While his father glared out the tall Georgian windows, as if the very view was a personal insult, Ronan looked daggers at his mother, who perched uneasily on the edge of the sofa, nervous hands clasped round her knee.

He was still in total shock, having learned ten minutes previously that she'd taken his father back. The happy reunion, apparently, had occurred over Christmas. Now, one month on, it was as if the errant parent had never strayed. Ronan's mother seemed to have extracted no price whatsoever for the man's infidelity in terms of humility or loss of status. His position as petty dictator had been well and truly restored.

The happy couple had simply arrived on Ronan's doorstep unannounced, at ten o'clock on a Saturday morning. Still in his pyjamas, he had donned his oxblood leather slippers and red quilted dressing gown to admit them. Now the Doherty family was together again, in a scene all too familiar from the last quarter-century of Ronan's life – both he and his mother cringed while his father fumed.

'Sorry – I didn't quite catch your answer.'

Ronan cast his mother a final appealing, accusatory look. She studied her untouched coffee and twisted at her wedding ring. Ronan cleared his throat.

'Ah, uh, a few hundred.'

'How much?'

'Four. Four hundred a month.'

His father yelped like a kicked terrier, then resumed his patrol of the room.

'For that kind of money, you could rent a mansion in Belfast! Do you hear that, Margaret? Did you know how much he was wasting on rent?' His mother cowered and Ronan hated her.

'I need to be in central Dublin for the magazine to stand any chance of success.'

'Ah! The magazine! This famous magazine!' His father swooped on the coffee table, scooping up a copy of *Avalon*. 'Louis le…Louis le…' he boomed, stumbling.

'Louis le Brocquy,' Ronan sighed. 'Ireland's greatest living painter.'

'Ireland's greatest living chancer, more like! After you, of course.' His father held the magazine at arm's length. 'What's that supposed to be?'

'A portrait of Samuel Beckett.'

'Looks more like something he wiped his face on! How much is this costing a month?'

'How much is what costing a month?'

'This!' His father waved Beckett dangerously close to Ronan's nose.

'Well, it's hard to say, really. The cover price, as you can see, is two pounds – that's down from five – and we've only really been going since August, so circulation is just beginning to—'

'*How much is it costing a month?*' his father bellowed.

'Well, uh, each print run is costing me about fifteen hundred pounds, but I expect that to come down, if I can increase…'

The blood ran from his father's face and for a few moments, Ronan's long-standing prayer that the man might one day suffer a sudden, fatal heart attack seemed on the point of being answered.

'Margaret...' He physically reeled, as if ready to faint. 'Margaret – please tell me this isn't true. Our savings! Please tell me you haven't...'

'Well, Ronan did promise to pay me back,' his mother chirped, as if her son had only borrowed a few pence for sweets.

'Margaret,' his father's voice shook slightly, but took on a patronising tone, as if he were addressing an uncomprehending child – which in a way, Ronan knew he was. He strutted to the living room door, pulled it open and gestured with one hand. 'Do you see those cardboard boxes stacked in the hall? Do you see them, Margaret?' His mother nodded. 'What do you think is in those cardboard boxes, Margaret?' His mother blinked and shook her head. With sudden violence, his father reached out and toppled one of the stacks into the living room. It landed with a floor-shaking thump and the top box split open, pouring a neat flood of magazines around the legs of the coffee table. Seamus Heaney's face stared up in narrow-eyed surprise. Ronan's father pursed his lips.

'Pick one up and read it, Margaret. Read it out loud, please.'

Slowly, his mother obeyed. 'Seamus Heaney, Ireland's greatest living—'

'No. Not that part, Margaret. The bit at the top.'

'Oh, yes, *Avalon*, it's called. That's a nice name,' she smiled at Ronan. 'What does it mean?'

Ronan's father rubbed his forehead. 'The date, Margaret. Is there a date?'

'Yes,' she nodded. 'August 1989.' Ronan felt as if the floor had disappeared and the chair he was sitting on was falling through space.

'There's our money, Margaret.' His father pointed at the spilled magazines. He sounded tired. 'It's gone down a black hole and we'll never see it again. Come on, we're leaving.'

'But Alan, we've only just arrived.'

'We're leaving.' He turned to Ronan and held out a hand. 'The car keys, please.'

'What?'

'The keys to you mother's car. The one parked outside. You've taken everything else – the least you can do is give us back our car.'

'Wait a minute,' Ronan sprung up, stung. 'You can't just go screwing your secretary then expect to walk back into everyone's lives, as if—'

'Ronan!' his mother interrupted, raising her voice for the first time. 'I've taken your father back, and we're not going to talk about it!'

His father snapped his fingers, as a boorish diner would summon a waiter. 'The keys, please.'

Ronan stalked to the mantelpiece, grabbed the keys and flung them across the living room.

'Ooh!' his mother gasped and bent to lift them.

'The money stops now, boy.' His father shepherded his mother out of the room. 'You're nearly thirty years old – you should be ashamed of yourself.' The door closed. Ronan heard their footsteps on the communal staircase. He lifted one of the big sash windows fronting onto the street and took a dose of dank Dublin air. He felt as if he might faint. His parents emerged down the steps of the building and his mother went to unlock her car. His father pointed up the street, obviously towards where his own car was parked. Doubtless, he was telling the woman to stick close behind and not get lost in the traffic. Ronan turned and lifted a box of magazines from his hallway. He carried it to the window.

'Hey! Alan!' he called. His father looked up just in time to see the box hurtle down towards him and dove to one side. The box hit the pavement with a bang, scattering its consignment of magazines onto the road. Ronan's mother screamed. His father looked appalled, but nonetheless picked himself up and shook his fist at the window.

'You bastard!' he roared. 'You nearly killed me!'

Ronan retrieved another box. When his father saw what he was doing, he began to run. Ronan threw it anyway. It missed, but landed close enough to make his father run even faster. As the street filled with back copies of *Avalon*, Ronan reflected how odd it was that every time his major relationships ended, his most beloved possessions should end up lying in the gutter.

In February, Myles O'Brien, the senior partner at O'Brien Fanning Tate, summonsed Dionne into his office. He told her to close the door and sit down while he pretended to write, that tired old ruse for making an employee squirm with uncertainty. Dionne didn't squirm, but pondered O'Brien's oversized head.

'No matter how much dye you put in your hair, no matter what you paid for that shiny suit, you still look like a fat, middle-aged gobshite to me,' she thought.

O'Brien looked up suddenly, as if he'd heard her thought, and wrapped his ample lips around the top of his tortoiseshell pen. He was in the habit of speaking with that pen jammed in his mouth, as if it were a cigar. He looked her up and down, settled his gaze on her breasts and addressed them.

'I hear you sold your house in Donnybrook.'

'That's right, I did.'

'Why?'

'I have my eye on a place off Camden Street, I'm nearly there with it.' Dionne resented being quizzed on her private affairs, but knew that O'Brien was going somewhere with this, and opted to play nice until she found out where.

'Camden Street is nowhere near as good as Donnybrook.'

'Which is why I can afford a much bigger place – the one I'm looking at has four bedrooms and a back garden.'

'Oh,' he grinned, and a drip of saliva literally ran down the side of his pen, 'do I hear the sound of wedding bells?'

Dionne shook her head. 'Not at all. If I buy it, I'll extend at the rear and turn it into two decent flats – live in one and rent out the other.'

'Do you mind me asking – how much did you make on Donnybrook?'

Dionne felt her cheeks start to pink. 'Enough.'

He extracted the pen from his mouth. 'And is it true that you used one of our regular contractors to do it up?'

Dionne shifted in her chair. 'Mooney's did a bit of work for me, yes.'

'Is it true that they might have used a few odds and ends on your house that they'd saved over from other jobs, carried out for this practice? You know – wood, windows, light fittings – that sort of thing?'

Dionne's cheeks felt ready to explode. 'I didn't ask where anything came from – they gave me a price, and I left them to get on with it, just like any other client.'

O'Brien grinned maliciously. 'Is that right? A newly qualified architect, doing up her own precious little house for the very first time, and she doesn't source every last tile for herself?'

Dionne felt a cold streak of fear, but forced herself to smile seductively. 'Ah now Myles,' she cooed, leaning forward, 'sure, you have me working so hard in here, where would I get the time?'

O'Brien laughed, but only briefly. 'So tell me, how much did you make on the Donnybrook sale?' He waved the pen in a rectangle. 'It won't go beyond these four walls.'

'I, uh, doubled my original investment.'

He tapped his teeth with the pen for quite some time, then informed her breasts, 'That's what I thought.' There was a silence, as if he was expecting her breasts to reply. When they didn't, he forced himself to look back into her eyes. 'Tell me something else. If I told you that I had, ooh, roughly fifty or sixty grand kicking about in the bank, what would you say to that?'

'I'd say, lucky you.'

'And what would you say if I thought you could put that parcel of money to work for me, much better than any bank? No strings attached,' he added hastily, when he saw her sudden suspicion. 'A purely business relationship.'

'What kind of business?'

'Well, for example, you might want to buy two houses off Camden Street and turn them into four flats, or maybe more, if you could find adjoining properties.'

'I suppose I could.'

'I don't see why not. Economy of scale, and all that.'

'Would I be allowed to use Mooney's?'

'I wouldn't give a monkey's who you use, just so long as no paperwork comes back to this office.' He waved his pen in a rectangle again, then grinned. 'Apart from the paper my money's printed on, naturally.'

Dionne put her game face on. All the redness had now drained from her cheeks. 'How much?'

'How much what?'

'What percentage would I earn, for managing your investment?'

He shook his head. 'This would be a try-out, a chance to see how you do.'

'Not interested.' Dionne picked herself up and O'Brien's lower jaw stopped just short of his stomach. She turned to leave.

'Wait! Wait! Sit down! Five. Five per cent of whatever you make for me.'

Dionne sat back down. 'Ten.'

'Get a grip!' O'Brien blustered. 'You're just a wee girl!'

'I'm twenty-six, Mister O'Brien, and, with all due respect, you wouldn't be putting your money my way if you thought I was going to lose it on you. Seven and a half, or you can ask one of those idiots out there,' she jerked her thumb in the direction of his door, 'to do your dirty work for you.'

'It's yours,' he grinned, pulling himself up from behind his desk to shake her hand. 'Will you come for a drink after work,' he asked her breasts, 'to seal the bargain?'

'Ah, go on then, I'll find the time,' her mouth answered.

By March, Ronan was too poor to cover his rent, so he moved his books from his flat in Herbert Street into a garret room at the back of a rotten old house down on the quays. It had a crooked bed, bare floorboards, a wooden table and chair and a window that didn't shut properly. Not unlike his bedroom at the Pier House, but somehow, a damn sight less appealing. All the other rooms were occupied by a group of engineering students from Meath whose studies, it seemed, centred entirely on the beer taps of the grimy pub around the corner. There was one communal bathroom, a horror beyond words. Two days after he moved in, Ronan realised that he had just enough money either to invite Dionne out for dinner or buy groceries for the week. He rang her at work. Sorry, she couldn't make it – up to her eyes, try again soon. He told her nothing of *Avalon's* sudden demise, nor his reduced circumstances.

By April, he was starving and it occurred to him that he might actually have to find a job. He spruced himself up and trudged around the offices of all the city centre newspapers, gamely trying to project the image of a highly paid, London-based arts correspondent who'd taken a sudden caprice to live in Dublin. But nobody was hiring, not even freelance. However, one stressed-out assistant editor told him that there might be a spot of subbing work closer to the summer, and to call back then.

By May, relations with the engineering students had deteriorated badly. For his part, Ronan felt justified in reading the riot act during their noisy weekend parties. For their part, the engineering students felt justified in behaving any way they pleased, given that Ronan was behind on the rent and only emerged from his garret at mealtimes, in order to scrounge a plate of whatever they had on the go. Ronan also rang the stressed-out assistant editor to inform him that it was one whole month closer to summer, and the man somewhat crossly told him not to ring back again until the end of June, when the regular staff would be starting to go on holiday.

Manual work was, of course, out of the question, and the Dublin of 1990 was not exactly awash with employment opportunities anyway. Ronan wondered what he could do to kill four whole weeks before the engineering students either killed him, or he killed one or all of them. He briefly contemplated throwing himself on Singer again, but feared that if he did, word might get back to Dionne about his narrowed straits. Where could he go, what could he do, to tide himself over until these putative subbing shifts came through? There was always London, but that was way too much like history repeating itself, only backwards. Plus, if there was one thing worse than being poor in Dublin, that was being poor in London. And ultimately, he needed to be in Ireland to have any hope with Dionne. There was no chance whatsoever of going back to his parents, but London...now, there was the germ of an idea.

From the payphone outside the house, he rang his mother when he knew that his father would be at work and beseeched, bullied and blackmailed her into sending him a hundred pounds. Enough to scrape by for a month – provided he didn't have to pay any rent, and somebody else did all the shopping. The day the money arrived, he gave up his room, paid one of the engineering students a tenner to store his books and rang Frisby in southern England.

After a bit of small talk, during which the events of the previous Christmas were not mentioned, Ronan told Frisby that, because of his thriving arts magazine, he had oodles of research to do around the museums and galleries of London, but that he needed somewhere to stay, and wouldn't this be a good opportunity to for the two of them to catch up? Frisby sounded dubious.

'Hold on, I'll need to ask my mum.'

'Your mother?' Ronan exclaimed, but Frisby had set down the phone and his voice could be heard in the distant background. After quite some time, he picked up again.

'That's all right, my mum says you can have the spare room for a bit.'

'Great! It's Tunbridge Wells you live, isn't it?'

Frisby sounded uncomfortable. 'Well, it's not quite Tunbridge, more like Crawley, actually.'

'Crawley, as in beside Gatwick Airport?'

'Should be no problem meeting your plane.'

'I'm, uh, coming by boat, because I hate flying.'

Frisby laughed. 'Takes forever, but it's much cheaper, I suppose.'

Singer woke up in his suite in One Devonshire Gardens, a boutique Glasgow hotel discreetly hidden inside a row of Victorian-era town-houses. As ever, when he found himself somewhere strange, at first he imagined he was in the Pier House, until the more opulent curtains and wallpaper on this occasion told him otherwise. He pulled on a bathrobe and wandered into the lounge, where he smelled coffee. Breakfast stood on a table in the corner. Before an enormous bay window, Melissa sat in her black leotard, finishing her stretches.

'Guess what we have?' she asked as Singer rummaged in the drinks cabinet.

'All the jammy luck in the world?' he enquired, holding up a crystal decanter of Scotch.

'No, something much better than that, right here, in this suite.'

'I dunno,' he yawned and pretended to look around. 'An army of willing maidservants panting to obey my every depraved command?' She picked up a nearby slipper and threw it at him. He tried again. 'Cute bars of soap in the bathroom?'

'You're warm. The bathroom is massive – it has a Jacuzzi and a sauna.'

Singer laughed. 'No way.'

'What time are we meeting your man?'

'Casting director is picking us up at eleven. We're meeting Gardiner close by.'

'She's coming to the hotel?'

'I'm the one with the budget, so people come to us. But I didn't pick this hotel for its Jacuzzis, it happens to be right beside one of our locations. Great place to do a read, and see what this fellow's made of.'

'Goody,' Melissa declared, walking across the floor, 'that gives us two hours. Do you fancy sweating out some of last night's booze?'

The casting director was a blonde-bobbed, grey-suited woman of about fifty, called Burgess. With a bundle of scripts under one arm,

Singer held open the door of the waiting black taxi and she leapt nimbly in after Melissa.

'Derek Gardiner has done quite a bit of television,' she explained to Singer during the short ride, 'but he hasn't boxed himself into any corners – the public doesn't think of him as a cop or a doctor or anything. He's very versatile, and always looks different in every role. And because he's done nothing outside of Scotland, if you want him, you'll get him cheap.' The taxi pulled up outside a big modern building, with a full-sized concrete copy of an old terraced house tacked onto its side.

'The Hunterian,' Singer informed Melissa. 'Just wait until you see what's inside that concrete lump.'

The lump contained a partial reconstruction of Charles Rennie Mackintosh's old Glasgow home. Melissa stood in the white, upstairs drawing room, overwhelmed by its other-worldly elegance. She studied a gesso panel above one of the fireplaces, which showed a highly stylised, ghostly young woman holding roses.

'You made that,' Singer teased. 'Margaret McDonald worked alongside her husband. She was just as accomplished an artist as he was.'

'The talent was all hers, I'm afraid.' The sweeping Glasgow brogue came from behind them. 'It was she who inspired all my greatest work.' The hair on Singer's neck stood on end. For there, in the doorway, stood Mackintosh himself, alive after sixty years of death. The same head of dark, thick-curled hair, the same handlebar moustache, the same Italianate nose and chin and the same sad brown eyes. He wore an old-fashioned suit jacket with a plain white shirt, jeans and red trainers. Burgess jumped forward and took his arm.

'Gareth Singer, Melissa Montgomery, I'd like you to meet Derek Gardiner.'

Gardiner had a confident handshake and an easy way about him. Singer liked him immediately. He opened his scripts and asked Melissa and he to read a scene where Mackintosh comes home drunk, having lost his job as an architect – in spite of his outstanding ability. Margaret prevents him from smashing their gorgeous furniture as he rails against the miseries of Scotland. When he calms down, he advocates leaving Glasgow for London, where he hopes to be appreciated. Margaret promises to help him create heaven no matter where they go.

Singer already suspected that he'd found his leading man. By the time the scene ended, he knew that he had. He also knew that, sometime within the next few weeks, Melissa would sleep with Gardiner and that his eight-month affair with her would be over. He felt a pang of jealousy, but, watching the pair of them act at being husband and wife, his jealousy was far outweighed by his excitement at their performances. His film came first, second and third in his affections.

Leaving the Hunterian, Singer showed Melissa, Burgess and Gardiner a blow-up of an old photograph hanging on a wall. A young Mackintosh sat on a lawn, staring boldly at the camera, as no fewer than six women in summer hats and long, flowing dresses stood sideways on either side of him, the two middle women holding hands, in an arch above his head. Singer explained that the seven, all art students, had formed a group called the Immortals, and that the photograph had been taken before Margaret, who stood beside Mackintosh, became his lover. At that time, he was engaged to one Jessie Keppie, also present in the picture. Keppie had never gotten over losing Mackintosh, and had never married – although she had outlived the couple by decades.

'There they are,' Singer patted the wall beside the photo, 'young, talented and good-looking, bursting with friendship and optimism, with no idea of the sadness the future holds. I've called our film after this picture – *The Immortals*.'

Crawley wasn't as bad as Ronan expected – it was worse. A heartless, architectural mess, the conurbation had been thrown together as a so-called 'new town' in the 1950s. Frisby lived with his parents in a brown-brick, three-bedroom semi-detached, in a street utterly indistinguishable from dozens of others, all privet hedges and Ford Escorts parked out front. Frisby's mother – from whom he obviously took his physical build – was a happy, plump woman who welcomed Ronan the way the Aztecs must have welcomed visiting spacemen, with a mixture of awe and immense sacrificial offerings of food.

'James has never had a friend to stay before, you know!'

'James?' Ronan thought he had misheard.

'James,' she smilingly affirmed, reaching a meaty arm around Frisby's shoulders.

'James,' Ronan nodded. 'Of course.' Frisby grinned foolishly and stared at the floor.

The house smelled of cabbage and boiled meat, but had obviously been spruced up for Ronan's visit – he noticed, for example, that the red paint on the front door was sticky to the touch. He was shown a tiny bedroom at the back that was spartan but comfortable, and judging by the piles of angling magazines in the corner, the place where Frisby's father normally slept. Eddie was tall, suffered tonsure-like baldness and had the facial demeanour of a basset hound. He smoked a pipe and drove a bus at Gatwick Airport. When he wasn't working, he was angling in an artificial reservoir stocked with trout.

The trout that Eddie supplied for dinner were, as Ronan was to discover, by far and away the best thing about life in Crawley. Frisby father and son did not frequent the pub together; indeed they seemed to have nothing to say to one another. Frisby himself worked in a food-processing factory and was gone every morning at seven. His mother told Ronan over breakfast how proud she was that James was finally holding down a job.

'Head in the clouds, that boy. A dreamer, like his father.' Ronan tried briefly to imagine what Eddie Frisby might dream about. Trout, perhaps.

'You must be glad to have James home again.'

'From Ireland? Oh, he had me tortured last year, wearin' ladies' make-up and prattlin' on about ghosts. But he's all right now, seems like he got that rubbish out of his system, spending Christmas with you lot.'

'Yes. But I meant, you must be glad to have him home from London – all that time he lived up there, selling yachts.'

'Yachts? London? James has never set foot on a yacht in his life, and he's never lived anywhere but here, with us.'

Ronan opened his mouth to ask about Leamington Spa, then thought better of it. But as he crawled into bed that night, he wondered what it must have been like, growing up in a place like Crawley. For anyone with an ounce of sensitivity, he decided, the urge to reinvent oneself would be downright irresistible. Uncomfortably, he caught a fleeting glimpse of himself in that analysis, then tossed and turned, wishing he hadn't gained that particular insight.

On his first day, Ronan loftily explained to Mrs Frisby that he had important research to conduct up in London and set out, after breakfast, for the train station. Purchasing a return ticket, he received an enormous shock – it cost him one-fifth of all the money he had left in the world. If he were to survive financially through the next month, he couldn't be travelling up to London every day. When he arrived at Victoria, he walked in a daze up The Mall to the National Gallery, which he knew to be admission free. He spent the rest of the morning there, but exited to Charing Cross Road for a sandwich and a coffee because the gallery café was so expensive. Then, on a sudden whim, he took a Tube from Leicester Square out to Clapham and walked across the Common to the street where he and Linda had once lived. It looked the same, but not. The trees and bushes were bigger and the parked cars newer than the ones he remembered. There was a 'For Sale' sign outside their flat, with the smug addendum 'Sale Agreed' attached to the bottom. The curtains were closed. Ronan stood across the road for fifteen minutes, as if he somehow expected Linda to emerge. She didn't, so he sauntered to the top of the street and poked his head into his former local, the Britannia. It had been completely gutted, the old, organic interior replaced with polished wooden panels, cheap brass lamps and faux-Victorian armchairs. It was also empty of customers, the traditional clientele obviously having either died or decamped elsewhere, so when the young barman immediately approached him, Ronan frowned, pretended to look around as if fruitlessly searching for someone, and left. He didn't belong in this place, and felt as if he never had.

Whatever about London, Ronan definitely did not belong in Crawley, and on more than one occasion wished he'd taken his chances and stayed in Dublin. Trying to spend as little money as possible, he spent the next few days in the municipal library, a grey, glass-fronted box thrown up in the 1960s. Books made the tedium bearable. Every evening over dinner, he dropped casual mentions about the weather or the crowds up in London, where the Frisbys still believed he was doing important research. But his second major shock – after the London train fare – came the following Saturday, when Frisby announced at the breakfast table that, since it was his day off, the two would play golf.

'But I've never played golf in my life!' Ronan quailed.

'Just taken it up myself,' Frisby grinned, 'and I'm hooked! I'm out every spare second I have! If you're staying with me, you gotta play golf!' Sure enough, without his eyeliner, with his hair short but no longer shaved and wearing a pink Pringle polo shirt with a pair of gloves sticking out the back pocket of his slacks, the plump little Frisby looked, to Ronan's eyes, every inch the suburban Englishman who enjoyed a good old round of golf.

'But is golf not very expensive?'

'My old man knows the greenkeepers,' Frisby tapped his nose. 'He brings them free duty free from the airport. Fags and booze for green fees – it's a nice little arrangement. They'll slip you a set of clubs and all.' Ronan tried to assimilate this new image of Frisby's father as a kingpin of local crime, and once again, his imagination failed him.

However, one thing was for certain – Ronan stank at golf. Frisby seemed able to hit the ball exactly where he wanted, whereas Ronan could barely hit the ball at all. And Frisby hadn't lied – he played every spare second that he could, and Ronan had no choice at the weekends but to accompany him, or find some other cost-free way of entertaining himself that didn't involve watching daytime television with Mrs Frisby in that stifling, tiny house.

Towards the end of June, with precisely twelve pounds left in his pocket, Ronan walked into central Crawley and rang Dublin. The stressed-out assistant editor took a while to remember who, precisely, Ronan was – but yes, there were subbing shifts coming up – only a couple a week, mind, and they were nights. Ronan thanked the startled man so profusely that he sounded taken aback, muttered something about a deadline and hung up. Ronan staggered from the pay phone kiosk and collapsed to his knees in the middle of the pedestrianised shopping street, crying tears of relief so torrential that he was obliged to rip his glasses from his face and snuffle into a hanky.

'I know just how you feel, sonny.'

A blurred object stopped before him and spoke in a wavering, high-pitched voice. 'It's these immigrants – they get the best of everything, and honest English men and women like you and me are left with nothing.' He pushed his glasses back onto his face. A veinous hand extended a coin beneath his nose. 'Here, buy yourself a nice cup of tea. Things always seem better after a nice cup of tea.' The hand pressed the coin into his and he looked up to see an elderly lady in a petrol-green greatcoat toddle off across the anonymous plaza, dragging a skittish, rodential dog by the neck.

O'Brien paid Dionne a site visit, something he had never done before. Yet there he stood, outside the building site off Camden Street, wearing a totally unnecessary yellow hard hat that was way too small for his head. His big blue Mercedes was double parked on the road, hazard lights flashing. A man stood beside him, someone Dionne had never seen before, a small, older fellow with a pepper moustache and shrewd, pale blue eyes.

'Ah, Miss Brady!' O'Brien interrupted her conversation with the foreman, who took the opportunity to disappear into the bowels of the gutted houses. 'I'd like you to meet Mr Ryan, a valued associate of O'Brien Fanning Tate.' The little man wore only a nondescript navy suit with a plain red tie, yet there was an obvious deference in her boss's manner towards him. And it was most unlike O'Brien to defer to anybody.

'Call me Mick,' the newcomer shook Dionne's hand vigorously. 'All my friends do.' O'Brien, Dionne noticed, didn't.

'Mr Ryan wanted to cast an eye over our little project here. I've been explaining our arrangement, and he's keen to know a bit about costs and completion dates. As, indeed, am I.'

'Of course you are!' Ryan guffawed, and elbowed O'Brien in the ribs. 'Since it's your own readies that's tied up in it!' This truly was a day of firsts, because Dionne had never seen anybody elbow O'Brien in the ribs before, and the action left him with the expression of a miffed, overweight schoolboy. She couldn't help smiling.

'We're under budget and well ahead of schedule. I've managed to squeeze eight units in there, and I reckon I can have them on the market before Christmas, instead of next March, as originally planned.'

Ryan leered at her. 'Got that through the planners with remarkable speed, didn't you?'

'It's arguably an interior refurbishment, and still residential, so no change of use. Plus, I was nice to them.'

'Were you, now?' Ryan's eyes twinkled. 'So tell me this – how would you fancy taking on something a little bit bigger?'

'How much bigger?'

'Old warehouse, down by the docks. Has the potential for fifty units, maybe more.'

Dionne made a superhuman effort not to bat an eyelid. 'That's a lot – do you think they'll sell?'

'The time is coming, Miss Brady, when we won't be able to build flats quick enough in this town, or sell them dear enough, for that matter.'

She addressed her boss. 'Is this a company project?'

Ryan answered for him. 'Not as such.'

'I'll do it for a percentage of final sales, then.'

'Do you see, Mr Ryan,' O'Brien boomed pompously, 'what did I tell you? The arrogance of youth.'

But the twinkle hadn't left Ryan's eyes. 'Can I ask you, Miss Brady, what you consider to be the best hotel in Dublin?'

Dionne shrugged. 'The Bristol-Regis, I suppose.'

'I'm glad to hear you say that, because I happen to own it, amongst other things. Now, if we were to meet there in the restaurant tomorrow night about eight? To discuss your terms?'

Ronan detested subbing, but he detested being poor even more, so he stuck at it through the summer, taking every shift offered. He was given all the filler copy – mind-numbing dross, most of it – and quickly became aware how few people do so many different jobs in newspaper offices. One morning, just after he'd arrived for an extra shift, his saviour, the stressed-out assistant editor, slammed his phone down with a choice selection of oaths. The court reporter had phoned in sick and there was nobody to cover a minor but nonetheless newsworthy trial. The editor hollered around the office, 'Does anyone here have shorthand?'

Ronan timidly raised his arm, and next thing he knew, he was jogging towards the Four Courts, clutching a pen and notebook. By the time September rolled around, when by rights his subbing shifts should have dried up, he'd made himself so useful in so many ways that the newspaper kept him on – not with a full-time job, but with a series of part-time ones that meant he worked longer hours than most. The creeping terror engendered by his time in Crawley had transformed him from a gadfly into a worker bee. This, of course, was a superficial mutation, brought about by necessity, rather than a profound transformation of the soul. *Avalon* lived, but only as a daydream.

As soon as he could afford to, he rented a tiny one-bedroom flat in Christchurch. In truth, it was more of a broom cupboard than a flat, but at long last, he didn't have to share a bathroom with anyone from Meath. He even summoned up the courage to telephone Dionne, ready with his 'off in London doing important research' excuse for when she would inevitably ask where he'd been. But she didn't – his absence had not been noted. He brought her up to date about the newspaper, embellishing his dogsbody role into that of highly paid features writer, and she was sufficiently impressed to agree to a lunch date for the following week. She didn't mention *Avalon*, nor any of their mutual friends, so neither did he.

However, the very next evening, just as he was about to leave the newspaper office for his broom cupboard, an extension on a nearby desk rang, and since there was nobody else around, he lifted it.

'Subs.'

'Hello, I'm not sure if I have the right number.' The female voice was faint, but familiar. 'I'm trying to reach a Ronan Doherty.'

'Oona? Is that you?' She sounded as if she was calling from an echo chamber somewhere on Jupiter.

'Ronan, I didn't recognise you. How are you?'

'Fine, fine.'

'Listen, I'm just off the phone to Dee, and she told me you were working here.'

'Yes, they made me an offer I couldn't refuse.'

The old Oona would have made a crack about him finding a horse's head in his bed, or maybe even an entire horse. Instead she sounded tired, almost monotone.

'Sorry to bother you, but I was hoping you'd know where I could reach Singer. I've rung Belfast, but I don't think he's there. Has he moved house or something?'

'He's probably away, making his film. Have you tried Melissa?'

'Yes, but she's not around either.'

'Now there's a surprise.'

'Look, if he should happen to contact you, would you pass on a message from me?'

'Of course.'

'Would you tell him...' there was a pause, as she seemed to catch her breath. It wasn't until she started speaking again that he realised she was crying. 'Would you tell him that I'm back in St Eunan's again?'

'What's St Eunan's? What's the matter?'

'St Eunan's is where they send you,' she sobbed, 'when they don't know what's the matter with you.' There came a series of electronic beeps, the sound of a pay phone demanding more money, and the line went dead.

17

The Immortals cost less than two million dollars to make, and earned fourteen million back in two years, following its release in late 1992. The producers were gobsmacked. By clever choices of location and by hiring the best production designer he could afford, Singer had managed to make the film look much more expensive than it was. He also used computer effects in an unusual way, occasionally decorating the screen with Rennie Mackintosh's and Margaret MacDonald's distinctive designs to bring their creative ideas to life. But what really made the film work were the performances he extracted from Melissa Montgomery and Derek Gardiner, both complete unknowns who, as Singer had predicted to himself, were in the middle of a raging affair by the time principal photography got under way. They set the screen on fire, transforming what risked being a minor arthouse curio into a respectable hit, especially in Europe. The film took an award at Cannes, and in spite of his antipathy towards the place, Singer found himself spending a lot of time in Los Angeles, discussing bigger and bigger deals for his next picture.

Melissa fared better still, with offers of work flooding in off the back of The Immortals, including several from different Hollywood studios. There was a period in early 1993 when her face graced the cover of practically every women's magazine in Britain, France and

Germany, countries where *The Immortals* did particularly well. In America, she was still a nobody, but a leading New York agent called Granville Flannery, well known for his shrewdness, nonetheless snapped her up. Her next leading role, he maintained, would be the one to break her in the States – if properly chosen. While her new Svengali wheeled and dealed on her behalf, Melissa amused herself by accepting a supporting role in a rather po-faced historical drama shot by a moderately famous English director, set in colonial Egypt. Her affair with Gardiner, who had landed a television series that kept him in London, didn't survive her four months in Egypt, and a fling with the moderately famous English director.

In June 1993, Melissa's agent flew to meet her in London. He booked himself into the Dorchester, where Melissa arrived to meet him after a sad, recriminatory lunch with Gardiner that she wished she'd never agreed to. She'd had a few glasses of wine and was in no mood for niceties. Flannery, a sandy-haired, freckle-faced Wasp type with eyes like titanium drill bits, plonked a pile of paper down on the smoked-glass coffee table of his suite.

'Okay, way I see it, we have ourselves two options.'

'But I've had more offers than that, surely?'

'You've had eighteen worth a damn, but these two have been green-lit by the studios, and are definitely happening real soon. This,' he pushed a script across the table, 'will make you the next Sharon Stone.' *Love in a Forbidden Place*, read the cover.

'Sounds painful,' Melissa muttered.

'One point two mill, plus two points – it's by far and away your biggest offer. These guys love ya, they want you in their movie.'

'Have you read it?'

'Yup.'

'What do you think of it?'

'Porn for yuppies – it's gonna be huge.'

'I don't want to be the next Sharon Stone. I want to be the next Meryl Streep.'

Flannery curled his upper lip in what Melissa took to be a smile. 'But you look like Audrey Hepburn.'

'I think we'll say no.'

'I'm real glad to hear you say that.'

'Then why did you suggest it?'

'Because I'd have failed in my duty to you as a client and to me as an agent who makes a lotta money outta his clients if I hadn't run it past you.'

'What else have you got?'

'This, I like.' He pushed over a script with a powder-blue cover, *To Live and Shop in Manhattan*. 'Romantic comedy, great part, lotsa good lines – and you get to keep your clothes on. You can do a British aristo, right?'

Melissa gave him a throatier version of Frisby. 'Well yah, dahling, one simply does posh English accents all the time.'

'Okay, you're an upper-class Brit who hits New York to party, but then Daddy cuts off your allowance. To make ends meet, you wind up working in a big store on Fifth Avenue, your first-ever job. You meet a customer, a funny guy, he likes you, you like him, you date, you fall in love. But there's a problem.'

'There always is.'

'He's engaged to be married to this total rich bitch in one month's time. But by the kind of coincidence that only happens in the movies, your boss appoints you personal shopper to the store's biggest spender.'

'The total rich bitch?'

'You got it.'

'So let me guess – I spend the next month trying to sabotage this woman in the eyes of everyone she knows, by getting her to shop for her wedding in the worst possible taste.'

'It's a take on rampant consumerism, I guess.'

'But in spite of my motives, I gain an entrée into her eccentric but loveable family, and begin to see her for the vulnerable girl that she really is?'

Flannery grinned. 'Keep goin'...'

'I also discover that the man I'm trying to steal is actually a bit of a bastard, and I develop a secondary romantic interest, probably with her brother, and the whole thing plays itself out in a mish-mash of comic errors into a happy ending where true love saves the day.'

'Kid, you coulda wrote the script.'

'I'll do it.'

'I thought you wanted to be the next Meryl Streep?'

Melissa donned her faint smile. 'Ah, but this is very Audrey Hepburn. And while I'm making this,' she patted the script, 'you can go out and find me something low-key and serious to follow up with. Speaking of which…'

Her agent interrupted. 'Don'tcha wanna talk money?'

'One point two mill, plus points.'

'No, that was the other guys.'

'Tell these guys,' she patted the script again, 'that that's what I'm being offered elsewhere, but obviously don't tell them that I'd rather stay celibate for the rest of my life than endure *Love in a Forbidden Place*. Be prepared to come down a bit, but one point two seems a good place to start. Now, as I was about to ask you – did you talk to Gareth Singer's producers in LA?'

The agent shook his head. 'Nix. Nada.'

Melissa felt suddenly sick. 'You mean he doesn't want me for Zelda?'

'Oh, he wants you all right, but those guys are still fighting over the script. They won't be making movies any time soon, that's for sure.'

'Pity,' Melissa pouted, 'sounds like a wonderful film, and it's never been done before.'

'A biopic of F. Scott Fitzgerald? Now why do you think that's never been done before?'

'No idea.'

'Can you imagine how stupid you'd look if you screwed up on F. Scott Fitzgerald?'

On Christmas Eve 1994, Dionne parked her car on the gravel drive in front of Liscloone, a Palladian-style country house set in three hundred acres of virgin countryside, deep in County Carlow. She switched off her mobile phone, which hadn't stopped ringing on the drive down from Dublin – niggling problems with a fair-sized project she was financing herself on the city's south side. The phone took up most of the space inside her Moschino handbag, but she squeezed it in anyway and stepped out of the car, a bulky Mercedes Benz coupe, which, when Johnny Roache had first clapped eyes on it, he'd denounced as far too big, fast and thirsty for a young single woman. Dionne had laughed and explained that new business contacts always took her seriously when they saw what she drove. A car like that, along with the right outfit, could save months of bullshit. Anyway,

Johnny's father owned a Bentley, so he was hardly one to be grumbling about conspicuous consumption.

Johnny emerged from the house, onto the sandstone steps of the colonnaded front portico, smiling like the master of all that he surveyed. As it happened, Johnny's father still owned everything he surveyed, but one day…As she climbed the steps and kissed his handsome cheek, she couldn't help but sneak a final look at all that lovely, rolling parkland. The things you could do with a place like this, if you ever got your hands on it…

Four hours later, still wearing her high heels and black evening dress, she stormed down the same portico steps in the dark, trying hard not to trip. Nothing ruins a dramatic exit like falling on your arse. She popped the boot lid with her electronic key fob and it yawned open as she stalked towards the car. She flung her little Vuitton suitcase in and slammed it shut. Johnny came crashing through the front door of the mansion, took the steps in a single bound and sprinted across the gravel towards her.

'Dee! Dee! What on earth is the matter?'

Dionne yanked open the door, threw her handbag in and began to remove her earrings – big, stupid, sterling silver pendants that looked great, but had annoyed her all evening.

'What's the matter, Johnny, is that you're pretending you don't know what's the matter. I'm not staying here a moment longer.'

'Look, I'm sure my mother didn't mean what she said – at least, not the way you're taking it.'

'Oh, but she meant exactly what she said. She's yammered on about your ex-bloody-girlfriend since the moment I arrived. Lucy this, Lucy that…'

'But Lucy and I are ancient history – my mother knows that!'

'Your mother knows that Lucy's daddy breeds horses on a big fucking farm, while mine breeds children on a housing estate.' She put on a shrill, falsetto voice. 'How many brothers and sisters did you say? My! That's rather a lot, isn't it?' She flung the earrings into the car.

'Look, please don't leave, I'll go back in there and set her straight.'

'Forget it. The woman can already see the wedding pictures in her head, and she's horrified. The oh-so-perfect Roaches, with their oh-so-perfect son, beside a tribe of savages from darkest Dublin. Believe me, it's better this way.' She jumped into the car, conscious that Johnny wasn't moving, hand on hips.

'Well, I think you're over-reacting.'

She pressed a switch and her window whined down. 'Johnny, you're going to end up married to Lucy, whether you like it or not.' She twisted her key and the enormous engine rumbled. She gunned it for effect and the exhaust roared. 'Have a good life.' The car sped off, spraying gravel in its wake.

Five miles up the road, she pulled into a lay-by and allowed herself to cry for a few minutes. She unzipped her handbag, snuffled into a hanky and switched on her phone. It beeped, with one message, which she deleted without reading. She scrolled through her directory until she found the number she wanted. She pressed call. The number rang three times before being answered.

'Hi. It's me. I wasn't sure if you were in town for Christmas. I know it's late, but can I call past and see you?'

It took her a couple of hours to drive back into the city, and then a good ten minutes of manoeuvring her luxury barge around the narrow, dirty streets behind Christchurch before she finally found the block of flats, which were dingy even by Dublin standards. When she buzzed, Ronan came down to admit her – the entry system was broken. Framed by the fluorescent light from the corridor, his hair looked rumpled, as if he'd been sleeping. He pushed his glasses up onto his nose and blinked at her car, as if it were a flying saucer. Then he took in her evening dress and blinked all the more.

'Dee – is something wrong?'

'I hope not. I bought some wine,' she held up two bottles, one in each hand, 'just in case you didn't have any.'

'Come in, come in.' He held the door open for her. 'Wine is one of the few luxuries you'll never find me without.' She stepped past him.

'So, have you written any poems about me lately?'

To Live and Shop in Manhattan was a major hit for Melissa, both commercially and critically. 'The new *Philadelphia Story*,' the *New York Times* cooed, 'only with Audrey, instead of Katherine.' She had chosen well, because the film did exactly what both she and her agent wanted, which was to break her in America. It also showed that she could do comedy, as well as act. Once again, she was on the cover of all the women's magazines, but this time, the truly important ones.

In 1994, before *To Live and Shop* was released, she shot a low-budget film called *Territory*, about a woman campaigning to save a small Canadian town from an unscrupulous mining company. Hard on the heels of *To Live and Shop*, but completely different in every way, *Territory* cemented Melissa's reputation for versatility, leaving her, by early 1995, with a choice of plum parts. Continuing her strategy of making one surprise independent film for every mainstream role, in 1995 she shot *Pacific Freeway*, a straight, big-budget romance set in 1970s California, and then spent the summer in France, on location for *La Vignoble Perigourdine*, a dynasty saga centred on a family-owned winery during the great French vine epidemic of the 1860s.

During *La Vignoble*, Melissa entered into the first relationship that she knew she wouldn't be able to walk away from again as soon as filming was over. He was a cameraman called Guy. He hadn't a penny to his name, but Melissa was besotted and was in the process of buying a farm in her new lover's native Dordogne, with the full intention of settling down and having bilingual babies when the call came through from Singer about *Scottie & Zelda*.

'I haven't bothered ringing your agent.' Singer's voice was broken by transatlantic static, but Melissa detected his deadpan tease, nonetheless. 'Because I assume that you're now outrageously expensive.'

'Oh, you know me – always available, for the right sort of man. What about you? Found any nubile young starlets willing to grace your arm?'

'I've found the odd one willing to grace my expense account, but every woman I meet in LA thinks I'm a degenerate because I like a few drinks. I hate this place. They're all total health freaks. They consult their personal trainers before they have sex.'

'Well, I'm glad to hear that your Fitzgerald film is happening at last.'

'It would be wonderful to have you – somebody sane, from the old days. Please say you'll do it.'

'Singer, tell me this. After *The Immortals*, you could have made anything you wanted. It's taken you three years to get this one together – why are you only interested in stories about doomed couples?'

'Because doomed people are interesting, and two doomed people are twice as interesting as one.'

The massive sound stage at Premier Studios, Burbank, Los Angeles contained a faithful reconstruction of a luxury suite in the New York Plaza Hotel from the early 1920s. Scott Fitzgerald and Zelda had lived there on and off during his first flush of literary success. Melissa, who looked stunning in a flapper dress, was meant to be having a petulant argument with her husband, played by a famous young star called Nick Danver. Instead, she sat flopped on a chintz sofa as Danver argued with Singer. Danver, as well as being young and famous, was a noxious boor with a serious cocaine habit and had been hell to work with from day one. It was now day twelve. Singer had been trying to shoot this particular scene all morning – he was now on his thirteenth take and still hadn't managed to get what he wanted. To make matters worse, Kaspar and Leon Kaminski, Singer's all-powerful producers, having heard about the arguments, had dropped in to see a bit of filming for themselves. They sat off to one side in the shadows as fifty other highly paid people stood around, waiting to reshoot the scene. Melissa had a headache. She had been surprised at how much weight Singer had lost since they'd last met, but not in a healthy way. He looked tired, his untidy mop of black hair had begun to grey and he wore a stained white shirt tucked into black jeans, his scruffiness a deliberate protest, she suspected, against the burnished perfection of everyone around him. He stood, arms folded, as Danver, dressed in a beautifully fitted jazz-age suit, paced up and down, waving a script.

'Nobody calls anyone "my darling",' he protested querulously. 'I mean, who the hell says that? Why can't I call her "honey" or "baby"?'

'Because,' Singer closed his eyes and massaged his temples, 'as you might be able to gather from the costumes and the set, the events we are depicting occurred over seventy years ago, when educated people spoke more formally to one another. Also, because the use of "my darling" is a deliberate affectation. Because the couple are fighting and using the term sarcastically, and finally, because you are being paid to act, not fucking well write the script.'

'Kas! Leon!' Danver shouted off set. 'Did you hear what he just said? Do you hear the way this guy treats me?'

The Kaminskis, a pair of obese brothers, shifted in their seats. Kaspar, the older, uglier and wealthier of the two, raised a hairy arm, revealing a sizeable patch of sweat on his expensive shirt. Although not twins, they were close in age and had a habit of dressing in similar outfits. Today, they both wore cravats, bulging white slacks and black, open-necked shirts worn loose at the waist.

'Everybody take five!' Kaminski Senior bellowed. Slowly, he pulled himself to his feet. The crew didn't move, but looked to Singer.

'Kas,' Singer called over, 'on a studio set, the director traditionally decides when people work and when they don't. I'm trying to shoot a scene here – do you mind?'

'I need a word, Gareth – please. You too, Leon. Follow me.' Grumbling, Kaminski Junior struggled upright. Singer turned to his first assistant director, a woman called Reagan. 'Call make-up, and freshen these two up. Keep everyone in position, I'll be right back.' Reagan nodded. 'Danver,' he addressed the younger man, wearily. 'In a few minutes, I'm going to give this scene one more try. If you deliberately screw me up again in front of all these people, I'm going to break your pretty face.' Danver, who had been smirking with satisfaction, frowned as Singer followed the Kaminskis towards the studio door.

'Asshole,' he snarled. 'Where does he get off, talking to me like that?'

'Can I offer you a word of advice?' Draped across the sofa, Melissa studied her false, painted nails. 'I've never heard Gareth Singer say he'll do something and then not do it. If I were you, I'd try to get it right on the next take.'

Danver sneered. 'Don't you worry, baby – ain't nothin' gonna happen to me. Kas looks out for me. He's gonna tell your fuckin' buddy exactly how it is.'

Singer resented having to step from the dark cool of the studio into the bright heat, summonsed like a schoolboy by a pair of fat, foul-mouthed prefects. He squinted in the sunlight, which bounced mercilessly off the concrete around the lot. The Kaminskis had sunglasses hanging on chains around their necks, which they donned in unison. They stopped, swivelled around and glared at him.

'What do you two want with me?'

Kaminski Senior waved a fat finger. 'Listen you, there's twenty million of my dollars and three whole years of my life tied up in this picture—'

'Mine too!' growled Junior.

'Shuddup, Leon!'

'No, Kas, you shut up.'

'Both of you shut up.' The weariness gone from his voice, Singer stepped up to his patron, looming over him, in spite of the man's bulk. 'I've spent three years telling you I don't want that little shit in my picture. He's a spoiled brat and he can't act. You've been watching him all morning – you can see for yourself, he's completely out of his depth.'

'But his last movie grossed forty-two million!'

'His last movie was a pile of teenage trash with more explosions than dialogue. This, on the other hand, is a nuanced portrait of one of the greatest writers who ever lived!'

'Gareth, please!' Kaminksi Senior spread his hands in a placatory gesture. 'We told you before – we have Nick contracted to make three movies. We gotta do somethin' with him!'

'Well, commission some gung-ho secret agent bollocks for him, you have enough money to make whatever you want. He's not right for this film, Kas, and you know it.'

'I don't believe it!' Kaminski Senior addressed his younger brother, pointing to Singer with a pudgy index finger. 'We give this guy a box-office star, and he complains about it!'

'Yeah, you shouldn't complain about it,' growled Junior.

Kaminski Senior, having tried nice, turned nasty. 'What do you know about movies anyway, you crazy Irish bastard? You've only made one!' Passers-by slowed their pace, peering over their sunglasses at the three men arguing, hoping to see a fight. 'We was makin' movies when you was still jerkin' yourself off on your grandaddy's farm in fuckin' Ireland! Do you see that car? Do you see that fuckin' car?' Purple in the face, Kaminski gestured at a black Ferrari, one of the few cars parked in the reserved places beside the studio door. 'I came here today in a half-a-million-dollar car!'

'So did I!' Kaminski Junior gestured at a red Ferrari parked beside it.

'How did you get here, Mister Big Shot?' Senior demanded. 'If you know so much about movies, where's your half-a-million-dollar fuckin' car?'

Singer rubbed his temples. He could barely see, in the sun. 'Actually, I took a taxi here this morning. It cost me thirty-nine dollars and fifty cents.' He turned on his heel and walked back through the studio door. The cool dark enveloped him. He clapped his hands. 'Okay, everyone, let's get ready to go again, please!' All around the studio, crew handed cups of coffee to runners and resumed their posts. Four make-up women parted like frightened finches, swooping away from Melissa, who looked as good as new, in spite of having worked eight hours straight. Melissa watched Singer stride towards the set and saw the Kaminskis waddle through the studio door behind him, their rotund bodies momentarily silhouetted in the California sun. She walked to the mantelpiece of the artificial fireplace, turned her back to the cameras and found her mark. Squinting over at the Kaminskis, whom he could not properly see beyond the studio lights, Danver leaned his elbow on the mantelpiece and smiled smugly at Melissa. A camera homed in on him and a soundman held a boom high above their heads.

'Okay,' Reagan announced, 'everybody ready? Mac? You rolling? John? The light's okay? This is a take, everybody, silence on set!' The loader stepped forward, snapped the clapperboard in front of the camera and retreated.

'When you're ready,' Singer nodded at Melissa and Danver. He refused, under any circumstances, to say 'action'.

Danver coughed, cleared his throat, looked around one final time, then settled his face into an expression of haughty contempt.

'But surely, cutie pie, you're not too sick to go for a few drinks?'

'Cut!' Singer called, sounding tired again. 'Nicholas, just to remind you, it's "my darling". The line is, "But surely, my darling, you're not too ill to go for cocktails?" Fitzgerald is being sarcastic, because he knows that Zelda would rather eat her own leg than miss out on cocktails, and anyway, he would not have called his wife "cutie pie", at least not in the context of an argument. Now, would you please deliver the line, as it appears in the script, so we can shoot this scene and go home to our swimming pools?'

'Ready, everyone?' Reagan called.

'One more time,' Singer breathed.

Danver stuck his tongue out at Singer and composed his face again. He took a deep breath, then said, 'But fuck me sideways, cutie pie, surely you could suck my dick for good old Ireland?' Melissa turned away in frustration and disgust. Singer stepped onto the set and took her hand. He lifted it to his mouth and kissed it. His expression was unreadable.

'I'm sorry to have wasted your time. Good luck with your next film.' He gently let go of her, then stepped up to Danver. His arm moved so fast that she didn't really see it, but the actor's face literally exploded and a whip of blood spattered the wallpaper above the fake mantelpiece as his head snapped backwards, gurgling a scream. Something small and hard bounced across the mantelpiece, and she looked down to see a white porcelain tooth. Danver spun across the set, demolishing a replica Louis XV dresser as he fell. The crew froze. The Kaminskis looked at one another. Calmly, Singer studied his knuckles, which Melissa could see were badly skinned. With a sigh, he turned around and walked slowly across the studio and out the door. By the time Melissa had recovered her wits sufficiently to follow him, he was climbing into a yellow taxi from the rank in front of the studio gates. The taxi moved away, and he was gone.

18

The first major difference that Oona noticed was in the quality of the cars parked beside the houses. Driving through the village in her own car, a battered little saloon, she saw that many homes had big, gleaming new jeeps outside their front doors. Most of the village's scattered old bungalows had been renovated, repainted and dickied up. Conservatories had been added. About a dozen new buildings stood down by the road where there'd been none before. They were odd, upright, townhouse affairs that managed to look both ostentatious and cheap. Again, these played host to a contingent of spanking new 2002-registered cars. Coloured Christmas tree lights winked on and off in the windows. Dunaldragh was obviously prospering – and she had imagined fishing to be a dying industry. Then she saw a young man lifting a case of beer from the boot of one of the gleaming new cars – by his trendy-casual clothes, an unmistakable urbanite, no more a grizzled Donegal fisherman than she. His car was Dublin registered, and that was annoying, because Oona had always imagined that she, Dionne and Melissa were the only Dubliners who knew about Dunaldragh.

The old corrugated-iron shop on the left of the road was gone, in its place a white-painted supermarket, again with a rash of new cars parked outside. She gritted her teeth, but supposed she couldn't begrudge the place a few of the conveniences of the modern world, especially since this was her first visit in thirteen years. Authenticity is nice, provided you don't have to live with it every day. The old grey stone church, at least, still looked the same, tucked in the trees behind the supermarket. On the car radio, George W. Bush massacred the English language, drawling about Saddam Hussein and weapons of mass destruction. Oona switched him off.

Then, at the edge of the forest that separated the village from the valley, she saw something that caused her to brake to a halt. It was a large stainless-steel sign – the kind of sign one might expect to see outside the corporate headquarters of some hi-tech manufacturing company. The blue letters cut into its surface were lit from within, making them seem even more alien in the midst of the December countryside. The sign read,

Welcome to
Barclay Golf

With a knot in her stomach, Oona drove on. Emerging from the forest, as the road descended into the valley proper, she caught sight of the sea. Peering to catch her first glimpse of Dunaldragh Bay, she nearly smashed into a big, tank-like jeep coming onto the road from the left. For a second time, she skidded to a halt, her heart thumping. The driver of the jeep, a man in his forties, glared down at her as he roared off up the hill. Oona looked around – the jeep had come from a car park that had been blasted out of the hillside. Now that had definitely not been there before. Then, when she realised the enormity of what she was seeing, she whispered, 'No…'

McFall's pub had completely disappeared, to be replaced by a building many times larger. Constructed of wood, glass and concrete, it was three stories high, and another stainless-steel sign stood in front of it, almost identical to the one up at the village, with the same illuminated blue lettering. It read,

Barclay Golf Hotel ★★★★

The stark new edifice was surrounded by brutish, chrome-bedecked jeeps of the type that had narrowly avoided hitting her, mixed with Mercedes saloons and the occasional sports car. As she watched, a pair of automatic doors slid open and three men emerged, pulling golf bags on trolleyed wheels and wearing the gaudily coloured clothing that the game demands. They crossed the road in front of her car and walked through a gap in an aluminium fence opposite. Leaving her engine at idle, Oona climbed out and followed them. Disoriented, she remembered the little iron gate and the spinney of trees that had stood in front of McFall's. Like the pub, it was as if they had never existed. She reached the fence and gasped.

With the trees gone, the entire vista of Dunaldragh Bay stretched beneath her. The sea-grass dunes had been landscaped and manicured and little red flags fluttered at regular intervals. Tiny figures dressed in yellows, pinks and blues walked or stood in groups below. Numbly, Oona realised that she was looking at a golf course. At the eastern end of the bay, a new road had been gouged into the foot of the mountain. Along it, several looping streets of neat, white-painted holiday homes were strung out like shoelaces. Most had cars parked outside. To the west, to her relief, she saw that the Pier House, at least, was still standing, but it looked very different, boxed in on both sides by blue glass rectangles. One of the modern extensions had completely replaced the old outhouses, and the other, which overlooked the golf course, was two storeys and almost as big as the Pier House again. She could also see that the property was completely surrounded by high black security fence.

A car horn blared behind her. A hard-faced woman in a BMW glared over, eyes obscured behind a pair of sunglasses, even though it was a dull day. Oona's saloon was blocking the entrance to the hotel car park, so she crossed the road, climbed in, and was about to move off when an even louder horn sounded and an enormous stone lorry drove past her, the road shaking under its weight. She followed it down the hill. Halfway down, she picked up the black security fence on her right, then, just before the harbour, an ostentatious new gateway, red brick pillars supporting black barred gates topped by gold-painted spikes. The lorry continued onward, apparently heading for the harbour, but it swung right at the last second and drove down an earthen ramp onto the pebble beach. Oona stopped and watched as the lorry bounced onward, sliding and skidding, churning up debris as it went. Halfway along the bay it stopped, reversed and tipped its load of grey quarry boulders at the top of the beach, just below the golf course. Beyond, the boulders stretched into the distance, a crude imposition on the natural, wave-formed undulations of the pebbles.

The harbour, she noticed, had several white, sleek cabin cruisers moored inside it, but no fishing boats, and nor were any hauled up for the winter. As the lorry rumbled towards her on its return journey, Oona walked up to the conspicuous new gateway. It had a black marble plaque mounted in the brickwork, with gilded lettering which read,

THE PIER HOUSE

She pressed an intercom beside the plaque. Nobody answered, but after about a minute, the gates clicked, then opened in the middle and swung slowly back. She drove her car through. A glistening tarmac drive had replaced the old laneway, and although the sea-grass itself still persisted on either side, it had been completely cleared from all around the house and replaced by a wide apron of pink brick. The sundial was gone – indeed, the entire front porch of the house had been removed and replaced by a large cube, made from the same blue glass as the new extensions. Oona parked her car beside two gargantuan black jeeps and a very expensive-looking Mercedes coupe. She killed the engine and stepped out slowly, feeling by now as if she was in the middle of a strange dream, one in which a familiar place is distorted and shifted to the edge of recognition. Then she spotted the sundial.

It stood in the centre of a rockery, which rose out of the neat pink brick driveway like a wart before the glass extension where the outhouses had once stood. Two enormous ship anchors lay on either side of the rockery, which contained scorched-looking miniature pines and deflated clumps of heather. Brick steps led up to the sundial, and Oona climbed them. The sandstone plinth had been cleaned and repaired. *Tempus mutantur, nos et mutamur in illis.* The broken copper plate had been replaced with a chrome one, which had a solid triangular gnomon resembling a shark's fin. The sandstone façade of the Pier House had been cleaned too, giving it the raw, uniform appearance that old buildings assume when the shadows of time have been scrubbed away. The uneven roofline had been straightened, and new, smaller slates heightened the building's neater, neutered demeanour. The wooden sash windows had been replaced with double glazing. Oona saw that a woman was watching her from inside the glass-box porch. Her blonde hair was cut medium-length with a side parting, in a style similar to her own, which was still mouse-brown. The woman wore a patchwork bo-ho style blouse, with jeans and boots. She smiled and waved. It was Dionne.

'And this was taken just after we exchanged our vows. The photographer told us to run, holding hands, and it came out beautifully.' The giant canvas dominated what had once been the living room wall, previously occupied by faded snapshots of old lighthouse keepers. It was a blown-up shot of Dionne wearing a white dress with matching flowers in her hair, and Ronan in a beige linen suit, splashing barefoot together through the surf of a sandy beach. While she'd thickened slightly with age, Dionne kept her body in very good shape. Ronan was as skinny as ever, although his red hair had receded drastically.

'And where was this taken again?'

'Cousine Island, it's one of the Seychelles. Tiny. It used to be a private home – beautiful French-style villa, five star, but only room for eight guests – plus staff, of course, you know they really look after you. So we booked the whole place for a fortnight back in April, and had a beautiful wedding, just for ourselves.'

'That must have cost a bomb.'

'It did, but the way I look at it, we got our honeymoon at the same time. We're going to repeat our vows at a ceremony in Dublin next year, and we'll throw a big bash for everybody – that's a promise. But you know what wedding parties are like – you never get the chance to talk to anybody. So, I thought how nice it would be to get the old gang together for New Year's Eve. Now that we have the house, it's sort of apt, don't you think?'

'And Melissa's definitely coming?'

Dionne squawked and held Oona's arm. 'Coming? She's already here! Flew in last night, by helicopter! Landed at the ninth hole, if you please! She's shooting a film in Dublin, but they gave her a week off.'

'I'm surprised she didn't want to spend Christmas with her kids.'

'Oh, but she did – you wouldn't believe the life. They're in Bordeaux with Guy's mother, so she stayed there until Thursday, flew to Dublin yesterday for a meeting, then landed with us in the afternoon, in true movie-star style! The punters on the golf course fell over themselves when they realised who it was!'

Oona dropped her voice. 'So it's true, then, about her and…'

'They broke it off last year, but since the kids are French, she doesn't want to move them. She spends most of her time there, still has that place in the Dordogne.' Oona glanced around. 'Don't worry, she can't hear us, she's out for a walk. It's just you and me – the lads only went out an hour ago, they wouldn't even be halfway round yet. Course is pretty crowded, with the holidays.'

'I can't believe they talked Singer into playing golf.'

Dionne frowned. 'They didn't. He's not here, we haven't heard from him. I was hoping you'd have had more luck.'

'I e-mailed him at that address Melissa gave me, but he didn't reply. I haven't seen him since the last time we were…well, you know…here.'

'Sure, that was a lifetime ago, forgive and forget.'

'Don't get me wrong, I'd like to see him again. Could Melissa not call him up? She saw him in America, didn't she?'

'She tried his number, but it's stone dead. That old Hotmail address is all we have, but none of our messages have bounced back, so maybe it's still valid.'

'Maybe he doesn't want to come. I mean, we don't know where he is, or what he's doing. He could be dead!'

Dionne frowned. 'We'll give it one more try tonight – we found something that might tempt him.'

'What do you mean?'

Dionne smiled. 'I'll show you later. We're having dinner up at the hotel at eight, and when we return, we'll drop Singer a line and try to make him jealous about not being here.'

'So the hotel is yours, too?'

'Yes – or at least, the consortium which I head up owns it. And have you seen the holiday homes on the far side of the bay?' Oona nodded. 'We retained a few, but most of them went before the golf course was even finished, three hundred grand apiece. Worth a lot more now.'

'Is it true that Frisby helped to design the course?'

'He's quite a big name in golfing circles, you know.' Dionne laughed. 'Not that I play the shagging game myself, but when you're starting a new resort, these things matter.'

'I nearly chickened out when you said he'd be here. I'm nervous about seeing him again.'

'Ah, don't be silly – after all this time? He's a sweetheart. Completely changed, much more sensible now, though aren't we all?' It took Oona a moment to comprehend that the question was not purely rhetorical.

'Yes. Yes, of course.'

'He was a big help to us, getting this place off the ground, and he's great for keeping Ronan occupied. But you needn't worry, he only has eyes for Melissa.'

'Still?'

'Jaysus, he spent all last night telling her every single thing about every last film she's ever been in. He's married, though, wife and three kids back in England. Devoted to them – he's harmless as can be.'

'The house has certainly changed.'

'Oh, you haven't seen anything yet.'

Oona looked around at the white-painted walls and the immaculate pine floor of what had once been the living room. The hallway with the hooks had been completely removed, making most of the old downstairs open plan. One could stand by the big fireplace in the living room – now full of flowers – and look all the way to where the oak table still stood in kitchen, refurbished and surrounded by modern brown leather dining chairs. Following a brown-and-white theme, the huge space was replete with leather sofas, rugs, coffee tables and expensive-looking lamps, to the point where it resembled the lobby of a boutique hotel.

The wooden staircase still descended onto the flagstones of what had once been the hallway – it had been stripped back to its original oak and heavily varnished. Following Dionne across to the kitchen end, Oona was sad to see that the big iron range had been ripped out and a smaller, modern one put in its place. The kitchen itself was brand new, done in stainless steel and black marble. A new doorway had been knocked into the west gable wall – this led into the glass extension where the outhouses had stood and, Dionne explained, now contained offices, three ensuite bedrooms and, at the very end, a games room of which Ronan, apparently, was inordinately proud.

The bigger, two-storey extension at the sea-grass – or, as Oona would now have to think of it, golf course – end of the house was accessed both along the rear kitchen corridor and via the old upstairs, which was still given over to bedrooms, only these were now fewer, larger and completely modernised. The upper storey of this eastern extension was truly astonishing, consisting of a single room, glass-walled on three sides, the naked stone of what had been the outside gable making up the fourth. It overlooked the harbour, the entire beach and bay, the golf course and the mountain. Although home to another dining table, a full-sized bar and several sofas, seats and occasional tables arranged to take advantage of the views, it still felt underfurnished. On the stone wall beside the bar hung the biggest flat-screen television Oona had ever seen and two slender, futuristic-looking loudspeakers stood beside it on the floor.

'Are you not worried that everyone can see you up here?' she asked. With a smile, Dionne lifted a small remote control from a coffee table and pressed a button. The entire eastward view gradually dimmed until it had practically disappeared altogether, behind what resembled a grey, translucent wall.

'It's called electrochromatic glass,' she cooed. 'You can set it at any level between clear and almost completely opaque.' She pressed the button again and Oona saw the golfers rematerialise.

'Is that not incredibly expensive?'

'Yes, but every room has it. Now that the house is finished, we'll be spending quite a lot of time here – maybe as much as two months a year. But more importantly, I'll be using it to entertain. A lot of my projects are out in Dubai, and investors there, they like their luxuries, I can tell you. And their golf.'

'But you have a four-star hotel up the road.'

'Honey, four-star is for plebs.'

'What happened to Manus and his wife when you built the hotel?'

'Oh, they got one of the new holiday homes as part of the deal. You should drop over and see them while you're here. Which reminds me, there's something else we should mention when we e-mail Singer tonight. He ought to know that Manus hasn't been well – maybe that will persuade him to show.'

'What's wrong with him?'

'Well, Bronagh didn't really say, but I can tell you this – they're much better off in their new house, and she has enough money in the bank to look after him no matter what happens.'

'Bronagh?'

'Mrs McFall.'

Oona shook her head. 'I never thought of that woman as having a Christian name.' She crossed to the corner of the glass box overlooking the bay, where a telescope balanced on a tripod. 'Hey, I don't mean to be nosey, but when I arrived, I saw a lorry dumping boulders on the beach – what's that all about?'

Dionne stood at her shoulder. 'Last year, the spring tides ate into the twelfth and thirteenth holes – gobbled whole lumps from two fairways. So we're having a breakwater built to stop it from happening again.'

'You got planning permission for something as big as that?'

Dionne waved dismissively. 'Ah, sure, we don't worry too much about that sort of thing around here. We bring a lot of money into the local economy – we're the biggest employer in the area.'

Out at sea, Inistrahull light winked conspiratorially at Oona, like an only friend to have stayed true. But Dionne took her arm and led her to the top of a stainless steel staircase at the landward end of the glass box.

'You haven't seen the best bit.' Oona followed her downstairs. As she descended, she noticed a humming noise. 'Ventilation system,' Dionne explained. 'Cost a fortune, but I couldn't have my nice glass walls steaming up, now could I?'

Oona stopped in amazement. Most of the ground floor of the eastern extension was taken up by a turquoise-blue swimming pool, surrounded by potted plants, recliners and sadistic-looking pieces of gym equipment. Dionne beckoned her onward.

'I built showers and a steam-room along the old kitchen corridor – do you remember where the pantry was? Actually, I was about to have a dip before you arrived – fancy one?'

Oona laughed. 'So that's why you look like a million dollars, you crafty bag – your own private gym!'

Dionne nudged her. 'That, and I can call the beauticians from the hotel down here whenever I want!' She hugged Oona lightly, then held her at arm's length. 'We're going to have such a lovely time, I just know it! Now, come with me, I've put you in one of the new bedrooms in the western extension. I hope you like it – it's ground floor, but what it lacks for a view it makes up for in comfort. I've put a few of my swimsuits out for you, we're the same size, so let's see if we can find one you like.'

'I'll pass on the swim if you don't mind, but how's about I join you after yours, for a few drinks?'

Fresh from her walk, she wore a plain black jumper, jeans and woolly socks – the Dunaldragh uniform of yore. Nobody at the university would believe that Oona had gone to school with Melissa Montgomery, yet here she was, dressed like a friend, not a film star. She was still strikingly beautiful, and Oona was trying to decide whether she was wearing make-up, apart from a tiny bit around the eyes. Oona had seen more of Melissa during the nineties than she had of Dionne – Melissa had kept her house in Ranelagh and made a point of getting in touch during her annual visits from her permanent home in France. It also helped that, since she had become truly successful, instead of turning into a rampant egotist, Melissa had gone the opposite way and learned to relax more in herself. She spoke more freely and frequently than she ever had, and was much less reserved. Having children would tend to make you that way, Oona supposed. Perhaps – the end of her marriage to Guy notwithstanding – between children and a career, Melissa had finally got what she wanted out of life.

On the other hand, Oona detected that Dionne, in spite of her obvious millions, was trying was trying too hard to look like the woman with everything. She had changed her outfit after her swim and now wore a green and red gypsy dress with a miniscule, loose-knit white cardigan. Dionne, as Oona was to observe, changed her outfit several times a day. The three sat chatting in the upper seaward corner of the big glass box, soaking up the view and a bottle of chilled champagne from the bar.

'And how are Bruno and Daniel?' Dionne asked Melissa.

'Wonderful,' Melissa smiled. 'Bruno had a bit of a cold over Christmas, but he also had his cousins over, so he didn't want to be with his *maman* at all. But luckily I still have Daniel to give me big, long snuggles.'

'Don't you miss them?' Oona asked.

'Of course, but I discovered only yesterday that production has been delayed by a fortnight, so I'll stay here until New Year's Day, then get a whole ten days at home to see them back to school. That's a bonus I wasn't expecting.'

'Daniel is at school already?'

'*Ecole maternelle* – nursery. They start them at three. Bruno feels very grown-up because he started at the primary in September.'

'Good schools, are they?'

'I live near a small town called Saint Cyprien, and you couldn't ask for better.'

Dionne interjected. 'No plans for little ones yourself, Oons?'

Oona pouted. 'I doubt it, at this stage. Getting a bit late. Me and Rob – sometimes I wish we had, but more often I'm glad it never happened. I haven't been as lucky as you two, meeting the right man.'

'Oh, I wouldn't say that!' Dionne laughed, reaching for the bottle. Just then, the sound of male voices rose from below. She put her hand to her mouth, then sprung up, tottered to the back of the room and called down the steel staircase. 'Hoy! You two! We're up here! Come and say hello to Oona!' Oona threw Melissa a pained look. Melissa reached out and patted her hand. Ronan appeared at the top of the stairs. Dionne pecked his cheek.

'Well, how did you do?'

'Frisby made it round in six under, damn him. I, on the other hand, was quite a bit over.'

'Seventeen, to be precise.' Frisby's voice came from behind Ronan.

'But that's really good, Ro-ro! I mean, that's a big improvement, isn't it?'

'It certainly is. We'll make a scratch golfer out of your husband yet, Mrs Dockerty!' Frisby emerged into the room behind Ronan. Both wore check golf trousers – Ronan's blue and white, Frisby's red, white and blue. Frisby wore a blue top, Ronan's was green. Frisby also wore glasses, small, circular and gold framed, just like Ronan's. He was still podgy and his hair was short and dyed blond at the tips. He walked straight up to Oona with a broad smile and offered his hand. She stood, and took it.

'Lovely to see you again! What's it been – twelve years?'

'Thirteen.'

'Far too long! But Dionne tells me you travel a lot?' Nothing whatsoever in his manner or tone gave any indication that, on their last encounter, they'd done anything more intimate than shake hands, just as they were doing now.

'Yes, I travel a lot,' she echoed. 'I'm a lecturer now, but mostly I'm involved in research. I'm just back from a two-year sabbatical.'

'Lovely. Anywhere interesting?'

'Argentina, South Africa, Antarctica and Burma.'

Frisby laughed. 'And I thought I got around!'

'Play a lot, do you?'

'Most of the major US and European tournaments.'

'Dionne said you're a fully fledged pro.'

'Pays the bills, and keeps Sabina in the style to which she is accustomed – and that's all that counts, isn't it?'

'Sabina's Swedish,' Dionne rested a hand on Frisby's shoulder. 'She was over here during the summer, just after we finished the house. You'd really like her, Oons.'

'Well, Andy and Gertie loved it here, I can tell you.' Frisby smiled benignly. 'They had every stone on that beach carried up to the garden, didn't they?'

'Oh yes, when we were building the rockery,' Dionne agreed.

'What ages are they?' Oona asked Frisby.

'Andy's eight and Gertie is six – she's the same age as Mel's Bruno, actually, which is why we really must get them together some day.' Frisby beamed at Melissa, who smiled and nodded. He pulled a mobile phone from his pocket. 'Look, here they are.' The screensaver on the phone showed a boy and a girl, both fair and handsome in a Scandinavian way.

'They got their mother's looks, thank god,' Ronan muttered from behind.

'I don't care what they look like, mate, as long as they don't have your golf swing!'

'Bollocks to you, fatso. Good to see you again, Oons.' Ronan stepped forward and kissed her cheek. 'Thanks for coming.'

'I'm glad I could make it.'

'But she's had no luck with Singer,' Dionne chipped in, 'so we'll have to try again tonight.'

Ronan frowned. 'Maybe he just can't be arsed…'

'We've decided to e-mail him one more time when we get back from dinner – haven't we, girls?' Dionne didn't wait for an answer, but took both men by the arms. 'Now, you two fetch a couple of beers and follow me. You're going to get out of those horrible sweaty clothes and have a nice steam and a swim while we girls finish our chat. We have a lot to catch up on, and dinner's at eight.' Her voice echoed from the stairs. 'I just want to see what the cleaners have done with the towels. They never leave them in the same place two days running. Ro-ro, you're going to have to have a word with them, or else I will.'

Oona realised that she was still on her feet, facing an empty room. She flopped into her chair, let out her breath and ran the back of her hand across her brow in a theatrical gesture of relief.

'There, that wasn't too hard,' Melissa spoke quietly.

Oona, too, kept her voice low. 'I was crapping my pants – what did he call you?'

Melissa stifled a laugh. 'Mel! I know, I know, but he's grand. Very pleased with himself, has a nice family – I think he has even more reason than you to want to forget that particular episode.'

Oona gave a wry smile. 'Perhaps. To be honest, I'm not at all sure what I'm doing here. It's all bit...I dunno...contrived.'

'Dionne rang me nearly every day for two months to twist my arm into coming.'

Oona's eyes widened. 'Me too! I mean, I know you two see one another a bit, but there were quite a few years when I didn't hear from her at all. Then, all of a sudden, it's like I'm being love-bombed.'

'In my case, I think she's more taken with the idea of having a celebrity about the place than she is with me. I was the scarlet woman, remember? But recently, she's made more of an effort.'

'Well, I'm in Dublin a lot more than you, and I rarely see her. They have a big place out in Dalkey, and I've never set foot in it – never been invited!'

'What was that she said when you mentioned about meeting the right man?'

'That sounded like a dig, didn't it?'

'Yes, but was it a dig about me leaving Guy, or was she implying that...'

The door into the upstairs of the old house opened and Dionne came through it. Oona made a face, wondering whether their voices had carried, but Melissa recovered superbly – years of acting, Oona supposed – and greeted her casually.

'We were just saying, Dee, how lovely Frisby's children look. He's very lucky.'

Dionne let loose a tart little laugh. 'He certainly is.'

Dionne changed into a dark-brown velvet evening gown that Oona felt was perhaps a bit glamorous for a hotel dinner, but which she had to admit was perfectly stunning. There was no point in measuring herself against Dionne Brady any more – it was obvious who had won in life's race, but Oona was also through with measuring herself. Melissa, meanwhile, wore a modest black shirt and trousers, while she herself wore a white long-sleeved blouse and her best skirt, which had cost forty euros from Mango.

Dionne pretended not to notice how deferential the staff at the hotel were towards her, but a small, triumphant flush in her face nonetheless betrayed her pleasure. No doubt, her standing was further heightened by having such a famous actress in tow. People – staff and customers alike – literally stopped and stared at Melissa, but she did a very convincing yet graceful job of pretending not to notice. With no small amount of bowing and scraping, their gathering was shown into one of the marble-effect elevators in the lobby, complete with its own television, which was showing Sky News. A suicide bomber had killed seventy-two people in Chechnya. British Prime Minister Tony Blair spoke of the threat to world peace posed by Iraq.

It turned out that the front section of the top floor was quite a sizeable restaurant, which was very busy for what Oona had supposed would be a quiet time of year.

'Are you serious?' Dionne laughed as they were shown to a window table. 'This place has been booked solid since it opened. Good pre-publicity. People grab holidays when they can – do you notice there's no kids?' Sure enough, all the other tables were occupied by either groups of men or middle-aged women, with only a few couples, and everyone clad in costly casuals. There was not a child to be seen. 'You see, these people are here to play golf. That's the whole idea, to specialise. A guaranteed, four-star golf package. We hadn't quite enough space to go five-star, but it's in the pipeline.'

'What, for here?'

'No, for a site we're developing in Portugal.'

'I recommend the hake.' Frisby waved a menu in front of Oona's face. He had sat himself between her and Melissa.

'Pardon?'

'The hake. It's fish – very nice.'

Out to sea, Inistrahull light winked at Oona, telling her to keep it together. As they sipped their aperitifs, a big man in his sixties stood up from a nearby table and approached theirs. Dionne moaned.

'Ooh, sorry, Melissa – look, I'll tell the staff to keep the punters away.'

'It's all right, I get this everywhere.'

The man stopped, with an ingratiating smile on his face. 'I'm sorry to interrupt your evening, but I really felt I had to come over and say how flattered we all are to have such a star dining in our midst tonight. We'd heard a rumour that you were here, and when you came in,' he jerked his thumb at his table, 'one of my friends was literally just talking about your win at Woodlawn last year – amazing stuff, especially that putt on the fifteenth. So,' the man reached out, and patted Frisby's back, 'on behalf of all of us, welcome to Ireland.' For the first time since arriving, Oona's heart warmed to Frisby. She had never seen anyone look so utterly, irrevocably pleased. 'Incidentally,' the man continued, 'is it true that you went around today in six under? Are you going out again tomorrow?'

Oona burst into peals of laughter.

Two courtesy cars from the hotel dropped the five diners back to the Pier House shortly before midnight, and Dionne shepherded everyone straight through the kitchen and into the western extension, where the first door off the corridor opened into a sizeable, well-equipped office. A rather drunk Frisby was dispatched to fetch drinks, while Dionne switched on the computer.

'Now,' she announced, 'this is our last chance at getting the Christmas Club together for New Year's Eve, 2002. I expect everyone to do their bit.'

'But Dee,' Oona protested, 'we don't know that he'll even get this.'

'We can but try,' Dionne persisted. 'Why don't you go first?' Oona bent over the keyboard as Frisby returned with a precariously balanced tray. The message read,

To: garethsinger17@hotmail.com

Subject: Please come!

Hello, Singer – Oona here. Dionne is literally holding a gun to my head…well, more like a gin, actually, but it would be really, really nice if you could join us for NYE. This feels a bit silly, sending a message into the void. But I, for one, would like to hear from you, even if you can't make it this time, which I hope you can. xxx Oons

Hi, Melissa here too. Tempus mutantur, *but Dionne says she's solved the Sophia mystery, and won't tell us anything until we're all together. So I hope you're still alive. x M.*

Would be great to see you again, old man. Regards, JF

Hey, pig-breath, personally I hope that your black soul is rotting in hell, but please get these whining women off my back by shifting your ass. Orders from Central Command, stardate 28.12.02

Dear Singer, please forgive my husband's so-called sense of humour. Yes, can you believe I married the gimp, so miracles still happen. A couple of things you should know, apart from we're having lots of fun – Manus isn't well, and it would be great if you could see him. Also, what Melissa means is we found a letter when we refurbished the Pier House, which (we think) explains the Sophia Clements story. But we need your expert opinion. So please come,

Lots of love from everyone, even gimpy Ronan,

Dionne

'You didn't tell me you found a letter!' For an instant, Oona felt that delicious sense of mystery come flooding back.

'We had to renovate Sophia's room,' Dionne explained, 'and that involved removing the wooden panelling...'

'No!' Oona was horrified. 'How could you do a thing like that?'

'Don't worry – we didn't throw it away. In fact, we spent a fortune having it cleaned, and we used it in Ro-ro's den.'

'My games room,' Ronan leered.

'We found an old letter behind the panelling near the bed – it looked as if it had been hidden there.'

'What does it say? Is it from Sophia?'

'Ah!' Dionne gave a smug smile. 'Now that would be telling, wouldn't it?'

'Dee! Don't be such a rat-bag! Tell us what it says!'

'It's no use,' Melissa drawled languidly, 'I've already tried.'

'I want to keep it to see if Singer comes,' Dionne insisted, 'but if he doesn't, then I promise I'll show it to everyone on New Year's Eve.'

Oona scowled. 'But that's three whole days, and you know damn well he's not coming!'

'Come into my parlour,' Ronan put an arm around her waist. 'There's plenty more to see.'

'That's right, Oons,' Dionne commanded, 'keep Ro-ro happy by checking out his little hidey-hole, then you can join the rest of us upstairs for a night-cap or three.'

She followed Ronan further down the corridor, which had Dionne's beloved blue plate glass on the right, giving onto the front yard and the old façade of the house, dramatically floodlit in orange. To the left, three more doors were set into a wall, the second of which was her bedroom. However, the corridor terminated at a much bigger door that stretched from ceiling to floor. It was incongruously heavy, ancient and made of weathered oak. On the wall beside it, a key hung on a hook. A big, old iron key. Oona froze. His back turned to her, Ronan lifted the key and used it to open the wooden door.

'I take it you recognise this,' he said, pushing it open. 'Dee's very keen on architectural salvage where she can, and…what's wrong? Are you okay?'

Oona forced herself to speak. 'Sorry. Sorry. Just, ah, took a little turn.' She put a hand on the wall to stay upright. 'Is that what I think it is?'

Ronan waved the key before her eyes, then hung it back on the hook. 'Yup, it's the old front door, in all its glory. Dionne saved it when she demolished the porch. This room is a bit of a tribute to the way the house used to be, actually.' He reached in and flicked a switch. The room certainly was very different from the rest of the building. All four walls were solid, uninterrupted by windows or openings of any sort. Oona found that odd, since it was completely glass-clad on the outside. A burnished, antiseptic version of the panelling that she remembered from Sophia's bedroom covered three walls, while the fourth, at the far side of the room, was taken up entirely by old books.

'The library!' she stepped forward, away from the iron key. 'You kept the old library!'

'We're not complete savages, you know,' Ronan smiled, only half-jokingly. As she entered the room, she saw that the centre was taken up by a full-sized snooker table. Most of the subdued light came from an old-fashioned fringed canopy hanging above it. Around the three panelled walls was a variety of leather sofas and casual tables, a few modern lamps and in the far corner, a small bar counter, made of newer wood than the old panelling, but cut to match it in design. Oona walked across to the books and lifted one out, a bound tome of *The Illustrated London News*. She opened it randomly, at an exquisitely executed view of the pyramids at Giza, done in pink and pale blue ink, with silhouetted palm trees in the foreground. Framed lettering announced,

Egypt Number
Price one shilling, as usual

'February, 1923.' Oona stroked the page. 'The Tutankhamen exhibition opened in London – people were so thrilled, it caused an absolute craze. Wouldn't you love to live in an age where artefacts from a tomb were enough to drive an entire nation wild?'

'Wouldn't you love to live in an age where you can reach into a fridge and help yourself to a nice, cold glass of champagne?' Ronan produced two snipes from behind the bar and twisted at their corks. Oona replaced the volume. She wandered noiselessly across the red woollen carpet. She realised how quiet the space was – she couldn't hear the sea.

'Like something out of Edgar Allen Poe, this room.'

Ronan smiled indulgently. She lifted the black ball from its position on the snooker table and played with its satisfying weight. The wall opposite the bookshelves held a quantity of old photographs and framed posters.

'It's the lighthouse keepers – my god! This used to hang in the living room, didn't it? And what are these?' Seamus Heaney gazed meditatively at her from one of the framed posters. *Avalon*, it read across the top. Then, *Heaney – Ireland's Greatest Living Poet?*

'My old magazine covers,' Ronan answered wistfully. He walked over and handed her a brimming, sparkling flute. 'Only ran to six issues. Thank goodness *The Speckled Bird* is doing a bit better.'

'Oh, you're into wildlife now?'

Ronan lifted a thin magazine from a stack on a coffee table beside the nearest sofa. 'No, it's a reference to Yeats — *The Speckled Bird* was his unfinished novel. He wrote four different versions of it.'

'No wonder he never finished it.'

'Well, this is a quarterly review,' he handed her the magazine. 'Got a good readership. Small, but influential.'

'Good, I'm glad to hear you're still doing Ronan-ish things. Golf isn't you, is it? I mean, what's that all about?'

Ronan smiled. 'Anything that keeps Dionne happy — it's easier to play along than to argue.'

'Always was.'

'She's achieved a lot, Oona. All this,' he gestured with his glass at the world around, 'is entirely down to her. She's done it all, and a lot more besides. You should see some of the stuff she's built in Dublin—'

'I have,' Oona interrupted, flatly.

Ronan either didn't notice or chose to ignore her lack of enthusiasm. 'And she's doing deals in Dubai, Spain, Portugal — that girl has some head on her, I can tell you.'

'A very rich head by now, I should imagine.'

He appeared mildly concerned. 'Yes. I suppose we are. The question is, what do you do with it?'

'Build more golf courses.'

'It's providing a service that people want.'

The young Oona would not have bitten her tongue, but the older one had learned to. 'Of course it is. Look, I'm tired after that drive today. Would it be rude if I took my champagne to bed, and read your magazine?'

'Do you not want to join the others?'

'I do, but the other side of your house is just too far to walk.' She gave what she hoped was a convincingly weary smile. 'Tell them goodnight from me, and I'll see them for a jog on the beach at first light.'

He gave a wry smile. 'We'll probably still be drinking by first light.'

As they exited the room, he closed the door with the iron key.

'Why do you lock this room? Does Dionne keep her diamonds in a secret safe in there or something?'

'Not at all — it's a front door, remember? So no handles. Look.' He unlocked it and the door swung gently open. 'Dionne hates anything untidy.' He locked it again and hung the key back on its hook. Oona tried not to look at it. She stopped outside her bedroom and gave him a small hug.

'Night, then. It's great to see you all again.'

'Trudging around golf courses is a small price to pay.'

'Pardon?'

'For being with her.'

She gave him another hug. 'She's very lucky. You're both very lucky.'

Ronan nodded, apparently satisfied. She closed her bedroom door, flung the magazine onto a sofa and emptied her champagne into the sink of the ensuite. She drew the curtains across the picture-window wall and sat on the bed. Just like a hotel room, she thought. She reached into her holdall and came up with a tin of Tiger Balm. She rubbed some on her temples and below her ears. She took off her shoes, skirt and tights and crawled into the outsized bed with her blouse still on. She clapped her hands, like Dionne had shown her. The lights went out, plunging the room into total blackness.

19

'So, what happened between you and Guy? Where did it all go wrong?'

It was late afternoon. Dionne, Oona and Melissa sat on loungers near the pool. Dionne and Melissa wore towelling robes, Oona a brown shirt and jeans. The weather outside had turned vicious – wind and rain crashed against the glass wall. Beyond the security fence, the beach had disappeared under a miasma of dirty white waves. The cabin cruisers in the harbour had all been towed clear of the water, which was just as well, as the pier wall was barely visible for spray. Yet where the three women sat, it was warm – hot even, and the air draught free. It was strange to be surrounded by such commotion, lolling in balmy comfort, while the outside world went insane. Dionne had not surfaced until one, and had demanded the other two's company for a steam and a swim. Melissa had joined her, but Oona, claiming a mild headache, had declined. After her ablutions, rather than wrestle with her gym equipment, their hostess had telephoned the hotel and had a manicurist sent down. She was young and foreign looking – Polish, according to Dionne. She wore a blue and white uniform with the Barclay Golf logo on the chest. She had worked in total silence while Oona and Melissa had sipped, and Dionne quaffed, cold white wine from the upstairs bar. Melissa had insisted on tipping the girl generously before the hotel car whisked her off again. They were now on their second bottle and Dionne was quite tiddly. The other two were getting that way.

Formerly, Melissa would have answered Dionne's blunt query with a faint smile, but she pulled her towelling robe around her swimsuit and studied the fury of the gale.

'Guy didn't want me working any more, basically that was it. After we had Bruno, I cut down to one film a year, but that didn't satisfy him. He wanted me to give up acting altogether.'

'That's nuts! The only way a man can possibly object to his wife earning millions is if he's earning billions!'

'It wasn't about the money — he was never insecure about that, God knows. Kept him in fast cars and fancy clothes. It was more a jealousy thing — being part of the business, he knows what it can be like, during a shoot. I'm afraid his imagination supplied the bits that his macho French heart hadn't already invented for him.'

'And he had absolutely no reason to be jealous?' Dionne smiled lightly.

'It doesn't matter what you've done, it's what people think you've done that counts. I wanted to be with my children, but I wasn't prepared to stop working altogether.'

'So who are you seeing now?'

'Nobody.'

'Hey, what are we going to do, ring *Hello* magazine? She can tell us, can't she, Oons?'

'I haven't slept with anyone since I split up with Guy last Christmas.' Melissa's tone was matter-of-fact, but Oona detected a hint of annoyance. Perhaps Dionne did too, because she turned her attention towards her.

'What about you, Oons? What happened with you and whatsis-name — Rob?'

'I really don't want to think about Rob Maloney, to be honest.'

'Still a bit sore, are we?'

'Not any more, but it wasn't an amicable parting.'

'Did he do the dog on you?'

'Rob, as I discovered, would have done any dog that stood still for long enough. But by the time I realised that, he'd done three other women in the faculty, and God knows how many students. Rob was a mistake. Even by my standards, a pretty big mistake.'

'Is that why you're glad you didn't have children with him?'

Oona sighed. 'Sometimes I wish we'd had one. I mean, we were together for four years, but I refused to have anything to do with him for a long time afterwards, and that wouldn't have been good for any kid. Plus, this way, at least I'm free to travel, and do my research.'

'What about you, Dionne?' Melissa asked.

'What about me?'

'Are you and Ronan planning any little Dohertys?'

'She doesn't want to mess up her lifestyle,' Oona teased. 'Imagine the sticky fingerprints that children would leave on all this lovely glass.'

'Actually,' Dionne addressed her knee, 'we've been trying very hard since the wedding, but no joy.'

Oona grimaced. 'Oh, I'm sorry, I didn't mean...'

Dionne studied her wine. 'I can see why people might think that I'm a bit of a hard-headed bitch – I would have to be, wouldn't I, to do all those deals, but...'

Oona launched herself forward and took Dionne's hand. 'Dee, I'm sorry, that was really insensitive of me, I made a joke about something I shouldn't have, and I apologise.'

'No, I'm sorry – I shouldn't let it bother me.'

Melissa spoke gently. 'You can sometimes get infertility treatment, if you've left things a bit late.'

Dionne laughed tartly. 'It's not me who needs the infertility treatment.' She took a glug of her wine, then reached to top up her glass. Oona and Melissa exchanged a glance. 'Don't worry,' Dionne continued, 'he can't hear us. He's playing snooker with Frisby down in his bloody den.'

'That's definitely the problem?' Melissa asked.

'Oh, we've had all the tests. Not so much a low sperm count, as no sperm count whatsoever – nada, nothing, zilch. Me, I'm fine. I could still get pregnant by sitting on a warm seat on a bus. But not by my husband.'

'That sucks,' Oona sympathised.

'We've tried that too,' Dionne gave a wry smile. 'Nothing works. It pisses me off,' she looked around, 'to think that I'll have built all this up, then have nobody to pass it on to. What would you do, if you were me?'

'Adopt?' Melissa suggested.

This is why she wants us here, Oona thought. For all her money, she has no one to talk to.

At eight o'clock, a buzzer sounded in the kitchen. It was a van from the hotel, bearing dinner. Via the intercom, Dionne ordered it to drive around to the back of the house, as the wind was now blowing with such violence that she didn't want to use the front porch. Two waiters in Barclay Golf blazers carried the food into the kitchen, heated it and served them as they sat around the old oak table with its new leather dining chairs. Oona recalled the first meal she'd eaten at that table, Ronan's foul-tasting salmon curry. She wanted so badly to be eating it again, with all of them sitting around – young, poor, in a semi-derelict house, cynical little fledglings sizing each other up, with no idea how lucky they were. Instead, here she was, a so-called grown-up, making polite conversation with other grown-ups.

'Mmm, fillet.' Sitting opposite, Frisby waved a lump of red, dripping meat around on his fork. 'Nothing like a nice bit of steak when you've been drinking all day, isn't that right, Dockerty?'

'This plaice is a bit cold,' Ronan muttered, poking at his fish.

'Then turn the central heating up!' Frisby guffawed.

Afterwards, as the staff cleaned and departed, the company repaired to the upstairs lounge, where the glass walls were as black as the devil's waistcoat and streaming with rain. Once again, Oona had that weird sense of detachment from the outside world. The orange spotlights shining on the front of the house made it impossible to see the beach, but the noise from the shore was tremendous. The general idea was to watch a film, but everyone had drink taken and consensus was proving hard to reach. Melissa fetched a DVD from her room, of a film she said was all the rage in Hollywood. It was called *Ivan's xtc.*

'Is it one of yours?' Frisby was keen to know.

'I wish I'd been asked,' answered Melissa, 'but I wasn't. It's a stunning piece of work.'

'What's it about?'

'A man who dies of cancer.'

'Oh, cheer-*ful*,' Dionne drawled. She sat on a stool at the bar. 'Ro-ro? Fix me a brandy and Coke there, with lots of ice. And lots of brandy. Actually, forget the Coke.'

'Don't you think you should take it easy now, my darling?'

'No, I don't. But Jay will fix me a drink if you won't.' She threw an arm round Frisby's neck and ruffled his blond-tipped hair.

Ronan sniffed. 'I like the sound of that film, let's watch it.'

'Of course you like the sound of it,' Dionne cawed from her barstool, 'it's all artsy-fartsy.' Frisby went behind the bar.

'Brandy makes you randy.'

'Then make it a treble – if that's okay with my husband here.'

Ronan, Oona and Melissa tried to watch the film, but between the noise of the storm and Frisby and Dionne perched cackling at the bar, it was impossible to concentrate, so halfway through, Oona pleaded sleepiness and made to leave. Melissa stood and followed her. Dionne and Frisby appeared not to notice, engrossed in a rather loud and repetitive conversation about the market for golf resorts in Portugal. Oona and Melissa exited into the upstairs corridor of the old house, leaving Ronan looking forlornly at the television. Melissa stopped by the first door on the right.

'Come on in a minute.'

Sophia's room was painted entirely white, and even bigger than Oona remembered it, with an ensuite bathroom added on the left-hand side where a smaller, neighbouring bedroom had obviously once been. The four-poster bed was gone, replaced by a sleek, Scandinavian affair with built-in units. The new space was tastefully furnished with a black leather suite and a brace of abstract paintings on the replastered walls. The window where she'd sat and gazed at the harbour for hours on end had mixed cushions nestling in it instead of the naked, dusty wood of before. Every last trace of Sophia was gone, except perhaps…no, even the stubs of the metal bars had disappeared from the outside windowsills, which had been replaced with freshly cut stone.

Melissa smiled. 'That's the first thing I looked for, too. I guess Dionne didn't like the idea of her master bedroom being a former prison.'

'I don't think she's very happy. I don't think either of them are.'

'I shouldn't gossip, but their room is next to mine so I can't help hearing – there have been arguments.'

'All couples bicker.'

'Have you noticed how much she's drinking?'

'I feel sorry for her. That's very tough, if they can't have children.'

'Poor Dionne – it's obviously what she so badly wants.'

'And she's very good at getting what she wants, but...'

'Babies are one of the few things money can't buy, which must make it all the more frustrating, for someone with her energy and drive.'

'It's nice to see everybody again, really it is – but it's not the same, is it?'

'No. It's like being on a corporate golf junket, only none of us likes golf, corporations or junkets.'

'Except for Frisby.'

'I think Dionne's torn between wanting us to see how well she's done and needing a shoulder to cry on. I feel bad, talking about her behind her back.'

'So do I – but that won't stop us, will it?' They shared a laugh, then Oona pouted. 'Seriously, though – I really put my foot in it earlier, when I teased her about not wanting kids.'

'Forget religion and politics – children are the most sensitive subject in the world. It's so easy to say the wrong thing.'

'You must miss yours.'

'Terribly. I'll be out of here like a shot on New Year's Day. I just want to go home to them.'

'It would be different if Singer were here. He always had a knack of making everything seem okay.'

'Most of the time.'

Oona sighed. 'Most of the time.

'Can I take it you've forgiven us, then?'

Oona stared at the storm beyond the glass.

'I'm sorry. I was selfish, then. Selfish and stupid. I expected every-thing to be exactly how I wanted – even when I had no idea what I wanted.'

'That's called being in your twenties.'

'I knew Singer liked me, but I put him off because I didn't feel quite the same way and couldn't cope with a heavy relationship. Then I was gutted when I found out about you two.'

'You'll be glad to hear that we weren't together for very long.'

'But it must have been good while it lasted.'

'We both kept large parts of ourselves to ourselves. We collaborated, but we never really shared.'

'Where do you think he is?'

'I have no idea. But I'm glad he's not here.'

'Because you'd be uncomfortable about seeing him?'

'Not at all. Because he would hate the way this place has changed.'

'I hate the way this place has changed.'

'I think Dionne would be genuinely shocked if she heard us say that.'

'Are we snobs, or what?'

'I suppose we are. But now that we're here, we may as well make the most of it – take the time to catch up and chill out.'

'Let's start tonight. Can I sleep here with you?'

'That would be nice – we can chat until we nod off.' Melissa crossed to a chest of drawers. 'You can have my spare pyjamas.'

But Oona shook her head, kicked off her shoes and jeans and crawled under the duvet. 'I'll sleep in my shirt,' she yawned. Melissa changed in the ensuite. By the time she re-emerged, Oona was fast asleep.

Dionne woke with a raging hangover. The clock beside her bed said half-past eight. No wonder she felt awful – she'd had five hours' sleep. Her mouth was horribly dry, so she groped around for a glass of water, then realised that she'd forgotten to bring one to bed. She pictured the nice, cold bottles of fizzy mineral water that stood in the kitchen fridge. Ronan lay huddled on the far side of the bed, snoring lightly. She prodded him, and he mumbled something that sounded like 'Joyce has a working trout', but stayed asleep. So she sighed, sat up, swung her feet out of the bed and stood on her dress, which lay in a mangled heap on the floor. She squinted around for a dressing gown, couldn't see one and thought she'd skit downstairs in her bra and knickers. From the silence straddling the house, no one else was up.

She held the wooden banister as her feet negotiated the cold varnish of the staircase. At the bottom, she turned left into the kitchen area, scuttled to the fridge and grabbed a plastic bottle by the neck. She turned to run back to the staircase. A man with white hair sat at the kitchen table. She screamed and dropped the bottle on the floor. It bounced and rolled away, hissing. The man didn't speak. He looked to be in his early fifties, with a pale, bloated face. He wore a brown corduroy jacket over a blue shirt. Looking speculatively at her, he puffed on a cigarette, which Dionne now saw he held in his left hand. Modesty suddenly overcame fear, and she shielded her chest and groin with her hands. The man took his eyes off her and glanced around the room.

'Love what you've done with the place,' he murmured.

'Singer!' she shrieked. She rushed over and bent to hug him. He half-stood and they embraced awkwardly. 'But how did you…? Never mind – wait there, okay? Don't go away, I'll be back in thirty seconds!' She dashed up the stairs and dragged jeans and a jumper from her wardrobe. She yanked on the fluorescent light of the ensuite – last night's make-up still clung to her face. She swore and performed a lightning patch-up job. Ronan rolled over in bed.

'Whass goin' on?'

'Singer!' she exclaimed and fled for the stairs. The kitchen was empty. For an instant, she panicked, thinking maybe she'd been dreaming or sleepwalking…but no, there he was, standing in what had been the old living room, before her giant wedding portrait on the wall. She ran over to him.

'It was taken in the Seychelles – fills that space nicely, don't you think?'

'It's a big space.'

'How did you get in?'

He looked at her casually, as if he, and not Ronan, had been married to her all these years. 'The back door was open.' His voice was gravelly, as if he needed to cough. His eyes carried heavy bags beneath them, and his face had turned jowly.

'Bloody hotel staff…no, I meant, how did you get in through the security gates, without buzzing?'

'I didn't come through the gates. I parked on the harbour and walked.'

'But there's a fence.'

He drew on his cigarette. 'No, there isn't.'

She laughed. 'What?' He gestured at the front window. Dionne peered out of it. Between the house and the beach, a huge section of her security fence had vanished. 'What the freakin'…'

'Most of it's down there on the pebbles, but I think some bits might have been washed away.'

'I don't believe…I mean, how…oh, bloody fucking *hell*, that thing cost a fortune to put up!' She ran off into the back kitchen corridor and returned wearing a pair of green Wellingtons and a purple fleece. Singer followed her out through the glass porch. They crossed the driveway onto the sea-grass, to where the fence had stood until sometime early that morning. The sea had eaten a sizeable chunk of the sea-grass dunes, causing the structure to collapse. As Singer had said, most of it lay strewn on the beach, like laundry blown from a washing line. Already, several people wearing various hues of golfing wet wear stood around the harbour, as if enjoying a morning constitutional after yet another salubrious evening at the Barclay Golf Hotel. But really what they were doing was inspecting the damage the storm had inflicted on that incredibly exclusive house down by the water, which was rumoured to be jam-packed with celebrities.

'Global warming,' Singer muttered and took a hip flask from his jacket pocket. He offered it to her. She accepted, swallowed, then coughed and patted her chest. 'Either that, or you should fire your architect.'

'I can't,' she wheezed. 'I was the fecking architect.'

He accepted a cup of tea and topped it up from his flask. He sat at the kitchen table, fielding a flurry of questions from the three women.

'Where are you living these days?'

'London.'

'So, you're still in film?'

'Not quite – just advertising. I help to sell cars, toilet roll and mortgages.'

'Are you married?'

'No.'

'Kids?'

'No.'

'Girlfriend?'

'No.'

Ronan made a fresh pot of tea on the range while the women fussed over the new arrival. Singer held up a pouch of rolling tobacco and offered him a cigarette.

'I smoked my last one four years ago,' Ronan admitted, with the false satisfaction of the reformed addict who secretly spends the rest of his life craving his former poison.

Dionne pinked. 'Actually, we don't allow smoking in the house at all, normally. It makes the furniture smell...'

Singer stood. 'You're absolutely right – it's a disgusting habit.' He shambled to the front porch. Dionne thought he'd put on weight. Melissa was taken aback by how old he looked. To Oona, he seemed tired. She followed him out to where he stood looking at the beach and saw the damage the sea had wrought.

'No offence to our hostess, but I didn't like that fence anyway. It cut the house off from its surroundings, and that was always the beauty of here, the way you always felt part of the landscape – don't you think?'

He squinted over at the golf course, where play was in full swing. 'Not much of the landscape left, is there? Where's Manus?'

She pointed. 'Do you see those holiday homes across the bay?'

'Hard not to.'

'Dionne says he's in one of those.'

He started through the gap in the fence. 'Tell them I've gone to visit Manus, will you?'

'But shouldn't you...I don't even know which house he...'

'I'll find it.'

She ran after him. 'Wait! I'm coming with you.'

He guided his hire car around the bulky white cabin cruisers squatting on their trailers above the harbour.

'So, did Frisby get a job selling yachts after all?'

'Better still – he's a professional golfer. Apparently quite a famous one.'

'No better man.'

As they drove up the hill past the hotel, a bevy of players made to cross the road. Instead of slowing down, Singer stepped on the accelerator and sped past, narrowly avoiding them. He glanced in the rear-view mirror and smiled when he saw two of the group gesticulate angrily after the car.

'Hey – those are Dee's paying customers! She owns the hotel too, you know, and the golf course. At least, her consortium does.'

'Then she wrecked a perfectly good pub, along with everything else.'

'True – but you can't expect places to stay the same forever, now can you?'

'No,' he sighed, 'but somehow you don't expect them to become infested with arseholes.'

They drove out of the valley almost as far as the village before they saw where a new road had been opened at the edge of the forest, opposite the Barclay Golf sign. The surface was still not properly paved, so Singer took it slowly, and eventually they emerged from the pines down at the eastern end of the golf course, with a reverse view of the hotel and the Pier House across the bay. The road hugged the foot of the mountain, then abruptly its roughness met slick new tarmac. They were surrounded by dozens of modern bungalows, built in a perfunctory imitation of the cottage style, with small conservatories and postage stamps for gardens. A high mesh fence separated the houses from the golf course, to prevent stray balls from smashing their windows.

'So, which do you suppose it is?'

'Well, I think we can discount any with Dublin-registered cars. What about down there on the left?'

'Why that one?'

'Because there's turf smoke coming out of the chimney.'

Oona opened her window, closed her eyes and sniffed the air. The smell of the burning turf mixed with salt and the scent of the wet seagrass instantly swept her back to the first time she'd ever stood outside the Pier House, how it had emerged from the night like some crumbling, enchanted castle, a dream in solid form. Then she remembered how a very young Singer had held her hand slightly longer than necessary, when she'd first stepped off the Dublin bus. She opened her eyes again. They had pulled up in front of the bungalow with the smoke. A repetitive, mechanical whirring noise came from behind it. They stepped from the car and she followed his lead around the side of the building, in the direction of the sound.

Manus had his back to them and was pushing an old-fashioned, upright lawnmower across a patch of grass so short it resembled the felt on Ronan's snooker table. He was bent into his task, and although his shoulders looked as powerful as ever, when he turned around, Oona could see that age sat upon him. He had lost a lot of hair, his face had swollen and gone from ruddy to a mild shade of purple, and he carried a heavy pot belly. He wore a pair of carpet slippers, dark blue tracksuit bottoms and a mangled black jumper.

'Mr McFall,' Singer greeted him. 'We warned you we'd be back, one day.'

Manus appeared not to see or hear them, and set off across the garden again, gaze fixed on his already balded grass. Oona glanced at Singer, who shrugged. This time, the lawnmower's return path took Manus right to where they stood. He stopped just in front of their shoes, and looked up slowly, as if somehow shy.

'Manus,' Singer tried again. 'It's Singer, and Oona. Do you remember? From the Pier House?'

'Sersamann!' Manus barked. 'Corpus sersamann!' His eyes contained no spark of recognition, indeed no sign of anything, except unalloyed confusion.

'It's been a long time...'

'Sersamann!' Manus glared at Singer and waved an arm for the two of them to step out of his way.

'Manus!' Oona stepped forward and gave him a hug.

'Ooooooh!' he roared, dropping the handle of the mower. He shoved her away and backed off, looking around in panic. 'Sersamann!'

'Manus! You're all right now! You're all right!' Mrs McFall came out of the conservatory door behind them. She took Manus by the arm and made soothing noises. He responded as a young child might to its mother, allowing himself to be placated, although he still mumbled and looked around as if frightened and vexed. 'It would be easier if you let him get on with the grass,' Mrs McFall informed them. 'Come in here a minute.' Stunned, Oona and Singer followed her into the conservatory. Outside, Manus picked up the handle of his mower and started to push.

Singer frowned. 'There's no grass left to cut.'

'Ah, sure, don't I know,' Mrs McFall stated matter-of-factly. Her salt-and-pepper hair had turned white at the sides, but otherwise thirteen years had done little to change her. 'But it's all I can do, to keep him distracted. Up and down, up and down, over and over – the doctor said to let him get on with it.' Oona started to cry. Singer patted her hand. 'I'd say it would be a shock now, if you haven't seen him in a while,' Mrs McFall continued, as casually as if she were discussing the weather, 'but it's been eating away at him for a long time.'

'What is it?' Singer asked. 'Alzheimer's?'

Mrs McFall nodded. 'It started with him being forgetful, but I put that down to the drink. Then he would go to his chores at the Pier House, and not come up for dinner. I'd go down and find him sitting there, in that old place, alone in the dark. Then it got so he was confused about simple things, so I took him into Letterkenny and had him seen to, and the doctor said he was well past the early stages of Alzheimer's.'

Oona dabbed her eyes with a tissue that Singer offered her from his pocket. 'I'm sorry,' she sniffled, 'I'm just a bit...'

'The speech went earlier this year. The more it goes on, the divil he knows any better. He can't be left on his own any more – the last time I did, he nearly burnt down this house. That old mower is the one thing that keeps him occupied, and thank god for it, because I don't know what I'd do without it.' Outside, Manus trundled on a fresh circuit, oblivious to the two dazed faces watching him from the conservatory.

'Have you been given any indication how long...'

'The doctor says I'll be lucky to still have him by next Christmas, but I'm praying that God sees fit to end his suffering before then.'

Singer looked as if he, too, might cry. An awkward silence followed. Since Mrs McFall didn't offer tea, or any further information, they took that as a hint to leave.

'If there's anything we can ever do...'

'Sure, what could you do? I'll let you out by the front, to save upsetting him.' She led them through the house, which was furnished and decorated in a sub-Laura Ashley style, with no trace of the exotic paraphernalia that had once graced the old pub. They stopped on the doorstep, Singer clutching for straws of familiarity, anything at all to bridge the yawning gulf that now separated him from his former friend.

'Michael, the setter? I suppose he's...'

'Dead. Dead these many a year.'

'I'm sorry,' Singer breathed lamely.

He turned to leave and a golf ball whacked off the tarmac a few paces in front of him, narrowly missing the car, before bouncing off into the garden of the house opposite. Oona hesitated.

'Can I ask you something, Mrs McFall?' The woman cocked her head in enquiry. 'I don't mean to be nosey – but when you sold all your land to my friend Dionne Brady, did she tell you what she was going to do with it?'

Mrs McFall gave her a cold look. 'Why do you ask?'

'The place has changed so much.'

'Let me tell you something – ever since Declan died, I've hated this place with all my heart. But my husband wouldn't leave. Instead, he wasted his life looking after a big old wreck of a house that was no use to anyone, when he should have been looking after me and my Declan. And where did it get him? When your friend came to me with her money, I gladly sold her every inch. This place is hers, now – she can do what she likes with it, and may it bring her more luck than it ever brought me. But sure, what do you care? You're just a blow-in, like all the rest.' At that, she closed her front door.

They drove back towards the Pier House in silence. Again, Singer parked on the harbour.

'I need a walk.'

'So do I.'

They climbed the hairpin path to the top of the headland, where the stone watchtower still stood, bricked up and lonely, high above the sea. Singer patted its wall.

'Nice to see something that hasn't been yuppified.'

'No doubt they'll get round to it.' Oona gave a sardonic laugh. 'Probably convert it into a coffee bar and sell overpriced lattes to stray golfers.' They walked to the edge. The sea was up, whipped into majestic life by the previous night's storm. Huge rollers obliterated the snout of the headland, forcing themselves into the gorge, choking it with spume. 'It's funny,' she sighed. 'If we look over our shoulders, the world has caught up with us. But if we look straight ahead, it's as if nothing had ever changed.'

'Are you up for it?'

'I am if you are. You've put on a bit of weight – can you still climb?'

He patted his tummy. 'I'll have you know that's pure muscle.'

Grunting and gasping, they made it onto the top of the pinnacle, where they stared into the frothing maelstrom, each thinking their own thoughts about what they'd seen at the McFall home. But the drop had lost none of its primitive, dizzying magic, and eventually, Oona had to take Singer's arm.

'I hope you don't mind – but do you ever get that crazy urge just to chuck yourself off a high place?'

'Every time I stand upright.'

'Do you know, the last time I felt like this was on top of the Twin Towers, in 1994. I married an idiot called Rob, and we went to New York on our honeymoon.'

'There you go. I was in New York in 1994, but I had no time for sight-seeing – it was all meetings.'

'Would you mind if we went back down again? This is making me nervous.' She shivered and turned her back on the chasm. At the base of the pinnacle, Singer huddled into a niche in the rock to roll a cigarette.

'Hey, can I have one too?'

'Thought you were part of the anti-smoking league?'

'Not today. Poor Manus.' The pair sat in a sheltered spot out of the wind while Singer busied himself.

'Poor Manus. Still, at least he's got someone to look after him.'

Oona frowned. 'I wouldn't fancy being looked after by her.'

'Better than no one.'

'She's the kind of person that would put arsenic in your tea.' Singer laughed. 'So,' she continued, 'you never married yourself?'

'I did, but only for a while.'

'Was she nice? Sorry, tell me to shut up if I'm being nosey.'

'You're not being nosey. Yes, she was nice.'

'Did you love her?'

'For a while.'

'What do you mean, for a while?'

'From about eleven o'clock the night we met, until I woke up the following morning.' He brought out his hip flask and offered it.

'You're such a liar. Why did you split up?'

'Because I shouldn't have married her in the first place.'

'So why did you, in the first place?'

'Because it seemed like a good idea at the time.'

'If you don't give me a bit more information, I'll be forced to ask more questions.'

'I take back what I said – you are being nosey.'

'Well, you still have to answer. Was she nice?'

'Kate? She was pretty, she was posh and I wasn't spoken for, so I sort of went along with it.'

'Was she rich?'

He lit their cigarettes and handed her one. 'Nowhere near as rich as Dionne, but I found out after we'd slept together that her daddy owned a big advertising agency.'

'Ah. She didn't tell you, because she wanted you to love her for herself. I bet she was a nice person.' She blew smoke from her mouth. 'Man, that feels good.'

'It was all a bit too easy. I'd left America, and I'd been kicking around London for about a year, avoiding anything that required an ounce of effort on my part.'

'So, did her family gobble you up?'

'I allowed it to happen – I blame myself.'

'That's big of you.'

'I was sleepwalking. The west London dinner-party circuit, where everyone is something in the media, and it's all tickety-boo, until you realise that beneath those sophisticated exteriors, they're all wracked with chronic status anxiety.'

'So you dumped her?'

'I tried to play along, but I'm crap at pretending. I engineered it so as she could dump me, for the sake of appearances. What about you?'

'Hold on, we're not finished with the subject of you yet.'

'It's your turn. What did you say his name was?'

'Rob.'

'Was he any good in bed?'

She slapped his leg and reached for his hip flask. 'Yes, he was, actually – he was spectacular. Too spectacular for his own good.'

'Sorry to hear that.'

'Of course you are. Men hate hearing about other men being great in the sack.'

'I came looking for you, you know.'

'Pardon?'

'That year, after we…when was it? Ninety? Ninety-one? Ronan said you'd rung him, out of the blue, from that St Eunan's place.'

Oona blanched and felt sick from the cigarette. 'That was November 1990. What do you mean, you came looking for me?'

'You know how practical Ronan is. It took him a whole month to tell me you'd rung, and only then because I was passing through Dublin, and took him out for a pint. I was up to my eyes, editing my film in London. But yes, he told me you were in St Eunan's, so I went there the next morning. On Christmas Day, as it happens.'

'You were in that dreadful place?'

'Just as a visitor, I'm glad to say. But they told me I'd missed you by a fortnight, so I didn't get to see the facilities.'

'I can't believe you did that.'

'Well, I did.'

'Sorry, what I meant was, I can't believe I'm only finding out now, after all this time, that you came to see me.'

'Ronan didn't know your home address, Melissa was in Egypt and Dionne wouldn't speak to me, so I just went back to London. I'm sorry I didn't try harder to find you.'

'I was in St Eunan's for three months.'

'God. What for?'

'Oh, the usual. Another chronic attack of glorified self-pity. I had it bad that year, much worse than before.'

'Do you still...'

'Suffer from depression? Yes – but I've learned to live with it. I had another horrendous episode after I split up with Rob, but that was when I decided that if you have an open wound dripping blood, you have a responsibility to yourself and to other people to get it bandaged up, don't you?'

'I suppose.'

'Well, after Rob, I spent two years in counselling. I take my medication without fail, and when I feel a bout coming on, I have distraction techniques. I travel a lot, which helps. When I'm doing my research, that takes me out of myself. I'm never going to let it get the better of me ever again.'

'Good for you.'

'It becomes your identity, if you let it. You know, "there goes Oona, she's always depressed". But now, I'm just boring Oona who gets on with her job at the university. And now I'm going to prove how boring and responsible I am by saying that I think we should go back down to the others. I mean, you just arrived, then walked straight out the door again.'

Singer stood and smiled. 'You have changed, haven't you? The old Oona would have pulled a bag of magic mushrooms out of her pocket and stayed up here all day.'

'Yes, and then spent the next three months in a mental hospital. I can't believe that you tried to come and see me. Why did nobody tell me?'

'Because nobody knew – I went straight back to London and then on to America. I didn't even see Melissa for a long time afterwards.'

They started on the grassy slope towards the watchtower.

'I've spent the past thirteen years thinking that you just didn't care.'

When he offered his hand to help her up the steep bits, she accepted it.

Looking back on it, Oona often thought of the dinner they shared that night as a sort of last supper. Singer told Dionne that he didn't want to go to the hotel, and was amused at the suggestion that the hotel should come to them.

'It's about time this kitchen was christened, don't you think?' He looked about at all the virginal appliances and worktops. 'Miss Montgomery, you're not too famous to be seen in a supermarket, I hope?'

'Do you think I'd trust a grown man to shop by himself?'

So Singer drove himself and Melissa up to the village and they returned an hour later, laden with bags. They had decided to make homemade pasta with a complicated sauce, homemade garlic bread, a selection of starters and salads and a homemade lemon cheese-cake. Oona smiled inwardly, because she could see what Singer was up to. By cooking everything from scratch, he was deliberately making the preparation of their evening meal a labour-intensive task, so that everyone would have to gather in the kitchen and slice, stir or, in Frisby's case, use tooth-picks to pierce anchovies, slippy tinned olives and cubes of feta cheese, 'because,' Singer told him with a straight face, 'I need someone with superb hand-eye co-ordi-nation to make the appetisers.' He then circulated with a bottle in each hand, issuing instructions, keeping glasses topped up, and a combination of wine and work dropped everyone's guard and turned the tentative atmosphere warm with smells, smiles and noisy chatter.

Dionne glowed with pleasure, thoroughly enjoying her role as *châtelaine*, showing Singer where knives, bowls and chopping boards were kept, and jars of dried herbs and spices that had never been opened. Much to Singer's approval, Ronan put Vaughan Williams on the CD player, then proceeded to chop garlic into wafer-thin slices and argue with Frisby about the wisdom of invading Iraq. Frisby was for, Ronan was against.

'But Saddam is an evil dictator!' Frisby protested.

'Whose only crime in America's eyes is that he stopped obeying orders. Sure, wasn't Bush Senior busy punishing another former bum-boy the last time we were here, in Panama?'

'I don't remember.'

'No, you probably don't.'

Oona also noticed how Singer refrained from mentioning Manus, as if not to kill the delicate illusion of long-lost chums happily reunited that he'd temporarily invoked. The upbeat mood prevailed all the way through the meal, which went on for hours. As they polished off their cheesecake, Ronan popped yet another handful of Shiraz corks and Melissa reminded everyone of something that, in their festive spirit, they'd hitherto forgotten. She tapped her fork against her wine glass until she had silence.

'Can I just say,' she raised her glass, 'how lovely it is to see what I never thought I'd see again, and that is everyone sitting around this table, enjoying each other's company as much as we did when we were still young, slender and attractive.'

'Speak for yourself!' Frisby hollered.

'I am,' Melissa smiled. 'But I wonder whether you agree with me that it's time for our most gracious hostess to share her little secret...'

'What,' Frisby chortled, 'how much she's worth?' Dionne threw her napkin at him.

'I seem to remember some mention of a letter that allegedly resolves a one-hundred-year-old mystery – the identity of Sophia Clements, to whom we arguably owe our presence here tonight. If the Pier House had not existed, Singer could never have invited us in the first instance, and Dionne and Ronan would not be married, and I might not have had a career. So, Dee, it's denouement time.'

'Does that mean she has to take her clothes off?' This time, Dionne threw a wooden coaster at Frisby's head, off which it ricocheted smartly.

'Jay Frisby, I'm a married woman, and if you don't stop making lewd remarks, I'm going to get my husband to come around the table and give you a right good seeing-to.'

'Can't wait – it will make up for the one I gave him on the back nine this afternoon!'

'We're getting away from the point,' Melissa reprised. 'It's just that once, a very long time ago, I spent an entire week of my life in the National Library researching Lord Leitrim, and found no mention of Sophia, so I'm dying to know who she was.'

'I was hoping to save this for the party tomorrow night.'

'Ah,' Oona chipped in, 'but you also promised to reveal all, if Singer showed.'

Dionne turned to Ronan, who shrugged. '"Knowledge comes, but wisdom lingers".'

'Whatever that means.'

'It's Tennyson. Follow me, everybody.' Ronan stood and opened the door into the western extension. He led them down the glass corridor to the huge old oak door that darkened the far end. Oona averted her eyes and the others carried their glasses and chattered excitedly, while Ronan took the iron key from its hook and admitted them into the games room cum library. He lifted a small, blue book down from one of the upper shelves – a 1913 Methuen edition of Wilde's *An Ideal Husband*. He set it on the snooker table and the others gathered around. With a conscious degree of ceremony, he opened the cover, and inside it sat a creamy-brown envelope, frayed around the edges, which bore no stamp or postmark, but had been addressed in black ink by a firm hand.

Miss Caroline Sophia Clements,
The Pier House,
Dunaldgragh,
County Donegal

Carefully, Ronan extracted a letter from envelope.
'His sister,' Melissa breathed. 'Sophia was Lord Leitrim's sister.'
'How do you know?' Oona asked.
'He disinherited his immediate family, except for a sister called Caroline.'
'But I thought Sophia was very young, and Leitrim much older?'
Melissa pressed a hand to her head, remembering. 'There was nearly a forty-year gap between them. But his father, the second earl, married twice. So it's not impossible.'
'That would make her a half-sister, then.'
Ronan laid the letter, written on matching paper, on the table. They all huddled around, with the exception of Frisby, who toyed with a snooker ball. The letter read,

Lough Rynn,
March the 30th, 1878

My dearest Sophia,

At my direction, Kincaid carries these words to you with all haste. As you read them, do order your housekeeper give him ample fare, as he has travelled two days' journey in one. The situation here in Mohill grows graver by the day – in spite of my many protestations, or perhaps because of them, that fool Carlisle has done nothing to quell the murderous gangs of Ribbonmen and 'Molly Maguires' that take into their bloodied hands the run of this wretched, misfortunate country.

Only yesterday, there was another attempt on my person, in plain daylight, in the main street of Mohill itself. Although I have been loath to, it is now unwise for me to travel anywhere without the escort of two constables, who quickly disarmed the ruffian, but not before he had discharged a pistol in my direction – I can only thank God, as before, that my tenants are as poor at their shooting as they are at tending their fields. However, I deem it expedient to quit Lough Rynn as a temporary measure, as rumour reaches me that other, more serious plots are afoot in the wake of last month's evictions.

I am fully aware that what I now propose will come as a surprise to you, having banished myself from your presence these many years. For the indelicacy you suffered, I have apologised fulsomely and tried to make ample restitution, and long contemplated with sorrow and anguish how I abused my stewardship of you. What happened was a moment of contemptible weakness on my part, and you were too young to have it in mind how a lonely old man, a rough army captain, might have been susceptible to your unwitting charms.

But now, I hope we can agree – 'Tempus mutantur, nos et mutamur in illis'. Your condition is much improved and your circumstances are of a more appropriate convention, permitting me to break my vow and come to you, at this very short notice. My home county is not safe, as evidenced by the events of yesterday. Dublin is not safe – a mob dared to cast stones at my carriage when last week I went hither to purchase seed for the estates. Should I return to London, then that would become widely known, and my tenantry, detecting a weakness, would cause the collection of rents to be yet more arduous than it is at this present time. The only path open is to remain in Ireland, availing of the secrecy in which you dwell, and, for a few short weeks, join you at Dunaldragh. Kincaid, who is to be trusted, may then carry instructions to my agents for the administration of my properties, until the popular mood has subsided.

I leave tomorrow for Milford, where Kincaid shall meet me in order to arrange safe conduct on to Dunaldragh. Please have

your housekeeper ready a room for myself, and a lesser room for
Kincaid who shall also be staying with us. Do not be alarmed
on my behalf, as my intentions are known only to Kincaid, and
now you. It may also interest you to learn that I have redrawn
my will in the presence of Reynolds, Thom & Co., my Dublin
solicitors, for the purpose of apportioning a substantial benefit
to my beloved half-sister to thank her for the succour that I
know, from the goodness of her heart, will be forthcoming.

Yours in anticipation,

Sydney

'He was on his way here when he was killed,' Melissa murmured.

'How do you know?' Dionne demanded.

'The date — the thirtieth of March, 1878. Leitrim was ambushed outside Milford on the second of April, early in the morning — less than two days after he wrote this. He'd stayed overnight in the town and was travelling in this direction.'

Singer lifted a red ball from the neat triangle on the table and rolled it into one of the pockets. 'Do you think she betrayed him?' he asked.

'Why do you say that?'

'Where did you find this letter?' Singer asked Dionne.

'Behind this panelling,' she pointed around, 'when we had it removed it from Sophia's bedroom.'

'Did it look as if it had fallen there by accident, or had it been placed?'

'I wasn't there when it was found, but I'd say it was placed. That panelling was well built, with few gaps — it's hard to see how anything could have slipped behind it by accident.'

'Okay, try this — I think it's fair to say the letter confirms Melissa's theory about some sort of inappropriate relationship between Leitrim and Sophia — especially now that she turns out to be his half-sister.'

Melissa interrupted. 'Then why did her coded poem talk about "her father", and not a brother?'

'The letter mentions "stewardship". If she was made Leitrim's ward after the death of their father, then, given the age gap, their relationship almost certainly would have been more paternal than fraternal.'

Melissa nodded. 'Go on.'

'So let's say I'm Sophia, and the man who abused me, gave me syphilis and locked me away as a young woman is, more than a decade later, running to my house, in fear of his life. He's evicted so many tenants, everyone's out to kill him, and I still hate him for what he did.'

Ronan scratched his head. 'Who's the "fool Carlisle" he mentions?'

Melissa answered. 'Lord Lieutenant of Ireland, at the time. Come on, Singer, I'm quite enjoying you pretending to be poor Sophia.'

'Leitrim tells me in a secret letter that he's coming here, and he thinks I'm still a naïve goody-two-shoes who'll do what he says. To be sure of my loyalty, he throws in a bribe – the change of will. I dread the prospect of seeing him again, but he has stupidly informed me that I stand to benefit from his death. So there's no shortage of motive. I only have one chance to stop him, but it's a good one. He needs to break his journey in Milford, because it's a long way. How hard would it be for me to inform his many enemies of his movements? Remember, this man is a despot, hated throughout Ireland, but he owns my house and pays my bills, so I can't refuse him. I have to act fast.'

Melissa clapped her hands. 'Great pitch – love it, darling.'

'If I were Sophia,' Dionne interjected, 'and I did something as sneaky as that, then the first thing I would do would be to dispose of the evidence, and burn this letter.'

'Not if it was the only evidence you had, in Leitrim's very own hand, that he had included you in his will. Better to hide it somewhere safe, just in case there's any dispute.'

Oona frowned. 'I've always imagined Sophia as a sympathetic victim – but now you're saying she was a treacherous, murdering bitch?'

Melissa laughed. '*Tempus mutantur, nos et mutamur in illis*. Singer, we have to turn this into a script. I just know I could get it made if I tried hard enough.'

He smiled. 'It has all the elements of a good old bodice-ripper, doesn't it?'

'Needs a young, dashing love interest.'

'Kincaid has seduced Sophia, behind his master's back. No, better the other way around. She seduces him, and gets him to do her dirty work.'

'The name Kincaid rings a bell. I'd need to check, but I'm almost certain that there was a Kincaid with Lord Leitrim when he was ambushed, and that he survived.'

'So maybe Kincaid betrayed him, and Sophia had nothing to do with it.' Oona sounded relieved. 'But tell me, if you've quite finished writing your movie – how come she used her middle name, and not Caroline, her first name?'

'The aristocracy often did that amongst themselves, because the same Christian names kept recurring. Leitrim himself was William Sydney Clements, but you can see he signs his letter "Sydney".'

'How do you remember all this stuff?' Dionne asked Melissa.

Melissa curtsied. 'Most actresses have an astonishing array of useless information committed to memory. Comes with the territory.'

'If Leitrim was that hated by the peasantry,' Ronan pushed his glasses onto his nose, 'then most likely they would have acted without any help. Those were troubled times. Maybe Leitrim wasn't betrayed at all, other than by his own arrogance, thinking he could move around the countryside and nobody would notice.'

'You're probably right,' Singer agreed, 'and I'm probably being totally unfair to her – but you've got to admit, the Sophia theory makes a great story. Get your revenge on your tyrannical half-brother, while ensuring that his juicy new will comes into force immediately. Sorted.'

'Planning your comeback, are you?' Dionne asked him.

'Planning a large whiskey, actually.'

She laughed. 'Okay, everybody to the upstairs lounge, where hopefully my husband will continue to make himself useful by serving drinks at the bar.'

'Jolly good idea,' Frisby offered her his arm. 'I haven't a clue what you lot are yammering on about.'

'Of course you haven't,' Dionne ruffled his hair, 'because you're thicker than a brick shithouse.'

'Bloody top-class golfer, though.'

'Yes, you are.' Dionne hauled him off up the corridor. 'And a fine advertisement for Barclay Golf, which is why we're going to find you a very large gin and tonic.' Oona followed quickly behind, so as she wouldn't have to watch Ronan use the iron key to lock the door.

However, a few hours later, Oona found herself back in the western wing, searching for Singer, who had slipped away from the party in

333

the upstairs lounge. His room door was open, and she saw him sitting on the end of his bed, fiddling with the remote control that darkened his picture window. As the glass blackened, the night seemed to solidify, and a mirror image of Singer and the dimly lit room replaced the sea-grass outside. She watched from the corridor before tapping lightly on the door. He looked over his shoulder.

'Hi. Nice toy, huh?' He tossed the little remote onto the duvet, as if he hadn't really been playing with it. She sat beside him on the bed, took a tin of Tiger Balm from her skirt pocket and rubbed some below her ears.

'Sorry, I know it stinks. But I'm still addicted to it.'

'It doesn't stink − it just reminds me of you.'

'Cheaper than Chanel, and much more memorable. So what's wrong? Why are you hiding? Had enough already?'

'I feel like an idiot, sitting up there in that big glass box. So I thought I'd come down here, and sit in this slightly smaller glass box.'

'Come on, you're doing so well. Everyone's enjoying themselves, now that you're here to order them around.' He smiled, but it was a tired smile. More than ever, he looked like a beaten man.

'I can't believe what they've done to this place. Not just to the house, but to the entire valley. It's as if they've raped it.'

'Funny, Melissa and I had this very conversation only last night.'

'I feel so sorry for Manus, but there's a part of me that's glad he has no idea what's going on.'

'Do you wish you hadn't come?'

'Do you?'

'I asked you first.'

He sighed. 'I don't know who Ronan is any more, and I still think Frisby's a cretin. But it's really good to see you and Melissa, so I suppose I'm a bit sad, but not sorry.'

'I notice you didn't mention Dionne.'

'She hasn't changed a bit, has she?'

'Meaning?'

'She knows what she wants, and she knows how to get it. I don't mean to sound immodest − God knows I have plenty to be modest about these days − but I was worried she might...you know...'

'Start hitting on you again?'

'Yes.'

'Are you getting any hint of that?'

'Not at all. But I still can't help wondering why she's brought us all here. I had no contact with her for over a decade, in fact I thought of her as someone who just hated me and whom I'd never see again. Then, all of a sudden, she starts bombarding me with e-mails. There's something odd about that, don't you think?'

'Some people just adore reunions, especially when they get to a certain age. Have you heard of that Friends Reunited website? All these forty-somethings getting back in touch with their old school chums and even copping off with them.'

'Everyone has two lives – the one they've lived, and the one they wished they'd lived.'

'Do you realise that we're neighbours? My bedroom's next door, and what's more, we're the only guests in this wing.'

'Well, fancy that.'

'I wonder if our hostess is trying to play matchmaker?'

'Between me and you?'

'No, between me and Benjamin bloody Netanyahu – who d'you think?'

He laughed. 'Well, in that case, maybe I should be thanking her, instead of suspecting her motives.'

Oona crossed to the bedroom door and closed it. 'When I first arrived, I thought she just wanted to show off.' She started unbuttoning her blouse. 'She projects this image of her and Ronan as the perfect couple...'

'What are you doing?'

'I'm taking my top off...buttons are fiddly, though...but now that I've been here a few days, I can tell you that things are far from perfect.'

Singer looked concerned. 'Listen, I'm not so sure that we need to...'

'Don't be frightened, I'm keeping my bra on. I just want to show you something.' The last button gave and she peeled off her blouse. She stood before him, and held her left arm out for inspection. His eyes widened in surprise.

'Holy...how did that happen?' He took her wrist and studied the three identical scars that sat at regular intervals, in a melted plasticky red, against the flesh of her inner forearm. 'Who did this to you?'

'I did.'

'What?'

'I did this to me.'

'How? I mean, that shape – is it some sort of key?'

'Yes. As it happens, the same key that's hanging on a hook at the end of the corridor, almost outside my bedroom door. I was rather hoping I'd never see it again.'

'You think they put it there deliberately?'

'No. Dionne and Ronan don't know about this. I've never even told Melissa. I've been gagging for a swim since I got here, but I can't, because I don't want anybody to see my arms. You're not to tell them, by the way.'

'Of course not – but why…?'

'I started self-harming, the night I sent you all away from here. I was so annoyed at myself, for behaving like a spoiled child.'

'We were all children, back then. Highly mobile children.'

'This arm,' she held out her right, 'has healed much better, but then I only did little razor-cuts on it, over a longer period of time.' Singer saw a white tracery of lines on the surface of her right arm, but his eyes were drawn back to the awful imprints on her left, which still looked sore, although he knew they couldn't be. She sat down beside him again. 'I know it looks really, really stupid, but in a strange way, the pain helped. It was a release. But this is why I ended up back in St Eunan's.'

'Jesus, I feel awful.'

'Precisely. And if you'd visited me, I'd have used these to blackmail you. That's why I rang Ronan, so you'd come to me, and I could make you feel awful. But these marks aren't your fault, they never were.'

'So why are you showing me now?'

'Because I want to be totally honest with you.'

'Okay…'

'And because I want to prove that I've changed. I'm in charge now.'

'In charge of what?'

'Me.'

'May I?'

She nodded, and gently, he touched the livid old burns. She looked at him, but he didn't meet her eyes, gazing instead at her skin as he moved his fingertips across it.

'I wish I could say the same thing.'

'What?'

'That I'm in charge of me.'

'You were always in charge.'

He snorted. 'In charge of nothing.'

'Would you like to kiss me?'

He hesitated before answering. 'Oons – I'm a forty-year-old nobody. I live alone in a shitty little flat in north London, almost right back where I started as a student. I freelance for poxy newspapers and cheapskate advertisers. I had my chance, but I threw it away because, like I told you, I'm crap at pretending.'

Oona shrugged. 'Well, I live alone in a nice little flat in south Dublin, and I'm right back where I started, at university. And I'm not pretending – I know it's been a long time, but I guess I'm hoping that you still like me.'

'I wasn't going to come, until I saw from that e-mail that you were definitely here, too. You're the only reason I bothered.'

'So, what are you waiting for?'

They kissed, slowly and softly.

'Mmm. Brandy and ginger?'

'Yes. Neat whiskey? It's a wonder you can taste anything.'

'We should have done this years ago, when I still had tastebuds.'

She grinned. 'I like to make them wait – keeps them keen.'

Just as their mouths met again, the bedroom door opened. They leapt apart, but Dionne gasped and put a hand to her face.

'Sorry! Sorry!' she yelped, half-withdrawing. Oona hid her arms. 'Sorry, but we're having such great fun upstairs and everyone was wondering where the pair of you had got to, so I just…err, sorry.' She closed the door. Oona swore softly, pulled on her blouse, pecked Singer on the cheek and pursued Dionne up the corridor, fumbling with her fiddly buttons.

20

Oona and Singer walked along the beach.

'So, what did she say to you?'

'Absolutely nothing, it was as if she hadn't seen anything.'

'But she did.'

'Of course she did.'

'I'm sorry I didn't follow after you. I wasn't embarrassed, just feeling tired and thoughtful, really.'

'How sweet. You went to bed and thought of me?'

'Um. I suppose so, yes.'

She reached out and squeezed his arm, then returned her hand to the pocket of the black and red ski jacket she'd borrowed from Ronan. It was at least three sizes too big, but snug and reassuringly waterproof, and had a generous hood. Broken gusts of rain blew in from a pewter, white-capped sea, and a wall of swollen grey clouds hid the horizon, auguring another storm. Singer still wore the same brown cord jacket and blue shirt from the day before. He seemed not to notice the cold.

'Well, I got back upstairs,' Oona continued, 'just in time to say goodnight to Melissa, who was off to bed, which is probably why Dee came looking for me, to have someone to talk to. Ronan and Frisby were still arguing about Iraq, so she sat me at the bar and yammered endlessly about her new projects in Portugal and Dubai, and some house she's bought in Dubrovnik. Or was it a flat in Rome? Both, I think. To be honest, I wasn't paying attention. She lives in a completely different world from me now.'

'She must think I'm a sleaze. Every time I come here, I cop off with one of her friends.'

Oona grinned. 'You are a sleaze. I saw you topping up your flask at the bar, after breakfast.'

'In that case you won't object if I take a nip – want some?'

She shook her head. 'If we're having a New Year's party tonight, I'm not touching alcohol until at least seven o'clock. That way, I stand a chance of seeing in 2003. I can't handle drink any more.'

'Bollocks to New Year's Eve.' He took a swig. 'I hate that whole thing of forced enjoyment. You must have fun because the clock on the wall says you must.'

A growling, crunching sound came from behind, and they turned around to see a stone lorry come crawling along the beach towards them. They stood to one side as the dirty, smoke-belching leviathan crunched past. It stopped up ahead and shed its load of rude grey boulders where the sea-grass met the pebbles. Singer stared in disgust.

'What the feck is that all about?'

'That,' Oona sighed, 'is Dionne playing King Canute. You saw what the tide did to her silly fence. Coastal erosion isn't my field, but I do know that once it gets going, it's hard to stop. Building that breakwater will put more pressure on the beach, and if the beach goes, then that pile of stones will be as much use as an ashtray on a motorbike.'

'Have you told her that?'

Oona smiled. 'No.'

'Now, wouldn't that be poetic justice – if the sea just came and washed everything away? When I look at the Pier House now, I feel as if it's ashamed of itself. As if it wished she'd torn it down instead of vandalising it.'

'If you liked it so much the way it was, how come you never bought it? At one time, you must have had the money.'

'For about ten minutes, I probably did. But I put it all back, into my next film.'

'Melissa said it didn't get made, because you quit.'

Singer nodded. 'When I walked away from that, I waved goodbye to the money.'

'She also said you put *the* Nick Danver in hospital.'

'Did I?'

'Didn't you?'

'I hit him a dig.'

'She said he was in hospital for a month afterwards.'

'Good for him.'

She laughed. 'But I thought he was a tough guy!'

'He wasn't, but his stuntmen probably were.'

'Whatever happened to Nick Danver, anyway? He used to be the biggest thing since sliced bread.'

'Sliced bread gets eaten, and forgotten.'

'And what about you – any chance of another film? I loved your Rennie Mackintosh one, by the way. I cried at the end.'

'Thanks, but I've no plans.'

'But what about Melissa's suggestion?'

'What suggestion?'

'To turn the Leitrim story into a script?'

'That was just a bit of banter.'

'Melissa's not the kind of person who talks empty talk – you know that.'

'True.'

'So, what if she was for real? Would you write a script if she asked you to?'

'Not if I thought she was offering me work out of pity.'

'Maybe she respects your talent, even if you don't.'

'Look, Melissa has influence in the film industry, but not even she can get a film made by just clicking her fingers. Turning out a good script is just the start – usually the start of several years of bullshit.'

With a metallic roar, the stone lorry bounced past them on its return journey. They waited until it was far away, then followed it back towards the house.

'I don't mean to badger you. Just tell me to mind my own business.'

'What good would that do me?'

She smiled. 'None whatsoever. It's just that I've been where you are now. I got horribly down in myself, and walked away from the only thing I was good at, which was geology.'

'Because it wrecked your head.'

'Just like you and the film industry. But I went back to it.'

'Because you were good at it.'

'No, because it required perseverance. And the same perseverance helped me rebuild myself – do you understand?'

'Yes. It's really good to see you've overcome your illness, I'm delighted for you.'

'Well, if I can do it, so can you.'

He sounded indignant. 'But I don't suffer from depression!'

'You're suffering from something – something that made you stop trying.' He took his hip flask from his jacket pocket. She nodded at it. 'And that isn't helping.'

'What is this? We share a kiss, so now you're running my life?'

'I know self-pity when I see it. I'm the expert, remember? I bet if you drank a bit less, you could write something brilliant.'

'In Spain, it's perfectly civilised to have a little drop with your breakfast. And lunch.'

'Still using that tired old excuse, eh?'

'Why do you care what I do with myself?'

She didn't answer immediately, but instead tapped his arm and nodded. Dionne stood on the beach up ahead, wrapped in a white fur coat, talking into a mobile phone. Oona stopped walking, while they were still out of earshot. Dionne waved down the beach at them. Oona waved back, then turned to face him.

'Come with me to Galicia.'

'Pardon?'

'Next month, I'm off to Galicia on a research trip – three weeks in northern Spain. Come with me. It's wild and beautiful, just like this place used to be – lots of rugged Atlantic coastline, only with no newly minted yuppies to screw it up. We'd stay in a little hotel – you could come on my field trips, and write if you felt like it.' Her face was pale, upturned, grey eyes searching his.

'Jesus – you're serious, aren't you?'

'Yes. Do you remember that second Christmas? Those wonderful weeks we had alone, before it all went to hell?'

'Of course.'

'I want us to try that again, and see what happens.'

'Really?'

She nodded. 'Make up for missing time.'

He pouted and stared out to sea. 'I don't know if I'd be any good in a relationship.'

'That's what I said, the last time. Do we have to wait another thirteen years before we're even?'

He gave a thin smile. 'No, I suppose not.'

'You said last night that you came here because of me. Did you?'

He looked at her. 'I told you, the very first time, when Dionne came, I was hoping you'd come too, and you did. It was always about you.'

'The Pier House is over now, for good. The six of us will never come together here again, you know that.'

'Yes.'

'But maybe that would be fitting, if we all finally got what we wanted − Ronan got Dionne, Dionne got rich, Melissa got her career, Frisby got a life, and now, maybe we could have each other. Come with me to Galicia. I'll even let you keep your hip flask.'

'Since you put it like that...'

Dionne was walking towards them, still talking into her mobile phone.

Oona gave Singer's hand a furtive squeeze, then stood back from him. 'We probably won't get a chance to talk tonight. But you think about what I'm saying, and tell me for certain in the morning.'

'I don't need to—' he began, but then Dionne was upon them, squalling.

'So what if tomorrow is New Year's Day? I'm trying to run a business here, I have customers all over the place, and your fence is lying on my beach and it looks second rate and downright shoddy! If your company wants any more contracts from me, you better get your boys up here and fix it ASAP! Are we clear? Good! Ring me when they're on their way!' She snapped the phone shut, raising her eyes to heaven. 'Sorry, folks, but you know what it's like − if you want anything done, you have to do it yourself!'

At that, four men wearing Barclay Golf uniforms emerged from the sea-grass at the front of the Pier House, lifted a heavy piece of fencing from the pebble beach and dragged it up towards a stack they had made in the dunes.

'Now!' She wrapped one of her white, furry arms around Oona's. 'I'm very much afraid, Mister Singer, that I'm stealing this fine young woman away from you. We have beauticians and hairdressers coming down from the hotel to help us get ready, then the costumes arrive at five, and the food shortly after that. Your two little chums are out there somewhere,' she waved towards the golf course, 'but they'll be back soon enough, and then you can do men's things together. But in the meantime, I suggest—'

'In the meantime,' Singer interrupted, 'I'll just keep on walking.' He patted his hip flask pocket, winked at Oona, and ambled off towards the hairpin path. Dionne called after him, 'The next time you see her, you won't recognise her!'

'Singer!' Oona shouted. 'Would you not need a coat?'

But he strode on, as if he had not heard either one of them.

Later that afternoon, Ronan noticed that Singer already seemed under the influence when they played snooker together and Singer missed lots of easy shots. Frisby was keen for a game, so when Singer inevitably lost, he abandoned play to the sportsmen and flopped on the sofa, sipping a cold beer from the fridge behind the bar.

'Living in London, you won't be familiar with this, but I'd value your opinion nonetheless.' Ronan handed Singer a copy of *The Speckled Bird*.

'What have we here?' he squinted at the cover. '"The quarterly journal for Irish arts?" Fascinating.'

'The successor to *Avalon*.'

'*Avalon*? Yes – your esteemed organ of the nineties, of course. Well. *The Speckled Bird* – Yeats?'

Ronan simpered. 'Of course.'

'Must have a read, so.' Singer rolled a cigarette and put his feet up on a coffee table. Ronan returned to his game, which became quite engrossing when Frisby missed a pot and left the table wide open. Fifteen minutes later, when he looked up from a most satisfying clearance, he saw that Singer had dozed off, with the magazine open on his lap and his cigarette burning slowly into an empty matchbox. Frowning, Ronan stubbed the cigarette out.

At half-past four, the security gate buzzer sounded in the kitchen and Ronan admitted a black van with the name *Richardson's* inscribed in gold lettering on the side. A clearly harrassed driver unloaded several white boxes and three suit bags into the glass porch, got Ronan to sign a docket and sped off down the drive again. Dionne's voice came from the top of the old staircase.

'Ro-ro? Was that Richardson's?'

'Yes. Who are Richardson's?'

'Outfitters from Dublin. The suit bags are for you, Frisby and Singer. Bring everything else up here, would you?'

'There's rather a lot – can you give me a hand, my love?'

'No. Stop yakking and hurry up, would you?'

Ronan pulled a sulky face, lifted a few of the boxes – which admittedly weren't heavy – and trudged up the stairs. Dionne's voice was now coming from Melissa's bedroom, so he opened the door to be confronted with one of those snapshots that most men tend not to forget – the three women stood around in their underwear, with their faces exquisitely decorated, complexions as smooth and pallid as bone china, in contrast to the rest of their bodies. Their hair, too, looked different. Oona was marginally less exposed than his wife and Melissa, in that she wore an unbuttoned white blouse. She held a bottle of champagne and poured for the other two. From an ashtray on the dressing table, a lit cigarette tapered a thin ribbon of smoke from its tip. Ronan coughed.

'I'll just set these here, then.' He put the boxes on the bed. Dionne squealed and ran over to him, her champagne glass slopping.

'Out! Out!' She shoved him in the chest and he flew backwards through the doorway. 'God, you are such a ninny!' She used the door to shield herself, so that only her painted face and ringleted hair were visible. From within, he heard Melissa and Oona giggling. 'Leave the stuff in the hallway, and go away! Do you not know by now not to walk in on ladies while they're changing?'

'Are you smoking?' he asked querulously, but the door slammed in his face. Dionne's laughter joined that of the other two, while Ronan stomped off to fetch the rest of the boxes.

'Singer – wake up!' Singer still slept on the games room sofa, his feet propped on the coffee table. Ronan put a hand on his leg and shook it.

'Mmmm?' he opened his eyes, which were pink. 'Bloody hell. Ro – how's it going?' Ronan held up a suit bag.

'Your clothes are here, everyone's getting ready for the party.'

He sighed. 'Victorian capitalist time again, eh?'

''Fraid so.'

'Can I not just go like this?'

'If you're prepared to spend the evening arguing with my wife. Me, I'm getting changed.'

'Bloody hell,' he repeated, hauling himself off the sofa. Instead of accepting the suit bag, he crouched down behind the bar counter, rummaged in the fridge and came up with a fresh beer, which he cracked open. 'Want one?'

Ronan shook his head. 'I'll wait until I'm dressed.' He pointedly held out the suit bag, which Singer now accepted.

'Haven't had a chance to chat since I got here, Ro.' The pair sauntered to the games room door and Ronan locked it. 'How's everything with you? Are you a happy bunny?'

Ronan hung the key on the hook. 'Yes, I am a happy bunny. See you at the party.' He walked away, up the glass corridor. Singer shrugged and let himself into his bedroom, which had been tidied to exhibition standards by the small army of hotel staff that invaded the Pier House on a daily basis. He dumped his suit bag on the bed and stripped to shower, then realised that anyone looking at the back of the building would clock a fine view of his pallid, overweight body in the picture window, so he fumbled for the remote and used it to darken the glass.

Upstairs, Ronan carefully draped his suit bag over a chair in the bedroom he shared with Dionne. Judging by the female laughter coming from Melissa's room next door, the party had already begun. As he stepped dripping out of the shower, he heard the intercom buzz impatiently from the kitchen below. He swore, hunted for his glasses, found them and peered out of the window. A hotel van waited at the gates. He wrapped a white towel around his waist, and poked his head out the bedroom door.

'Hello?' he called. 'Dee?' No reply, only more laughter. 'Frisby? Singer? Can somebody please let the caterers in? I'm just out of the shower! Can anybody hear me?' Muttering viciously under his breath, he descended to the kitchen. As they carried plates, pots and platters into the house, the hotel staff, if they found the sight of their boss's husband amusing, were careful not to show it.

By ten o'clock, the party was moving from the buffet on the ground floor up to the commanding lounge in the eastern extension. As they climbed the steel staircase beside the pool, Singer whispered in Oona's ear, 'Hey, you look amazing.'

'Thanks, but this is all Dionne's doing. We went online, and we all chose a dress from this ludicrously expensive outfitters. She insisted on paying, even for Melissa.'

'You all liked the same dress?'

'They are not the same dress!'

'I'm not complaining, it's a gorgeous look.'

'It was Dionne's idea to co-ordinate.'

As well as long black evening dresses, the women also wore black, elbow-length gloves and silver jewellery. The men wore standard black suits and bow-ties, although Frisby's bow-tie was multi-coloured. Singer laughed and poured the champagne that waited in chrome buckets on the upstairs bar into six traditional, wide-brimmed coupes.

'A toast!' he announced as the others stood around and fell silent. Rain from the mounting storm tapped heavily on the glass walls. Singer had asked Dionne to turn the orange spotlights off, so outside, all was darkness, save for a distant phalanx of blue lights on the front of the hotel, which was throwing its own New Year's party. 'There's a sundial in the front garden,' he continued, 'which has a motto carved into it. Melissa?'

She delivered the line portentously, as a ham Olivier. '*Tempus mutantur, nos et mutamur in illis.*'

'Thank you, we can see why you're one of the most respected actresses in the world.' Melissa bowed and the others tittered and gave a light round of applause. '*Tempus mutantur* – times change, and we change with them. I have a picture in my head, from many years ago, of three women sitting around a kitchen table, making beautiful dresses by candlelight, from scraps of cloth they'd salvaged from second-hand shops in Letterkenny. Now, I look around myself, and things have certainly changed.' The company nodded and murmured. 'Times have changed, and we have changed, but one thing has remained the same.' He raised his glass, and the others followed. 'Ladies and gentlemen, Dionne Brady – or Mrs Doherty, as she is now known – still knows how to throw a great party. To our hostess, the mistress of the Pier House!'

'Hear, hear!' Frisby bawled as the others cheered and drank the toast.

Dionne reddened, which made the dull gold of her hair shine all the more. 'Thank you, Mister Singer, thank you very much.' She addressed the room. 'I'm no good at speeches, so I'm going to keep it tight.'

'Phwoarr!' Frisby interrupted. Dionne ignored him.

'I just want to say that it's so nice, after thirteen years, to see the Christmas Club back together again!' More cheers, and more champagne swallowed. Singer slapped his forehead.

'God! I'm an idiot! I completely forgot!' He handed Ronan his glass and made for the stairs.

'Where are you off to?'

'I left something in the car, I'll be back in a minute.'

Singer was gone for more than a minute – it was more like ten, and he returned with his hair tossed, his shoulders damp and spots of mud on his shiny black shoes. He carried a canvas bag over one shoulder and a scrappy plastic shopping bag in his hand.

'Look at you,' Oona chided. 'Where have you been?'

He held the plastic bag aloft. 'I left this in my glove compartment. I knew there was something I meant to do before the party.'

'What is it?'

Singer reached into the bag, and withdrew a battered old book with a brown leather cover. Oona shrieked. It was *Chambers's Miscellany*.

'I don't believe it! You still have that!'

'I've moved house eleven times since 1989, and this is the only item of personal property I've never managed to lose. And the irony is, it's not even mine.'

Oona took *Chambers's Miscellany* from his hand and the others gathered round as she opened it at the flyleaf opposite the title page. It still read,

The Christmas Club
Rules
Oona, Dee, Melissa, Singer, Ronan and Jay hereby agree to:
1. Always spend Christmas at the Pier House.
2. Always dance formally on New Year's Eve.
3. Always respect the Pier House and its memories.
4. Never forget how beautiful the girls are.
5. Never forget how virile Ronan is.
6. Never let anything screw it all up.

Signed – Oona Tyler, Club Secretary and Commodore-in-Chief, Sunday the 1st of January, 1989, in her very own blood.

N.B. The rest of the blood in this book isn't mine, but you have to be a member to know about that.

Oona couldn't help it. She sat on the nearest sofa and cried.

'Oons!' Melissa sat with her and held her hand. 'This is a happy occasion – look, everyone's here. Nobody's dead, or sick, or any of the other horrible things that could have happened to any one of us. Now dry your eyes, before you ruin that lovely make-up.'

'I'm sorry,' she sniffled. 'I'm very happy, yet I feel very sad.' She dabbed at her eyes with a napkin that Singer fetched from the bar.

'Mister Singer?' he felt a tap on his shoulder. It was Dionne, smiling impishly. 'I hereby invoke rule number two of the Christmas Club.' She nodded across the room, and Frisby pressed 'play' on the wafer-thin stereo system mounted on the wall below the plasma television. A Chopin waltz came lightly to life and then surged, mingling with the patter of raindrops on the glass. Singer necked his champagne and set his glass down as Dionne led him into the middle of the floor.

She smiled up at him. 'I hope you've been taking dancing lessons.'

'I'm thirteen years older, three stone heavier and ten times less co-ordinated.'

'Oh well, just follow my lead and try not to tread on my toes. A one-two-three, one-two-three...'

Ronan sat on a barstool in the corner, watching them dance. He pushed his glasses into position on the red notch above the bridge of his nose.

They drank quite a lot of champagne before midnight, when they turned on the television for just long enough to cheer in 2003. Then Singer extracted a camera and tripod from his canvas bag and set it up in one corner to take a posed picture of all of them, the men standing at the back, the women at the front and Oona in the centre, holding open *Chambers's Miscellany*. After the photograph, Oona closed the book and handed it to Dionne.

'Here. It belongs in this house – in your house, in the library. And thanks for bringing us all together again.' They embraced. Ronan tapped Oona on the shoulder.

'S'cuse me, but I should like to dance with my wife.'

Dionne gave Oona the book. 'Put this somewhere safe, while I try to make an old man very happy.'

At the bar, Oona spotted Singer tip a measure of brandy into his champagne. She sidled over. 'Take it easy, big boy, otherwise you'll be no use to me later on.'

He smiled. 'I seem to remember something about Galicia.'

Half-jokingly, she flashed a leg from under her dress, showing a black, thigh-length stocking. 'Are you prepared to wait that long?'

'I feel a powerful urge to undress you with my teeth.'

'Well stick around, and I might let you.' He put an arm around her and pulled her to his side. 'Hey! Everybody's watching!' He immediately released her, which is when she realised that he had merely been moving her out of Frisby's way, who, scrabbling and grunting, had climbed up onto the bar counter behind her. He stood, waving a bottle of champagne.

'My turn to make a toast! My turn!'

Dionne shouted up at him. 'Get down off there, you clown! You'll hurt yourself, or worse, someone else. Ronan – make him get down!'

'What do you want me to do, bite his leg?'

'Quiet! Everybody quiet! My turn!' He put his hand on his chest. 'I'd like to thank Dee, the hostess with the mostest, for givin' me lotsa, lotsa money.' He held the champagne bottle like a golf club and pretended to swing. The bottle barely missed Singer's head.

'Jay,' Dionne admonished again, 'get down!'

'I'd also like to say,' at this, he clutched his free hand to his heart, 'how much I miss my lovely wife Shabina, and my two lovely chil'ren, Andy and Bertie. I mean, Gertie.' No one applauded, but Frisby raised the bottle to his head and took a large swig anyway. He teetered and would have overbalanced had Singer not grabbed him by the ankle.

'Come down, old man, or you'll do yourself an injury.'

'Let go my leg!' Frisby shouted. 'Why d'you always think you can tell me what to do?'

Singer released him. 'Relax the head, Frisby. Just don't want anyone to get hurt.'

'You always tried to tell me what to do, and now you can't, 'cos I'm ten times richer than you. You're not the boss here any more.' He gestured with the bottle at Dionne. 'She is.'

Dionne stood below him, hands on hips. 'Damn right I'm the boss of here and I'm telling you now – get down off my fecking bar, or I'm going to get really annoyed. You're after toasting your wife and children – well, what would they think if they could see you now?' Frisby, flummoxed, sat down heavily on the bar counter, then slid his feet onto the floor.

'I love my chil'ren very mush,' he informed Singer, solemnly.

'Good for you.' Singer raised his glass and took a sip.

'Are you sayin' I doan' love my shil'ren?' Frisby gave an exaggerated frown.

'I believe I said "good for you". Lucky children, to have a father who loves them so much.'

'Izzat why you doan' have chil'ren? 'Cos you only love you?'

Singer's voice turned frosty. 'I'm not the only person in this room who doesn't have kids, Frisby, so let's drop the subject.'

'No!' Frisby whined. 'You always looked down on me because you doan' like me, but you have no shill'ren 'cos you're not a nice person.'

'Jay!' Dionne intervened. 'You're being obnoxious and I want you to stop!'

'Jus' wanna know why ol' bossy boots doan' have chil'ren, if he's such a wunnerful guy.' Oona put a hand on Singer's arm, but it was too late. He growled, oozing contempt.

'So you've managed to reproduce – congratulations, Frisby, you've justified your existence. We say we love them, but speaking for myself, I don't want to bring children into a world that we're destroying on their behalf. Because love doesn't conquer everything – greed and stupidity do. Does that answer your question?'

Frisby opened his mouth to respond, but Dionne grabbed him by his lapel and physically dragged him across the room, towards a distant suite of chairs. They bumped into Ronan, who stood out of the way.

'Thanks for the help,' she snarled in passing.

Singer stared after them while Oona tried to sound breezy. 'I can't disagree with a single word you said, but let's just leave it at that, eh?'

Melissa joined them. 'More drink, I think.' She reached over the counter, and lifted a dripping champagne bottle from its ice bucket. 'Last one, by the looks of it. Would you mind?' She handed it to Singer, who seemed to snap out of a reverie.

'Of course, of course.' He dried the bottle with a napkin and began picking at the foil around the cork.

'Well, thank goodness.' She gave him a punch on the arm. 'For a few seconds, I thought we were about to witness another Nick Danver.'

Singer smiled wanly and topped up their glasses, but stayed silent. When Oona glanced at his eyes a few minutes later, she could tell that he was somewhere far away.

Half an hour later, Oona fetched Frisby from his purdah in the corner and brought him back to the bar, where he and Singer shook hands and apologised to one another for being drunk and silly. The company gathered again, in a suite of comfy chairs, except for Singer, who said he would step outside for a cigarette. Oona was half-tempted to join him and spent the rest of her life wishing she had, but Dionne cornered her and it was a good twenty minutes before she remarked that Singer hadn't returned.

'He's probably keeled over,' Dionne opined. 'He looked a bit wrecked.'

'I think I'll go and check that if he has keeled over, he's done it in bed, and not on the driveway.'

'Good, because I'd like you to do something for me – we're out of champagne, but there's more downstairs. Do you know the bar in the games room?'

'Yes.'

'While you're down there, would you be a love and grab a bottle from the fridge behind it? Melissa, you'd drink another glass of bubbly, wouldn't you?'

Melissa smiled faintly. 'I'm off to bed in a minute, Dee, but thanks, it's been a wonderful party.'

Dionne patted Oona's knee. 'Lookit, fetch a bottle up anyway, because I fancy some, and if I can get another dose into my husband,' she gave a sardonic laugh, 'I might get lucky later on.'

'Champagne makes him amorous, does it?'

'No, darling, it makes him unconscious.'

Oona let herself into the old house, descended the wooden staircase and stepped into the porch to peer outside. The storm hadn't lived up to its earlier promise, but it was still windy and the rain blew around like salvoes of black bullets. Nobody – not even Singer – could be out there smoking for any length of time. So she continued into the western extension. Sure enough, Singer's bedroom door was slightly ajar. A faint light glowed from within, so she tapped and, receiving no answer, let herself in. He was lying sideways on the bed with his back turned towards her, fully clothed and breathing slowly. His bow-tie had been cast to the floor. She kicked her shoes off beside it, making, she felt, a small but significant tableau.

She whispered. 'Singer?'

He didn't stir. She noticed that the window-glass was dimmed, but she pulled the curtains closed nonetheless and removed his shoes. Sleep had eradicated every trace of weary scepticism from his face, and she felt as if she owned him. She bent and kissed his cheek.

'I'll be back,' she whispered.

'Good,' he muttered, making her jump.

'I thought you were asleep!'

'I am,' he yawned, and rolled over.

'Here, sit up a second and let me get that jacket off you.' Eyes closed, he half-obeyed, and with a bit of tugging at the sleeves, off it came. He collapsed back on the pillow and she doubled the duvet over him as best she could, then clicked her fingers at the bedside lamp, which extinguished, making the darkness complete. Shagging Dionne and her shagging champagne, she thought as tiredness swept over her. All she wanted to do was crawl into bed beside Singer and sleep. Instead, she gently closed the bedroom door.

It was only when she reached the end of the corridor that she remembered she would have to touch the key. It hung on its hook, dull and discoloured, daring her to pick it up. Once again, she considered abandoning her task, but it occurred to her that if she delivered the bottle and announced her immediate retirement, she could be back down in a few minutes, with no excuse for Dionne to come searching for her, as she had the previous night. So she swallowed and seized the key. Holding it made her feel dirty. She slotted it into the big wooden door and the lock turned smoothly.

She pushed the door open, found the light switch and padded noiselessly barefoot around the snooker table to the small wooden bar. She crouched down behind the counter to get at the fridge. She extracted a bottle of champagne and was halfway back across the room before she saw that the door had somehow swung shut. She ran over to it. There was no internal handle, but she put a small finger into the keyhole and pulled. The door didn't budge. She laughed, not in amusement, but disbelief. Then she thought, Singer – the arse. She rapped smartly on the wood.

'Singer! It's not funny! Let me out!' No answer. 'Come on, pretending to be asleep and then locking me in with that nasty old key isn't my idea of a joke!' She rapped the wood again, this time sharply enough to hurt her knuckles. Still no answer. Singer had looked pretty crashed out, and somehow she couldn't see him getting his kicks from locking her in a room. A draught of some sort – that had to be it. The door had been blown or sucked shut, and only needed something slid between it and the jamb to lever it open.

She went back to the bar and hunted around for a utensil of some sort, but the thinnest, stiffest object she could find was a plastic biro. When she tried to wedge the door open with it, it snapped. She cursed and threw the remnants to the floor. The door *was* locked – it was fearsome, almost, in its size and solidity, and she had about as much chance of forcing it from the inside as she had of lifting the entire room and moving it ten paces to the left. Perhaps she could wake Singer? She pictured herself closing his bedroom door and cursed again. Still, there was nothing for it. So she shouted and hammered with the palms of her hands. Nothing, except sore hands. She rolled up one of Ronan's magazines and slapped it against the door, but no joy. She felt bad about doing it, but the heaviest object she could physically throw was one of the collected volumes of *The Illustrated London News*, which she fetched from the shelves and flung against the door with all her strength. It made a sizeable bang, but no one heard it.

Feeling herself panic, she took snooker balls from the table and threw them at the wood. Each one rebounded with a crack, leaving a pockmark. She didn't care – she'd pay for the fucking door – she just wanted out. When the balls didn't work, she took a cue and whacked it, screaming, until it broke. Weeping with rage, she damned Dionne's grandiose Pier House to hell – in any normal-sized home, she'd have been found by now. It tortured her to think that her mobile phone was lying in her bedroom several paces away.

She dropped the broken cue onto the rest of the debris around the door and wandered back to the bar in a daze, where she fixed herself a very large brandy and Coke. The champagne bottle stood on the counter like an exclamation mark – for a few seconds, she contemplated tossing it against the door as an act of pure revenge. But then she remembered that Dionne would almost certainly come looking for it, and cheered up slightly, sitting down on a sofa to sip her drink. Her heart started beating at its normal speed again. Who, she wondered, if not Singer, could have locked her in? Had Ronan gone around closing up for the night and not realised she was here? Or had that evil key imprisoned her of its own, demonic accord? She put her feet up, telling herself she'd stay awake, but within minutes, fell asleep.

She came to him later – he couldn't tell when, because the room was pitch dark. He awoke as she slipped into bed beside him.

'Hello, you,' he muttered, but she didn't answer, other than to move the warmth of herself against him, and rub her hand over the front of his trousers. She smelled of Tiger Balm – the sharp scent cut through his tobacco-clogged nostrils. He rolled over, to kiss and embrace, but her massaging hand flitted up to his chest and pushed him back against the bed, and when he obeyed, it undid his belt, opened his trousers and slipped inside to resume its task. When it was satisfied with its work, the hand held him as she straddled him, carefully yet quickly inserting him, then he gasped, as she slowly leaned her full weight and put her hands on his chest. She still wore her stockings and dress, so he slipped his fingers under the fabric and held her bare hips as she moved herself up and down. He gasped again and pressed into her, so she moved faster, with greater confidence, leaning more and more weight into each downward stroke. She did not pant or make any other noise as he flexed into her harder and harder and then groaned as if stabbed, pushing himself upwards, as she pressed herself fully down, and sat upright on top of him. She waited for his spasms to stop, then took one of his hands and kissed his fingers. She climbed off him and slid over to edge of the bed. She had her feet on the floor and was about to stand when he rolled towards her, caught her in a bear hug and pulled her back towards him. She struggled and he laughed.

'Where do you think you're going? I've waited a long time for you to do something as nice as that.'

She didn't reply, but lay limp and allowed him to kiss the back of her neck and stroke her cheeks. His big hand moved onto her left arm and stroked it down to the wrist. Suddenly, it stopped and she felt his fingertips climb again, rubbing her inner arm.

'Oona, where have your...' he began, and with all her strength, she launched herself forward out of his relaxed embrace, out of the bed and onto the floor. She heard him click his fingers and the bedside light revealed her scrabbling to her feet, and his squinting face, contorted in disbelief.

'Dionne! What the...what the *fuck* do you think you're *doing*?'

She hurled herself at the bedroom door, twisted it open and went to run up the corridor, but staggered into the blue glass wall, drunker than she'd allowed for. He flew out of the bedroom behind her, but his trousers were falling down so he had to stop, and she recovered and dashed up the corridor, crashing through the kitchen door. She thumped up the wooden staircase, making more noise than a child being chased by imaginary monsters. Singer reached the bottom of the stairs and roared up after her.

'Dionne! What have you done?'

She glanced backwards at him as she climbed the last step, which is how she collided with Ronan, who stood in the dark at the top, wearing a burgundy bathrobe.

'Oof! Dee! What's the matter?'

'Get out of my way!'

Ronan's expression as his dishevelled, barefoot wife pushed past him mirrored the shock on Singer's face below. Dionne slammed the bedroom door.

'What did you do to her?' Ronan demanded of Singer, who had stopped with his foot on the bottom step.

'Why don't you ask your fucking succubus of a wife what she's just done to me?' There was no contrition in his voice, just astonished anger.

'Dionne! Are you all right?' Ronan exploded into the bedroom. Fully expecting to see a violated woman lying weeping on the bed, instead he was confronted with the truly bizarre sight of Dionne, who had donned a pair of pyjama bottoms, lying on the floor with her feet up on the bed, using her hands to support her hips in the air. Her black dress, which still covered her upper body, was spread like a cloak on the floor.

He wailed. 'Will someone please tell me what the *fuck* is going on here?'

'Shut the door!' she barked. 'Now, go to bed and leave me alone – I stand a better chance if I stay like this for an hour or so.'

Bewildered beyond measure, Ronan ran back out onto the landing to confront Singer. But he was gone from the bottom of the stairs.

'Crazy…crazy…' Singer stumbled around his bedroom, throwing random objects into his overnight bag. 'Got to get out of this crazy bloody house!' He was sober enough to know that he was still a bit drunk. He reeled mentally as well as physically as he tried to absorb what had happened. Then the thought struck him – if he walked out the door and drove away, to everyone except the two people who knew the truth, it would look as if he'd done something really horribly wrong. She could say what she liked, with him not there to defend himself. And Oona – where was Oona? He would have to tell her immediately, no matter what the consequences. He abandoned his chaotic packing and went to the room next door. He rapped on the door. There was no reply, so he burst inside.

'Oona!'

The room was in shadow, tinged with the grey light of dawn. The curtains were open, and he could see the wet sea-grass, stooped in the breeze behind the house. Not only was Oona not in the bed, but the bed had not been slept in. Items of clothing lay strewn on the sofa, and on the dresser, a mobile phone was plugged into its charger. Beside it, a small, circular tin lay open – someone, he noticed, had dug a finger deep into the Tiger Balm. He checked the ensuite – nothing.

Outside in the corridor, he saw that the door to the games room was closed, with the iron key – *that* iron key – hanging on the wall beside it. He pressed the wood with his fingertips just to make certain, but it was locked and no noise came from within, so he didn't bother to open it. He returned to his room and put on the black dress shoes. He remembered how Oona had pulled them off him in the night, along with his jacket – yes, there it was, bundled at the foot of the bed. He remembered her kiss, and how she'd promised to return to him, which was why he'd assumed, in the dark…what the hell was going on in this madhouse?

He checked the third bedroom along the corridor, just in case she'd stumbled into the wrong one. Empty, as was the office. In the kitchen, the remains of their buffet dinner had been cleared onto a sideboard, and what had been the old living room sat wide open, deserted and neutered, full of sofas that nobody ever sat on. Or slept on, by the looks of it – not this time. As he let himself down the back kitchen corridor, past the tiled changing rooms, he was assailed by a sudden mental image of Oona floating face down in the pool, so he ran and burst through the extension door, but the water was like glass, attended by its guardian gym machines and the steady hum of the air-conditioning.

He climbed the steel staircase into the upstairs lounge. The bar counter was crowded with empty bottles and glasses, but there were no signs of the carnage that he somehow expected to find. *Chambers's Miscellany* sat open on a coffee table, Oona's dried blood neatly ordered into the Christmas Club rules. A loud, strangulated snore made him jump. It came from behind one of the sofas, where he found Frisby, starfished on the floor, still fully clothed with his glasses and coloured bow-tie askew, breathing heavily through his mouth. This was both a disappointment and a relief – he'd hoped to find Oona, but at least she hadn't thrown herself at the little Englishman. Suddenly, he felt guilty about Dionne, but then remembered the smell of the Tiger Balm. She'd tricked him, quite deliberately. He had nothing to feel guilty about, yet… The absolute calm of the house, underscored by Frisby's snores, suddenly seemed like an insult. After what had happened, he expected noisy chaos. Where the hell was Oona? Should he wake Melissa, and then confront Dionne? What about the police?

'Hello – I'd like to report a rape…' He shook his head and laughed abruptly, as once more, disbelief washed over him. He looked through the glass wall at the harbour. The sea smashed into it enthusiastically, rather than violently. The landscape was empty – it was too early for even the wildest fanatic to be out on the golf course. With the grey sky and the rain, it was as if the very bay itself had a hangover. The lighthouse blinked at him, offering comfort, but no clues. Just then, he caught a flicker of movement to the left, at the top of the hairpin path. It was the black and red ski jacket she'd worn yesterday, on the beach. And then, he remembered where he'd found her on New Year's Day, 1990.

He dashed through the top corridor, thundered down the wooden stairs, barged through the glass porch and sped off across the driveway, onto the sea-grass, through the missing fence and onto the beach. He ignored the wind and the rain on his shirt. He waded through the pebbles and crossed the tarmac apron where the boats were parked, then started up the path at a run. By the time he was halfway up, he was reduced to a fast walk as he cursed the weight he'd put on, the thick heaviness of his body. He decided that he despised running even more than golf. Fighting for air and with a stitch in his side, he made it to the watchtower, then to where the headland fell away, and the twisted rocks mounted their doomed defence against the sea. She sat on the pinnacle, hood up against the rain, dangling her legs over the far side, into the gorge. He cupped his hands and roared.

'Oona! Oona!'

But the wind was against him – down at the house, it blew in gusts. Up here, it whipped in from the sea like an infinite armada of billowing sails. He dropped over the edge and slid down the soaking grass hill – he was now so wet, he barely felt it. He scrambled onto the rocks and began his frantic climb up the pinnacle, panting through the hot raw bags that were his smoker's lungs. He reached the flat summit and pulled himself onto it. She sat a few paces away, at the very edge, arms braced as if uncertain whether to push forward, or pull back. He threw himself across the slippy surface and grabbed her nearest arm.

'Oona! It's me! Get back from there!' The sickening drop gurgled with rock-sucked sea. The figure writhed in surprise at his touch. The face under the hood was long, thin, wore circular glasses over red-rimmed eyes and had cheeks that ran with a mixture of rain and tears.

'Ronan? What are *you* doing up here?'

21

Oona wandered around the grounds of Trinity College, past the ancient oaks behind the campanile, through New Square and the neat little garden that gave onto College Park. Usually, she just strolled in circles around the park, oblivious to the rain and the lawnsmen gathering leaves. She'd taken all of January off, cancelling her trip to Galicia, and had now been back at work for over a month, but couldn't settle. She retreated into herself and stayed there, delivering lectures on autopilot to the featureless blobs that were her students' faces. And as she made her daily, unseeing circuits of the campus, she replayed events again and again in her head, trying to understand how, and more importantly, why.

She'd woken up in the games room to find the big wooden door lying wide open and the iron key hanging on the corridor wall, as if nothing had ever happened. She had tumbled into Singer's bedroom, ready to cry her eyes out. Someone had locked her away, like Miranda from *The Collector*, and she felt entitled to a mini-nervous breakdown. But Singer hadn't been in his bed, nor, as she conducted an increasingly puzzled search, could she find him anywhere else around the house. It was still early, but light outside, and she had just discovered

Frisby sleeping in the upstairs lounge when she'd spotted a tall, hooded figure in a black and red ski jacket out the panoramic window, approaching the house from the direction of the harbour. Out for a walk – of course! She'd dashed down to the porch to fling herself into Singer's arms, but the figure had turned out to be a very surly Ronan, who had barely returned her greeting before disappearing upstairs into one of the bedrooms.

Eventually, she had woken Melissa, who had comforted her, made her take a shower and fixed some breakfast. But when Singer had still not materialised by eleven o'clock, she had started fretting again. Ronan had resurfaced around midday, and Dionne shortly afterwards. They'd both seemed in very bad moods, but the assumption was that they'd simply had another spat, and anyway, the mystery of Singer's whereabouts was taking precedence. His car was still parked on the harbour, and his belongings were in his room, so he hadn't departed. Oona was now certain that he'd met with an accident while out walking or climbing, and suggested calling the police. But Dionne had argued against doing so, and had instead dispatched Ronan to search the hotel bar and check with the McFalls, and Oona and Melissa had scoured up around the headland, climbing through the rocks and calling his name.

When those searches yielded nothing, Oona had turned frantic, but eventually it was Frisby, of all people, who had persuaded Dionne to telephone the police, pointing out that Singer could be lying somewhere injured and that that possibility outweighed any image considerations for Barclay Golf, whose customers swung happily away, as yet oblivious to the minor emergency unfolding around them. Indeed, it was only when a coastguard helicopter started clattering around the bay that heads were raised on the fairways and putting greens. The moments slid by for Oona in a nightmarish blur, until she knew, when the helicopter started hovering out to sea near the island, that her worst fears were on the point of being realised.

Dionne and Melissa fought to restrain her in the upstairs lounge as the helicopter set down on the sea-grass in front of the house and four men in bulky orange outfits unloaded a cradle-like stretcher that contained a long blue canvas bag, held in place with thick straps. She had broken free and pelted down the stairs to meet the stretcher coming through the front porch. Directed by Frisby, the men set it down on the kitchen table, and Ronan seized her around the waist, trying to stop her from clawing the canvas bag open. She could hear screaming, she couldn't see properly and a hammer was pounding down on her insides. Dionne ran from somewhere with a white linen sheet and the men helped her spread it over the object on the table, then as the cloth settled over the vaguely human form, she'd remembered a dream, a dream she'd had over a dozen years ago. So she'd stopped struggling and accepted what she knew to be the truth. Her legs buckled and Ronan couldn't take her weight so he'd let her slip to the floor, where she gratefully buried her face against the cold flagstones of the old hallway.

She came to to find herself standing before a group of statues in St Stephen's Green, green-bronze effigies of three sightless women, spinning an invisible thread. The women are the *Moirae* – the Three Fates. Clotho, who spins the thread of life; Lachesis, who measures it, and Atropos, who cuts it. The statues, Oona knew because of her interest in such matters, had been gifted to Ireland after the Second World War by the German people in gratitude for the treatment of refugees. Without realising it, she must have wandered out of Trinity, up Kildare Street and all the way across the Green.

Standing before the statues, she understood that she had two choices. The first was to check into St Eunan's and abandon herself to the black hole that had swallowed her heart. If she followed that path, there was every possibility she might never check out again, but it nonetheless seemed the easiest. By far the more difficult option was to try to keep on going and live a life of regret, aching for what could have been. She nodded to the women and walked through the nearby gate. Preordained, a free taxi sailed towards her, and as she settled into the back seat, she almost told the driver 'St Eunan's', but instead, the word 'Dalkey' passed her lips, as if the women had made the decision for her.

Singer's funeral now seemed like a distant event. His Uncle Lucius, an unexpectedly small man with swept-back grey hair, had presided at an anonymous crematorium called Roselawn, in Belfast. Dionne, Ronan, Frisby, Melissa and she had sat grim faced and almost guilty, as Lucius Singer had spoken of his nephew's love for wild places and a sense of adventure that had unfortunately cost him his life.

The police had declared themselves baffled as to how Singer ended up in the water – although the tides, as the coastguards had pointed out, were strong, and anyone swimming, or falling off a cliff, could have easily been swept out to sea towards Inistrahull. So they simply concluded that at some stage early that morning, Singer must have either gone for a walk or a swim in the dark and got into difficulties, through inebriation. The coroner had recorded the cause of death as accidental drowning, and that was it – case closed.

The other mourners were a mixture of Singer's relatives – who seemed like quietly prosperous, understated types – and a smattering of journalists and photographers who had known Singer back in the good old, bad old days. Northern Ireland's long, dirty war was finally over, and they, just like Singer, had had to find other, less barbarous subjects to explore. Moments before the plain, dark wood coffin descended into the plinth to begin its journey to the flames, Oona had stepped silently forward and placed a book on top of it – a tatty, brown leather-bound 1858 edition of *Select Poetry from Chambers's Repository and Miscellany*.

The taxi stopped at a set of black-barred gates on the coast road between Dalkey and Killiney, where mansions rub shoulders – allowing pop stars, stockbrokers, barristers and tech-sector millionaires to see into one another's gardens. Denuded beech trees leaned over a beige sandstone wall on either side of the gates, which were similar to those at the Pier House. As Oona peered up the pink gravel drive in front of the Edwardian villa, she saw a young woman of about twenty lift a suitcase into one of three large saloons parked close to the main doorway. She pressed the intercom by the gate, and the buzzer must have been just inside the front door, because the woman immediately looked up, saw her and entered the house.

'Hello?'

'Hello. My name is Oona Tyler. I'm here to see Ronan Doherty.'

'Do you have an appointment?' The pronunciation was precise, but had an Eastern European lilt.

'I'm a friend of his, Oona Tyler.'

'Please to wait, and I will see if Mister Dorty is available.'

'Look, I'm—' but there was a loud click and the intercom died. Oona kicked a stray piece of gravel at her feet. The wind blew off Dublin Bay, and the branches of the trees reached down as if to grab her. She pulled the collar of her navy raincoat up around her neck. After a bit of a wait, the intercom clicked to life again.

'Please to come in.' The gates crackled, so she pushed through them and trudged up the drive. The young woman was strikingly beautiful, with a broad, Slavic face and short, henna-dyed hair. Her mouth was full, her eyes like almonds, and her skin too flawless for make-up. She wore black trousers and a purple blouse, like a private secretary who had shed her jacket for lunch. With her own hair hanging damply about her cheeks, Oona felt like a dowdy pensioner. The woman did not offer to take her coat, but led her into a bright, white-painted hallway and up a red-carpeted staircase to the first floor, where she knocked on a wooden door.

'Yes?' Ronan called from within.

The room overlooked the front garden and driveway through two large, multi-paned windows. Ronan sat behind an immense antique desk, typing on a black keyboard into an ultra-slim computer screen. On all other sides, the walls were lined with books. The desk itself was admirably tidy, with a brass reading lamp, a telephone and a couple of framed photographs clustered together for company at the edge of its polished expanse. He gestured at a pair of red leather office chairs, and she chose one. She sat, feeling more as if she were attending a job interview than visiting a friend of many years' standing. He hit a key with a flourish and swivelled around to face her.

'Oons. How are you? Unusual to see you in this neck of the woods.'

'It's unusual for me to be in this neck of the woods.'

'Tea or coffee?'

'Neither, thanks, I'm fine.'

He looked over her shoulder. 'That will be all, Helena, thank you.' The door behind her clicked shut. 'Sorry,' he continued, 'just putting *The Speckled Bird* to bed. Contributor dropped out at the last minute, and you know how it is, muggins has to write the missing copy. Look, Dionne's not here, she's actually in—'

Oona interrupted him. 'I'm here to see you, not Dee.'

'Oh.' He looked taken aback, but recovered quickly. 'How's life at the university?'

'What happened to Singer?' she countered, ignoring his attempt at small talk.

He pushed his glasses into position on the bridge of his nose. 'Sorry?'

'You heard me. I want to know what happened to Singer, and I'm not leaving until you tell me.'

He slowly placed his hands on the armrests of his swivel-throne. 'Oona, I'm not with you.'

'I want to know what happened between you and Singer, and if you don't tell me, I'm going back to the police to have the case reopened.'

He lifted a hand, ran it through what was left of his hair, then forced it back onto its armrest, flexing his fingers as he did so. 'Pardon?' As a riposte, it was pretty feeble, even by Ronan's standards.

'Do you remember that first Christmas at the Pier House, the night that you, me and Singer sat up until morning? We drank my gin, and we went for a walk up to the watchtower. And you made a pass at me, and pushed Singer down the hill.'

He made a show of thinking, pulling a pained expression. 'I'm afraid I don't remember anything of the sort, but that was a very long time ago. I don't understand what it has to do with—'

'Shut up,' she snapped. 'If you don't answer my questions, you'll be hearing them again, only from the police. But if you tell me the truth, I won't report you – I just want to know why.'

They locked gazes for a good five seconds before he slumped and shook his head. When he spoke, his voice was gentle and conciliatory. 'We all gave exhaustive statements to the police, and I'm just as upset about what happened as you are. Don't forget, Singer was my friend for many years. Now, I share your sense of loss – we all do. But I really don't see what gives you the right to—'

She stood, slapped the edge of his desk and shouted. 'If you don't tell me why, I'm calling the police! I'm going to tell them about the time you made a pass at me, and pushed Singer off the headland! I'm going to tell them how upset you looked when I saw you coming back from your walk on the morning he died. I don't care what happens, I just need to know the truth!'

'Oona—'

'No! Stop talking to me like I'm some sort of child! Singer's dead, and I don't know why! The rest of my life will be just so much missing time!' Her voice rose to a scream. 'But for the sake of my sanity, I need to know why!' She heard the study door open behind her but didn't turn around. Ronan looked over her shoulder again and raised a hand.

'It's all right, Helena, thank you.' After some hesitation, the door closed. 'Now please – sit down and stop shouting at me.' His voice oozed reason, but no warmth. 'I genuinely don't know what you want from me, but if you would just sit down and take the time to explain, I—'

'You think you've got away with it.' She disobeyed his command to sit and set out around the room, pretending to study the book-shelves, super-sensitive to every nuance in his tone. She sensed fear, and so pressed on. 'By the way, I've told Melissa what I think, so you may as well know that if anything happens to me, that will be as good as a signed confession.'

Sure enough, he tensed. 'What have you told Melissa?'

'That I think you killed Singer.'

'Oona!' Now he tried to sound cross. 'Please see this from my perspective. I'm sitting here, busy with my work, trying, like every-body else, to get back to a normal life after losing a close friend. You walk into my house, uninvited, and without saying why, without a single shred of evidence, you accuse me of killing him. Why are you doing this to me?'

'Because I've been thinking about it for weeks, and I know that you did it. I just don't know why.'

He snorted. 'Well, that's great, just great. "Your honour, he's guilty because I think he's guilty." Look – Melissa happens to be a very good friend of ours...' at that, she gave a sharp, sardonic laugh, '...no, Melissa is our friend, and we all share your grief, but you have no right to be ringing her up and spreading wild stories about me. No right whatsoever. Now, we're all fully aware that you haven't been well in the past, so I'm prepared to be—'

She laughed again. 'That's your way out, isn't it?' She walked around the side of his desk to the window. He didn't look half as impressive without his big lump of polished wood to protect him. 'That's the first thing you'd say if the police asked you more ques-tions. "Oona's mad. She's been in the looney bin – long history of depression, and probably worse."'

His tone softened. 'Oona. Nobody wants to start flinging mud around, to what purpose? Can we not just—'

'Somebody locked me in your room that night.'

'I swear on my mother's grave that I did not lock you in that room. I swear it on my mother's fucking grave.'

For the first time since arriving, she found herself believing him, and so felt her façade begin to crumble. Her gamble – that he would crack if confronted – wasn't working, and now she began to wonder whether her instincts had betrayed her. None of it – absolutely none of it – made any sense whatsoever.

'Well, somebody locked me in,' she sighed, 'but the cops didn't take me seriously when I told them, because I didn't take me seriously. I was so upset, I felt silly even talking about it. But I've been thinking about it ever since, and I believe that whoever locked me in that room wanted me out of the way while they did something to Singer.'

Ronan placed his elbows on his table, removed his glasses and rubbed his face with his hands. His eyes always looked much bigger, and his face somehow harder, without his glasses. 'Oons, it's been a terrible time for all of us. Everyone has been punishing themselves, wondering if they'd acted any differently whether Singer would still be alive. But it's in the nature of accidents that you never see them coming. We were having a quiet, civilised reunion – how could anyone have foreseen that one of us would end up dead? I don't think we'll ever know what happened, and that's the hardest part of all.' He put his glasses back in their rightful position on his nose. 'How can we be sure, for example, that Singer didn't commit suicide?'

Her temper flashed. 'Don't say that! Don't you dare say that! If you say that again, I'll tear this place apart with my bare fucking hands!'

'I'm sorry, but he seemed somewhat down to me, and he was drinking a lot.'

She shook her head, eyes stinging. 'He didn't kill himself. I know for a fact that he didn't.'

'How?'

'From things he said to me. He was sad, but he wasn't unhappy.'

'Oh. I thought that sad and unhappy were more or less the same thing, but if you say…'

'They're not, and I do say, so shut up.'

Ronan opened his mouth, but then obviously decided not to provoke her any further. She wiped her eyes with her knuckles and stared out the window. Helena the servant, or secretary, or whatever she was, had resumed packing one of the big black cars on the drive-way below. Surrounded by all this money, Oona was beginning to feel like an interloping idiot. But still, she tried one more trick.

'Do you think maybe Frisby locked me in the room?'

'Why would he do that?'

'We never told the police about the argument he had with Singer. He was really drunk, and drunk people do really strange things.'

Ronan pouted, as if pondering her theory. 'You could be right, but I don't see it. Nobody mentioned that tiff, because that's all it was, a silly little tiff about nothing. You got them to apologise – remember? And you're right, Frisby was drunk – so drunk he couldn't make it to his bedroom a few doors away, let alone to the far side of the house. But let's say, for the sake of argument, that he did sneak down to Singer's bedroom to try something. How would a shrimp like Frisby get someone the size of Singer all the way down to the sea – even if Singer didn't fight back, which he most certainly would have? It just doesn't make sense.'

Either Ronan was telling the truth, or else he was too smart. Had he denounced Frisby, then she could have been certain he wanted the spotlight off himself. She sighed,

'You're right. It doesn't make sense.'

He stood, and approached her. He made to put an arm around her, but she turned abruptly and marched to the middle of the room. Still, his voice was gentle and persuasive.

'When bad things happen, we like to have a reason. But some-times, there is no reason.'

'I'm sorry to have bothered you. I just don't, for the life of me, understand. Give my love to Dee, wherever she is.'

'I'll get Helena to see you out.'

'I'll see myself out, thanks. She's a very pretty girl – what is she, Polish?'

'Romanian.'

'Secretary?'

'Au pair, actually.'

'Au pair? But you only hire an au pair when you have…'

Ronan blushed. 'Uh, yes – well, we were about to tell you. That's where Dionne is, in London, at a top obstetrician. She's fourteen weeks, but because she's nearly forty and this is our first, we're taking no chances.'

'*Dionne*? But how could that happen?'

His blush deepened. 'How do children usually happen? At the Pier House, over Christmas, you know, we…well. It's fantastic news, and we're over the moon. Dionne says she'll call it Gareth, if it's a boy.'

'But Dionne told us that—' She stopped in mid-sentence. He studied her. 'Dionne told you what?'

She shook her head. 'Nothing. Never mind. I'm very pleased for both of you, congratulations.'

He smiled beatifically. 'We have Helena in, helping us to make the preparations. Top au pairs are hard to get, and she came highly recommended, so we snapped her up. It will be good for us to get to know her, before the baby arrives. She's flying with me in the morning, to meet the doctor and be there for Dionne.'

'How wonderful for both of you. I mean, for the three of you. Four, if you count the baby.'

Ronan laughed. 'Yes it is – wonderful. Just a shame that it's happened at such a difficult time. But everything changes, and life must go on. You know, maybe there's something symbolic in this – a soul leaves, just as a new one arrives.'

'That's certainly one way of looking at it.'

'Dionne has decided to sell Barclay Golf. She says there's no way she could ever stay there again, after what happened.' But Oona wasn't really listening as she reached for the office door. 'In fact, we're thinking of selling up in Ireland altogether, and maybe basing ourselves at this new place in Portugal. You know, for tax purposes. We can both work just as easily from there.'

She flashed him a smile. 'Super. Keep me posted, won't you?'

'Are you sure you won't stay for a coffee?'

'No. You're busy and I should get back into town.'

'I can get Helena to drive you.'

'No need. I like to walk, and there's a bus from the village. Bye – see you guys around.' And she was out the door, and down the stairs. He watched through the window as she bustled off along the drive. When she reached the gate, the buzzer sounded and she left quickly, without looking back.

He stood at the window, weighing his performance, analysing every word. Had he given anything away? He didn't think so, but there was something about the abruptness of her departure that…that what? The woman was mad – who would believe her? Shaken as he was, perhaps her visit had been a good thing, because now he could be certain there was no hidden proof, some detail he hadn't foreseen, waiting to jump up and bite him. If that was the best anyone could do...

Directly below, Helena bent over to arrange something in the car. She really did have the most stunning ass. He could see a hint of white thong above the waist of her fitted trousers, and imagined that ass without the trousers, and then without the thong. He sat down again and looked at the computer screen, without really seeing what was on it, because in spite of Helena's ass, his mind was still racing, throwing up memories he'd tried his utmost to forget. He could never allow himself to think about Singer on the pinnacle – everything he had, all his comfort, security and wealth – everything depended on being able to forget about that.

But the one image he couldn't banish was that of Singer looking up the stairs. The way he'd stood, foot on the bottom step, clutching the banister, his clothes dishevelled, his face angry and surprised. Dionne had fled into the bedroom, but Singer hadn't climbed after her, instead he had shouted something – what was it again? What had he called her? Suck your bus? Being a literary man, Ronan felt he ought to know what that meant, but of course, one can hardly retain everything...hold on, just a few clicks and we can summon up the online *Oxford English Dictionary*, handy thing to subscribe to...there we are...now, what have we got?

Sukiyaki – a Japanese dish of fried meat.

Sukkur – a city in south-east Pakistan.

Perhaps not, but a quick scroll upward...

Succentor? No...

Succory – an old word for chicory? Interesting, but not...

Succotash – a dish of maize and beans.

succubus, n. (pl. succubi) a female demon believed to have sexual intercourse with sleeping men. [LL. succuba prostitute, succubus f. succubare (as SUB- cubare, lies, lies beneath.)]

He sat back and contemplated the framed photographs of Dionne across his desk. One was a black-and-white shot of her supervising work on the Pier House, a picture she liked because, she said, it had caught her naturally. She looked beautiful yet capable, the kind of person who'd be very good at getting other people to do exactly what she wanted them to. The other was a formal studio portrait, in which she wore a black evening gown – not unlike the one she had worn *that* night, only without the gloves. She was leaning on a studio prop, a white alabaster bust of a leering Pan – poised, posed, pleased, smiling into the camera from behind her immaculate make-up, confident and most of all, in command.

I'll be seeing you tomorrow, he thought.

Succubus…